MARC ALAN EDELHEIT

LEGACY'S EDGE

I

THE CLAIMED REALM

aethonbooks.com

ACKNOWLEDGMENTS

I wish to thank my agent, Andrea Hurst, for her invaluable support and assistance. I would also like to thank my beta readers, who suffered through several early drafts. My betas: Steve Koratsky, Tim Adams, Marshall Clowers, Paul Klebaur, William Schnippert, David Cheever, Erin Penny, Sheldon Levy, Walker Graham, Jimmy McAfee, Joel Rainey, James H. Bjorum, Sally Tingley-Walker, Tom Trudeau, James Doak, Nathan Hildebrand, Jeremy Craig, Bradley Renfro, Tom Moore, Jacob Turner, Michael Brown, Lamarr Kelley, Dragos Emil Ramniceanu, Kieran Maisonet, Lance Dahl, Lee Adrian, Brian Thomas, Ed Speight, Rusty Juban. I would also like to take a moment to thank my loving wife, who sacrificed many an evening and weekend to allow me to work on my writing.

Editing Assistance by Hannah Streetman, Brandon Purcell, Audrey Mackaman

Agented by Andrea Hurst & Associates

http://maenovels.com/

ALSO BY MARC ALAN EDELHEIT

FANTASY

THE CLAIMED REALM

Legacy's Edge

THE STIGER CHRONICLES

Originally Published as Chronicles of an Imperial Legionary Officer

Stiger's Tigers

The Tiger

The Tiger's Fate

The Tiger's Time

The Tiger's Imperium

The Tiger's Fight

The Tiger's Rage

The Tiger's Battle (Coming 2025)

STIGER: TALES OF THE SEVENTH

Originally Published as Tales of the Seventh

Stiger

Fort Covenant

A Dark Foretoken

The Kingdom (Coming 2025)

THE KARUS SAGA

Lost Legio IX

Fortress of Radiance

The First Compact

Rapax Pax

Brothers of the Line (Coming 2024)

THE ELI CHRONICLES

Originally Published as A Ranger's Tale

Eli

By Bow, Daggers & Sword

Lutha Nyx

TBA

THE WAY OF LEGEND

With Quincy J. Allen

Reclaiming Honor

Forging Destiny

Paladin's Light

SCIENCE FICTION

BORN OF ASH

Fallen Empire

Infinity Control

Rising Phoenix (Coming 2025)

GUARDIANS OF THE DARK

Off Midway Station (Coming 2024)

Off Indigo Station (Coming 2025)

NONFICTION

Every Writer's Dream

The Insider's Path to an Indie Bestseller

AUTHOR'S NOTE

Writing **The Claimed Realm** has been a labor of love and a joy. It is my sincere hope that you love it as I do.

I also want to take a moment to thank you for reading and keeping me employed as a full-time writer. For those of you who reach out to me on social media or by email, I simply cannot express how humbling it is, as an author, to have my work so appreciated and loved. From the bottom of my heart… *thank you.*

Reviews keep me motivated and help to drive sales. I make a point to read each and every one, so please continue to post them.

You can reach out and connect with me on:

Facebook: Marc Edelheit Author
Facebook Group: MAE Fantasy & SciFi Lounge
Twitter: Marc Edelheit Author
Instagram: Marc Edelheit Author
Amazon Author Central: Marc Edelheit Author
Patreon: Marc Alan Edelheit
Newsletter: www.maenovels.com

Again, I hope you enjoy this book and would like to offer a sincere thank you for your purchase and support.

Best regards,
Marc Alan Edelheit

1

Alaric's arm muscles tensed as he raised his sword, its polished steel surface catching the dim light of the day through the overcast clouds. He met the incoming attack with a resolute block, the collision of metal against metal producing a jarring, echoing clang. The impact sent a wave of sharp pain radiating up his arm. His fingers, wrapped tightly around the cord grip of the hilt, tingled.

His adversary, a figure clad in black leathers, bore the distinctive marks of the ash men, his face obscured under a heavy smear of ash and charcoal. With a snarl that matched the ferocity of a beast, his opponent drew back his sword as he prepared to unleash another strike. But Alaric, fueled by a blend of adrenaline and sheer will, refused to be bested by this animal. He surged forward, taking a stab at his opponent, driving the ash man back even as he hastily blocked the attack.

With lightning speed, Alaric lunged again, pressing his advantage. Caught off guard, the ash man backed up a step, giving ground. He took another step backward, and a rock, concealed amongst the grass, became his downfall. He stumbled, arms windmilling to keep his balance. Seizing the fleeting moment of his adversary's vulnerability, Alaric advanced. He took several rapid steps, channeling the force of his momentum into his shoulder. Like a battering ram, he collided with the ash man's chest, the impact resonating with a pained grunt that drove the man backward and to a knee.

The battlefield around them was a maelstrom of violence and chaos. Men's voices rose in a tumultuous blend of screams, yells, shouts, and curses. The desperate chorus was underscored by the relentless clashing of metal as swords struck against swords and the duller, reverberating thuds of impacts taken on shields.

Amidst this chaos, the wounded were rendered invisible in the press of the battle line, their bodies trampled underfoot as they screamed out their agony, their fear, their pleas for help. The air was thick with the acrid stench of spilt blood, sweat, and excrement.

Yet, for Alaric, this bedlam was a familiar landscape. To him, the chaos of battle was an old companion, its rhythms and demands something to which he had long since become acclimated.

In the midst of the chaos of the line, Alaric found a grim sort of homecoming, a place where, despite the horror and the bloodshed, he knew exactly who he was and what he was capable of doing.

Lightning tore through the darkening sky, its brilliant flash illuminating the battlefield in stark, fleeting contrasts of light and shadow. Alaric executed a slash, his sword carving through the air with lethal precision to bite deeply into the kneeling ash man's thigh. Alaric's enemy cried out in pain as the blade cut deeply, a singular note of suffering amidst the cacophony of the fight.

As the ash man fell, Alaric was without mercy, his movements fueled both by necessity and a grim familiarity with the dance of death. He drove the point of his bloodied sword into the man's exposed throat.

The result was a fountain of thick, oily blood that sprayed into the air with a gruesome beauty that only one familiar with death could truly appreciate, showering Alaric in its warm, metallic-scented mist. The taste of blood on his tongue, strong and tangy, mingled with the adrenaline coursing through his veins, prompting a triumphant shout from his lips.

Yet there was no respite, no momentary break. Even as Alaric stood over his fallen opponent, another enemy was upon him, fueled by rage, his scream piercing the tumultuous air. Alaric raised his sword in a block, just as the sky was yet again torn asunder by lightning, its brilliant illumination followed by the resounding crack of thunder.

Amidst the tumult of the heavens, with lightning cleaving the sky and thunder bellowing its ancient rage, the battle below took on an almost mythic quality. Alaric, locked in a fierce duel with this new adversary, found himself a player in a scene as primal as the storm itself. Each strike and counterstrike between them spoke to their skill and determination, a struggle for life under the watchful eyes of the gods, whose own battle seemingly raged in the skies above. Pressed hard by his opponent, Alaric retreated steadily down the slope of the hill, his boots slipping slightly on the blood-soaked grass. He was careful where he stepped, for he did not wish to trip over a body or unseen rock.

As if to add a layer of misery to the already dire situation, the heavens opened, releasing a slow drizzle upon the combatants. Blood mixed with rainwater rapidly created a slick veneer over the grass, a hazard that Alaric knew would soon prove treacherous. Hundreds of feet, belonging to both friend and foe, would rapidly churn the grass and dirt to mud as they struggled against one another. Soon, those battling would not just be fighting each other, but the very ground beneath them for purchase.

This fight for the crest of the hill, amidst the elemental fury and the mire of conflict, was reminiscent of a child's game of

King of the Hill, albeit with stakes incomparably higher. The ash men, currently in possession of the hill's summit, were the adversaries to be overcome, a force sent to block them from reaching and relieving the Cardinal's army. Alaric and his men, driven by a fierce determination, discipline, and faith, sought to claim that elevated ground for themselves.

The ash man, his wet features obscured by the remnants of war paint, ash, and the grime of battle, launched a ferocious attack, his broadsword descending with lethal intent, accompanied by a primal scream that echoed the chaos of their surroundings.

Alaric, with agility born of desperation and skill honed through countless encounters, executed a swift dodge to the left, evading death by mere inches. A rush of air nipped his neck, a ghostly caress of death, as the blade sliced by and embedded itself in the ground where he had stood a heartbeat before.

Seizing the moment of his enemy's overextension, Alaric counterattacked, jabbing out. His blade found its mark, piercing the ash man's side. The impact was met with a heavy grunt, along with a look of shock and disbelief in the eyes of his opponent, a powerful figure now vulnerable, who could only muster a guttural grunt of pain as the steel of Alaric's sword bit deep.

As he released his grip upon the broadsword, the man stumbled as he took a faltering step back and away. Alaric could read the pain and sudden fear in his opponent's eyes as he sought retreat.

"Give your hateful gods my regards!" Alaric advanced and lunged forward again, driving his sword into the stunned man's stomach. His opponent exhaled heavily as the sword went in. Alaric's senses were assaulted by the stench of the other's acrid breath. With a final, cruel twist of his blade, Alaric unleashed a storm of pain upon the ash man, a grimace of agony etching itself across the warrior's face.

An unseen assailant barreled into Alaric from the right, severing the moment of his triumph and sending him crashing to the ground. Sword ripped from his grip, he landed hard and awkwardly. Scarcely had he begun to gather his wits and recover when a crushing weight bore down on his arm—a merciless stomp that threatened to shatter bone beneath the weight of iron-clad and hobnailed boots.

Around him, many sandaled and booted feet—symbols of the varied factions clashing on this field—moved perilously close, each stomp a potential death knell. The sharp bite of fear, cold and visceral, flooded Alaric's veins. The dread of being crushed underfoot gripped him. He had witnessed the horror of such a fate befall others—warriors rendered helpless, their lives extinguished beneath a crushing tide of indifference. Determined not to meet such an end, Alaric struggled for purchase, for any advantage that might get him back on his feet.

A booted foot, devoid of any semblance of mercy, struck his helmet with a force that sent a blinding white shockwave through his consciousness. The world narrowed to a pinpoint of pain, leaving him momentarily adrift in a sea of disorientation. Fighting through the haze, he attempted to maneuver, to position himself in a way that might allow him to rise and face the onslaught with the dignity of a warrior standing his ground.

Yet before he could marshal his strength, another blow, this time to his armored side, sent him sprawling helplessly onto his back.

"Get back! I said get back!"

An unexpected reprieve enveloped Alaric, as if the chaos itself had momentarily recoiled, granting him a fleeting sanctuary of precious space. Within this bubble of calm, he found the opportunity to take stock of his surroundings, his gaze lifting to meet the chaos that raged beyond his immediate respite.

It was then that a firm grip seized him, a hand clad in a

black worn leather glove grabbed his shoulder. With a forceful yank on his armor, Alaric was pulled upright and to his feet. His rescuer was none other than Ezran, one of his Shadow Guard. Alaric let go a relieved breath. Ezran's presence, a beacon of steadfastness amid the storm of conflict, was a sight for sore eyes.

Mere steps away, Thorne, another guardian, sword drawn and with a shield held at the ready, shoved at one of their own men, forcing the man away from the bubble of protection the two men had created.

"Are you all right, my lord?" Over the cacophony of clashing swords and the cries of the embattled, Ezran's voice, laden with concern, pierced through. Ezran's gaze flicked over Alaric, searching for injury. "Are you all right?"

"My sword," Alaric bellowed back, desperation edging his voice as he scanned the battlefield around them, searching for the weapon. "Oathbreaker, where is she? Do you see her?"

As Alaric's gaze darted across the battlefield, his men continued their relentless push up the hill's crest, a living wave of determination, will, and steel moving around the bubble Ezran and Thorne had created. Each step was a struggle against not only the enemy, but the very ground itself, as they sought to claim the high ground.

Lightning flashed.

Thunder followed.

Ezran, a former ash man, stood out starkly in the black and comfortable leathers characteristic of his people. His dark eyes scanned the battlefield with a predator's precision. Then they stopped. With a swift motion, he extended his scimitar, the curved blade pointing. "Over there, my lord."

Alaric turned around, his gaze following Ezran's guidance and settling where his sword, Oathbreaker, remained embedded in the body of his fallen adversary, just steps away. The man lay motionless, his life's light extinguished, eyes frozen open in a final, vacant stare toward the heavens.

With a decisive stride, Alaric approached his fallen enemy. Grasping Oathbreaker's hilt with a firm hand, he placed his boot upon the man's chest. For a moment, the world seemed to stand still as the sword recognized him and the magic of its bond flowed into him, infusing his being. Then, just as abruptly, the world shifted back into motion, and with a resolute tug, he liberated the blade from its unwilling bodily sheath.

Breathing heavily from the exertion of the fight, he paused to allow himself a moment to grasp the ebb and flow of conflict, to get a sense for what was happening. It was easy to become hyperfocused on the immediate fight before him, but Alaric was responsible for the overall fight.

Nearby, Kiera and Jasper, the last two members of his Shadow Guard, remained vigilant, their gazes attuned to the chaos that swirled around them. Kiera, a Luminary, her stature imposing and her presence unmistakable in the dull gleam of her plate armor, stood as a beacon of strength. Her silver armor was splattered with a mixture of blood, grime, and mud.

Kiera's demeanor was somber, her gaze steely, a reflection of the resolve that had seen her through countless battles. The ritual scars and tattoos that adorned her face spoke not only of her order, but of a warrior's path, each mark telling a story of survival, achievement, and defiance. Armed with her longsword and shield, she embodied the martial prowess of the Luminaries, a dwindling order of female knights whose legacy for valor lingered in her every action and being.

Jasper, hailing from the forested realms of Likaysia, presented a contrast to Kiera's armored might. Dressed in light, studded leathers that allowed for nimbleness and speed, he carried a short sword in hand. His trusted and prized bow was strapped to his back. The man's quiver was empty, his missiles likely well spent.

Jasper's long brown hair was secured in a practical braid that fell across his back, while his keen eyes moved ceaselessly as he also scanned for threats that might come their way. Together, all four formed a circle of guardianship around Alaric, their sworn charge.

The tumult of battle had surged forward, leaving Alaric and his Shadow Guard momentarily in its wake. Under the rain and rapidly darkening sky, Alaric's men pressed hotly against the thin enemy line at the crest of the hill, who sought to block them from reinforcing the Cardinal's army. The rain had intensified, fully transforming the slope into a treacherous morass, each footstep a battle against both the enemy and the elements.

The standard of Alaric's company, the Iron Vanguard, was just a few yards ahead, waving and bobbing as its bearer labored just behind the line. The standard struggled under the weight of the rain, its once proud bearing now appearing burdened, sullen, as if echoing the somber mood of the skies above.

"Onward!" Captain Grayson, the company commander, stood with the standard, rallying the men with fervor. Waving his sword overhead, his voice, a clarion call amidst the cacophony of steel and thunder, spurred the men onward. He was the embodiment of leadership, his presence instilling a sense of purpose and urgency as he led the advance up the hill. "Push!"

Flanking Alaric's company were allies from the Twelve Realms, a coalition of northern kingdoms united under a common cause. They advanced with equal determination, gradually forcing the ash men back, step by step, inch by inch, toward the hill's summit.

Overall, the fight was going their way. That, Alaric knew, was a welcome change.

Upon the call of the Cardinal—a plea cloaked as a demand, woven with the gravity of desperation—Alaric, alongside a cadre of fellow lords, had been thrust into the role of savior. The missive, delivered by Father Kemm, had reached them as night was about unfurl its shadows over the city of Hawkani, Alaric's seat of power, located nearly twenty miles away. Without hesitation, he'd marshaled the available forces and set out, marching through the night toward battle.

The journey from Hawkani to the Cardinal's army had been difficult, for there were no roads. Alaric's force had traversed fields, negotiated forests, and forded streams under the cloak of darkness, their path lit only by the stars and the moon. It had been a punishing endeavor, each mile a battle against fatigue.

As dawn broke, they pressed on, driven by the knowledge that their arrival could help tip the scales in favor of the Cardinal's beleaguered forces as the battle was joined.

Beyond the hill they were now fighting to take, Alaric's scouts had reported that the Cardinal's army was in the valley on the other side, heavily engaged with the enemy army. It was reputedly being led by Sunara himself.

They were almost there.

"Come on," Alaric bellowed, starting to climb again, and calling to those on either side who were struggling toward the battle line. "Come on, boys!"

Lightning lit the sky. Thunder followed several heartbeats later.

Fighting uphill against a determined enemy was incredibly difficult. It was something you generally did not wish to do, something best avoided—but there had been no choice, no opportunity to choose their own ground, not this time. Besides, they outnumbered the enemy facing them by more than two to one, so that canceled out some of the advantages of elevation. Along with his company and their allies, Alaric had brought more than two thousand men to the fight.

Ezran chopped down at a wounded enemy, who had been trying to crawl away, taking the man in the back. The ash man stiffened. A moment later, he relaxed and went limp, falling still, as if going to sleep. Ezran spat on the vanquished man.

Ezran's disdain for the ash men was more than a simple expression of victor's contempt. It was a personal vendetta, rooted in a history as tumultuous as the landscape upon which they fought. But then, the man had good reason to loathe his former people and their gods.

"Push them," Alaric urged. "Push them hard, boys."

"My lord," Thorne said, drawing Alaric's attention. He was pointing with his bloodied sword off to the right. Alaric followed with his eyes and found himself scowling. There, more than a quarter of a mile distant, a contingent of mounted men had appeared, distinguishable even at a distance by the banner they carried—a symbol that struck a chord deep within Alaric's heart.

The banner, emblazoned with the symbol of Eldanar, stood out starkly against the backdrop of conflict. The Radiant Compass, more than just an emblem, was a profound representation of their faith and the divine guidance it promised. The outer circle of the compass was gold, symbolizing the holy light that encompassed all creation. From the center, eight rays of light extended outward, each pointing in the cardinal and intercardinal directions, signifying Eldanar's omnipotent guidance to his followers in all paths and stages of life.

Alaric's gaze locked onto the distant figures. His observation of the knights, from one of the many orders who had joined the Crusade, discerned through the telltale glint of plate armor and the careful maneuvering of their heavy mounts, sparked curiosity. The knights seemed to be withdrawing. Their careful descent down the grass-covered hillside, moving away from the fray, stirred a sense of unease within him.

"Where are they going?" Kiera inquired, her confusion plain. Under the dim light and her helmet, her blue eyes sparkled with an intensity that was almost mesmerizing. The shadows danced across her scarred and tattooed face, highlighting her features in a way that made her look otherworldly.

"I don't like it," Thorne responded gruffly, his voice laden with distrust.

"Neither do I," Jasper said.

Alaric shared their sentiments, feeling a knot of apprehension tighten in his stomach. It was an ominous sign, one that he could not simply ignore. Yet he knew dwelling on it would serve no purpose, for he had a job to do. "We need to focus on the fight before us," he asserted, his voice firm, slicing through the tension like a blade. He turned his gaze away from the puzzling scene, redirecting his attention back to what mattered. In the short time they focused on the riders, the advance up the hill had continued, and the frontline was now more than twenty yards ahead of them.

"Push them!" Grayson's voice thundered across the battlefield, a rallying cry that cut through the chaos like the crack of a whip. At the forefront of the line, he was a figure of relentless determination, his sword arcing through the air, gleaming ominously as he waved it for his men to see. "Come on, boys, we're almost there! Onward! Keep pushing the bastards. They'll break soon enough."

From his vantage point, Alaric observed the unfolding drama with the keen eye of a seasoned leader. Grayson was correct, for his instincts also whispered of the imminent collapse of their foes' line. The ash men were on the verge of breaking. Their numbers had thinned considerably.

Despite the weariness that clung to his limbs, a result of the grueling march and the fierce combat he had joined in when the two lines had met, a surge of resolve steeled over Alaric. He resumed his ascent, following the path carved by his men.

Moments later, the inevitable happened. The holy warriors of the enemy, once unified in their fanatical zeal, broke ranks in a collective realization of defeat.

With a thunderous cry that seemed to shake the very ground beneath their feet, his men unleashed a primal roar and gave chase to the retreating and fleeing enemy. It was in this moment, as the once cohesive lines of their foes disintegrated into chaos, that the true carnage and killing began as his men ran the enemy down. Once more, the one true faith, a light in this shadowed and cursed land, had guided him and his men to victory.

"Eldanar, thank you for your many blessings," Alaric breathed.

As he made his way up the hillside, his gaze swept over the scarred landscape. The ground was littered with the fallen, many of whom he had to step over. Among the hundreds of bodies, the dead of the enemy outnumbered his own, yet this did little to alleviate the heavy burden of sorrow that weighed on his heart.

The reality was that with each clash, with every drop of blood spilled, his ranks thinned. What was more disheartening was the dwindling stream of reinforcements from their homeland. Over the last three years, the flow of men willing or able to join the Crusade had slowed to a trickle, a phenomenon not unique to his realm but felt across all allied lands. This alarming trend, coupled with losses suffered during campaigns, had gradually eroded the Cardinal's army, diminishing its numbers at a time when the enemy seemed only to swell in strength, ferocity, and boldness.

Every soldier lost was a precious resource they could ill afford to squander, let alone replace. The dwindling reinforcements meant that each victory, however significant, came at an increasingly unsustainable cost. Alaric's once formidable force, a proud assembly of four companies from Dekar, numbering nearly a thousand warriors, had been eroded by the relentless tide of war.

At the end of the previous campaign season, recognizing the need for unity and strength in the face of diminishing numbers, Alaric had made the difficult decision to merge the remnants of these once proud companies, now totaling little more than two hundred souls. The outcome of this consolidation was a new formation, one he'd named the Iron Vanguard. This new unit was composed of the most hardened, experienced, and resilient of his warriors, those who had survived ten hard years of war.

As Alaric continued to make his way up the slope, his boots stained with the mud and blood of the fray, he encountered a wounded soldier from his own ranks. The man, Jessen, lay on the ground, his breaths shallow, labored, a hand pressed tightly to his thigh, covering an ugly wound from which blood flowed liberally.

Alaric's heart clenched at the sight, knowing well the man's pain and fear, yet also understanding the brutal necessity of their situation. The wounded would have to wait, their cries for help echoing in the back of his mind as he pushed on, passing by the man, another soldier he could ill afford to lose.

The battlefield demanded cold priorities, and the living who could still wield a blade took precedence until victory was assured. This was the unforgiving equation of war, where mercy had to wait for the silence that followed the storm of combat.

The thought of continuing this seemingly endless conflict filled him with a weariness that went beyond physical exhaustion. It was the fatigue of the soul, a yearning for peace, escape, and a return to a life unmarred by the constant shadow and specter of death.

The idea of returning home, of abandoning the Crusade that had consumed so much of his life, flickered in his mind like a bonfire of hope in a storm-ravaged night. Yet duty and loyalty anchored him firmly to his current path.

Of late, he had received no word from his father, nor any directives from his king, or even, for that matter, queries concerning the Crusade's progress. The silence from his homeland, the Kingdom of Kevahn, was as disconcerting as it was isolating, leaving him to navigate the murky waters of his conscience and duty with no guiding star other than faith. The absence of communication, the lack of guidance or acknowledgment of his own letters, only deepened the chasm of uncertainty that threatened to swallow him whole.

Alaric's resolve, however, was as ironclad as the name of his newly formed company. Despite the doubts that plagued him, he was a leader, a noble warrior bound by honor, duty, and the unspoken oaths that tethered him to his men and their shared cause. The possibility of retreat, of abandoning their sacred mission, conflicted with every fiber of his being.

Yet, as he looked upon the faces of his wounded and dead, the stark reality of their situation pressed upon him. In the quiet moments of reflection, he dared to contemplate a future where the swords could be laid down, where the echoes of war would fade into memory.

Until that day, or until orders commanded otherwise, Alaric and the Iron Vanguard would stand firm, facing whatever trials awaited them on this foreign soil, far from the homeland he and his men yearned to see once more.

"My lord," Ezran's voice cut through into his thoughts, urgent yet controlled. With a subtle gesture of his chin, he directed Alaric's gaze to a scene that immediately drew his full attention.

Ahead, just a few short yards away at the hill's crest, Alaric's men had inexplicably stopped. They were not engaged in the fervent chase he anticipated, the relentless pursuit to run down the fleeing ash men. Instead, they stood eerily still, their silhouettes outlined against the grim sky. Their postures were tense yet hesitant as they peered into the distance with a palpable sense of uncertainty. It was an unexpected sight, one at odds with the momentum of their recent victory.

A cold shiver of apprehension ran down Alaric's spine, a premonition of danger that he could not quantify. His mind raced with possibilities. Was there an unseen enemy force lying in wait just beyond the hill's crest, ready to spring a deadly trap on his men? The very thought that they might be walking into an ambush or facing a second line of the enemy set his heart pounding with a mix of fear and adrenaline.

Even Grayson, a pillar of strength and aggression on the battlefield, had come to a standstill. His inaction was out of character, signaling to Alaric that something was terribly amiss. With no time to lose, Alaric quickened his pace, urgency propelling him as he made his way up the hill. Each step brought a growing sense of dread, the kind that tightens its grip around one's chest.

As he moved toward Grayson, Alaric prepared himself for whatever lay ahead. His mind was a whirlwind of strategy and concern, ready to adapt to the situation, to lead his men through whatever new challenge awaited them.

"Make way for the lord," Thorne's voice boomed over the clamor of shifting armor and uneasy murmurs. His command rippled through the ranks like a wave, parting the sea of warriors as Alaric, driven by a mix of dread and determination, shouldered his way through the press.

As he reached the hill's summit, he found Grayson, a figure of unshakeable resolve, looking defeated, his shoulders slumped and his sword's point buried in the grass and dirt. Alaric's gaze followed his captain's, extending over the crest and down into the valley beyond.

The sight that greeted him was one of stark, raw impact. Below, the remnants of the enemy force they had routed were in retreat, a disorganized stream of figures scrambling madly down the hill's reverse slope, which was quite steep. Yet it was not the sight of their fleeing adversaries that captured Alaric's attention or caused his heart to sink. No, it was what lay beyond the immediate chaos of retreat.

The valley, sprawled out under the dying light of day, revealed a scene that reshaped the entire context of their victory into something much more daunting. The implications of what Alaric saw were chilling, forcing him to reassess their situation and the challenges they faced.

The heart of the Cardinal's Holy Army was engulfed in the throes of battle, their forces locked in a desperate struggle against a numerically superior enemy. The clash of arms and the cries of combatants filled the air, a cacophony of violence that resonated even to the hilltop half a mile away.

Beyond the immediate melee, Alaric observed with a sinking heart, the methodical advance of the enemy's reserves. Like dark, inexorable tides, massive block-like formations were in motion, moving across the battlefield and maneuvering to completely encircle the soldiers of the faith. Thousands of enemy cavalry, sounding from a distance like the low roll of thunder, were moving around and behind the Cardinal's army, pursuing the remnants of the allied cavalry, clearly sweeping them from the field.

It was a tactical nightmare realized: The Cardinal's army was completely surrounded, caught in a vise from which there seemed little hope of escape. He estimated their army was outnumbered, perhaps as much as three to one, likely more.

The reality of the situation was inescapable, the strategic implications dire. The enemy, in all their massive might, had not only engaged the Cardinal's forces, drawing them into battle, but had outmaneuvered them. There appeared to be no path for retreat, let alone victory.

Alaric searched the enemy banners and, after a moment, settled upon one that was crimson red. Sunara, the great enemy general, was on the field and in command. This was his doing.

"We've arrived too late." Alaric's words were barely more than a whisper, a stark awareness that settled heavily upon his shoulders and soul. The scene before him, with its raw depiction of chaos and loss, painted a truth he could no longer deny. Even as hope flickered dimly within him, he acknowledged the bitter reality: Their timing mattered little against the overwhelming force the enemy had marshaled and brought to bear.

"The Crusade is lost." Grayson's voice echoed Alaric's despair, imbued with a tone of disbelief and shock.

The battle, the Crusade, their sacred mission—everything they had fought for was slipping through their fingers like grains of sand in an hourglass. Alaric was powerless to change the dynamic, let alone stop it. Standing beside Grayson, he could only offer a wooden nod, his body reacting while his mind reeled.

There was nothing to be done, nothing he could do to help.

As the reality of their defeat settled in, Alaric's initial shock gave way to a deep, seething anger. He had led his men across the sea, fought with every ounce of his being, believing in the righteousness of their cause. And it was all for nothing.

"Ten years," Alaric said, his voice thick with emotion, each word imbued with sacrifice, struggle, and now, a pervasive sense of futility. The heat in his breath was not just from the exertion of battle but from the fire of frustration and disillusionment burning within him. How many had died for this failure? "Ten years…"

"What?" Grayson's response was a mix of confusion and concern, his brow furrowed as he faced Alaric, trying to decipher the underlying meaning behind his words. "What did you say, my lord?"

"We've been here for at least ten years." The weight of those years pressed down on Alaric with renewed force. A torrent of memories flooded through him—battles fought, comrades lost, victories and triumphs that now seemed hollow. The bitterness that welled up inside him was an elixir of regret and resentment.

"Aye," Grayson said softly.

"Ten wasted years." The finality in Alaric's voice was a reflection of his internal reckoning, a painful acknowledgment of the time and lives consumed by this Crusade. The dream they chased, the victory they sought, seemed now more elusive than ever, leaving behind only a trail of lost opportunities and what-ifs.

Alaric and his men had come to this land as bearers of a cause they believed just and holy, only to find themselves ensnared in the complexities and brutalities of a conflict that drained their spirits and questioned their convictions.

"We must press forward," a voice implored, imbued with a fervor that seemed almost out of place. "We have to keep going. By Eldanar's light, we must keep going."

Alaric, gaze still locked on the calamitous scene unfolding in the valley below, was for a moment untouched by the urgency of the plea. The battle raged on, a living animal ravenously consuming lives on both sides, yet he remained motionless, caught in a tumult of thought and despair.

"We must press forward!" The insistence in the voice finally drew Alaric's attention away from the battlefield, compelling him to find the source of this unyielding determination. Father Kemm had emerged from the ranks, his waterlogged holy robes a stark contrast against the backdrop of war. In his hand, he clutched a finely honed staff, a symbol of his office.

The priest was the Cardinal's direct representative. When he spoke, it was with the Cardinal's voice. Father Kemm, with the golden compass hanging around his neck—a delicate, yet powerful symbol of their faith—was here as the Cardinal's dog, meant to watch over Alaric, to ensure compliance and obedience. The priest pointed toward the embattled forces below with a conviction and authority that brooked no argument. "We must go to their aid—before it is too late."

Father Kemm's gaze, intense and unwavering, locked onto Alaric and Grayson, his staff directed toward the tumult below. His voice carried the weight of authority, a command that demanded obedience and action. "My Lord Alaric, we must press forward before it is too late. You cannot fail us now."

Alaric's response was a measured glance, first toward the chaotic dance of death below, then back to the priest. Kemm, for all his ostentatious display of piety and dedication, was a figure that Alaric had always struggled to respect. The priest's ascent from humble origins in the Kingdom of Gress to a position of considerable influence was a tale not of divine favor, but of political acumen and ambition. His involvement in the Crusade from its inception had served solely as a ladder to power, elevating him above his birthright and into the circles of the nobility. Kemm's reputation for greed, consumption, and manipulation was well-known to Alaric, who found such traits distasteful, if not outright reprehensible.

Yet for all his personal grievances against the man, Alaric could not dismiss the influence and power Kemm wielded. As the Cardinal's direct representative, his words carried the force of command, his directives shaped by the unseen hand of the church's highest authority in this land. In the complex hierarchy of their holy mission, Kemm's position afforded the man a degree of power and protection that could not be easily challenged, even by those of noble birth.

The irony of their situation was not lost on Alaric. The Cardinal, the spiritual leader of their cause, was likely somewhere in the midst of the valley's turmoil, his fate intertwined with the thousands of souls battling in his god's name. The distance between the lofty ideals of their faith and the grim reality of war had never been more apparent than in this moment, with Kemm urging them into a battle that was unwinnable.

Alaric's disdain for Kemm's character did not blind him to the gravity of their situation, the moment, and what was being asked. The call to rally to the aid of their embattled brethren posed a dilemma that transcended personal animosities.

"What are you waiting for? We must press forward. Surely you can see that. We can turn the tide!" Father Kemm's insistence pierced the heavy air, his voice a mix of command and desperation. His words, though laden with conviction, seemed to Alaric like the last flickers of a candle in a storm—doomed to be extinguished by the overwhelming might of the enemy.

"Going forward is nothing short of suicide," Grayson said.

Alaric's response was a silent shake of his head, a gesture laden with the weight of resignation. The Crusade, for all its lofty ambitions and divine aspirations, was over. The journey that began as a grand adventure, a holy quest to reclaim ancient and sacred lands and spread the light of their faith, had deteriorated into a quagmire of loss and disillusionment.

In the early years, the fervor of their mission carried them forward, driving them to remarkable victories and the establishment of a new kingdom in Eldanar's name, raising the Cardinal to new heights, making him a holy king. But as the years passed, the nature of their endeavor shifted. The focus strayed from the divine and the devout, corrupted by the very mortal failings of man—greed and power. The Cardinal, a figure who should have embodied the highest virtues of their faith, had instead steered their mission toward mortal concerns and political machinations.

About five years ago, the tide had begun to turn. The ash men, once scattered and subdued, rallied under Sunara with a newfound unity and purpose. With each passing campaign season, the momentum of the Crusade faltered, then gradually been reversed, until they found themselves retreating toward the very shores that had once seen their arrival as conquerors and liberators.

Now, standing on the brink of this final defeat, Alaric could not deny the evidence before his eyes. The infidels, so long branded as the enemy, had turned the tide, reclaiming their conquered lands and repelling the invaders. The faith, which once seemed an unassailable fortress of righteousness, had crumbled under the weight of its own hubris and misdirection.

The Crusade, indeed, their entire endeavor, was lost. The

dreams of glory and divine favor had dissipated, leaving behind a bitter legacy of conflict and loss. The proof of their failure was not just in the battered remnants of their army or the lands they failed to hold, but in the very soul of the Crusade itself, which had strayed so far from its original, sacred purpose.

The infidels had begun winning and the faith had started losing.

No, the enemy had won. The proof of that lay before him. It was undeniable now.

Alaric envisioned the inevitable downfall with a clarity that bordered on prescience. In the aftermath of the battle, which would see the Cardinal's complete defeat, the horizon bore the grim promise of a future where the cities along the coast stood on the precipice. The enemy would lay siege and methodically dismantle their powerful defenses, one after another, until those of the faith were gone from these shores.

The Holy Land of Divinara, a realm sanctified by the prayers and blood of the faithful, stood on the brink of being reclaimed by the enemy, once more plunged into darkness. The stark choices that awaited the defeated were dire: death beneath the cold edge of a sword or an executioner's axe, the shackles of enslavement, or the erasure of their beliefs under the weight of forced conversion.

Sensing movement in the distance, Alaric shifted his gaze to the left, looking down the line of his men. He caught sight of their so-called allies—their spirits clearly shattered—retreating in a disheartened exodus. They slipped away quietly, in ones and twos, without a backward glance, hurrying back down the hill. This retreat was not a mere physical withdrawal, but a symbolic fracture in their collective will to stand against the encroaching darkness.

Despite the disheartening scene unfolding before him, a surge of pride swelled within Alaric's chest as he observed his own men. Not a single man amongst them had succumbed to the instinct of flight. They stood as unwavering pillars of discipline and loyalty, in absolute opposition to the faltering morale around them. His men, forged in the crucible of countless battles, shared a bond with Alaric that was unbreakable. They looked to him for direction. Where he told them to march, they would march. His duty to them now outweighed any oaths he'd made to the Cardinal.

"We must go to our brethren's aid!" Kemm shouted, stepping forward, his face contorted with passionate zeal. Spittle flecked his lips as he brandished his staff, jutting it toward the battle in the valley below. "In the Cardinal's name, I command you, Lord Alaric, to advance."

"No," Alaric countered. Unlike Kemm's impassioned plea, Alaric's tone was hard, resolute. It carried a harshness that was foreign even to his own ears. "The fight here is over. Adding more souls to the slaughter will serve no purpose."

"Blasphemy!" Kemm screamed, his voice tearing through the air. His outburst was more than mere disagreement; it was a challenge to Alaric's authority, a denunciation of his decision. "The faithful will prevail by our divine righteousness alone!"

"Divine righteousness?" Alaric murmured under his breath, his gaze lingering on the priest. He took in the sight of Kemm, noting the opulence of his attire. The robes draped over the man's rotund frame were of a fabric so rich and finely woven, their value alone could surpass what the humble peasants of this land could hope to earn in a span of five years, maybe more.

As Alaric's scrutiny continued, a cold realization dawned upon him, painting Kemm's fervent plea in a starkly different light. It wasn't just spiritual conviction that fueled the priest's desperation; it was the looming threat of personal loss. Kemm balanced on a chasm's knife edge, facing the potential downfall of everything he held dear—his esteemed position within the church hierarchy, the opulent lifestyle to which he had grown accustomed, the companionship of those who catered to his basest desires, and perhaps even his very life. The stakes were far more personal for Kemm than they were spiritual, and he wanted Alaric to spend the lives of his men on the folly of it all.

This insight into Kemm's motivations filled Alaric with a profound sense of revulsion. Disgust welled up within him. In this moment of clarity, Alaric saw the true face of those who cloaked their ambitions in the guise of faith. It was a dour reminder of the corruption and moral decay that could fester within the hearts of those who professed to lead in the name of the divine.

"So be it," Alaric said. "The die has been cast."

"What?" Kemm asked, confused, his eyes narrowing.

"Grayson," Alaric intoned, his voice carrying the weight of command as he motioned toward the base of the hill behind them. There, in the relative safety of the rear, lay their baggage train, a lifeline amidst the chaos, stationed a quarter-mile away with a small guard. Within that assemblage of mules carrying their supplies and provisions were ten horses, among them Alaric's own steed—a majestic black stallion named Fire. "Detail some men to our horses as an escort. Thorne, you go with them. You are in charge."

Thorne gave a nod. "As you command, my lord, so shall I obey."

"Yes, sir," Grayson said. "And what are your orders for these men, for Thorne?"

"There are three ships currently in port. They put in the day before last. You know of which ones I speak, yes?" Alaric stated, directing his attention now to Thorne.

"Captain Magerie's ships?" Thorne inquired, seeking clarification.

"That's him," Alaric affirmed, determination and an undercurrent of urgency now in his voice. "Find that old pirate. Tell him we're on the way and want passage. Whatever he demands as a fee, I will pay it and then some. We need space enough for our company and those allies who desire to go with us," he continued, casting a sweeping glance at the nearest of his men. The weight of leadership bore heavily upon his shoulders. "Passage is to include our women and children. They will be coming with us as well."

Many of his men had forged bonds, taken wives, and started families in this foreign land, ties that he knew they could not bear to sever, let alone leave behind at the mercies of their enemies.

"Then tell the garrison to pack everything, and I mean *everything*, all of our supplies. When we go, we will bring with us several months of rations. Instruct the garrison commander to buy anything else we need or could possibly require and get on that immediately. Understand?"

"I do, my lord," Thorne said. "And what of you?"

"I will march back with the men. My intention is to board and leave as soon as the ships are loaded and the tide will bear us. We must move fast on this matter."

"Yes, my lord," Thorne said. "I will see your will done."

"Oh, and be wary of our allies," Alaric cautioned, his gaze shifting toward the unsettling scene of their erstwhile comrades-in-arms on either flank. The trickle of retreat had become a flood, with ranks thinning as more and more figures slipped away, a tangible sign of the crumbling alliance and the recognition that the Crusade was finally over. The sight foretold a grim future where the bonds of loyalty and duty dissolved into a desperate scramble for survival. "Soon it will be every man for themselves, even the nobility." His voice carried a note of somber realism, acknowledging the bitter truth that in the face of overwhelming defeat, the veneer of unity and honor amongst allies would quickly erode, leaving only self-preservation in its wake. "If I am any judge, some will be switching sides, and we don't want to be here when that happens. Be on guard."

"I will be, my lord," Thorne replied.

"Grayson." Alaric turned to the captain. He hardened his voice and raised it so it would carry. "Prepare to withdraw. First, we will look to our wounded. We will not be leaving them."

"Yes, my lord," Grayson said with a nod, then looked around. "Sergeant Miks. Form a detail to care for the wounded and get them ready for transport back to Hawkani."

"Aye, sir," came the response from Miks.

"You cannot leave!" Kemm shouted, tears in his eyes as he looked between Alaric and the Cardinal's army. His outstretched finger, trembling slightly, pointed accusingly at Alaric, as if trying to anchor the warrior to his spot with sheer willpower. "You must fight. You swore an oath to obey. I forbid you to go!"

Alaric's response was visceral, a primal surge of anger that welled up within him, mounting rapidly, like heat from a freshly lit and fired forge. He drove the point of Oathbreaker into the soft dirt with a force that left no doubt of his fury. He started for Kemm, each step deliberate, causing the priest to retreat instinctively, stumbling in his attempt to maintain distance between them.

As Alaric closed the gap, driving the priest to the edge of the steep slope, Kemm's defense was feeble at best—his staff raised more in hope than expectation, serving as a barrier between them. With a swift, contemptuous motion, Alaric brushed the staff aside, knocking it from the man's soft hands. It went clattering down the hillside, as if chasing after the retreating ash men.

"I—I forbid—" Kemm stammered. "I—I forbid—" Kemm's attempts to assert his authority were pitiful, his voice faltering. He looked to Grayson for help. None was forthcoming. And then, it came—an explosion of force as Alaric's fist connected with Kemm's face. The priest crumpled in a heap.

"I can and will leave." Alaric's voice sliced through the charged air, as cold and unyielding as the steel of his blade, his towering presence casting a long shadow over the fallen priest, even as the rain continued to pour around them.

From a split lip, blood was streaming down onto the man's wet robes. He stared up at Alaric in horror. "You struck me!" Kemm's voice was tinged with shock and disbelief, his words hanging between them. The notion that he, a servant of the cloth, could be subjected to such violence appeared to all but shatter his understanding of the world. "You struck one of the cloth!"

"Struck you? You are lucky I don't kill you. Long ago, your Cardinal turned from the faith, his focus, like yours, becoming greed and the accumulation of wealth and power. He worships gold more than anything else, and this day, our god is punishing him and everyone else with him for his avarice. Even someone as blind as you should be able to recognize that."

Alaric's gaze fell upon the golden compass around the priest's chest. He reached down. Kemm's instinctive reaction was to shield himself, his hands raised in a futile gesture of warding. Brushing the hands aside, Alaric seized the golden compass from around the trembling priest's neck and ripped it free, snapping the gold chain with a crack.

"You don't deserve this," he declared, voice echoing with finality, a renunciation not just of the man before him, but of a corrupted system that had strayed far from its divine path. Alaric waved the compass. "I will take this into safekeeping for someone worthy."

The look in the priest's eyes hardened.

"I curse you, Alaric of Dekar," Kemm hissed, his fear morphing into pure hatred. "I curse you to the end of your days."

"I am already cursed." Alaric turned away from the fallen priest, his focus shifting back to his men, eyeing them as he considered all that would need be done. But first, they had to make it back to Hawkani, before the enemy could catch them. He glanced back at the battle in the valley and judged it would continue for several hours to come. After it ended, the enemy would need time to regroup. That would give him a head start.

He turned his attention once more to his men. They had all seen what he'd just done to Kemm. The air, already heavy with anticipation, thickened further. He opened his mouth to speak, then was interrupted.

Behind him, a scream of pure rage and hatred shattered the momentary calm. Before he could turn, Ezran responded with a speed that belied human capability. His movements were a blur. Something flashed briefly in the dim light as it flew from his free hand, narrowly missing Alaric's shoulder—a missile guided by intent and years of practice.

The sound that followed was gruesomely distinct—a meaty thwack that spoke of flesh being forcibly united by steel. Alaric, reacting, spun around, his warrior instincts fully awakened.

Kemm stood just behind him with a dagger clutched in his hand, its blade glinting dully under the muted light. The priest's stance was frozen, dagger poised to strike at Alaric's back. Then the moment shattered. He stumbled backward, a look of shock painting his features, his eyes wide with disbelief. The cause of his halt—the hilt of another dagger protruded grotesquely from his throat, a silent arbiter of his fate.

Reaching up, Kemm grasped the hilt with his free hand. His mouth worked and then opened. The priest's attempt to scream never came, silenced by his own blood, which poured forth in a gruesome fountain that flowed over his rich robes. He took a step back, only to lose his balance and fall, tumbling down the rocky and grass-covered slope until a large boulder halted his involuntary journey.

Alaric gave a nod to himself. He should have known better than to turn his back on an enemy, especially one like Kemm.

"Nice throw," Thorne said to Ezran.

"I never liked him anyway," Ezran replied simply, then a

regretful look overcame his face as he stepped to the edge of the slope and looked down. He let go a heavy breath. "But I will miss that dagger, for it was well-made."

"Where will we go, my lord?"

The inquiry, laden with uncertainty, pierced the tumult of Alaric's emotions, carving a path through the remnants of his anger and bringing him to a moment of clarity. As he turned, his gaze fell upon Beechum, the man who'd spoken from the ranks. He was one of Alaric's veterans, his visage marked by the scars of war, yet alight with the steadfast loyalty that had seen them through the darkest of times. Alaric's eyes lingered on him, a silent acknowledgment of the bonds forged in the crucible of battle, before sweeping across the faces of his gathered men.

Every warrior's gaze was fixed upon him with a mixture of anticipation and hope. They were men who had followed him through the abyss, their faith in him unwavering, even as they stood on the precipice of the unknown. It was a responsibility that weighed heavily on Alaric's shoulders, a mantle he bore with the solemn dignity of a true leader.

"Home," Alaric said. "At long last, boys, we are going home. Home to Kevahn… home to Dekar."

2

The guard, with a swift movement, snapped to attention and swung the heavy wooden door to the keep open with a hard push. Without stopping, Alaric passed him by and strode inside.

Behind him, Ezran, Jasper, and Kiera—his personal guard—followed in weary silence, their steps heavy with fatigue. Outside, the courtyard came alive with the sound of orders barked by Grayson as he directed the men of his company with a firm and commanding presence to clean their gear before turning in for some sleep. The door, ancient and groaning under the weight of its own history, banged closed with a resounding echo that seemed to linger on the air. It muffled the sounds from outside.

"My lord," Kiera said, her voice firm and demanding attention. "Would you excuse us?"

Alaric halted his advance and faced his personal guard in the narrow corridor. To his left, a stone staircase loomed, its steps worn smooth in the center from countless years of use, a witness to the passage of time and the many feet that had trodden its path over the centuries.

The corridor itself was dimly illuminated by a pair of oil lanterns hanging from the walls, their flames casting a warm, flickering light that danced across the stone surfaces. The pungent smell of burning oil enveloped them in an almost tangible haze.

Before him, the three stood, the toll of their recent endeavors etched into their weary postures and dirt-streaked faces. Even Ezran, typically the most resilient amongst them, bore the unmistakable signs of exhaustion. The return march under a relentless rain had done little to cleanse them of the grime, mud, dried blood, and gore from battle. Fatigue clung to their beings like a second skin.

"I will not be needing you," Alaric announced, his tone carrying the weight of finality and a deep-seated weariness that mirrored his companions'. He was so tired, his right eyelid was twitching. "I plan on eating, cleaning up, and sleeping for at least four hours."

"Thank you, my lord," Kiera responded, her relief and gratitude clear. She turned away, her boots—fitted with hobnails that echoed her every step—striking against the stone as she ascended the staircase toward her quarters. The sound of her departure was a staccato rhythm that faded with distance. Ezran and Jasper, without a word, trailed after her, their own heavy steps speaking to the day's hardships and the promise of a brief respite that lay ahead.

Alaric let go a breath and navigated the short corridor leading to the heart of his domain, the great room of Hawkani's keep. The keep, while modest in size compared to the sprawling estates and castles of some of his peers, held a certain charm and warmth. Upon reaching the door, he pushed it open, the heavy oak swinging inward with a low creak that welcomed him back.

As Alaric crossed the threshold into the great room, he paused long enough to allow his eyes to adjust from the corridor's dim light to the bright ambiance of the room. Dozens of candles, mounted in six large candelabras to either side, lit the space with plenty of light.

The interior, though modest, was comfortably furnished, reflecting the practical and unassuming nature of its lord. The walls, constructed from thick, gray stone, stood solid and imposing. The room was suffused with the soothing aroma of woodsmoke, emanating from the large, open fireplace that occupied a place of prominence on one wall.

The fireplace, filled with crackling logs and glowing embers, radiated a warmth that contested the chill creeping in from the outside. Its flickering light, along with those of the candles, danced across the room, casting an ever-shifting pattern of light and shadow that seemed to bring the simple furnishings to life.

Here, in this humble great room, Alaric regularly found a refuge from the demands and dangers of his position. The warmth from the fireplace immediately enveloped him, easing the cold that had seeped into his bones during the long, rain-soaked journey back.

Central to the room were three long wooden tables, each able to accommodate more than ten people with flanking benches. This communal area, designed for both the daily breaking of bread and the conducting of council, stood ready to serve its purpose at a moment's notice.

Further enriching the room were various chests and cupboards arrayed against the far wall, each piece echoing the history of the keep through its weathered and worn appearance. Above these practical furnishings, tapestries of vibrant hues and intricate designs hung from the walls, their threads depicting scenes of valor, the tranquility of pastoral life, and the fervor of spiritual devotion. These woven artworks provided a much-needed infusion of color and narrative to the austere stone surroundings.

Dominating the head of the room and the main table was an ornately carved high-backed chair. This chair, more than any other item in the room, signified Alaric's undisputed authority within the keep and city, a physical embodiment of his leadership and status, conferred upon him by the Cardinal King. Soon, it would no longer be his…

Was that such a bad thing?

Upon entering, Alaric's gaze fell upon two servants, Michael and Missa, who awaited his return with clear unease. Their anxiety was not unexpected; the arrival of Thorne, sent ahead with news of the coming departure from this land, had undoubtedly set the stage for their apprehension. It was something Alaric could well understand.

"My lord," Michael greeted as he bowed his head in reverence. He took a shuffling step forward, the movement betraying the legacy of a past wound that had taken him from the ranks to this very hall to serve his house in a different manner. He gestured toward the long table, where the chair, resembling a throne with its elaborate carvings, waited.

On the table, a place setting, a loaf of bread, a pitcher of wine with several mugs, and a bowl of what looked like stew sat. The room was infused with the smell of smoke from the fireplace, tallow from the candles, and the subtle aroma of the stew.

"We have food and wine prepared."

Alaric gave a weary nod in acknowledgment. The rain had left him drenched and miserable, his clothes clinging uncomfortably to his skin. He walked over to the fire, its crackling warmth a source of solace. Holding out his hands, he sought the fire's welcoming embrace, a small comfort for his weary bones.

"Missa, kindly fetch me some dry clothes," Alaric requested without glancing over. He rubbed his hands together, trying to get the warmth back.

"Yes, master," came the soft, obedient reply from the girl with brown eyes. Missa, young and slender, with an unassuming appearance that belied her efficiency, bowed deeply. As she hurried from the room, her figure was a fleeting shadow against the candlelit walls, the bottom of her wool dress whispering secrets across the stone, her departure marked by the careful watchfulness of Michael. His eyes followed her before he turned back to attend to his lord.

Alaric moved away from the soothing blaze of the fire. With deliberate movements, he untied and lifted his helmet, a masterpiece of craftsmanship that had seen countless fights, and placed it on the table. The sound of metal against wood echoed hollowly in the room. Dented and scratched, the helmet had seen better days. Next, he unhitched Oathbreaker's scabbard from his harness, laying the sheathed weapon beside his helmet. Its presence was as much a part of him as his own shadow, a constant companion. He poured himself a generous mug of wine, the rich aroma filling his senses as he took a deep draft. Alaric let go a relieved breath. The poor-quality, vinegarish wine available in Hawkani had never tasted so good.

"Help me out of my armor, would you?" Alaric's request broke the silence. He set the clay mug down upon the table with a heavy *thunk*.

"Yes, my lord," Michael responded, shuffling forward. His hands moved to the straps of Alaric's breastplate. He began working on a knot along the side. "It is taking longer than it should, my lord. The leather is wet and has become resistant."

"It was raining through the night, though it's finally starting to taper off." Weariness seeped through Alaric's words. The desire to shed his armor and the soaked remnants of his journey was strong, each piece of metal and leather a burden he longed to be free of. His gaze drifted to the plate of stew, the steam rising invitingly, its scent promising comfort and sustenance. His stomach rumbled powerfully.

Michael got the first knot free and, rapidly after, had another undone. The armor began to yield, loosening its constricting grasp upon Alaric. Soon all the knots were untied. The relief was immediate as the breastplate was lifted over his head, a weight both physically and metaphorically removed from his shoulders.

Alaric's groan of relief, mingled with the sound of his armor being set aside, was a final release from the day's trials. Free of the heavy weight and feeling incredibly light, as if he weighed almost nothing, Alaric stripped off his soaked tunic, laying it upon the bench next to the table.

He settled himself on a wooden bench, its surface worn smooth by years of use, running along the length of the long central table that anchored the room. He turned his attention to his boots next, peeling them off with a grimace and a sense of real relief. Each boot was so sodden that it squished when he walked. He pulled off his socks and saw his feet white and badly wrinkled. He handed the boots to Michael, who limped over and placed them near the fire to dry out.

Stripped down to just his pants, Alaric allowed himself a rare moment of relaxation. The bench, though hard and unyielding, felt like a throne of comfort.

Missa reentered the room, her arms bearing the simple luxury of dry clothes, along with a towel. She placed the fresh tunic and pants on the stool beside him, her movements swift and unobtrusive, a dance of service and care that had become second nature. Alaric offered her a nod of gratitude, an acknowledgment of her contribution.

Sitting there, he fully inhabited the moment. The room was a personal sanctuary, warm and comfortable, as it had been ever since the keep became his seat of power in this land. The sensation of just sitting, of allowing his body to rest, was a magnificent indulgence that bordered on the surreal. The day's exertions weighed heavily on him; the march of nearly forty miles there and back in so short a time, along with the clash of battle, had taken its toll. Every muscle ached, a chorus of protests from his feet to his legs and back, a physical inventory of the day's demands. Even his hands, fingers, and arms hurt, not to mention his neck, which was incredibly stiff. He rolled his neck to work the discomfort out.

Yet, in this moment of stillness, there was an underlying current of satisfaction. The aches and weariness spoke of survival, of yet another battle fought and endured. It was a warrior's respite, brief and hard-earned, a pause in the relentless march of duty that defined his life. Alaric's gaze lingered on the flames, their dance a mesmerizing difference to the stillness within him, a warrior momentarily at peace with the tumultuous world outside and all its waiting problems.

"Is it true, master?" Missa's inquiry, soft yet laden with concern, bridged the gap between servant and master. Her brown eyes fixated on Alaric, and in them, he saw a depth that seemed to mirror her soul. Her features, kissed by the sun, bore the distinctive mark of the local populace, a blend of resilience and exotic grace carved by the harshness and beauty of their land. "Are you leaving Hawkani, master?"

Before Alaric could respond, Thorne's voice cut through the tense air, emanating from the shadows near a side door from which he emerged. The door led to the kitchen. "As I told you earlier, we are leaving, Missa. Lord Alaric has already given the orders and commissioned the ships to take his people home."

Alaric, wearied from the demands of the day, could only nod in confirmation. His acknowledgment sent a ripple of emotion across the room. Missa's gaze darted toward Michael, a silent exchange fraught with anxiety and unspoken hope. Alaric observed the momentary connection, a wordless conversation that spoke volumes of the bonds of shared fates formed under this roof.

Discovered on the unforgiving streets of the city, Missa, an orphan, had been half-starved. She'd been selling her body for a pittance, just to earn enough to eat. When they'd first met, one of her clients had just beaten her horribly.

Alaric could not put his finger on what had drawn him to notice her so many years ago, a pitiful figure amongst the press of the crowd, shuffling her way down the street in the opposite direction. Fate or perhaps divine intervention caused him to glance around and pick her out. There had been something about her that had spoken to him. Long ago, Alaric learned to listen to his instincts, his gut, and that had changed her life.

He had seen beyond the desperation of a starving and hurt girl just into her teens, to the soul residing underneath, and felt a moment of pity. He had taken her in and had her injuries tended to. Ultimately, he'd also seen her trained as a servant, and over the years she had made her own place amongst his household. In truth, with Michael, she ran it. More importantly, she was fiercely loyal, and he did not wish to part with her services now.

"Do you wish to go with us?" Alaric's question was gentle, offering her a choice, a crossroads between past shadows and the promise of a new dawn. "If you choose to remain, I will reward you with gold for your service. The amount will set you up with a comfortable life."

"That would be a life under the ash men," Thorne added. "There is no guarantee they will treat you right, especially given your history with the current lord of Hawkani."

Missa looked to Thorne, then at Michael, and finally, Alaric. Her bottom lip gave a slight tremble.

"So," Alaric asked, "what will it be? Will you come with us and continue to serve me?"

"I will, master," Missa replied, her voice steady, her resolve clear. Her glance toward Michael, Alaric's loyal manservant, spoke of the bonds of loyalty and affection that had grown in the unlikeliest of soils. "If Michael is going, I will go too."

"I am going," Michael said. "I wish to go home to Dekar, my lord."

"Then it is decided," Alaric proclaimed, his decision not just a command, but an affirmation of the family they'd become, bound not by blood, but by the deeper ties of loyalty, compassion, and shared adversity. "Missa, you will go with us when we depart for Dekar."

Alaric lifted the mug of wine once more and drank. When he set it down, he looked between his two servants. They were staring at one another, emotion and meaning in their gazes. He felt a softening in his heart. Both had been wounded, one physically and one in the heart and soul. Here was a chance to do some good.

"Right," Alaric intoned, the weariness of his bones seeping into his words. "I am tired and spent. Missa, I need to bathe before I get some sleep. Can you see to that?"

"I will draw the buckets, master, and have them waiting in your room." With a slight bow and unshed tears in her eyes, she glanced once more at Michael, her gaze deeper than ever, then moved to fulfill the request.

Michael's eyes lingered on the path Missa took. He shifted his gaze to Alaric. "I did not think you knew, my lord."

"Of course he knew of your affection for Missa," Thorne replied, his tone laced with gruff assurance. "Now, give us some peace. Take the armor and see that it is thoroughly cleaned, made free of rust, then packed and ready to be moved to the ship. As soon as it is, send me word."

"Yes, sir." Michael picked up the armor and, limping, followed after Missa.

"Any trouble coming back?" Thorne's question, casual, yet mired with the concern of a seasoned soldier, cut through the room's temporary reprieve.

"No," Alaric responded firmly. Rising from his seated position, he was greeted by a chorus of protests from his legs. With a groan, he shed his wet pants, the fabric clinging stubbornly to his skin, as if reluctant to part ways. He dried himself with the towel Missa had brought, then slipped into the dry pants. It was a small comfort, for the stone floor was cold beneath his bare feet.

Alaric pulled on the fresh tunic, then moved to his chair. Seating himself, he reached for the loaf of bread, tearing it in two with a decisiveness born of hunger. Dipping it into the stew, he watched as it soaked up the juice. The first bite was an act of reclamation, of grounding himself in the present, each chew a momentary escape. Not only was the stew fresh, it was also hot, which was more than welcome. He swallowed, then looked back up at Thorne.

"Sunara's cavalry did not trouble us," Alaric continued. "I think they were too busy keeping the Cardinal's forces from escaping the trap that had been laid than worrying about us. The rain—well, fortune favored our withdrawal."

"They had bigger fish to fry." Thorne gave a nod and poured himself some wine. He took a drink from the clay mug.

"I got your message on Bramwell's agreement," Alaric said. "Five thousand in gold is a lot, though, more than I anticipated spending."

"He wanted seven thousand, especially for a hurried departure, claimed on such short notice the food stores for such a voyage would cost a fortune. He said he was planning on beaching his galleys to work on their hulls and had reserved space, and that would cost too."

"You've not paid him yet?" Alaric asked.

"No, not fully," Thorne replied. "I gave him a thousand gold sovereigns as a down payment. He eagerly pocketed it and is looking forward to the rest."

Alaric nodded and took another bite of his bread.

"The garrison has already begun work on packing our equipment and supplies."

"Good," Alaric said. "Has there been any panic? Disorder in the city?"

"Surprisingly, no," Thorne admitted as he took another sip of his wine. "The word is out, but people are going about their lives."

"Really?" Alaric asked as he took another bite. He found that surprising.

"There have been so many reverses of late that I think it is hard to shock people these days." Thorne scratched an itch on his neck. "Lord Merrick came by to see you about an hour ago. I told him to come back in the morning."

"What does he want?" Alaric said between bites. He had never much gotten along with Merrick.

"What do you think he wants?" Thorne asked sourly.

"The city," Alaric surmised and set the bread down. "It is a good thing we have more men than he does."

"Yes, it is," Thorne agreed. "Otherwise, he would have moved against us long before. But now that we are leaving, he will get it without a fight."

"He's welcome to Hawkani, and all the headaches that come with it," Alaric said.

"Are you not concerned about leaving?" Thorne asked curiously. "You did swear an oath to the Cardinal King."

"I did," Alaric said. "Long ago, he betrayed that oath. I no longer feel obligated to honor it."

Thorne nodded as he took another swig of wine.

"It is time to go home to Dekar and Kevahn," Alaric said.

The door creaked loudly as it opened. Grayson entered. He closed the door behind him, the latch falling into place with a click.

"How are the men?" Alaric inquired, his voice carrying the

weight of responsibility for those under his command. The well-being of his soldiers was a constant concern.

"Tired, worn, which is understandable," Grayson reported as he made his way across the room, his gaze momentarily drawn to the stew, speaking to the hunger that mirrored their shared exhaustion. Alaric tossed him the other half of the loaf of bread, which the captain caught with practiced ease. "As you ordered, I sent them to the barracks to get some rest."

"Good," Alaric approved, his mind already moving to the next phase of their plans. "In five hours, we roust and put them to work alongside the garrison. We must load the ships rapidly before a panic can set in amongst the populace. We take everything we can with us."

"Yes, my lord," Grayson acknowledged. "What of the city's treasury?"

"That too. It's mine. We bring it all and leave nothing behind," Alaric declared. "Anything of value is to come with us as long as there is room on the ships."

"Merrick will not be happy about you taking the treasury," Thorne interjected. "When he takes control and finds the treasury bare, he will be put out."

"I don't care about Merrick. Besides, he has money himself. Let him spend his own funds on fixing Hawkani's problems for a change." Alaric turned his gaze back to Grayson. "See that it is done."

"I will make arrangements for that to happen," Grayson said. "We will do it quiet-like, under the cover of darkness. No one will know."

"Good," Alaric responded, a wave of exhaustion sweeping over him. At the moment, all he wanted was to eat and sleep some.

"It helps that the treasury is kept here in the keep," Thorne commented.

"With your permission, my lord, I will withdraw to clean up." Grayson glanced at the door to the left, his readiness to retire and change apparent.

"You don't need my permission," Alaric said. "We are long past that."

"You are still the lord and senior here," Grayson said. "Respect and honor demands that I ask."

Alaric gave a weary nod.

Without further exchange, Grayson took a bite of his bread and exited the room through the same door Michael and Missa had gone through, his departure leaving Thorne and Alaric alone in a contemplative solitude.

In the quiet that followed Grayson's departure, the room seemed to shrink around the two of them, the air charged with the unspoken understanding of warriors who had weathered countless storms together.

"I'm beat," Alaric confessed quietly.

"I can imagine," Thorne responded, his voice tinged with empathy. "I rode, but you marched all the way. Though, since I got back, I've only managed an hour of sleep myself."

Alaric, seeking solace in the simple act of eating, picked up the wooden spoon and took a hearty sip of the stew. The warmth of the broth seemed to seep into his very soul. Thorne, respecting the moment, remained silent. He drank a pull of his wine, the fire crackling cheerily in the background.

Before long, the stew was finished, the bowl empty—a small victory in the grand scheme of things, yet a significant one for a man who had spent the day battling both the elements and the exhaustion that threatened to overwhelm him, along with keeping his men moving and marching back to Hawkani.

Alaric sat back, a yawn escaping his lips, a clear signal of his body's demand for rest. The readiness for sleep was more than physical; it was a bone-deep craving for a few hours of escape from the burden of command.

"What is Dekar like?"

Alaric's gaze shifted to Thorne, the inquiry pulling him from the precipice of exhaustion into a moment of reflection. Thorne, with his origins in the Southern Isles, possessed a perspective shaped by seas and storms. Alaric dove into the recesses of his memory, where images of Dekar lingered like echoes of a song whose words were long forgotten but not the tune. The question stirred something within him. It had been so long, at times he felt like he'd forgotten himself what home was like, and that troubled him deeply.

"Well?" Thorne's voice was tinged with curiosity.

Alaric gathered his thoughts, the imagery of Dekar coalescing from the mists of his mind.

"It is a green land," Alaric began, his words painting a picture starkly different from the landscapes that surrounded them now. "With large forests and trees aplenty, not plains and grasslands like this one we find ourselves in... nor the vast stretches of baked sands to the south."

"Lush, then," Thorne pressed, seeking to clarify, his interest clearly piqued by Alaric's words. "No deserts?"

"No deserts." Alaric nodded, the affirmation carrying with it a sense of nostalgia, a longing for the beauty and tranquility such lands promised.

Dekar, in his memory, stood as a bastion of natural splendor, very different to the arid expanses and the relentless and seemingly unending sands they had known in this land.

"Yes," Alaric said. "Dekar is bountiful. My homeland is rich, and the ground is good for farming, very fertile. There is no real hunger, not like here in the south. The summers are nice, temperate, easy. It snows in winter, but that's generally manageable."

"I've never seen snow," Thorne admitted.

"I think you will like it. Everything is blanketed in a layer of white and seems clean."

Thorne gave a nod, then grew somber, his gaze going distant as he looked toward the crackling fire. "It was the sands that were our undoing."

"The desert?"

Thorne nodded gravely. "We lost many trying to cross their depths to reach the enemy's strongholds—too many good men. It bled us, the Crusade, white. That expedition was doomed from the beginning. The Cardinal should have heeded your warning."

Alaric took another sip of wine as he regarded Thorne over the rim of his mug. "It was the corruption, the lack of focus, turning away from the mission God entrusted to us—building a righteous kingdom in his name." Alaric stabbed a finger down onto the table. "That is why we lost, the greed for more than we needed."

Thorne nodded again. "He should never have looked that far south."

For several moments, they did not speak.

"What now? What comes after this?" Thorne asked.

"We go home," Alaric said.

"To Dekar." Thorne appeared contemplative as he rubbed his shaved jaw. "And then, tell me—what comes next?"

"I am hoping the end of war, at least for us—the end of the killing." Alaric took another sip from the mug. He let go a long breath. "I've seen enough to last me a lifetime. If I never pick up Oathbreaker again, I will be a happy man."

"Maybe." Thorne gave a shrug. "But no matter where we go, you and I know there will always be those who need killing. Besides, you seem to bring out the best in people"—Thorne grinned at him—"and then they need killing."

Alaric found himself scowling at Thorne. He set his mug down upon the table. With a decisive movement, Alaric brought both palms down onto the wooden surface, his family ring and signet on his right hand clunking heavily, the sound echoing slightly in the near quiet of the room. He stood, his body protesting the motion with a groan.

"Enough talk. Eldanar willing, what will come will come. I will not tempt fate by worrying about what has yet to materialize."

Thorne gave another decisive shrug.

"Besides," Alaric said as he started for the side passage that led to his quarters. He stopped at the door and looked back at Thorne. "I make my own fate."

"Don't I know it," Thorne said. "It is why I swore myself into your service—that and your faith in our god. Where you go, Eldanar's justice follows."

Resisting a scowl, Alaric held Thorne's gaze for a long moment. He turned away for his quarters, where he badly needed to bathe and then get some sleep, leaving Thorne and the great room behind.

3

Alaric placed his hands upon the galley's weather-beaten railing. The wood was rough, the result of extended exposure. He leaned forward slightly, peering out into the horizon as the ship, the *Magerie*, with her timeworn sails billowing softly overhead, rolled gently as she rode the current and wind. The oarsmen were below decks, rowing and pulling the ship forward. He could hear the muted sound of the drumbeat to which the two hundred slaves worked.

They were in the process of navigating their way out of Hawkani's natural bay—a majestic, half-oval inlet cradled by towering cliffs, its entrance guarded by a manmade water break that had been built long before Alaric had set foot upon these shores.

The harbor was choked with floating debris, the water murky and heavily polluted. Trash and flotsam jostled for space among the bobbing vessels at anchor, painting a grim picture of neglect. The water itself bore the brunt of the city's indifference, the surface dark and ugly, the direct result of the daily deluge of waste dumped by the residents into the harbor. Hawkani had no sewers. The air hung heavy with a sour odor bordering upon foul.

Alaric's gaze was fixed on the open sea, yearning for the moment they would break free from the harbor's grasp and put the pervasive stench firmly behind them like a bad memory. He imagined the clean, salty breeze of the open waters, a contrast to the fetid air trapped within the confines of the bay and city. The thought of sailing into the vast, unspoiled expanse, where the air was as fresh as a new day dawning and the water sparkled blue under the sun's embrace, filled him with eager anticipation. He longed for the freedom that waited beyond the bay, where the wind and waves spoke of ancient mysteries and untold adventures.

Alaric's gaze momentarily shifted from the boundless sea ahead to the gold ring adorning his right hand—a distinguished emblem of his lineage, the signet of his family. The metal, burnished by years of wear, emitted a continual warmth that seeped into his skin, a peculiar trait that had always intrigued him. This ring, oversized and conspicuous, held an inner power that was not merely physical; at times, it seemed to pulse with a hotness that nearly scorched.

The ring was a vessel of his heritage, imbued with enchantments that tethered him to his lineage and it to him. Crafted for his great-great-grandfather and passed down through generations, it was an artifact of power and significance. Like his sword, it was bonded to him.

He seldom removed it, and on the rare occasions when he did, Alaric guarded the talisman with a vigilant eye, never allowing it to stray far from his presence. Like the sword, the ring occasionally spoke to him, just not with words. It served as both a tool and a token of his family's enduring strength, the power that ran within their blood, along with their history.

Alaric's contemplation was interrupted by the sharp squawk of a seabird. Searching, he lifted his gaze toward the heavens. There, against the backdrop of a gray cloud-smeared sky, he spotted the flight of a white seabird. The bird's wings were outstretched, cutting through the air with effortless precision. For a fleeting moment, he allowed himself to be captivated by the animal's freedom. However, his attention soon returned to the depressing waters of the bay.

Nearly a decade had passed since Alaric first set foot in this harbor, a naive boy no older than sixteen, with eyes wide and eager to see the strange sights, sounds, and smells of a new land and adventures that lay ahead. Now, as he departed, he found himself a changed man—tempered by the trials of combat and politics he had faced. Those tests and the resulting experiences garnered in this foreign land had molded him into a seasoned veteran, a leader of men, a warrior forged in the crucible of a conflict ultimately rooted in survival of the fittest.

Despite the adversities, Alaric felt an undeniable sense of gratitude toward this land he was leaving. It was here, in this cursed and forsaken place, that he discovered his true self. Turning his gaze back to the city, a complex tapestry of emotions enveloped him.

From his current vantage, Hawkani appeared as a vast jumble of buildings, along with tightly clustered warehouses that ran along the water's edge. Hundreds of boats and ships littered the bay, some anchored, others moored along the wharf. Though it wasn't the largest city in the kingdom, Hawkani was walled, with powerful defenses, and home to more than thirty thousand inhabitants.

The keep, which had been his stronghold and home for the past five years, now stood as a silent bystander to his transformation, the change the holy land had wrought in him. A pang of sadness tugged at his heart at the thought of leaving it all behind, a symbol of the life he'd built here.

Divinara, for all her challenges and tribulations, had become a part of his soul. Yet Alaric was torn between the sense of unfinished business that gnawed at his conscience and the understanding that to stay would be tantamount to courting an early death. The city had shaped him, but so too had the land beyond in ways he was not fully sure he would ever understand.

Would he return?

"I hope not," Alaric breathed aloud as the wind gusted strongly around him, driving away the stench of the bay.

Just prior to their departure, news had arrived that the Cardinal King suffered a crushing defeat and been taken prisoner by Sunara. The messengers had also brought word that the ash men were marching on the capital, Hawkarwa, fifty miles to the east. It seemed, for the moment, Hawkani would be spared. Eventually, he knew, Sunara would turn his gaze this way, and when he did, Alaric would be long gone.

"They won't give any," Alaric uttered into the wind. His statement was not just a prediction, but a cold, hard insight into the nature of their enemy.

"Give any what?" a deep, yet unmistakably weary voice inquired from behind him.

"Mercy," Alaric responded, his voice steady, eyes still fixed on Hawkani. He didn't need to look back to recognize the speaker; the deep timbre, despite its current hoarseness, belonged to Grayson.

The captain of Alaric's company, dragging the weight of fatigue with each step, joined him at the railing. He leaned heavily against it, releasing a long, drawn-out breath, his gaze lingering on the receding outline of the city they were leaving behind as the ship worked her way out of the harbor toward the vast expanses of the sea ahead.

"Maybe," Grayson pondered aloud, the word laced with a mix of skepticism and hard-earned wisdom. "Our side rarely showed any, so why should they?" The older man paused. "Still, Sunara is smart, intelligent. He understands that one can conquer with the sweetness of honey just as through the sword and use of force. With the Cardinal King finished, there is a strong chance the coastal cities will surrender rather than contest the enemy by force. As the victor, he may surprise everyone and prove generous in his terms."

"I feel like we haven't done God's work here," Alaric confessed, his voice barely rising above the sound of the waves slapping against the ship's wooden hull and the wind as it gusted lightly. "Not for a long time."

There was a drawn-out moment where only the sea spoke, her timeless murmur a backdrop to their contemplation. Grayson, his forearms braced against the railing, gazed into the depths below.

"I fear you are correct," Grayson admitted, tone laden with a weariness that went beyond physical exhaustion. "It is good this venture is finally over for us. I long to return to the land of my birth, my family, my daughters. This cursed land..." His words trailed off, as if memories of what they endured had surfaced, moments when their moral compass had been tested, when the line between right and wrong blurred. "There were times I felt we almost lost who we were and why we had come."

Turning to face Grayson, Alaric observed the changes time had wrought on the man who had stood by him through countless challenges and been the voice of wisdom and courage in the darkest of nights. The once brown locks now bore the dignified mark of experience, a blend of silver and gray strands. The lines on Grayson's face, etched by years of campaigning, hard service, and the sun, seemed to deepen in the fading light of the day, marking him as a man who had weathered many storms.

"If I have not said it before, thank you," Alaric expressed, his voice imbued with genuine respect and a deep-seated fondness for the venerable soldier.

Grayson's initial response was a scowl, along with a slight furrow of his brow as he looked at Alaric. His expression, usually stoic and unyielding, hinted at a discomfort with the direction of the conversation.

"For what?" Grayson queried after a protracted moment, tone edged with the roughness of a seasoned soldier.

"You know for what. I would be dead and buried were it not for you. You helped make me the man I am today, the leader I have become. For that kindness, I offer my gratitude and thanks."

The moment stretched between them, charged with an unspoken acknowledgment of what they endured together, the battles fought, and the lessons learned. Grayson's gaze, usually so piercing and alert, softened as he met Alaric's eyes, revealing a rare glimpse of vulnerability beneath the mask of command the man normally wore. The older man's eyes grew watery, a window into the emotions he so fiercely guarded and hid from the world.

"I did nothing more than my duty, my lord," Grayson said, his voice thick. Turning away, perhaps to hide the emotions that threatened to breach his stoic facade, Grayson cast his gaze toward the horizon, where two ships, their sails billowed by the wind, were gracefully navigating out of the harbor with the outgoing tide and into the open sea. These galleys, already catching the favorable winds, were tacking hard to port.

Those two ships cutting through the water ahead of Alaric's galley carried more of Dekar's returning soldiers, battle-weary yet unbroken, alongside their families, embodying the fragile hope of a new beginning, one where the Crusade was a distant thing, nothing more than a memory.

Amongst their number were a handful of civilians from Hawkani, a mix of craftsmen, merchants, and ordinary folk, all believers of the true faith, who held the foresight to see the dark clouds gathering on their horizon, the end of the world they once knew. These were individuals wise enough, or perhaps desperate enough, to abandon their homes and livelihoods to escape the shadow looming over the city.

Notably absent from this exodus were Alaric's fellow nobles, the highborn men and women, Crusaders all, who chose to place their faith in the ancient stone walls of the city and the valor of her defenders. They had declined Alaric's offer of a berth, to return home, opting instead to stand firm in the face of adversity, a decision fueled by a blend of pride, duty, and perhaps a hint of denial about the true might of the approaching enemy. Most hadn't seen what he'd faced, and those who had thought the walls stout enough to hold back the enemy.

As expected, Lord Merrick of Gress had eagerly stepped into the void, seizing the reins of command of the city with a zeal that was characteristic of his ambition. Merrick, a noble whose appetite for glory and recognition was well-known, had always fancied himself a master strategist, a belief that was generously indulged more by his own vanity than by any notable military accomplishment.

To many, including Alaric, Merrick's tactical prowess was questionable at best, his strategies often teetering on the edge of folly. Describing him as a bumbling amateur might have been a charitable assessment, considering the critical whispers that often followed his plans and maneuvers. Still, for five years Alaric had done his best to keep Hawkani under control. He had passed that baton onward. Now, it was Merrick's responsibility, his burden to bear, and he was welcome to it.

This transition of power, with Merrick's eager assumption of control, left Alaric with mixed feelings as he watched his city. As the galleys pushed forward, leaving Hawkani and its new commander behind, Alaric pondered the fate of the last of the coalition that had rallied against the ash men. The Great Crusade had drawn many warriors from distant lands.

How the survivors from the other nations who joined in on the Great Crusade against the ash men would get home, Alaric had no idea. Divinara had consumed many lives in the name of religion, and before Sunara finished, many more would fall.

"It is their choice to remain," Grayson said, as if he could read Alaric's thoughts.

"As it is ours to go," Alaric said.

In a way, with all he'd seen, Alaric did not care, not anymore. It was a wonder, after all he and his men witnessed—the brutality of war, the harshness—that they managed to remain sane.

"The treasure is aboard this ship, our war chests?" Alaric inquired.

"Yes, my lord, it is," Grayson confirmed, his gaze returning to meet Alaric's. The hardness in his eyes spoke of the weight of responsibility he carried, ensuring the safeguarding of their material assets, the treasure accumulated over a decade of campaigning, a veritable king's ransom. "Our boys loaded and stored them in the hold. I have a strong guard standing over the cabin in question." His assurance was solid, leaving no room for doubt regarding the security measures in place. "The chests are all locked, with the keys upon my person."

"Good," Alaric acknowledged.

"There are also twenty men under arms." Grayson's gaze swept toward the aft of the ship. His soldiers, sprawled across the deck in various states of rest, bore the marks of their recent exertions. The last two and a half days had drained them—a hard march out, a battle fought and a hurried return, then the preparations for departure, followed by loading the ships—leaving them utterly spent. The limited space on deck, cluttered with the forms of weary soldiers, underscored the scale of their undertaking; so many had been brought aboard that finding an unoccupied spot to stretch out was a challenge. But his people were grateful for whatever they had, for they were going home.

"They are below decks and stand ready for action," Grayson added, then glanced over at a sailor heading their way. The brief interruption by the sailor, carefully navigating the crowded deck with a full bucket of water and a scrubbing brush, offered a momentary pause in their conversation. His careful steps were designed not to disturb the resting soldiers.

"I assume a similar guard and watch has been set on the other two ships," Alaric ventured, once the sailor passed out of earshot. "I'd not have any of our own end up slaves. They deserve to go home, all of them."

"I left orders for that to be done. Our people will remain vigilant and ready for trouble," Grayson assured. "You think Captain Bramwell would do that? Betray us? I thought you both were friends."

"We may be friends, but he has to know we are carrying a king's treasure, especially after what I paid him for this voyage," Alaric said. "That doesn't even take into account what he could make for our people on the blocks. The temptation may be too strong to pass up."

"I know he's a pirate," Grayson said, "but over the years, he has been good to us, especially after that incident in Antle."

"He has," Alaric admitted, "but I still don't trust him—well, not fully."

"I understand he has confined himself to raiding our enemy," Grayson said.

"That we know of."

They fell silent for a time, each lost in his own thoughts as the ship continued to slice her way through the dirty waters of the bay. The sun had just come up an hour before and it was painting the eastern sky a brilliant orange.

"I did take one priest," Grayson admitted. "The rest who wanted to come I turned away."

"Who?" Alaric inquired, his curiosity piqued.

"Father Ava," Grayson revealed, a name that brought a visible change to Alaric's demeanor.

"I like that man," Alaric responded, his approval evident. A smile touched his lips as he contemplated Father Ava's character. "He never fit in with the rest of the money grubbers. He went out of his way to minister to the poor, the untouchables. I always felt he was a true believer, one who'd journeyed to the Crusade to do good. Perhaps out of all of us, he managed to do just that."

"I thought so too," Grayson said. "It is why I sent men to find him. I explained we were leaving and why. I did not want to leave him behind. Favorable terms or not, Sunara is likely to deal harshly with our clergy for what they did, the purge and all. Besides, he is a good surgeon. He saved more than a few of our boys, Michael included, gave them a second chance."

"When we return home, I will find a place for that man and make him comfortable."

"And will you have a place?" Grayson asked.

"As in, will my father welcome me home?" Alaric glanced over. The thought had troubled him more than a little since he'd made his decision.

"We are returning from a failed crusade," Grayson said.

"I have not gotten a letter from him or my mother in over a year." Alaric played with the ring on his finger. "Something is wrong."

"Are you certain?"

"I can feel it in my bones." Alaric glanced at the ring. It had begun to grow hot. "I am"—he found himself hesitating—"being called home."

Grayson looked at him sharply.

The ring was almost burning. "We should have left long before now."

"And when we get there, if everything is fine, what then?"

"With all the gold and treasure we are bringing home? How do you think we will be welcomed?"

"There is that little fact," Grayson said.

As the white sails fully captured the wind with a resounding *whump*, the galley seemed to leap forward with newfound vigor, slicing with wind-driven power through the murky waters as she made her way out of the confines of the bay. All the while, the oarsmen continued to row. Alaric, feeling the ship's acceleration, straightened, a silent acknowledgment of the journey's next phase beginning in earnest.

His gaze swept the deck, landing on Ezran. Dressed in black, he was the embodiment of readiness and resolve. The wind played with his loose-fitting and comfortable clothes, ruffling the fabric, as one hand rested on the hilt of his scimitar, while the other stroked his clean-shaven chin. Ezran's sharp eyes missed nothing as he watched the nearest sailors.

"A little over a month traveling along the coast, then a two-day journey over open seas to our island kingdom, and we will be home," Alaric remarked, a note of eager anticipation in his voice as he envisioned the end of their arduous journey. The ring had begun to cool again.

"Have I mentioned how I hate sea travel?" Grayson grumbled as he stifled a yawn. "I've never much enjoyed sailing. There are so many things that could go wrong, an errant storm, running aground, falling overboard, encountering a vengeful sea monster… I don't swim so well. I'd rather have solid ground under my feet or travel by horseback."

"You could have remained behind," Alaric teased with a grin, lightening the mood with the banter that had often eased the tension of their shared trials. "Waited with Merrick for Sunara."

"Would you have wanted me to?" Grayson countered, a hint of seriousness underlying his question, probing the depth of their bond and Alaric's reliance on his presence.

"No," Alaric admitted readily. He then clapped Grayson on the shoulder, a gesture of camaraderie and concern. "Since we are sharing a cabin, why don't you turn in for some sleep, my friend?

I feel like watching the sea for a time." His suggestion was an offering of respite, an acknowledgment of the older man's clear weariness.

"Are you sure, my lord?" Grayson asked, his loyalty and duty prompting him to question the offer and defer.

"I am," Alaric assured him. "Go on, get some rest. We can take turns remaining awake and watchful of deceit."

As Grayson acquiesced, moving toward the promise of rest below decks, Alaric turned his gaze back to the vast ocean stretching before them beyond the bay. The sea, with its ever-changing moods and mysteries, offered a moment of solitude for reflection, thought, and prayer. Alaric intended to offer up thanks to his god.

The horizon, a distant line blending ocean and sky, held his gaze. Out there, somewhere, lay Dekar, the land of his birth and the home he longed to see once more. A sigh of longing escaped him, a mixture of anticipation and trepidation at the thought of his return.

His thoughts drifted back to his father, the Earl of Dekar, a man with whom Alaric's relationship had always been strained by expectations and the heavy weight of duty. The earl, a figure of authority and ambition, had envisioned for his son a path filled with achievement and leadership, pushing Alaric to excel in every task, including the study of warfare.

Yet, despite his efforts, Alaric always felt overshadowed by his father's towering standards, never quite fulfilling the legacy expected of him. It was this sense of inadequacy, perhaps, that propelled his father to send him off to the Holy Crusade. He'd seen it as a chance for Alaric to prove his worth on a grand stage.

"If the king had allowed," his father had said, "I would have gone in your stead and left you here with your mother. Alas, it is now up to you. Hold the faith and lean on God in times of need. Look after your men and listen to Grayson. Learn all you can, while you can. My son, you represent the honor and future of our house. Do not let your family down."

Over the years, those parting words had haunted Alaric something fierce. His mother, with tears in her eyes, offered only a hug and a kiss upon the cheek. Alaric had turned from her, more to hide his own tears than anything else, mounted his horse, and ridden away. That had been ten years ago.

Now, as he stood on the deck of the galley, Alaric pondered his imminent return. He was no longer the eager young noble sent off to war with dreams of glory; he had been tempered by the harsh realities of conflict, albeit leading a diminished force back from a campaign marked not by victory, but by survival and loss. The anticipation of facing his father, under these circumstances, stirred a complex whirlwind of emotions within. Would his father see the wisdom and resilience he'd gained, or would he only perceive something else—a man running from a fight?

The journey ahead was not just a physical return to Dekar, but a reckoning with his past and the expectations which shaped his path through life. As the ship carved its way through the waves, Alaric's resolve hardened. No matter the reception that awaited him, he was determined to confront the challenges of home with the same courage he faced the enemy on the battlefield.

Still, he could not shake the feeling that something wasn't quite right back home. He should have heard some news, and yet, there had been none. The sudden warmth of the ring on his finger, a surge of magic that seemed to resonate with his unease, only deepened Alaric's sense of foreboding.

"You seem preoccupied."

Turning, Alaric faced Captain Bramwell, a man whose presence commanded attention, not through imposing stature, but through an air of competence and internal strength. His face was not a kind one, but filled with a hardness that spoke of knowing his place amongst his fellow men. His eyes were perpetually squinted, likely a result of living at sea. Bramwell, of equal height to Alaric, was clad in civilian attire that included pants and a heavy coat over a tunic. His clothing was cut from the finest material and revealed the man's wealth.

His dark hair and nearly black eyes added to his enigmatic persona, a man whose origins were as obscured as his intentions. He was clearly from a foreign land, but Alaric knew not where and Bramwell had not said. Despite this, his fluency in the common tongue, which he spoke without accent, and his demeanor suggested a worldly man, one well-versed in the nuances of cultures and conflicts far beyond his own. He was also unarmed, or at least appeared so. Alaric suspected the man had a concealed weapon and carried one at all times.

Ezran's protective stance, a mere step away from the ship's captain, drew the other's attention. Ezran's hand gripped his scimitar, clearly prepared to defend his charge.

"Just thinking of home," Alaric offered, a simple yet loaded response that acknowledged his preoccupation without delving into the depths of his concerns. Bramwell nodded, then shot another cautious and concerned glance toward Ezran.

At Alaric's subtle hand signal, Ezran withdrew, loosening his grip on the scimitar and stepping back two paces. This gesture, small yet significant, served to lower the immediate tension, allowing Bramwell to relax marginally.

"Your Shadow Guard are more than intimidating," Bramwell admitted. "They make me nervous."

"You, nervous?" Alaric barked a laugh. "I find that surprising."

"Even I occasionally get uncomfortable, especially around that woman, Kiera," Bramwell added, then leaned forward and lowered his voice conspiratorially. "She scares me."

"Is that because you took her to your bed?" Alaric asked with a grin. "And you've since made yourself scarce? Perhaps that is the root of your unease."

"You heard about that?" Bramwell cocked his head to the side.

"I did," Alaric said. "She told me."

"I figured as a Luminary, she'd not be interested in marriage or a relationship."

"She's not," Alaric said.

"But, still—she's holding a grudge."

"It was how you left," Alaric said. "Abrupt-like and without the courtesy of a goodbye. It took her weeks to cool off."

"I had no choice," Bramwell said. "The authorities in Antle were onto who I was and, more importantly, what I was doing there. It was either run or face the executioner's sword. I chose to keep my head attached to my neck."

"Have you explained that to her?"

"No, I have not. I heard she came aboard, but I've not seen her yet." Bramwell glanced around the deck, his eyes narrowing, searching.

"She's sleeping below decks," Alaric said.

"I will have to make amends, then," Bramwell said, "before she takes it into her head to stick me with a blade."

"That likely would not be a bad idea."

"I have heard the rumors about them, your Shadow Guard." Bramwell glanced at Ezran again.

"You have?" His Shadow Guard had acquired a fearsome reputation, which suited Alaric just fine.

"They are famous in these parts. There are stories about them, especially Ezran, an ash man turned against his people."

That turned Ezran's gaze their way again. He raised an eyebrow at the ship's captain.

Bramwell studied Ezran for a long moment. "May I ask you a question?"

"You may," Ezran said. "Though I reserve the right not to answer."

"Fair enough. Is it true he"—Bramwell jerked a thumb at Alaric—"saved your life, and in return, you swore service to him? That he did the same for the others as well with the same result?"

"In my case, it is true," Ezran said.

"A life for a life, then?" Bramwell asked.

"It is more complicated than that," Ezran admitted, "but you may think on it in that manner if you so desire."

It was Bramwell's turn to raise a curious eyebrow at Alaric, seeking an explanation. It had been at least a year since they'd last seen each other. Alaric had been looking forward to renewing their friendship, sharing a few drinks, but then the Cardinal's call for aid had come and he'd been forced to take his men and march.

"If Ezran wishes to tell you his tale, I have no issue with him doing so," Alaric said. "He speaks his mind freely. I do not command him. I never have."

"And will you?" Bramwell looked over at Ezran.

"No," Ezran said with a small shake of his head. "I will say no more than has been said already."

Bramwell gave an amused grunt. "I expected no less."

"I will tell you something," Ezran said, "if you will but hear it."

"Oh?" Bramwell asked curiously, then gave a nod for Ezran to continue.

"If you betray us, I will make sure you die before your men take me down."

The ship's captain stiffened, his face hardening, shifting his stance uncomfortably. "I gave my word of safe passage for Alaric and all those who boarded."

"You did, and now I have given mine," Ezran said simply with a hard coldness. "I have only ever broken my word once. I shall not do so again, especially not for you."

Bramwell turned back to Alaric, a hint of uncertainty in his gaze. "If you were anyone else, I might be tempted to betray you. But you are my friend, and in my position—well, there are few I can truly count on."

"As a pirate?" Alaric asked.

Bramwell held out both hands to his sides. "I am an opportunist, nothing more." The ship's captain grew serious. "Besides, with so many trained killers aboard, it would not be the wisest move on my part to act against you, now, would it?"

"I have paid you a fortune," Alaric said.

"There is that also," Bramwell admitted. "With your funds, I will be able to buy two more galleys. Within a year, I will be even wealthier than I am now, the fruit of this journey."

"But with no place to settle down, no place to call your own," Alaric said. "Once the enemy takes Hawkani, they will not welcome you, for you freely prey upon their shipping. If I recall, there is even a sizable bounty on your head?"

"True—there is," Bramwell said sadly. "I must keep moving, for the free ports all know what, who I am. Those that still accept me charge exorbitant rates and ask few questions. They are more than eager to receive my goods and bribes, and I pay through the nose."

"And what of Dekar?" Alaric said. "You'd be welcome there."

"There are no ports in Dekar—Kevahn, yes, but in your earldom, only fishing villages. My ships need a safe harbor, one that I can trust, where I can rest my men and conduct repairs."

"And what if I built you one?" Alaric asked.

"Then I might come. Send word if you do."

"I will," Alaric said and then glanced out beyond the bay. The galley was almost clear and out to sea. "Shouldn't you be rather busy at the moment, you know, navigating the ship?"

"My first officer can manage well enough. I came to find you, for I was wondering if you would give me the pleasure of dining with you this evening."

"You mean drinking?"

"Food goes better with some grog, don't you think?" Bramwell asked. "At seven bells, come to my cabin. We will drink some, eat, and talk about this port you will build for me. Perhaps you might convince me to make Dekar my home, yes? Eventually, I would like a place to retire, settle down and start a family, own some land, and live out my remaining years in peace."

"I will join you," Alaric responded.

A shout from the aft end of the boat by an officer drew Bramwell's attention. He scowled. "Good. Now, as you rightly reminded me, I must get back to work. There is the Vakeran Reef ahead and the tide is going out. I want to make sure we pass through her channels safely."

"I will see you tonight," Alaric said.

"That you will. We will also drink to killing the infidels, something you and I do quite well." Bramwell, with a purposeful stride, turned on his heel and began to navigate toward the aft of the galley, his eyes set on the bridge and great wheel that lay beyond where the helmsman stood, along with two officers. Alaric had never met anyone who hated the enemy more than Bramwell. With him, it had become a passion.

"I like him," Ezran remarked, breaking the silence that had settled about them.

"I do too," Alaric admitted, exuding a mixture of respect and caution.

"But I would not trust him."

"Oh, I don't, but, in his own way, he is a friend," Alaric added, acknowledging the complex nature of their acquaintance. It was a friendship defined not by trust, but by mutual understanding and, perhaps, a shared sense of purpose, drive even, and respect for achievement.

"That he is," Ezran concurred.

Alaric's gaze drifted back to the horizon, a vast expanse that held both promise and uncertainty. The ship, having finally left the harbor behind, began to encounter the open sea's growing swells. Behind them, the coast was already fading, receding into the distance until it would eventually disappear. Alaric was leaving behind a tumultuous past, a tapestry of memories and experiences marred by pain and loss. These were memories that, despite his deepest wishes, he knew would forever linger in the recesses of his mind, shadows of a past that could never be completely erased.

As the ship sailed onward, carving her way through the ever-deepening swells, Alaric couldn't help but wonder about the future. The days and weeks ahead were shrouded in mystery, a path undefined and fraught with potential peril. Yet amidst the uncertainty, there was a glimmer of hope, a chance for new beginnings far from the ghosts of his past.

4

Alaric's gaze was drawn to the rugged coast less than a quarter-mile away. The sun had already dipped below the horizon to the west, painting the sky in shades of deep pink that gradually faded into a dusky purple. Aboard ship, the day's brisk activities had quieted to the point of stillness; the anchors had been dropped, the sails neatly and efficiently furled, and the long oars carefully brought in and stowed for the night.

This particular stretch of shoreline was a picturesque blend of beaches, followed up by rolling, sandy hills, over which clumps of sun-browned grass spoke of scorching days and cold nights. The ship had found her nocturnal refuge in a partially sheltered cove, the natural contours providing a semblance of protection against the unpredictable whims of the sea.

Not far off, the silhouettes of the two other vessels could be discerned. They were anchored a safe distance apart. To the east, about a half-mile away, the outlines of a fishing village were beginning to merge with the twilight, becoming nearly indistinct in the gathering darkness. A dozen small fishing boats lay hauled up onto the beach before the village, their day's labor done, resting like tired but content sea creatures on the shore.

From the modest huts and single-room houses of the village, thin wisps of smoke curled up into the rapidly cooling air. The heat of the day was beginning to wane, giving way to a refreshing breeze that occasionally blew strongly, carrying with it the promise of a peaceful night. The wind smelled of sand—the desert far to the south, a place Alaric had no desire to ever see again.

A week had elapsed since their departure from Hawkani, and already, a rhythm as consistent as the tide had been established amongst the three ships. Each evening, as the sun's fiery descent heralded the approach of dusk, the vessels sought sanctuary in safe anchorages, places cradled by nature's hand. Sometimes other friendly ships were present, but ofttimes not.

These havens were chosen with a mariner's keen eye for safety. When dawn painted the sky with its very first light, the crew would be mustered. The anchors were hauled up, the oars were run out, and the sails prepared and unfurled to capture the morning breeze as they navigated out of the night's anchorage and embarked on another day's journey along the coast, steadily creeping their way toward Dekar and Kevahn.

Bramwell, like most seasoned captains who navigated these treacherous waters, harbored a deep respect for the sea's latent dangers, especially under the cloak of night. The coast was a jagged line mixed with both beauty and peril, fraught with hidden reefs and underwater hazards that were not marked on any chart and could spell doom for the unwary.

Such risks dissuaded the captain from the notion of nocturnal sailing. That was a common practice amongst those who plied these routes, only sailing during the day when one could see what lay ahead. Moreover, Bramwell's navigation style was one of caution and proximity; he rarely allowed his ships to stray far from the reassuring sight of land. The vast, open sea, with its unbounded horizons and deep waters, was ventured into only when necessary, and even then, with a strong sense of reluctance and caution.

Through their nightly conversations, Alaric had come to understand the captain's unease about the final leg of their voyage, when they would have to strike out into the depths of the ocean to reach Kevahn. Bramwell's discomfort was born not of fear, but of respect for the unpredictable sea and the knowledge that safety lay in the familiarity of the coastlines and landmarks that typically guided their path.

As the sound of a bell tolled through the air, its purpose obscure to Alaric, he continued to linger, caught by the allure and beauty of the view laid out before him. The signal bell, a mystery wrapped in the rhythm of ship's life, was rung once again. The sound of it was jarring and prompted him to turn away, for he was expected. Ezran, his shadow for the night, followed. Alaric hardly noticed.

With a purposeful stride, he approached the stairs that descended into the ship, his destination lying within her wooden heart. Alaric instinctively ducked to avoid hitting his head on the low-hanging ceiling. The steps plunged him into a dimly lit, almost nocturnal world.

Alaric's relationship with the sea and the vessels that dared navigate its vast expanses was one of reluctant necessity. The sea, despite its beauty—which spoke to his soul, with its untamed nature and boundless mysteries—held little allure for him, a sentiment magnified every time he ventured within the close quarters of the ship. He much preferred to appreciate the ocean from the shore's edge.

As he descended the stairs, the air grew thick with an unmistakable stench. It was the odor of humanity pressed too closely together, of unwashed bodies worn by labor and chained by circumstance, unable to escape the confines of this floating prison and personal hell.

Despite the effort to alleviate this oppressive atmosphere by opening the rowing ports to the sea's breeze, the foul reek was overwhelming. It stung the eyes and clawed at the senses. Even breathing through his mouth did not help. The smell was so strong, he could taste it upon his tongue, and Alaric had to resist the effort to gag. He had been told that over time one got used to it, but he could not see how that would ever happen.

Pausing at the foot of the stairs, Alaric swept his gaze across the deck, taking in the grim view. Rows upon rows of benches running along each side of the ship stretched into the murky dimness. These benches, designed to accommodate four men apiece, were the stations of slaves, each one a small cog in the vessel's massive engine of wood and sail. With two hundred oars cutting through the ocean's embrace, the ship carried nearly eight hundred souls in bondage. They were chained to their fate, as surely as they were locked to their bench.

A few sparse lanterns did little to light the space under the dying light of the day. The illumination was meager in the extreme, casting long, eerie shadows across the deck and leaving much of the space enveloped in a near-impenetrable darkness. It was within this twilight realm that Alaric's gaze fell upon the nearest of the slaves, their forms barely distinguishable in the gloom.

The sight pierced him with a sharp pang of pity. Despite the commonality of slavery, Alaric had always found himself at odds with the practice. To him, it was a violation of the most basic principles of dignity and freedom, an affront to the teachings of Eldanar that he held dear. The notion of owning another person, as one might a dog, struck him as fundamentally repugnant, a betrayal of the inherent worth and potential of every individual. But not everyone of the faith saw things the same way, especially when it came to the enemy.

These slaves, stripped of their dignity, their self-respect, and clad only in the remnants of their former lives, not to mention the rags they wore, were the enemy. He had learned they were mostly prisoners, captured at sea or during raids conducted by Bramwell and his crew on unsuspecting coastal villages and towns in enemy territory.

Yet knowing the context of their captivity did little to ease Alaric's discomfort with the notion of his friend's business. But that was the way of the world, and Alaric was powerless to change it. The realization that these men, now reduced to mere cogs in the machine, had their lives measured in the span of weeks—expendable and forgotten souls—deepened his sense of discomfort.

Turning his back on the dimly lit realm of chained souls, Alaric continued on, the weight of his thoughts heavy upon him. His path led him through the crew quarters. Here, just before the entrance, a contingent of five guards stood watch upon the slaves. They were armed to the teeth, a necessary precaution in a world where the line between captor and captive was as thin as the blade of a knife or the link of a chain. Among their number was a man with a crossbow, loaded and ready, cradled loosely in his arms—a potent reminder of the lethal seriousness with which they approached their duty.

Slave uprisings were a grim reality. Such events were not rare, but rather alarmingly frequent, a shadow that hung over every journey and a serious worry for the crew. The desperate struggle for freedom, should the slaves ever break their bonds, was a scenario fraught with extreme violence and chaos, one in which the captives would fight with ferocious determination, preferring death over the return to bondage.

The guards, despite the gravity of their role, appeared disinterested, the monotony of their duty etching a look of boredom upon their faces. Yet as Alaric approached, they shifted, acknowledging his presence with a blend of respect and routine. No words were exchanged. One of them moved to open the door for him, revealing a brightly lit room that served as a threshold to another world within the ship.

Beneath this deck lay the quarters of his people and his own cabin. Farther below, the belly of the vessel held their supplies and equipment, securely stowed for the long journey ahead, along with the animals they'd brought, a mix of horses and mules.

In the relatively brief period Alaric had spent aboard, he had quickly familiarized himself with the ship's layout, including the positioning of the crew quarters both fore and aft. The ship was a hive of activity, sustained by a crew, not counting the slaves, that numbered just over two hundred men. Someone was always doing something. Their existence was one deeply intertwined with the rhythm of the sea, a life that demanded resilience and bred a unique kind of camaraderie.

As Alaric crossed the threshold into a room distinctly marked by the practicalities of seafaring life, he found himself amidst a scene that spoke volumes of the daily lives of the crew. Dozens of hammocks were slung across the room. At the heart of this communal space was a long table.

Around this table gathered more than a dozen men, their attention momentarily diverted from the simple, if not Spartan, meal before them by his entrance. The day's fare, a type of green gruel served in clay bowls, was a humble offering that Alaric had come to recognize as the standard sustenance aboard for at least one meal a day. The type of gruel varied, but its quality, or lack thereof, was a constant reminder of the harsh realities of life at sea, where provisions were often limited to what could be preserved over long durations, not to mention what Bramwell considered affordable and appropriate for his men. He had told Alaric more than once he operated on a budget and had complained repeatedly of the cost to feed so many hungry mouths.

The crew, a rugged assembly of individuals, bore the unmistakable marks of their profession. Their hands were calloused from the relentless grip on ropes and oars—tools of their trade—and their faces, weathered by the salt and sun, told stories of countless voyages. As Alaric moved through the room, a few of them lifted their gaze from the evening meal, acknowledging his presence with a brief, albeit indifferent, glance before returning to their food, drink, and the low murmur of conversation that accompanied it.

This detachment was not born of rudeness but rather a reflection of their nature; they were men hardened by the exigencies of a life spent navigating the ocean. Their resilience was forged in the face of the waves and stormy skies, shaping them into a formidable, if not insular, brotherhood. As Alaric passed among them, he was acutely aware of the divide separating his world from theirs, a chasm bridged only by the shared, transient membership aboard this vessel.

Alaric's journey took him through three distinct sections, each echoing the previous in its utilitarian design, yet unique in the snippets of life it harbored. He traversed additional communal areas where the rhythm of sleep had enveloped other members of the crew, their snoring forms swaying gently in hammocks while the ship moved with the waves as she rode at anchor.

Finally, Alaric arrived at the very end of the ship, what the sailors called the aft of the vessel. The absence of a guard outside the captain's quarters spoke to a certain level of trust, or perhaps they simply feared Bramwell enough that a guard wasn't warranted. The closed door stood as the final barrier between Alaric and the purpose of his visit. He paused, collecting his thoughts. Ezran stopped a few paces away and leaned against the wall, seeming to meld with the shadows. He would not be following further. Alaric gave the door a solid knock.

"Enter," came the captain's voice from beyond, firm and inviting.

Lifting the latch, Alaric pushed the door open and stepped into a realm that felt worlds apart from the rest of the ship. Inside, he found Bramwell and his first officer, Caxatarus, standing at a table. They were engrossed in study of a navigational chart that bore the creases and marks of extensive use.

The first officer was a tall man, well built and muscular. There was a hardness about him that spoke of someone confident in who he was and what he was about. Alaric had never seen the man go about the ship unarmed. He wore a short sword on his right hip. The weapon had a well-used and worn cord grip. There was no doubt in Alaric's mind that Caxatarus could use the sword, for his forearms and hands were heavily nicked and scarred from weapons training. He had learned the man was a former Crusader, one who could read, write, and do numbers. That hinted at a noble birth, for most were illiterate.

The cabin was illuminated by oil lanterns that hung from hooks in the ceiling, their light casting a warm, flickering glow that danced across the room with the ship's gentle sway. The captain and his first officer, leaning in close, appeared as two scholars in the midst of a debate, their attention intently fixed upon the parchment that held the key to their navigational strategy. Bramwell had his finger on a spot and was tracing a line with it.

"I think here," the captain said and looked over at Caxatarus, who nodded in reply after a moment's hesitation. "This is the spot we will put in tomorrow evening. We can get fresh water from a stream that empties into the anchorage."

"We've been there before," Caxatarus said, his voice hoarse

and raspy from a wound he'd taken on the neck. Puckered and red, as if perpetually irritated, the old scar was an ugly thing. "If the winds favor us, we can be there in ten—maybe eleven hours once we weigh anchor come morning."

The large and oversized, aft-facing windows of the cabin, now unshuttered and fully open, provided not only an excellent view, but invited the sea's breath into the room, filling it with the fresh, briny scent of the ocean. This influx of air swept away the heavier atmosphere that lingered like a shadow over the ship's lower decks, where men were bound to their laborious existence or confined to narrow spaces and cabins.

At the heart of the captain's quarters was a large table, its surface weathered by time and heavy use, currently serving as the foundation for the discussion. The presence of a sturdy desk of dark wood near the windows further emphasized the captain's role as both commander and lead navigator. This desk was cluttered with the tools of his trade: navigational maps, books that held the wisdom of the sea, and scrolls of various types. On it also lay a sextant and compass.

The walls, if they could speak, would have told countless stories of conquests and defeats. They were adorned with a varied collection of swords and shields, each, Alaric was sure, with its own unique history. In one corner of the room, a pair of large, brass-bound chests commanded attention. Each was secured with an iron lock that gleamed dully under the lantern light.

Alaric supposed the chests contained spoils from raids intermingled with the ship's operating funds and Bramwell's own treasure, what he called his retirement fund. Opposite this, a simple cot was pressed against the wall and secured to the deck. Along the left wall were several cabinets, their contents hidden behind fastened doors.

"I am not interrupting, am I?" Alaric asked when the two men did not look up from the map they were studying.

"We were just finishing up," Bramwell remarked, his eyes momentarily shifting from the map to Alaric and then back again. "Food should be here soon, but we already have drink."

"We are done," Caxatarus announced, straightening. "As discussed, though the moon won't be overly bright tonight due to that bank of clouds moving in, I will place additional men on watch throughout the night."

"Very good, Cax," Bramwell said. "See to it. I will stand third watch. You can take second."

"Do you want me to put a few men ashore, get them farther to the east and west of our position?"

"As lookouts?" Bramwell asked as he glanced down at the map of the coastline they had been studying. He rubbed his stubbled jaw. "Yes—I think, given the circumstances, that might not be a bad idea."

"I will see to it immediately, sir." With that, Caxatarus nodded respectfully to Alaric, then left, closing the door behind him.

"Extra watch? Men ashore?" Alaric asked. "I thought we were in friendly waters."

"We are." Glancing down at the chart once more, Bramwell sucked in a breath and let it out slowly, then carefully rolled it up, tying it with a faded blue ribbon. He set it on the far end of the table. "I sent men ashore when we dropped anchor to barter with the people in the village for some fresh fish and meat. They told us an enemy galley had put in, anchoring for the night, in this very spot, two days before."

Alaric straightened. "Raiders? Is there any danger?"

"At sea, there is always risk and danger, my friend, especially in these waters," Bramwell added, moving around the table and clapping Alaric on the arm. He grabbed the pitcher and poured one drink, then another. "The enemy is growing bolder by the day, and these waters, which were once safe from raids and attacks, have become dangerous for some."

"But not for you?" Alaric asked.

"Even for me," Bramwell acknowledged almost regretfully as he handed Alaric one of the mugs filled with a dark liquid. "Then again, I am dangerous myself, and I have three ships. The enemy primarily operates alone, isolated raiders looking for easy prey, smaller ships sailing by themselves and not in a convoy. If they happened across us—they'd run, or at least try to."

Alaric's acknowledgment was measured, his mind already racing through the implications of their conversation. The possibility of encountering an enemy warship or falling prey to pirates was a concern. These waters were a complex weave of alliances and enmities, where the flutter of a friendly or hostile sail on the horizon could mean the difference between safety and peril. Alaric gave a slow nod as he wondered what the chances were of encountering an enemy warship or pirate.

"Let us toast," Bramwell said, his tone lightening, "to an easy journey."

"One without incident," Alaric added.

Bramwell raised his mug in a casual gesture, the liquid inside sloshing slightly before he took a hearty swig. Alaric, following suit, lifted his own mug to his lips, the aroma of the grog hinting at its potency even before he tasted it.

The drink, a favorite among sailors for its warming qualities and the ease with which it could be made aboard a ship, was a curious blend. It carried a sweetness that was almost surprising, a richness that coated the palate, only to be followed by a robust aftertaste that lingered assertively in the mouth.

Bramwell seemed to relish the drink, a small nod of satisfaction after swallowing. Alaric, on the other hand, found his thoughts drifting to the wine he preferred, where each vintage told a story of the land it came from. The grog, for all its interesting qualities, lacked the subtlety and depth he had come to appreciate in a fine wine. It was not without its merits, however. In the chill of the sea air and the company of sailors, it provided a certain communal solace, a shared reprieve from the rigors of their journey and toil of their hard life.

Yet, as he took another sip, allowing the warmth to spread through him, Alaric couldn't help but reflect on the differences between the worlds he had navigated—the refined courts of his fellow nobles, where fine wine was a symbol of status and sophistication, and the deck of a ship, where grog served as a lifeline to warmth and friendship. Each had its place, and while he might prefer the former, he understood the value of the latter in the context of their current endeavor. The drink, like their journey, was a blend of necessity and choice. It was also cheap, which was how Bramwell preferred things.

"If it comes to a fight," Bramwell said as he lowered his mug and looked levelly at Alaric, "I trust I can count upon your men, for it will mean a boarding action."

"Of course," Alaric said, "though we have never fought in one."

"It is not terribly different than fighting on land. We steer for the enemy ship—all of mine are equipped with a solid bronze ram. Once we drive into them, planks are lowered from the bow and we board the enemy ship, rushing it, killing everyone who resists. It's simple, really, and this is one of the fastest ships afloat. There are few out there that can out-row us."

"And what of those who don't resist?" Alaric asked.

"We always have need for more rowers," Bramwell said with a shrug. "If there is anyone valuable, they will be cared for and ransomed."

"What of the goods?"

"We take what we can before the other ship sinks," Bramwell explained simply. "Most times, their ship is stuck fast with ours, which keeps them afloat and gives us time to unload the cargo before we need to back away. Sometimes the damage is too great, and the ship sinks rapidly. If that happens, we lose most everything of value but send a few infidels to the great beyond, which is always a bonus."

Alaric gave a nod. "You can count upon my men, if it comes to a fight."

"Excellent. I figured I could but felt the need to ask." Bramwell glanced at the floor, and when he looked back up, he studied Alaric for several heartbeats before speaking. "May I touch upon a personal matter? There is a curiosity I wish to satisfy."

"In relation to me?" Alaric found himself mildly surprised.

Bramwell gave a nod.

"I don't see why not. I consider you a friend."

"As I do you."

"Then ask away."

"In my travels, I have heard whispers, tales…"

"About me?" Alaric asked, raising an eyebrow and wondering what was coming.

"Yes…" Bramwell hesitated once more, as if unsure. "Suggesting the blood of great and ancient leaders courses through your veins."

The air around Alaric seemed to thicken with an unspoken gravity, a shift that was almost immediate in its effect. His body, previously relaxed in the act of a shared drink, became a portrait of tension, every muscle tightening as if bracing against an unseen blow.

This reaction was more than just a momentary lapse of composure. The Cardinal King's realm was one of intricate politics and delicate alliances, a labyrinth of power where secrets were both currency and weapon. Bramwell's words, perhaps innocuous in intent, had unwittingly pierced through his defenses, evoking a response that was as involuntary as the subject of conversation was unexpected.

The chord struck by those words resonated with silent fears, worries, and the burdens of concealment that Alaric carried, a reminder of the precarious balance he had maintained in his quest to safeguard his own truths amidst the ever-watchful eyes of the Cardinal King, his spies, and the sycophants of his court. And yet, the Cardinal was now a prisoner of Sunara, the Crusade was on the verge of disaster, and Alaric was headed home.

"So, it is true?" Bramwell said slowly, clearly gauging Alaric's reaction. "You hail from an ancient line."

"Who told you such things?" Alaric asked.

"I make it my business to listen to the words whispered in dark corners," Bramwell said. "Information can be power."

Alaric eyed the other man for a long moment. He knew he would not get an answer. Bramwell was like that, for he always played things close to his vest and seemed to know more than he should.

"So?" the ship's captain pressed.

"This subject is something I generally do not speak on, with anyone," Alaric said firmly, feeling almost pained. "My family has a long history, one we take pride in but rarely discuss, let alone advertise."

"How far back do you trace your ancestral line?" Bramwell asked.

Alaric found himself hesitating. He considered making a denial, but Bramwell would surely see through that, for it was far too late. After a moment, he gave a mental shrug. "All the way to the Ordinate."

"The empire?" Bramwell asked, clearly surprised, for his dark and bushy eyebrows rose a tad. "Your lineage goes back to the Great Empire of the Ordinate—the empire that ruled all? Are you serious?"

It was now clear to Alaric that Bramwell had not believed what he'd heard concerning his family and its history. Alaric gave a slow nod of confirmation, hoping he'd not made a terrible mistake though fearing he had.

"Nobility of the empire? That is what you are saying—claiming?"

This time, feeling deeply uncomfortable, Alaric did not reply.

"Well, well, well." Bramwell shook his head slightly and set his mug down upon the table. He poured himself more grog, topping his mug off, then stepped forward and refilled Alaric's mug. "Perhaps some drink will loosen your tongue some, eh?"

Alaric eyed him as he took another sip. It was time to put his foot down. Though Bramwell was a friend, he had no need to know more, let alone the line Alaric descended from. "I've said all I am going to say on the subject."

Bramwell scowled. "There are more than a few orders of knights and holy warriors that would give anything to see the Ordinate restored—even some of our enemy. You realize that, right? They believe in the prophecy of the second coming of the empire."

"I do," Alaric said. "But I wish no part in that nonsense. Drawing such attention is—would be dangerous, not to mention unhealthy."

"I don't doubt it, for there are few who can trace their lines that far back. Those orders aim to see a restoration, and as the years have passed, they have gained in strength and power. The Second Ordinate—I have no doubt people would rally around such an effort should it come to pass. I might even rally to such a cause myself."

Alaric felt the ring on his finger begin growing warm, intensely so. Both his father and grandfather had warned not to discuss this subject outside of immediate family.

"And there would be those who rally against it." Alaric took another sip from his mug. "I would appreciate you dropping the matter. Let us talk on something else."

"All right." Bramwell's eyes had narrowed as he regarded Alaric.

There was a knock at the door.

"Enter."

The door opened and the ship's cook stood there holding a steaming pot with a thick towel. He was a large, burly man with a heavily stained tunic and apron. He spoke with a gruff and thick accent, from one of the southern kingdoms. "I have your food, sir."

"Put it on the table."

"Yes, sir."

Alaric was grateful for the interruption. The ring on his finger had grown hot enough that he feared it might burn. As the cook placed the iron pot upon the table, Alaric noticed the captain's gaze resting upon him in a speculative manner.

"Do you require anything else, sir?" the cook asked.

"No," Bramwell said. "Leave us to eat."

"Yes, sir," the cook said and retreated, closing the door behind him with a thud.

Bramwell went to one of the cabinets, opened it, and drew forth two plates, along with a pair of metal spoons and a ladle. He set them down upon the table and turned his gaze fully upon Alaric.

"Your secret will remain in my confidence," Bramwell assured. "My friend, should you ever wish to discuss the matter, you can count upon my discretion."

"I appreciate that," Alaric said, wondering on how Bramwell had learned of the matter in the first place, for he thought few knew beyond his immediate family. Who had the man been talking to? Worse, how many knew the actual truth and how had they learned of the secret? "I doubt I shall put that burden upon your shoulders." Alaric turned his focus to the pot. "What are we eating tonight?"

"I asked the cook to prepare something special for us, pea soup with salted pork," Bramwell said, with a pleased look. "My favorite. Shall we eat?"

The captain pulled the top from the pot. Alaric resisted a groan, for it looked very much like the green gruel the rest of the crew was eating.

5

The early evening air, cool and laced with the essence of the sea, caressed the cheeks of the crew and Alaric's men as the sun dropped behind the horizon, painting the sky in hues of fiery orange and deep purple. The oars, which had rhythmically cut through the water throughout the day, lay silent and secured. The anchor had also found its rest in the sandy seafloor.

Alaric stood at the prow. Leaning heavily on the rail, his keen eyes traced the outlines of a tragedy nestled among the cruel embrace of jagged rocks that guarded the cove like ancient sentinels. There, embraced by the relentless grip of the sea, was the partially submerged wreck of another galley, a ghostly silhouette against the backdrop of the day's rapidly dying light.

The hull of the forsaken vessel told a tale of violence. She had been brutally breached and battered by forces both seen and unseen, her side gashed open at the waterline amidships, exposing the heart of the ship to the cold embrace of the sea.

The remnants of her sails, now no more than tattered shreds, hung mournfully from what remained of a splintered mast, fluttering feebly in the gentle breeze. Seabirds perched solemnly on the fractured remnants, their mournful calls weaving a haunting melody that filled the air, a somber reminder of the unforgiving nature of both the sea and man.

As Alaric's gaze lingered on the remains of the wreck, his thoughts ventured into the realm of those who once called the doomed vessel their own. The shadow of the ship whispered questions that stirred the depths of his imagination. Could she have been a merchant galley, he pondered, her hull once filled with the bounty of distant lands, treasures untold, and exotic wares destined for markets far beyond the horizon? Or perhaps she had been a vessel of war, a pirate receiving her comeuppance?

The very sight of the wreck, her eerie silhouette etched against the fading light, sent an involuntary shiver cascading down his spine. As Alaric's gaze shifted from the melancholic scene of the wreck to the beach, he noted the evidence of the ocean's ruthless handiwork scattered along the shore. There were crates, large and small, that might have once held trade goods and supplies, along with fragments of the ship's once proud form—planks, lines, torn sails, and other debris. Among the wreckage were bodies of the crew, a sight that spoke of lives abruptly ended. The birds had already arrived and were picking and worrying at the flesh of the dead.

Amidst this picture of destruction, two survivors had stood out against the desolation, waving for their attention. A longboat had been dispatched with haste toward the shore, taking to the waves with determined strokes. Alaric watched as the longboat now made its return journey, the survivors safely aboard.

The land behind the beach, with its backdrop of undulating, sandy dunes, stretched away into the distance, untouched by the hand of civilization. All day, while they had sailed, this desolate stretch of coast revealed no sign of settlement.

Grayson, standing at Alaric's side, shared in the solemn

reflection of the moment. His eyes, too, were locked on the returning longboat, observing the rhythmic dip of oars as the crew pulled, driving the longboat rapidly back to their ship. Among the oarsmen, Caxatarus stood prominent at the aft of the vessel, his presence commanding as he steered them home with a steady hand on the tiller.

The other two ships of Bramwell's fleet lay at anchor a few hundred yards from their own vessel. These behemoths of wood and sail were bathed in the fading light of the day. Nearby, the captain stood alongside one of his officers. Their attention was unyieldingly focused on the longboat making its way back to them.

"What are you thinking?" Alaric's voice broke the silence, his question to Grayson hanging in the air.

"That this is a bad business, and we are still far from home."

"Bramwell seems to think this is a friendly ship," Alaric mused.

"I imagine she is or was," Grayson said, referring to the ship and gesturing at the beach, "especially after how Caxatarus handled the survivors ashore."

"They were treated like long-lost crewmates," Alaric breathed.

As the anticipation of the crew mounted, Alaric's gaze swept over the deck of the ship, where it seemed every soul aboard, that could, had congregated to witness the unfolding drama. The air was thick with tension and curiosity, their collective breath held in suspense as the longboat made its steady return approach.

"I will feel better when my boots are firmly on friendly soil," Grayson added.

Alaric gave a nod. They had been at sea for more than two long weeks, days filled with monotony and the occasional passing of a friendly ship. He was already eager for the voyage to end.

The days had passed by slowly with no excitement—that was, until now. Instead of replying, he turned back to the longboat and, like most everyone else, watched.

The moment the longboat came within arm's reach, a line was expertly cast, arcing through the air with precision, slapping down upon those within, before being securely caught and taken up. At Caxatarus's command, the oarsmen, with a synchronicity that spoke of their practice, skill, and discipline, lifted their oars out of the water before securing them.

Using the rope, the longboat was drawn closer by two of its crew, until the little craft nestled and bumped against the ship's hull with a heavy thud. A rope ladder, the bridge between the two crafts, was lowered, dangling like the strands of fate.

Alaric leaned slightly over the side of the ship to observe. Against the ship, the longboat bobbed on the water, which was so clear, he could see straight to the sandy bottom. Caxatarus was first off. He grabbed the swaying and swinging ladder and began climbing. His ascent up the rope ladder was swift and sure, demonstrating an easy grace, each movement reflecting a life lived at sea.

As Caxatarus neared the top, the deck above buzzed with subdued anticipation and much whispering, with everyone's attention riveted. Bramwell, standing at the forefront, stepped closer to the ship's edge in readiness. The captain extended his hand toward his first officer. With a firm grip, he pulled Caxatarus up and over the railing, assisting him in the last stage of his journey from the precarious embrace of the rope ladder to the solid, welcoming deck of the ship.

"She was the *Lady's Grace*," the first officer announced curtly, his tone carrying the weight of unsaid words.

Bramwell's response was almost visceral, his face contorting into a grimace. "Hanson's vessel? Truly?"

"Aye," Caxatarus affirmed with a nod, his voice a deep rasp

that sounded very much like rocks grating against one another. "The attack happened last evening. He was a good man, a proper sailor."

Bramwell scowled. "He was a proper bastard, and we will toast him later."

"As I said, a proper sailor," Caxatarus said. "And I will be honored to drink to his memory."

"Last evening, you say?" Bramwell echoed, eyes roaming once more over the scene of destruction. The scattered debris along the beach and torn sails painted a bleak picture, one that spoke of chaos, death, and loss.

"Yes, sir," Caxatarus said. "They'd sought refuge in the cove, anchoring for the night. The enemy struck shortly thereafter, taking them by surprise and under the cover of darkness."

"That's a bold move, especially considering the dangers of this anchorage." Bramwell scanned the coastline. "They must have had lookouts ashore, watching."

"It is what we would have done," Caxatarus said. "And they might still have them in place."

Bramwell gave a grunt.

Another figure made his way onto the deck, clambering from the ladder to the railing and then over, dropping heavily onto the deck, wearing nothing but a pair of trousers. His bare feet trod on the wooden planks. The sun had left its merciless mark upon his skin, painting him with deep, painful reds and browns. His state of undress and evident sunburn spoke of his ordeal.

He was one of the survivors, that much was clear. Looking back at his former ship, his eyes dull from fatigue and suffering, he took in the remnants of what had once been his sanctuary, his home. Exhaustion clung heavily upon him, each step an effort as he moved with the lethargy of one who had stared into the abyss and found it staring back.

His arrival silenced the group, a living reminder of the tragedy that had befallen the *Lady's Grace*. Here was a man who faced the fury of the sea and the cruelty of their enemies yet had lived to tell the tale.

"What is your name?" Bramwell demanded.

"First Mate Keeler, sar," the man replied, his voice hoarse and raspy, as if each word scraped against his dry throat.

"And the ship that attacked *Lady's Grace*? What kind was it?" Bramwell probed further.

"A hundred-oar war galley, sar," Keeler managed to say, his voice barely above a whisper now.

That caused a reaction from those gathered. There was much whispering and more than a few gasps. Scowling, Bramwell held up a hand for quiet. He waited a moment. "Continue."

"They came upon us shortly after we dropped anchor. It was one of Caston's galleys. At least that was the standard they was flying."

Bramwell's brow furrowed at the mention of Caston, a name synonymous with formidable naval prowess, one of Sunara's many allies to the far south. "A warship? Are you certain?"

"Yes, sar," Keeler affirmed, the weight of his survival seeming to bear down on him with his every word. "I am sure as the sun shines and sharks gotta eat. I saw her with me own eyes."

"What happened to your captain?" Bramwell asked, his voice growing softer.

"He died fighting, sar, run through the middle by the bloody bastards. I seen it happen. He died with a sword in his hand."

"And why didn't you die as well?" Bramwell's gaze was fixed on Keeler, searching not for judgment, but understanding.

"The ship was lost. I dove over the side and swam for shore. I did not want to end up a slave or lose me life for a lost cause."

Alaric, who had been observing the exchange, found himself nodding in agreement.

Another man, haggard and worn, stripped to the waist and barefoot, managed to haul himself onto the deck, adding his voice to the chorus of survival. "From shore, we watched while they looted the ship, sir. They didn't even bother none coming for us," he recounted, his voice a mixture of relief and bitterness.

Bramwell, clearly deep in thought, stroked his jaw as he gazed up the coast. "When did this Caston galley set sail? How long ago did she weigh anchor?"

"Late afternoon, sar, maybe no sooner than two hours ago. We hid from 'em and watched them bastards. They didn't even come ashore."

Bramwell's eyes moved to Caxatarus. Their eyes locked. "They can't be too far off, maybe five or six leagues at most."

Caxatarus cast a glance toward the heavens. The sky was clear of any cloud cover. "The moon is gonna be good, sir, potentially a fine night for navigating. We may be able to catch her, if she puts into a cove up along the coast."

"Why didn't the enemy spend the night here?" Alaric, puzzled, voiced the question.

Bramwell turned his attention to Alaric, expression reflecting a mix of contemplation and the burden of command. "This cove is on the smaller side and can accommodate only one ship, and a smaller one at that. It's high tide, and you can't see them, but there are plenty of hidden rocks. It was likely why Hanson thought he was safe." The captain's gaze briefly swept over the constrained waters that cradled their temporary haven. "That makes it risky for larger ships like this one to spend the night here, especially if a storm comes up and the anchor drags. We might easily find ourselves run aground with the hull ripped open and stranded in the middle of nowhere."

"The enemy got what he wanted and left for a better anchorage." Caxatarus's statement was simple, yet laden with the harsh reality of their situation, a grim acknowledgment of the ruthlessness that governed the actions of those who cruised these waters in search of prey.

"He did," Bramwell affirmed, a trace of bitterness in his tone as he looked back at his first officer.

"I wonder if it's Fina's boat that did this," Caxatarus mused, his statement turning heads. "He hunts in these waters."

"If it is him, I would love to take him down." Bramwell looked over his crew clustered nearby, along with Alaric's soldiers, their attention fixed on him. He fell silent for a long moment, then with a decisive nod, as if solidifying his intent, Bramwell glanced once more at the wreck. "First officer?"

"Sir," responded Caxatarus, his posture straightening in readiness.

"Haul the longboat out of the water and secure her posthaste. Signal the other ships to prepare to weigh anchor and continue up the coast a few leagues in search of the enemy. We will take the lead."

"Aye, sir," Caxatarus replied, acknowledging the command.

"We're going on the hunt, boys," Bramwell announced, raising his voice so all could hear while turning to address them at large. His proclamation was met with a robust cheer. The air was charged with a newfound energy, a blend of anticipation and solidarity. "We're going to find the enemy and pay them back in kind for the *Lady's Grace*."

That elicited another cheer. Alaric noted his own men were cheering enthusiastically alongside the captain's.

Bramwell turned his attention to the survivors, those who had borne the brunt of the calamity firsthand. "Get these men some water and food. See that they rest and enter them into the books. They now have a home with us."

"Thank you, sar." Keeler touched two fingers to his sunburned brow in salute.

"Aye, sir," Caxatarus's voice, rough as gravel, affirmed the command before he called out with authority, "To your stations."

His directive sent a ripple through the gathered crew, prompting them to scatter, each man moving with a sense of purpose and urgency toward their designated roles, leaving Alaric's soldiers behind. The deck buzzed with the activity of preparation, the air filled with the sound of footsteps and the clunks of gear being readied for the pursuit ahead.

Bramwell, however, appeared detached from the flurry of activity. He took a few steps away, focus fixated on the coastline that stretched ahead, almost as if he could see beyond its immediate beauty to the potential dangers and rewards that lay hidden in its embrace. His was a look of calculated hunger, a reflection of his thoughts on the opportunities that the night's endeavor might unveil.

Alaric, noticing Bramwell's contemplative stance, approached him, stepping close. "I thought you didn't like traveling at night."

"I don't, not one bit," Bramwell admitted, his voice carrying a hint of reluctance tempered by conviction. "But I know these waters well. There is some risk, but it is not overly great, especially on how clear a night it will be. More importantly, we have an opportunity here. If she is a Caston warship and the one I am thinking of, *Mysteeri*—a true raider—one that's plagued these waters for years..." He trailed off, leaving the implication of his words hanging between them, a tantalizing prospect of what they might achieve.

"Quite the prize?" Alaric ventured, words laced with both curiosity and the thrill of the hunt.

"Yes, a prize worth bragging on," Bramwell affirmed with a certainty that underscored the gravity of their potential undertaking. His eyes shimmered with the reflection of the fading light on the water. "If it is her, she should be full of treasure she's taken. Fina is a good captain, one of the best the enemy has..."

"I see," Alaric said, his intrigue and concern clear as he processed the magnitude of what they were contemplating. Bramwell wasn't intent upon attacking a simple transport or merchant.

"If she is a true warship," Bramwell elaborated, his tone growing more serious, "the Castons don't use slaves to man their oars." This detail wasn't just a footnote; it spoke about the kind of resistance they could expect. Standing just to the side of Alaric, Grayson stiffened.

"They are all warriors, then?" Alaric sought clarification, the implications of Bramwell's statement dawning plainly upon him.

"Correct."

"How many?"

Bramwell momentarily glanced to the survivors, now being cared for by his crew, before returning to Alaric. "If she is a hundred-oar galley, as Keeler said, maybe four hundred to five hundred swords."

"A significant challenge, then," Alaric remarked with a mix of awe and apprehension at the daunting odds they faced.

"In normal times, yes, they would outnumber us fighter for fighter," Bramwell admitted. "I'd likely avoid a boarding action and just focus on sinking her and sending her crew to the depths of the ocean, for we would likely not have the sword power, let alone strength to fully overcome her."

"Now you are thinking of taking her," Alaric said, piecing together Bramwell's thinking, "and looting her?"

"I have your trained soldiers aboard, veterans all," Bramwell pointed out, exuding a confidence that seemed to fill the space between them. "And three ships. A predator like *Mysteeri* won't expect an attack, especially if we move quickly."

"And if they have lookouts?" Alaric asked.

"Then, as I said, speed is of the essence,"

"And what about the women and children on the other two ships?"

"If we are to catch the enemy, there is no time to put them off and ashore," Bramwell said with a pained expression. "This ship doesn't have any of the families aboard. We will be the first one to attack, to get stuck in. The others will join as soon as the fight has begun, but we will face the brunt of it. That is the best I can do. We have a real opportunity here, and I don't aim to miss it."

Alaric's eyes briefly met those of Grayson, who maintained a discreet distance yet remained observant throughout their discussion. The older man gave a nod of agreement to the plan. Ezran was standing a few steps off. So too were Thorne and Jasper. Kiera was nowhere to be seen. She had been spending her nights with the captain. They had long since made up, which had been a relief to both Alaric and Bramwell.

"How many men do we have aboard?" Alaric asked Grayson.

"One hundred on this ship alone," came Grayson's prompt response.

"Break out the weapons and begin getting the men ready," Alaric commanded. "It will likely be some hours yet, but let's start preparing anyway."

"It will be hours," Bramwell confirmed, his gaze momentarily drifting to the wreckage of the *Lady's Grace*. His eyes narrowed as he studied her in the dying light. "I've always wanted to take on a real warship, and now I have my chance. I just hope she puts in for the night where I think she will."

"And where is that?" Alaric queried, seeking insight into Bramwell's chosen battleground.

"An anchorage five leagues distant, called the Well of Tears," Bramwell disclosed, a scheming smile touching his lips. "I've used it myself. There is fresh water to be had there, but no settlements. The anchorage is also large enough for maneuvering where I can bring more than one ship to bear upon the enemy."

"I see," Alaric said. He was feeling some unease with the prospect of this action but had already committed himself and his men to it, giving Bramwell his word.

Bramwell clapped Alaric on the shoulder. "Tonight, with some good fortune, we will turn the tables on our enemy." The resolve in his voice was infectious. "Now, if you will excuse me, I have a ship to prepare for battle."

6

Alaric stepped aside as one of the crew, with a bucket, carefully scattered a load of sand across the deck. He had been moving toward the bow of the ship, gazing out at the darkened, moonlit ocean. The ship itself was a hive of activity; the crew moved with a sense of urgency in preparation for battle.

The deck, now veiled in a thin, sandy film, served a dual purpose: Not only did it offer a primitive grip underfoot, countering the slick sheen of seawater that occasionally splashed aboard, but it was also designed to deal with the inevitable spillage of blood, where the wooden planks could quickly become as treacherous as ice.

Sitting on the deck and lining the railings, hundreds of buckets had been brought up from below. These were filled to the brim with seawater. Attached to each lay a neatly coiled length of rope.

"What's the purpose of the rope?" Alaric inquired, his attention momentarily shifting to a crewman who strode past, his arms laden with a bundle of arrows.

The crewman paused in his tracks, confusion briefly clouding his features as he turned to face Alaric. "I beg your pardon, sar?"

Pointing toward the array of buckets that lined the ship's railing, Alaric repeated his question. "The buckets, the ones filled with seawater—why are they attached to ropes?"

"Oh, that," the crewman responded, a flicker of understanding crossing his weathered, grimy, and sun-tanned face. "The ropes are there so we can lower the buckets into the sea to quickly fill them. Then we can haul them up again, without much hassle. That speeds up fighting any fires the enemy try to set." With this explanation, he offered a congenial nod, touched two fingers to his forehead, and continued on his way.

Alaric absorbed this information, gaze drifting back to the ocean as the ship crested a large swell, only to inevitably descend the opposite side, the bow landing in a muffled crash that sent spray into the air. Such movements, unnatural at first, had become familiar to Alaric, almost comforting in their regularity.

Beneath him, the rhythmic beating of the drum pulsed throughout the ship, a constant heartbeat that kept the rowers pulling in perfect harmony. This steady cadence, crafted by the drummer nestled within the galley's depths, reverberated through the wooden deck, a vibration that Alaric could feel underfoot through his boots. It was a powerful reminder of the human effort which propelled them—slaves who, chained to their benches, tirelessly worked the massive oars. Each stroke dipped into the ocean's embrace before emerging into the air, a cycle repeated endlessly as they drove the ship toward where the captain expected to find the enemy.

Alaric's attention shifted back to the water-filled buckets. The threat of fire aboard a vessel surrounded by the very element that could quell it was an irony not lost on him. Yet he knew all too well the chaos an untamed fire could wreak in the wooden belly of a ship, how quickly a vessel such as this one could burn, for he had once seen it happen and almost died as a result.

Fire was every sailor's greatest enemy. Even amidst an

expanse of water, a blaze could spread with ferocious speed, consuming everything in its path. This knowledge etched a line of worry deep within him. The prospect of flames dancing across the deck was a haunting image he found he couldn't shake off.

"Give me a battle ashore any day over this," Alaric said to himself as his eyes wandered to the shore, barely discernible under the silvery glow of a near full moon. The dark outline of the land seemed both a tantalizing promise of safety and a long way away. Alaric was a good swimmer, but the thought of being forced to abandon ship due to a fire and cross that distance through the cold currents of the ocean, with the currents and waves, was a daunting prospect on even the best of days.

He caught sight of Grayson making his way toward him, his approach marked by a calm assurance and steady gait. Absent was the cumbersome armor. Instead, the captain of Alaric's company wore a simple tunic and pants. His sword hung at his side, as did a dagger.

Alaric's men were already on deck. They too had not donned armor. This decision, inspired by Bramwell's pragmatic wisdom, reflected a sobering reality of naval combat. "Men wearing armor sink right to the bottom if they fall in," the captain had plainly stated, his words carrying the weight of undeniable truth. "Wearing armor may save you from the enemy, perhaps, but you're just begging for the sea to take you into her arms and keep you if you go overboard."

Still, Alaric couldn't shake off the discomfiting sensation of vulnerability that came with not wearing his armor, especially before a fight. He felt naked without it.

"The men are ready," Grayson announced, cutting through Alaric's ruminations as he came to a halt in front of him.

Alaric acknowledged Grayson's statement with a nod. The deck was a flurry of activity as the crew worked to ready her for battle. Bramwell and his officers, who had formed a half-circle about their captain, stood together on the bridge. Bramwell was likely passing along his final instructions.

"Fighting on a ship is so different than on land," Alaric said.

"Is it?" Grayson mused aloud, just as another crewmember hustled by, his arms laden with several leather-wrapped bundles of arrows. "Killing is killing, no matter where it is done."

Alaric took a moment to absorb the simplicity of Grayson's words. Just a few feet away, dozens of bows and crossbows had been arranged with meticulous care on the deck, accompanied by a steadily growing stack of arrows and the deadly bolts that could pierce armor and were the bane of infantry. Nearby, a collection of throwing spears lay next to one another, their pointed steel tips gleaming under the moonlight.

Every sailor aboard had taken up arms, carrying either a sword or an axe. A few had both. The air was charged with a near-physical tension, a blend of fear and determination that bound every soul on board into a shared brotherhood. No one ever liked putting their life at risk, but it was the business they were in.

Four large boarding planks had been brought up from below decks. These structures, now fitted into hinges on the bow—the very front of the ship—and held by cables, stood erect. Their ends pointed nearly straight up at the sky but leaned forward slightly, awaiting their moment of action. Each had large steel spikes at the end, for when the cables were cut. The planks would drop onto the enemy ship, the spikes crashing into and through the deck, locking both ships fast. Raised vertically, they served as a reminder of the bridge between life and death they would soon become.

"As we approach, while the ship increases speed for a ram attempt," Grayson added, "I imagine the crew will rain missiles down upon the enemy's deck—arrows, spears, bullets from slings. They have small catapults and ballistae, which they have not set up, but I understand those are for defensive purposes.

They send flaming balls of pitch and burning material at enemy ships. Since they want to take this ship and plunder her, Caxatarus told me they won't be using them."

Alaric nodded, his mind painting a vivid picture of the coming clash: a rain of arrows and spears as the vessels drew perilously close. He could easily imagine, amidst the shadows, death and dismemberment would arrive, cloaked as nearly invisible projectiles that fell from the sky.

"The enemy will no doubt respond in kind," Alaric mused aloud, the weight of the moment and the impending action pressing upon him.

"Indeed, which is why I've ensured our men are equipped with shields," Grayson continued. "Once we ram the other ship, those boarding planks will be dropped, and the men will charge over. Then the work begins."

"I expect this is going to be a hard and ugly fight, quite possibly the ugliest we've ever been in. Surrender will not be an option for the enemy—at least, they will not want to. I expect them to sell their lives dearly."

Grayson acknowledged the grim truth of what lay before them. "Indeed, it will be. But remember, no battle is ever pretty," the older man remarked, his gaze momentarily shifting toward the mast, where two archers began climbing with the agility of monkeys, bundles of arrows attached to their backs with ropes. "We will be outnumbered until one of the other ships joins in."

"I know it."

The captain, with Caxatarus by his side, navigated through the bustling deck with a sense of intent and urgency that moved the air like the sharp prow of their ship, passing them both by. Bramwell's expression was one of grave seriousness. Alaric and Grayson, left in the wake of this focused procession, exchanged a brief glance before Alaric decided to follow.

As Alaric caught up, he found Bramwell had stopped at the

railing, eyes locked on the horizon and path ahead. The moon cast a silvery sheen over the sea, transforming the waters into a magnificent display of light and shadow. It was a scene of haunting beauty.

Bramwell, aware of Alaric's presence, glanced over, but did not turn to greet him. Instead, he pointed toward the darkened shoreline that lay ahead, where a prominent hill rose against the night sky. "Past that hill and around the bend in the coastline is the Well of Tears. That, with any luck, is where we will find our quarry."

"And what if this ship is not there?" Grayson asked.

"Then"—Bramwell blew out a long breath—"we will anchor for the night. I would not feel comfortable pressing onward in our hunt, as the coastline ahead becomes quite rugged and rocky."

Caxatarus suddenly stiffened.

"What is it?" Bramwell asked, glancing over.

"Look there." The first officer pointed. "See it?"

Alaric's eyes, guided by Caxatarus's outstretched finger, caught sight of a small, flickering, orange light that crowned the hilltop. It pierced the darkness with its modest and low-hanging glow, a small spot of light in the sea of night, one that was nearly invisible.

"A fire," Bramwell breathed. "A campfire. This stretch of coastline is not settled. That's a watch post."

"The fools," Caxatarus said.

"They are blinded by their own firelight," Bramwell said with sudden excitement. "They must think it too late for anyone to sail."

"She's going to be in the bay," Caxatarus rasped, "right where you thought her to be."

"And we're going to give them one hell of an education." Bramwell turned to his first officer. "Ready the men. I want our boys to go first. They've done this before and know what they are doing. Alaric's soldiers can follow."

"Yes, sir," Caxatarus responded.

Bramwell turned to Alaric. "I mean no disparagement of your men. I know they are killers, but they've never fought at sea."

"I understand," Alaric said.

"Cax, you lead the boarding operation," Bramwell added. "I will handle the ship, then join you once we ram her and are stuck fast, understand?"

"Aye, aye, sir. I do."

Bramwell then regarded Alaric. In the darkness, the captain shot him a grin. "Mind the arrows and spears. I would hate to lose my drinking partner due to carelessness."

Alaric gave a grunt in reply and Bramwell left, brushing past Alaric, his silhouette merging with those waiting on deck for the action to begin as he made his way toward the aft, where the bridge awaited his command.

"Lads," Caxatarus called, moving to address the waiting sailors. The enemy watch post was over a half-mile away. There was no chance they could overhear him, what with the sound of the sea and wind. "Grab your shields and form up for boarding on me. Archers to your positions, ready yourselves for action."

The deck rapidly became a rush as the men moved to obey the first officer's commands. Shields were swiftly grabbed, bows and crossbows taken up. The sound of metal and wood clattering against the deck punctuated the night air.

Alaric found himself glancing toward the distant glow of the campfire. The absence of any light source aboard their own ship to betray their position minimized the chances of detection from the shore. However, a mere shift in the enemy's attention— moving away from the light of the fire to relieve oneself, along with a single glance toward the darkened sea—could reveal their presence and added a layer of tension to the atmosphere.

Caxatarus, who stepped away from Alaric, toward his men, held up his hands as the sailors pressed forward. "I want four lines for the boarding parties, one for each plank. The first man in line gets an extra cut of the spoils and two additional rations of grog from my personal store, and you know that's the good stuff. Now, enough lollygagging. Let's go. Get your asses moving."

Alaric's gaze followed the men as they swiftly fell into lines as directed. The moon, hanging in the sky above, cast a silver glow over everything that lent an ethereal quality to the activity unfolding on the deck. In the moonlight, the faces of the nearest men were illuminated just enough to reveal expressions of grim determination and fear.

"I will assemble our men and get them similarly organized," Grayson said, to which Alaric gave a nod. The older man left.

Alaric took in his guardians, who blended seamlessly into the fabric of his life—his Shadow Guard, all standing close at hand and ready for trouble.

Ezran, with his black attire almost melding into the darkness, seemed less a man and more a wraith at the edge of visibility. His attention was directed forward, out to sea, clearly looking for the first glimpse of the enemy ship. A few feet from him, Jasper's relaxed posture belied the alertness in his eyes. His bow, already strung, was casually hung over his right shoulder, while a bundle of arrows rested at his feet. Thorne and Kiera, each in their own way, completed the circle of vigilance around Alaric, their presence a constant reminder of the silent pact they shared with him.

These protectors, each distinct in their manner but united in their purpose, were more than mere bodyguards. They were the unseen shield against threats invisible and overt, a dedicated group whose very existence was intertwined with Alaric's own fate. The fact he often forgot their presence spoke to their skill in blending into the background.

Yet their impact on his life had been immeasurable. On more

than one occasion, they had been the difference between living and dying. In the dark alleys of political intrigue of the Cardinal's court and on the battlefield, they were his unseen edge, thwarting attempts on his life with a blend of foresight, skill, and unwavering loyalty.

The muffled, rhythmic thrumming of the drum, a heartbeat beneath the deck, intensified, sending vibrations through the soles of Alaric's boots and into the core of his being. It was as if the ship herself responded to the call of the drum, her pace quickening with each and every beat, an ancient creature stirred to life by the will of her captain. The rowers, unseen but deeply felt, matched the drum's tempo with powerful strokes, their collective effort propelling the vessel with increasing velocity through the night-shrouded waters toward their destination, the Well of Tears, and the prey the captain hunted.

Alaric, standing near the prow, felt the surge of acceleration as the ship cut a swift path through the dark sea. The water, illuminated only by the faint touch of moonlight, flowed past in a shadowed blur, the ship navigating the swells with a determined grace. It was a moment of singular focus, the world reduced to the sound of the drum, the rush of the sea, and the steady forward motion of the ship.

As the coastline drew nearer, Alaric noticed the subtle shift in their course. They were angling closer to land, steering toward the end of the hill where the rugged coastline bent and promised to reveal the hidden anchorage.

With another increase in the drum's tempo, the ship all but leapt forward, her speed escalating, as if eager to uncover what lay ahead. As they approached the hill, anticipation tightened in his chest. The cove, gradually coming into view, held the promise of discovery and, potentially, confrontation.

Yet as the ship drew nearer and the cove began to reveal itself, the expected silhouette of the enemy vessel at anchor did not materialize. The absence of any visible threat did not ease Alaric's vigilance; rather, it heightened his awareness of the unseen dangers that might still lurk in the shadows or lie in wait beneath the surface of the seemingly tranquil bay, rocks that could rip open the hull.

The drumbeat increased yet again, and with it, the ship began to move even faster, picking up the pace rapidly. The dark water began to move by at a startling speed. Alaric found himself surprised at how fast the ship was traveling. They drew closer and closer to the hill, and more of the cove became visible. Alaric saw nothing ahead, no ship at anchor, just moonlit water and, beyond that, the shoreline.

He glanced around and saw the two other ships of Bramwell's little fleet, almost in a line, following close behind. The sudden blare of a horn, distant yet unmistakable in its urgency, pierced the quietude of the night, drawing Alaric's attention sharply toward the hill.

The call, muffled by the distance, yet clear in its intent, rang out a second time. With the hill now looming less than a quarter of a mile away, the significance of the signal was undeniable. The watch post had clearly spotted the flotilla.

Alaric felt a chill grip his heart as the reality of their situation settled in. The element of surprise, so crucial, had evaporated into the night air, swallowed by the foreboding sound of the horn. The enemy were now forewarned of their approach, likely mobilizing, even as the echo of the warning faded and another call from the horn rang out.

The course was set, the die cast. With their presence known, all that remained was to press forward, to meet whatever awaited them in the cove with the courage and cunning that had carried them this far. The alarm had been sounded, the challenge laid bare.

"There." Caxatarus's voice, a harsh hiss in the tension-filled air, drew Alaric's gaze to the cove unfurling before them. His initial glance revealed nothing but the serene dance of moonlight on water, a peaceful scene at odds with the sense of urgency in the first officer's tone. Yet as he focused, guided by Caxatarus's outstretched finger, the shadowy outline of another vessel began to materialize from the darkness, anchored a mere mile away.

"There she is," Caxatarus hissed in mounting excitement. "There she bloody is!"

The ship, a galley, presented broadside to them, her sails neatly furled, oars shipped, betraying no immediate sign of activity. Despite her size, smaller in comparison to Bramwell's commanding vessel, there was an undeniable menace to her. Sleek lines and a low profile suggested speed and agility, characteristics of a ship built with a singular purpose in mind: war. In the dim light, she appeared not just as a ship, but as a predator at rest, her very form exuding a silent threat.

Alaric's eyes remained fixed on the distant silhouette, assessing, calculating. The quiet before the storm was over. Now, the confrontation lay ahead.

"Ship spotted," someone hollered back.

"There she is," Caxatarus repeated with feverish excitement. "*Mysteeri.* By all that's holy, we have her." The first officer punched a fist lightly into his palm. "We have her, and this time, there will be no escape for Fina. We are going to kill that bastard dead."

The repeated blare of the horn was now infused with a sense of urgency that bordered on desperation. As the rhythmic pounding of the drum accelerated, the ship responded with a nimble agility, veering onto a new course that aligned her bow and ram directly with the enemy vessel.

The passage of time seemed to slow, each moment stretched thin by anticipation, and the rapidly dwindling distance between their ship and the war galley. The sea itself appeared to part in acquiescence to their advance, the ship barreling at a speed that spoke of an eagerness to attack and get stuck in. The cadence of the drum, now echoing Alaric's own heartbeat, served as a relentless motivator for the rowers, each stroke bringing them inexorably closer to their prey.

When the gap had narrowed to a half-mile, then a mere quarter-mile, the activity on the deck of the war galley became visible. Men moved with a frantic energy. The deployment of oars in a hurried attempt to gain maneuverability, coupled with the effort to raise the anchor, spoke volumes of their readiness—or lack thereof—for the engagement that loomed and was now upon them.

"They're too late," Caxatarus said fiercely, then raised his voice savagely. "Archers, ready yourselves for action. Loose as soon as we are in range."

It was then that Alaric noticed the flicker of light that flared on the enemy's deck—a glow that stood out against the backdrop of the night, unusual and out of place. The sight puzzled him, until the chilling realization hit: The enemy was preparing to launch fire arrows and possibly worse. Alaric's gaze inadvertently drifted back to the buckets filled with water, a precaution that now seemed wise.

"My lord." Ezran had found a shield and approached. The rest of his Shadow Guard held shields too and had closed upon him. "Perhaps it is time to move back to your men?"

"What?" Caxatarus asked, looking over at Ezran, then back at the enemy warship, which was less than three hundred yards distant now. They were closing frightfully fast. A bell could be heard ringing urgently from the other ship, as well as a beating drum calling the crew to quarters. Someone over there was shouting frantically. "Right, time to move you behind the men. It's gonna get ugly at the bow."

Caxatarus grabbed Alaric's arm and started to guide him

away. Alaric afforded himself one final, contemplative glance at their adversary before turning to navigate through the ranks of sailors. These men, poised for battle, awaited the ram and the expected command to board the hostile ship. Releasing his arm, Caxatarus matched his stride. As they moved beyond this sea of anxious anticipation, Alaric was greeted by the sight of Grayson and his men. They stood divided into four distinct lines. Each warrior was armed with a rounded shield, sword still sheathed. They looked grim, but they were ready for a fight. That much he knew. A fierce stab of pride ran through his heart, for they were his men and he their leader, their lord.

In the midst of the drum's relentless and fast-paced rhythm—a heartbeat all its own—Alaric collected himself. It was time to address the concerns of his soul. With a depth of reverence and a fervor born of both hope and his faith, he lowered his head and offered up a prayer. The nearest men of his company, eyeing him and clearly understanding what was happening, dropped respectfully to a knee. Then the rest took a knee and bowed their heads. Even some of the sailors knelt.

"Lord above and beyond, on this day of battle, we seek your favor, your blessing," Alaric said, raising his voice so all could hear. "Grant us the strength to vanquish the foes who stand before us, those who have rejected your faith and are infidels. Watch over our brave warriors and spare them from the clutches of death. May our victory be a testament to your glory. In your sacred name, we place our souls, trust, and our hopes."

"Amen," Grayson said.

"Amen to that," Caxatarus echoed.

The men stood. Alaric looked over at the first officer, who was craning his neck to look toward the bow and the enemy ship. With the press of sailors before them, Alaric could not see much himself, other than the enemy ship's masts, which appeared quite close, almost on top of them.

"It will not be long now," Caxatarus said, looking back around. "Better brace yourself when the call comes."

With that, the first officer left them, heading back to the bow and the way they had just come. Pushing through the nearest men, he disappeared into the press. Alaric spared a glance at Grayson, then turned to face his men.

"You saw what these bastards did to the *Lady's Grace*," Alaric called, raising his voice again. "Fight like demons."

"What are you going to do?" Grayson roared to the men.

"Fight!" came the massed reply.

"What are you going to do?" Grayson roared again, even louder.

"Fight—fight—FIGHT."

A sudden, jarring sound of impact echoed across the deck as the massed shout died down—a meaty thwack. A sharp cry of pain came from a sailor in the forefront, quickly followed by another, their voices laced with shock, fear, and agony.

"Shields!" The command from near the bow cut through the din, urgent and commanding. "Shields!"

Swiftly, Grayson grasped a nearby shield that had been lying upon the deck at their feet, extending it toward Alaric while taking another for himself. Without hesitation, Alaric took it and hoisted the shield protectively above his head, adopting a defensive crouch. All around, men were doing the same. The deck about them began to be pelted with a series of heavy thuds and cracks as enemy arrows rained in a deadly shower, burying themselves into the wooden planks.

A pained outcry pierced the air, signifying another casualty somewhere in the ranks of his company. Alaric caught sight of one of his soldiers falling, dropping his shield, and writhing in agony on the deck, an arrow embedded deeply in his side.

Above, amidst the entangled silhouettes of the masts, came the distinct twang of a bowstring being released, followed rapidly by more, as the men perched up there fired directly down upon the enemy's deck. Bramwell's archers, standing just behind the boarding party, unleashed their own volley. The sound of bowstrings twanging and crossbow mechanisms snapping rang out.

Another barrage of arrows sliced through the air, their presence announced by a sinister hiss as they descended with lethal intent. The deck bore the brunt of this assault, transforming it into a pincushion of arrow shafts as the missiles hammered home. Alaric felt a jolt against his shield—a direct hit.

Surprised, he saw the point of an arrowhead that had punched through the barrier of his shield, mere inches from his hand's grip. The proximity of death, so tangible, immediate, random, and close, sent an involuntary shiver down his spine. Around him, the air was rent with the cries of the wounded and the dying, a grim chorus that underscored the brutal reality of their struggle, which had truly yet to begin.

"God, I've been hit." A choked cry shattered the tense air behind Alaric as a man screamed. The voice, strangled by pain and shock, belonged to one of their own. "Sarge, I've been hit. Help me."

The air was once again split by the sound of defiance—a series of sharp twangs as Bramwell's archers retaliated, sending their own arrows soaring toward the enemy vessel. The swift exchange was punctuated by another scream, this one emanating from across the water, one that was alarmingly close.

"Brace! Brace yourselves, boys!"

This urgent call rolled forward from the bow, a dire warning that permeated the charged atmosphere. Alaric's hands shot out, grasping for the nearest solid anchor—one of the ship's masts, its sturdy form offering a semblance of stability. Grayson, mirroring Alaric's actions, secured his own hold beside him.

Barely had they anchored themselves when a catastrophic

cacophony erupted. The harrowing crashing sound of splintering and shattering wood filled the air as the very structure of the ship groaned around them. It was as if the sea itself rebelled, abruptly halting their forward momentum with shocking force, one that felt like the hand of some wrathful deity.

Alaric's arms, clamped around the mast for dear life, were pried loose by the sheer ferocity of the collision. Propelled forward by the ship's abrupt halt, he was flung onto the deck with a force that tried to knock the breath from his lungs. Around him, the scene descended into pandemonium. Men had been hurled from their positions, their feet; bodies had been thrown forward and down to the deck in a terrible tumble.

Then, there was a sudden moment of absolute quiet, for even the drum had ceased.

"Cut the cables! Drop the boarding planks," Caxatarus's voice, raspy and urgent, roared into the silence. "Kill them all!"

7

Her timbers groaning, the ship gave a violent shudder. Alaric rolled from his side, where he had landed, onto his stomach. A series of heavy crashes came in rapid succession, one after another, four in total. Feeling more than a little shaken up, he dragged himself onto his hands and knees. All around him, men were doing the same.

Caxatarus's voice rang out, urgent and commanding. "Go, go, go! Kill them all! Kill them all!"

Understanding the attack had begun, Alaric pulled himself to his feet, though the ship beneath him was far from finished protesting. Groaning some more, she gave an ominous lurch, as if the very ocean sought to claim her and she was resisting, actively fighting against the pull of the depths. By God, he hoped she wasn't sinking. He looked up. Ahead, the sailors—swords and axes at the ready and back in their lines—advanced steadily in the direction of the boarding planks.

"Look out!" Ezran shouted, shoving him roughly and unexpectedly aside. Stumbling, Alaric almost fell again but managed to keep his feet. Out of his peripheral vision, he caught sight of something massive descending from the sky, falling fast. It landed with a powerful crash, merely two feet away, shaking the deck violently. Turning, he blinked, eyes widening in disbelief. It took a fleeting heartbeat for the realization to dawn upon him—he was looking at a mast, a colossal timber torn from the heart of the enemy's ship.

The air was thick with the men's voices. They were screaming—some in terror, some in pain, and others in absolute agony. Bewildered and still slightly disoriented, gathering his senses amidst the chaos and confusion around him, he took a couple heartbeats to assess his surroundings.

The boarding planks were now forcefully laid down and locked in place, bridging the gap between the two ships. Caxatarus's assault party had already begun surging forward, their boots thudding against the wood as they worked their way across the planks and over to the enemy ship. Several dozen had made it, dropping onto the enemy's deck. The sound of metal clashing against metal was strong on the air.

Alaric's gaze swept over his men. He could read the fear, uncertainty, and confusion as they picked themselves up from the deck. This was not the type of fight they were used to. Realizing the critical moment had arrived, he had to take command, to get his people organized for when they must charge over the planks and board the enemy vessel.

"On your feet!" Alaric roared, turning to his men. "Back in your lines. I said, get back into your lines!"

Grayson was suddenly standing beside him, a cut bleeding freely on his chin. "Hurry up, boys. Reform! Reform into lines. There are enemy over there that need killing and those swabbies will need our help doing it. Reform."

Battle was on the air, the sound of it intensifying with every passing moment. From the other ship, voices rose in a tumult of screams, shouts, and curses as men battled one another.

"Come on, boys," Grayson encouraged. "Hurry up. Miks,

move your ass or you will be on latrine duty until we get to Dekar. Understand me?"

"Yes, sir."

The sergeants began to work, shouting and shoving those who did not move fast enough into position. Alaric found himself well-pleased. Order was beginning to be restored.

Nearby, a couple of warriors lay silent and motionless, arrows lodged within their chests. Not counting those who had been crushed by the falling mast, mostly Bramwell's sailors, there were a few who were down and wounded, the work of the enemy's missile fire.

A *thunk* drew his attention as an arrow hammered into the deck five feet away, the shaft quivering with unspent energy.

"Get your shields up, boys! The fire coming down is hot." Grayson's command thundered across the deck and through the noise of clashing metal and screaming just yards away. He hoisted his shield over his head, a bastion against the incoming onslaught of arrows, which was still raining down as invisible death.

Alaric realized with a jolt of worry that his shield lay abandoned a short distance away. He had dropped it when the ship rammed the enemy vessel. His heart raced as he darted toward it, seizing the shield just as a streak of orange light hissed by perilously close, its brilliance flaring in the night like a shooting star before finding its mark in the ship's deck. Another fire arrow shot by, leaving a streak of light in his night vision as it landed somewhere behind his company.

Alaric raised his own shield over his head for protection and surveyed the scene. His gaze fell upon the ship's railing where, in the aftermath of the violent collision, the buckets had been upended, the water spilled uselessly over the side or across the sand-covered deck. He locked eyes with the nearest soldier.

"You!" Alaric barked. He pointed first to the man, then to the overturned buckets, and finally to the burning arrow, its pitch coating flickering with malevolent intent. The fire had yet to spread. "Grab a bucket. Use the rope to lower it into the sea. Fetch water and douse that flame before it claims us all. Quickly now!"

"Yes, my lord." The soldier nodded, understanding flashing in his eyes as he rushed to execute the order.

"Forward." Grayson's voice cut through the tumult, cracking like a whip. "Press forward, my brave lads! We're moving up behind the sailors. Soon it will be our turn to go over to the enemy. Forward now."

Alaric wheeled around. His men had finally reformed into neat lines. With shields raised overhead for protection, they moved as one, inching toward the treacherous boarding planks, which Bramwell's men were struggling over.

Above them and flanking both sides of their vessel, sailors, armed with bows and crossbows, unleashed a continual barrage of death. Arrows and bolts sliced through the air, a deadly rain aimed at the enemy around the planks. They were also providing cover for those in the process of crossing the makeshift bridges and those seeking to broaden their foothold on the enemy warship. Amidst this storm of missiles, others had taken up spears, hurling them at the enemy.

"Draw swords!" Grayson's command boomed once more. "Draw swords!"

Nearly in unison, the company's blades were yanked out. Just ahead, the last of the sailors were in the process of climbing with determined haste up and onto the boarding planks. Using their shields for cover, they moved across the narrow span between ships, each step a gamble against fate.

"What are we going to do?" Grayson roared to the men.

"FIGHT!" came the massed response, a powerful shout that for a moment drowned out the sound of fighting on the other ship.

"I want to hear it again!" Alaric shouted. "What are you going to do?"

"FIGHT!"

Alaric's gaze went to the planks as he advanced, coming closer and closer to his turn, when he would move across and into the fight. Arrows, loosed from the enemy, found their marks with deadly precision. Men, struck by the forceful impact, were plucked from the planks as they attempted to cross and cast into the sea's cold waters.

Then, Alaric stood at the brink of the crossing, waiting for the last two men to go. He reached for his sword, his hand wrapping around the cord grip. In that moment, for a fleeting heartbeat as he gripped his sword, the world seemed to pause, suspended in time.

Alaric's senses heightened. Every detail around him became more real, more vivid—the metallic tang of blood on the salt air, the anxious breaths of the nearest men, the screams and cries of the wounded, the clash of swords. As the magic from the sword flowed into him, the moment was almost surreal, otherworldly.

Blood me, Oathbreaker's voice spoke in his mind, a seductive female whisper. *Slay the enemy in Eldanar's name. Send their souls onto your god to prove you are worthy of* HIS *faith and love. In return, you shall be rewarded.*

The blade, dormant in its demands upon him for months, now surged with a dark hunger, which Alaric felt compelled to feed. Then, reality, which had seemed to hold its breath, catapulted forward. The world around him snapped back into motion.

Alaric found himself before the plank. It was now his turn. Thorne had gone before him and was already moving across in a crouch, shield up and held ready. Jasper, bow in hand, stood off to the side. He loosed an arrow toward the enemy, then drew another and, in a smooth motion, nocked it, took aim, then released again. Alaric did not look to see where it had gone. He glanced back as he climbed up and onto the plank. Kiera and Ezran were right behind him.

With Oathbreaker's thirst for blood echoing in his mind and drawing him forward, he took his first step. The wood underfoot shifted as Alaric advanced. It trembled uncomfortably with each step. The divide between the ships, a mere stretch in the physical realm, was a chasm that meant the difference between life and death.

With the absence of railings, the plank's width seemed to diminish with each step. He glanced down and wished he hadn't. Below was the visible portion of the bronze ram, now buried deep within the hull of the enemy warship. The breach it created was a gaping maw, around which the sea frothed and churned angrily.

A man screamed as an arrow took him. He fell into the gap between the two ships, where the water frothed and boiled violently. He disappeared and did not come back up.

As Alaric advanced, a chilling realization washed over him: He was willingly going onto a vessel that seemed fated for the ocean's depths, one that was likely in the process of actively sinking. What he was attempting seemed far from sane.

Lifting his gaze, the deck of the enemy ship came into view, a mere ten feet away, yet seemingly a world apart. The deck was a maelstrom of violence. Hundreds of combatants were locked in a chaotic and swirling battle, one without any organization, mostly clustered around where the boarding planks had come down.

The enemy, in a desperate bid to repel the invaders, pressed forward with relentless ferocity, fighting like madmen, seeking to stem the tide of attackers and push them back. Alaric realized this was a critical moment. If the assault failed, they would lose.

Thorne had already reached the other side. Sword in hand, he jumped down onto the enemy vessel. Alaric steeled his resolve and continued forward, the plank beneath him swaying ominously with the ocean's swells.

Something sliced through the air, hissing by like an angry bee. An arrow had narrowly missed. Instinctively, Alaric raised his shield in the direction he thought it might have come from. A heartbeat later, a hard *thunk* against the shield announced the strike of an arrow.

Then, he was over to the other ship. He jumped down, boots landing in a slick of blood that nearly betrayed his footing. The deck, tilted at a slight angle, was a scene of carnage, littered with bodies and the press of the enemy against the friendly forces attempting to take their ship. The noise of the fight was incredible, nearly overwhelming in its intensity. The sound of it clawed painfully at the ears.

No sooner had Alaric steadied himself on the blood-slick deck than he was thrust into close quarters combat. An enemy attacked him, a behemoth of a man, muscles bulging, screaming a battle cry, axe raised and in the process of slicing down.

Alaric's instincts took over. With a sidestep, he evaded the axe's arc. In the same fluid motion, he brought Oathbreaker to bear, driving the blade deep into the assailant's abdomen. He could feel the blade's insatiable hunger as a guttural groan escaped the man's lips, his eyes widening in shock and pain as his gut was violently punctured. The grip on the axe loosened, then it was dropped, where it went clattering to the deck.

Alaric gave the sword a cruel twist, then with a forceful shove, threw his enemy back and away. The man collapsed in a heap before Alaric. The grim reality of their situation left no room for mercy, not when it was close quarters fighting. A wounded enemy was a threat that could not be ignored, a lesson long since etched into Alaric's very being. Without a moment's hesitation, he delivered a final, decisive thrust. Oathbreaker found its mark in the man's neck, opening it to the bone and finishing him.

Alaric was jostled a step as another man crashed into him. An arrow had punched clean through the man's chest, the point emerging from his back, along with a piece of curved rib bone that gleamed under the moonlight. He collapsed over the man Alaric had just finished. In the darkness, Alaric could not tell whether the man was friend or foe.

Scarcely a moment passed before another assailant challenged him, wielding a longsword. The clash was immediate and brutal; Alaric's shield met the incoming strike, absorbing the force of it. The blow was powerful, and a jolt of pain coursed through Alaric's hand and arm. Gritting his teeth against the pain, he used the shield to deflect the attack, forcing the sword aside and creating an opening. His counter was swift, Oathbreaker finding its mark in the attacker's hip, sending the man staggering away. He was immediately swallowed up in the press.

There was no respite, no break. The fight was relentless, brutal, unforgiving, each enemy falling before his sword, only to be replaced by another, a never-ending tide of resistance and rage. Alaric met them all, his sword an extension of his will. He jabbed, slashed, and thrust, blocked attacks—every action driven by the primal need to survive and protect. His shield was not just a defense, but a weapon in its own right—bashing and creating openings for Oathbreaker to deliver the weapon's judgment, one more soul collected for his god.

Lost in the tempest of violence, Alaric's senses narrowed to the clash of steel, the opponent before him. Yet even as he became an avatar of death and holy justice, part of him remained dimly aware of his comrades-in-arms fighting around him. They were shadows at the edge of his vision, a presence felt rather than seen, each one locked in their own struggle for survival.

This was the essence of battle—a maelstrom of chaos and violence where only skill, will, personal strength, and a measure of fortune separated the living from the dead and dying. Amidst the fray, a nagging awareness crept into his mind, a suspicion that they were heavily outnumbered, a realization that hung on the periphery of his consciousness. The possibility of losing the fight was a very real one, and Alaric could feel himself beginning to tire.

Suddenly, the very world seemed to jump beneath him. The deck lurched violently, catapulting Alaric toward the ship's railing. He collided with the unforgiving wood, his shoulder absorbing the brunt of the impact painfully. The air was pierced by the sounds of men being hurled into the sea, their splashes and screams a grim punctuation to the chaos.

Then, a few feet away, a deep cracking sound filled the air as the ship's last standing mast succumbed and, like a felled tree, came crashing down upon the deck, crushing all in its path, then snapping like a twig, the excess falling into the sea with a splash.

What had just happened?

Having been thrown into the railing, Alaric managed to remain upright. Thankfully, Oathbreaker was still in his hand. His shoulder ached. Still, that was a concern for later. He had to focus on survival, killing the enemy before they killed him.

Instinctively, he stabbed out, dispatching an enemy who had fallen at his feet, the sword's point finding a deadly purchase in the nape of the man's neck. Through the grip, he felt his sword blade grate against the spine. Just feet away, another was attempting to rise and stand. Alaric kicked him in the face, his boot connecting powerfully with the jawline. There was a crunch of bone as the jaw snapped and teeth flew across the deck, along with a spray of blood.

An unexpected blow then struck him from the side; a shield, wielded with intent, sent him reeling. Stumbling over a fallen body, Alaric managed to keep his feet, just barely, as he turned to face his next foe. He went to raise his shield, only to realize with a jolt it was gone. He'd dropped it.

As this new opponent advanced, shield raised and sword ready to strike, Alaric braced for the coming exchange, settling into a combat stance while sizing his opponent up. In that fleeting moment, Ezran, a mere ghost, materialized from amidst the chaos, his dark clothing making him nearly invisible in the night. With his scimitar, steel catching the scant light with a dull flash, he delivered a ruthless strike to the attacker's back, sending the man crashing to the deck.

The battle's tempo changed abruptly with a series of resounding crashes that tore through the chaos. Alaric glimpsed planks falling from the other side of the ship. A fresh wave of combatants stormed forth, screaming, yelling, and jumping down onto the deck. In a moment of clarity, Alaric pieced together what had happened. One of the other vessels had maneuvered around and rammed the enemy warship, finally joining the fight and bringing badly needed reinforcement.

This unexpected maneuver shifted the tide before him. The enemy's ranks, previously a suffocating press, now frayed at the edges as many turned and scrambled to meet this new assault. The density of foes around Alaric lightened, then fully abated, granting him a precious reprieve. Gasping for air, his lungs burning with the exertion of sustained combat, he found himself in a fleeting bubble of respite amidst the storm of steel and bloodshed as his men fought almost shoulder to shoulder before him.

Even as his chest heaved with rapid breaths, Alaric's instincts compelled him to assess his surroundings. He was near the bridge of the ship. There were several men fighting there. Alaric recognized Bramwell, sword in hand, amongst those attempting to take the bridge from determined defenders.

But why? Having been rammed and stuck fast, this warship was going nowhere.

Alaric's gaze swept the chaotic fighting still raging around him. With the press having eased, Alaric's and Bramwell's men were beginning to push the enemy back, one painful and difficult step at a time. Grayson, Ezran, and Kiera were nowhere to be seen. Only Thorne remained within arm's reach, flanked by a handful of his soldiers, their expressions set in grim determination. All were breathing heavily from the fight and taking advantage of the moment to catch their breath. Was the enemy captain on the bridge? Was that why Bramwell was there? Alaric glanced once more in that direction and made a snap decision.

"This way," he commanded Thorne and the others, pointing his sword toward the bridge.

A knot of enemy stood between him and Bramwell's contingent. They were actively fighting with several of Alaric's soldiers and trying to reach the bridge themselves.

"Make for the bridge!" he bellowed over the din. He plunged once more into the fray, leading his small band forward. Alaric picked out an opponent who was partially turned away and engaged. Catching the man unawares, Alaric brought his sword down in a powerful arc. The blade bit into his shoulder, going right to the bone. He went down, hard.

Alaric stepped over the man he'd just dropped and jabbed his sword into the side of another whose back was to him. The sailor the man had been fighting seized the moment and thrust his own blade into the man's chest, allowing Alaric to press onward without pause.

He engaged the next enemy combatant, who spotted him. Alaric deftly exchanged a series of rapid strikes and counterstrikes, the metallic song of their swords clashing loudly on the air. With a keen eye, he spotted an opening, driving his sword into the man's thigh. The force of the strike sent his opponent tumbling backward onto the deck, writhing in agony.

Without missing a beat, Alaric advanced, pinning the downed man's sword arm beneath his boot and delivering a thrust to the stomach with his sword. In that moment, a blade emerged, its sharp point slicing through the air to open the man's neck in a lethal blow. It was Thorne, fighting alongside him. Together, they moved past the fallen, the path to the bridge now clear before them.

Navigating around a lifeless defender sprawled on the staircase, Alaric ascended, taking the steps two at a time. He found an enemy waiting at the top of the stairs. An arrow hissed out of nowhere and embedded itself into the man's chest. With a look of surprise, he took several steps back before falling to the deck, where he thrashed and convulsed violently.

Alaric had a glimpse of Jasper on Bramwell's ship, another arrow nocked. He released and another enemy on the bridge was hit, the arrow driving deeply into his side, just above the hip. Eyes wide, this man staggered backward to the aft railing, where he fell and pitched over the side. The sound of a splash followed.

Alaric turned and was greeted by the sight of the last stand on the bridge crumbling. Two men fell in rapid succession, then a third, Bramwell delivering a killing blow. Only one man remained. Bramwell and his contingent of six sailors moved and stood in a tense semicircle, their focus converging on a solitary figure who confronted them with sword in hand.

Despite the odds, the man's posture radiated defiance and a calm determination that belied his precarious situation. Blood seeped through the fabric of his trousers, staining it dark around a visible wound in his thigh, an ugly gash several inches long. Yet, even injured, he retreated only a single step, his gaze unflinching as he assessed his enemies.

The man's appearance was striking. He was tall and built with the unmistakable strength of a seasoned fighter, his muscles taut beneath his well-tailored attire. His clothing, though marred by the fray, hinted at a status beyond that of an ordinary sailor, suggesting a man of significant standing and means, perhaps even nobility or scholarly distinction. There was an educated air about him, an aura of intellect and poise that contrasted sharply with the raw brutality of their surroundings, the ugliness of the fight. At the same time, there was also a hardness to him that reminded Alaric of Bramwell. In a way, the two men were eerily similar.

"It's over, Fina," Bramwell said, shaking his bloodied sword at the other man. "Your days raiding this coastline are finished, done."

The enemy captain spoke common with a thick accent, his voice laced with a profound and unmistakable bitterness, "All those years ago, I should have killed you when I had the chance. But, alas, an educated man is worth more than a dead one, and I was paid well."

Eyes narrowing, Bramwell tilted his head slightly to the side. "You should never have sold me into slavery. That was your first and, in a way, ultimate mistake."

Alaric glanced sharply at Bramwell. He had not known that his friend had ever been a captive of this man, let alone a slave of the enemy. That, he decided, explained a lot, especially Bramwell's hatred for the other side.

Fina's gaze was locked onto Bramwell with a mixture of regret and resolve. The battle continued unabated behind them. The clashing steel, the cries of the wounded, and the roar of determined fighters created a backdrop of chaos against where this personal confrontation unfolded. The enemy captain's gaze, sharp and calculating, darted across the expanse of the bridge, assessing each of his adversaries as he edged backward a step toward the protective railing. Beyond that, there was nowhere else to go, save the sea.

The severity of his injury was unmistakable. The wound in his thigh bled profusely, a dark, steady stream that was rapidly painting his leg crimson and pooling on the wooden deck beneath him. The grim realization that an artery had been compromised was evident in the volume lost, a predicament that left him pallid and strained.

Despite the acute physical pain that surely racked his body,

Fina's grimace bore the mark of a deeper, more intangible agony. "Like my ship, I am already done. My time upon this world is at an end, just as one day yours will be."

"For me, that day is not today, nor anytime soon either."

"I suppose not," Fina said with a heavy breath that was almost a pant. He grimaced in sudden pain.

"I will celebrate your death tonight—with a drink."

"Will you make it quick, old friend?"

"Old friend?" Bramwell's features contorted into a visage of distaste, as if he'd bitten into a fruit long since spoiled. The words that escaped him came with a venom that curdled the very air between them, his tone laden with the weight of wounds clearly unhealed by time. "I should make you suffer to the very last for all you've done to me, torture you as you have done to so many others."

"You should thank me," Fina said, waving a dismissive hand at Bramwell, "old friend."

"Old friend? Thank you?" Bramwell was incredulous. "You want me to thank you?"

"I made you into what you are today. You cannot deny that. I would be disappointed if you tried."

Bramwell froze, his gaze locked onto the other captain. After a moment, he gave a slow nod. "No, you are correct. I cannot deny it. Hatred tends to motivate one."

"Well, then, one captain to another—we've hunted each other for years, played a game of cat and mouse. You and I were the top predators in these waters. You know me as well as I you, and you've finally won the game," Fina said heavily, his words becoming hoarse. "Make my death a quick one—for the debt you owe me. I do not wish to bleed out, like a prize bull sacrificed to my gods."

Bramwell's features, initially etched with the bitterness of past grievances, softened as he absorbed the gravity of Fina's request.

With a slow nod that carried the weight of finality, he conceded. "All right. I will make your end a quick one. I suppose you've earned that much."

Fina released a long breath that was filled with resignation and relinquished his grip on his sword, tossing it forward, where it clattered against the deck. Slowly, as if with great weariness and exhaustion, he collapsed to his knees, his body heavy with the toll of his wound.

Under the soft luminescence of the moonlight, his complexion had taken on a ghostly pallor, signaling the proximity of death's embrace. The proud sailor and captain of his own ship, once formidable in strength and spirit, now appeared diminished, his vitality ebbing away before the eyes of his enemies as the lifeblood fled his body.

With his sword poised, Bramwell closed the distance between himself and Fina. As he stood before the kneeling figure, blocking the moonlight, his shadow loomed over the defeated man. Looking down upon Fina, his enemy, a complex tapestry of emotions played across his features—what appeared to be regret, sorrow, and an unspoken acknowledgment of the inevitable conclusion to their shared saga.

"You should know, I have prisoners below decks," Fina said, his voice growing weak, almost a whisper. He cleared his throat with some effort, the sound gurgling. "Amongst them—is a lumina."

"A lumina?" Alaric found himself surprised. He took a step forward. "You have a lumina? Surely you cannot be serious."

Bramwell glanced back at him and appeared just as shocked, for he blinked several times.

Fina shifted his pained gaze to Alaric before returning to Bramwell. "I took her a few weeks back from a transport. She was the only person of value aboard. Though my crew wanted otherwise, she has been cared for and not harmed. I give you my word on that. I know such a person, though cursed amongst my own, is valuable to your people."

"You were going to take her back to your dark priests?" Bramwell said. It was more a statement than a question.

"I would have been rewarded for such a catch, taking one of the last of her kind." Fina's eyes closed as he swayed upon his knees. He was losing his strength. He opened them, blinking rapidly, his breaths starting to become quick and shallow.

"I imagine so," Bramwell said.

"It was not meant to be." Fina's tone hardened as he gazed up at Bramwell. "Now, finish it. Send me on to my gods where I can rest for eternity in the knowledge that I lived a good life and served well."

"That wasn't the deal," Bramwell said with a shake of his head as he stood solemnly over Fina, his sword poised to strike.

"What?" Fina asked. "What... do... you mean?"

"I am claiming your soul for my god. There will be no rest for you." Bramwell raised his sword. "Eldanar, accept this humble sacrifice, one I make in your name. Take this infidel's soul as your own and purify it with holy fire."

Fina, caught in the grip of his inevitable fate, reacted with a flash of shock mixed with surprise and disbelief. The look turned to one of heat and anger. He opened his mouth to speak. Fina's attempt to voice a final plea or protest was cut short, as Bramwell, with a swift and unerring slash, delivered the finishing strike. His blade moved with lethal precision, slicing through the air to sever the tenuous thread of Fina's life with a swift, clean cut to the neck.

As the neck opened, a shock of dark, viscous blood spilled forth, pouring down and staining Fina's chest and the deck with its macabre hue. For a moment, the ship captain's mouth worked as if he were trying to speak. He began to choke upon his own blood. It was a feeble sound. As the light faded from his eyes, they rolled back into his head. A moment later, Fina collapsed onto his side. The twitching of his limbs marked the last, desperate signs of life's departure.

A surreal calm enveloped the bridge, creating a stillness that was very different from the ongoing tumult of battle mere yards away. Then Bramwell raised his sword and, with a powerful grunt and effort, chopped down onto the side of Fina's neck, almost completely severing it. He chopped down a second time and the neck came free from the body. Then Bramwell stooped and picked the head up by the hair. He went to the railing by the stairs and held up the head for all to see.

"Fina is dead! Your captain is dead!" Bramwell shouted in common at the top of his lungs. Then he switched to the Caston tongue and repeated it, shouting even louder as he gave the head a violent shake. For a moment, the fighting across the deck of the warship slackened as multiple heads turned his way. An audible groan went through the enemy, even as their own men gave up a mighty cheer.

Bramwell shook the head once more, then lowered it and turned away. He glanced down at the prize in his hands. Fina's eyes were open and staring sightlessly outward. Alaric was surprised to see tears in Bramwell's.

"Fina is dead," Bramwell whispered, more to himself than anyone else. He dropped the head, where it *thunked* hollowly onto the deck and rolled a few feet from him. "At long last, my oath of vengeance is fulfilled, my honor redeemed." He sucked in a ragged breath. "It is over."

Though the fighting continued throughout the ship, upon the bridge there was a hush, thick with finality and the weight of what had transpired. It was abruptly pierced by the sound of several nearby splashes. Alaric turned his attention toward the source of the disturbance and moved to the railing, looking over the side. A number of men had jumped overboard. His eyes widened as he observed more of the enemy, in a state of clear desperation, casting themselves into the sea's embrace.

The sight of these men fleeing into the watery depths, in a bid for survival by swimming to shore, was an indicator of the shifting tide of the fight. Though the air was still filled with the clamor of combat, the frenetic energy of the battle taking place a short distance away seemed to diminish a tad. With their captain's death, the enemy were visibly fracturing, their collective resolve crumbling under the weight of impending defeat, which was becoming clearer by the moment.

Then what Fina had told them registered with Alaric. He turned to Bramwell. "The lumina, we must find her."

"We cannot allow her to perish on this ship if it goes down prematurely," Thorne said with fervor. "She must be saved."

With tears still in his eyes, unabashed by them, Bramwell gave a nod. "As a high-value prisoner, she's likely being kept near the captain's cabin and close at hand." Bramwell gestured toward a set of stairs with his sword, leading downward into the innards of the ship. "You go for her. I will bring order to this struggle and end the fighting on deck."

"Got it," Alaric said and looked at those of his men who had followed him to the bridge. There were only four of them now. "Thorne and I will go for the lumina. You men, go with Captain Bramwell and do what you can to help."

"Yes, my lord," one of the men, a corporal, said.

Bramwell caught Alaric's arm as he started to turn away. Alaric looked back at his friend in question. "Watch yourself down there. A few always choose to hide rather than fight with the rest. They are the most dangerous, for they are desperate beyond measure. I have lost more than a few good men to such cowardly bastards."

As Bramwell released his arm. Alaric shared a look with Thorne, then moved for the stairs. It was time to find the lumina.

8

Alaric peered down the wooden steps. A solitary oil lantern hung from the ceiling at the bottom, swinging gently with the movement of the ship. It provided a poor but serviceable light. Glancing over at Thorne and sword held ready, he began his descent, his steps measured and cautious, scanning the way ahead.

Thorne was close on his heels, both of them illuminated by the soft, flickering glow of the lantern that cast elongated and shifting shadows along their path. The dim light carved out the way forward and through the darkness of the ship's interior, which smelled fetid and sour, of sweat and unwashed bodies, not to mention human waste.

At the bottom of the stairs, they were greeted by a short, seemingly deserted corridor with several doors to either side. The stillness of the passage was deceptive. Alaric reminded himself of the potential dangers lurking in the shadows and hidden spaces of the ship, one he did not know. He knew better than to let his guard down. The possibility of an enemy hiding within the gloom was a threat he could not afford to overlook, not if he valued his life.

To his right, a door stood ajar, swinging gently with the ship's sway. The room beyond was clearly the captain's cabin. Meanwhile, another staircase beckoned them deeper into the bowels, where another dim light glimmered below.

Alaric glanced into the captain's cabin, a space that mirrored the familiar comfort and utility of Bramwell's own quarters. The muffled echoes of the battle raging above was distant here, almost another world away, as he took in the room's features.

Large aft-facing windows stood open, inviting the cool night air and the soft murmur of the sea into the cabin. The furnishings, though sparse, spoke of a captain's pragmatic needs and personal tastes: a cot for rest with blankets and a pillow; a desk likely used for planning, accounting, and correspondence; and several locked, iron-bound chests that were essentially strongboxes for valuable possessions, loot, or sensitive documents.

The cabin's centerpiece, a central table, was scattered over with several maps, a sextant, and a crude compass. Two chairs were overturned, and a pitcher along with several mugs lay shattered upon the floor, the planks stained with a dark liquid—red wine, likely all the result of when *Magerie* rammed *Mysteeri*.

"Empty," Thorne said, peering over Alaric's shoulder.

Alaric started for the short corridor. Most of the doors were open. He glanced into the first two cabins, rapidly scanning. They were empty, small, cramped spaces. There were two bunks in each, a chest, and a small table. Unlit lanterns hung from the ceiling of each. Studying the bunks, complete with blankets and pillows, Alaric supposed these were officer quarters.

Moving forward to the next set, he discovered nearly identical rooms. These too were empty of anyone hiding. Alaric checked the last two cabins, having to open only one door.

"No one home," Thorne said and then glanced meaningfully at the end of the corridor. The door was closed. Alaric stepped forward and, lifting the latch, opened it partially and cautiously peered into the room. No one was there. Beyond was open space.

"The ship's kitchen," Thorne remarked as Alaric fully opened the door.

"Bramwell's people call it the cook room," Alaric said as he stepped into the galley's kitchen, a confined room where the air hung thick with the scent of salt and smoke. To his left was a large, crudely constructed hearth, its flames dancing wildly as they licked the bottom of a blackened cauldron. The liquid inside was bubbling.

Above the hearth, an assortment of dried herbs and salted meats hung from the ceiling, swaying gently with the ship's movements. The walls were lined with shelves cluttered with clay pots and wooden bowls, each filled with different provisions: likely grains, dried fruits, and roots. A couple of flickering oil lamps provided the only light.

Alaric noted the cramped quarters allowed for little movement. The cook would have maneuvered between the central hearth and a sturdy wooden table that bore the marks of countless meals prepared upon its surface. This table was currently laden with a motley assortment of vegetables and a large, partially butchered fish, its scales glinting under the low light.

Despite the simplicity of the surroundings, there was an undeniable efficiency to the setup. Hooks and pegs protruded from every available space, holding utensils and cooking implements within easy reach. The air, though smoky, was underpinned by the tantalizing aroma of stewing meat and herbs cooking. From the smell alone, Alaric decided the enemy's cook was better than Bramwell's.

Moving through the cook room, he peered into the vast space beyond, the galley's rowing deck, now silent and transformed under the cloak of night. The oars, once the ship's relentless heartbeat, lay dormant or partially deployed, their shafts resting in the shadows, most parallel to the deck. In the dimness, the long, narrow space seemed to stretch endlessly, a cavern of wood and rope suspended in time.

The rowing benches, which by day bore the weight of the ship's rowers, their sweat and toil etching stories into the grain, were now unoccupied. In their place, hammocks had been strung between the stationary oars and the hull's ribs, creating a web of sleeping quarters that hovered above the deck. These makeshift beds swayed gently, cradling their occupants in a fragile peace. It was clear they had fully caught the enemy unprepared.

This quiet was abruptly shattered by a chilling interruption—a woman's scream, piercing the relative silence and snapping Alaric's attention back the way they had come. Together, they hastily moved back through the cook room and to the stairs.

"Where did it come from?" Alaric asked in a low tone. "Below?"

"I think so," Thorne said, glancing at the stairs that led downward. The ship gave a heavy groan, as if protesting in pain at the damage that had been inflicted upon her. "Do you believe Fina really captured a lumina? A real lumina? I thought they were all gone."

"We'll find out," Alaric said, starting for the stairs, holding his sword ready.

Thorne followed. "I once encountered a woman pretending to be one. She was a charlatan, nothing more, a hoaxer in search of the gullible and selling fake love potions. The church officials, when they got their hands on her, tortured her to death."

Alaric came to a stop before the next landing. He saw two feet of dark and dirty water lapping against the last steps. Things floated in the water, including a boot, a towel, and a small wooden box.

"That's not good," Thorne said, eyeing the water warily.

"Help me!" the woman screamed in the common tongue, much closer this time. "Please help!"

Upon hearing the woman's desperate cries for help, Alaric's resolve hardened. The knowledge that the ship was taking on water, her eventual sinking inevitable due to the extensive damage to the hull, added a serious sense of urgency. She must be terrified of being trapped, likely locked in a cabin as the sea flooded in and the water level rose. He climbed the rest of the way down the stairs and into the frigid seawater at the bottom. His boots immediately became soaked through.

Another corridor ahead like the one above stretched out before him, dimly lit by several lamps, with doors lining either side. Bramwell's words gave him pause. Though he doubted it, there could still be an enemy or two lurking below. He had to be cautious.

"Watch it," Thorne cautioned, pointing with his sword at a railing that descended into the water. "There's another deck below this one."

Alaric glanced back at Thorne and met the other's gaze as he too stepped down the ladder and into the murky water. Sword held at the ready, Thorne gave a nod for him to proceed, his gaze shifting ahead and scanning the dimly lit corridor. Beyond, it seemed a much larger space, but it was eclipsed in darkness. Alaric could hear what sounded like the distant bleating of goats. He supposed, like Bramwell's ship, Fina's kept animals too.

"Help me!" the woman's voice, fraught with terror, echoed once more through the hull, urging him along. With Thorne close behind, Alaric moved cautiously forward, the water around his legs a chilling reminder of the ship's grave condition. He glanced into each cabin as he passed, searching for the source of the screams or any hidden threat, but found no one. These rooms were mainly used for storage. They were filled with crates, amphorae, and sacks.

Then, a slap, the sound sharp and clear, followed by another scream from the woman and an unintelligible utterance from a man. There was yet another scream, this one filled with rage. It was followed by a curse, then by the sound of another harsh slap. Alaric's heart hardened as he understood what must be happening. The sounds were close now too—just ahead. He approached an open door on his right and looked in.

A man stood naked, his intentions clear as he forced a woman, face down, over a rough wooden bunk. He had hiked up her dress, revealing her naked backside.

"I am going to give you what you deserve, bitch," the man said in heavily accented and rough common. "What you've been asking for all along."

"That is an uncommonly bad idea." Alaric's voice was firm and cold as he moved into the cabin. The assailant released the woman and turned to face Alaric, his expression morphing into one of surprise, shock, and sudden fear as he took in first the man confronting him, and then the sword.

Alaric exploded forward. He plunged his blade into the man's stomach with a force that drove him violently backward and up against the cabin wall. The unmistakable sound and feeling of the tip of the blade striking the wood of the wall resonated in the cramped cabin as a solid *thunk*. Alaric's grip tightened as the assailant's blood flowed outward in a gush, warming his hand and sword arm. He had pierced the man's bowels, ripping them open, and could smell the foul and rank stench of waste suddenly exposed to the air. He yanked out his sword, and as his did, the man collapsed into the water. Alaric stabbed down, ending his life.

Turning from the grim task, his attention shifted to the woman, who had managed to roll over on the bunk. The dim light revealed her features: long black hair framing a face marked by beauty and resilience. Her dark eyes, striking even in the face of trauma, met Alaric's with an intensity that spoke of the recent terror, gratitude, and the shock of sudden rescue and deliverance. Her left cheek was red from being slapped. There were marks about her throat, as if she'd been choked as well. Come morning, Alaric knew she would have a series of terrible bruises.

Her once fine dress, now marred by her ordeal, hung in tatters. She was also dirty and had not bathed in some time. Yet, despite the disarray and degradation, her dignity and spirit remained unbroken, underscored by the defiant lift of her chin and the clarity in her gaze. Her eyes flicked to Thorne then narrowed as she looked back at Alaric intently. Her eyes widened ever so slightly, then she blinked.

"Who are you?" she demanded in a hard voice, one accustomed to command. "Tell me."

"Lord Alaric, at your service, my lady," Alaric said with a slight bow. "I take it you are the lumina?"

Instead of answering, she shifted slightly, rolling onto her side to better expose her hands, which had been bound behind her back. "You will free me—now."

Alaric responded to her order with the immediacy it demanded. He sheathed his sword and drew his dagger. With precise and cautious movements, he cut through the bindings that held her wrists captive. The ropes fell away and onto the bunk, revealing raw sores and chafed skin beneath. She rubbed at them, as if trying to work the feeling back into her hands.

"My lord," Thorne said, speaking up and glancing down at their feet. "The water is rising. I think we should go. The sooner the better, if you take my meaning."

Sheathing his dagger, Alaric nodded and held out a hand to the woman. "You are safe now. We are going to take you to our ship. What is your name?"

"Rikka," she said, with a firmness that Alaric found remarkable, especially given what she'd been through. Her gaze was piercing and resolute as she took his hand. He was surprised to feel an unexpected warmth radiating from her, as if a hot fire burned within. He wondered if she was slightly feverish.

With a gentle, yet firm tug, he hoisted her to her feet. The top of her head came up to his chin. She stared up at him, as if looking for something, her eyes searching his face. It made him feel slightly uncomfortable, though why he could not say.

"We had best be going, my lord," Thorne said.

Rikka started toward the door as Thorne stepped out into the dimly lit corridor. Almost instantly, a whirlwind of motion and shadow collided with him. Thorne was hit as a form barreled into him, knocking him down the corridor and out of sight with a great splash.

A man, wielding a crude cudgel, pivoted to face the cabin's entrance. His eyes fixed on them. "I kill you," he said in rough and barely intelligible common.

Reaching for his sword hilt, Alaric made to shove Rikka aside, for she was before him and at risk. However, she resisted and stood firm. Before he could force the issue or this new enemy could marshal his thoughts into action, Rikka, with her fingers stretched wide, raised her hand toward the man. As she did, his eyes widened, and under the dim lamplight, Alaric could read the naked fear in his gaze. The man took a sloshing step backward.

She moved her fingers in a rapid and intricate pattern, then spoke a single word, a language not bound to the confines of their mortal world; it was ethereal, transcending the mere vibrations of air to form sound. To Alaric, the word was as fleeting as an indistinct whisper, nothing more, rapidly evading the grasp of memory, as if it had never dared to exist, slipping away upon the air like the grains in an hourglass.

A surge of brilliant, blinding light erupted from Rikka's palm. Hissing, it streaked through the air, striking the man squarely in the chest with a deep cracking sound. An explosive gust blasted by Alaric as the man was sent hurtling violently backward with such force that he collided with the corridor wall, smashing some of the planking. For a fleeting moment, his form was ensnared in a dazzling display of white light, a spectacle of power that starkly illuminated the darkened corridor and cabin. Alaric's skin tingled and the small hairs on his arms stood on end as the air seemed to crackle.

Then, as quickly as it had manifested, the light extinguished itself, leaving behind only the echoes of its existence as Alaric blinked away the spots. The man's body, devoid of the life force that inhabited it moments before, toppled into the dirty seawater with a splash.

As the echoes of the confrontation faded, she turned to look at him, her eyes impossibly deep, once more searching his face.

"I came—for—I came—I came—you…" She blinked several times, then her eyes closed, and Rikka's strength waned, her legs betraying her. In a graceful descent, she began to crumple into the water, but Alaric, despite his shock at what he had just witnessed, reacted instinctively. His arms enveloped Rikka in a secure embrace, catching her.

Concern etched deeply into his features as he studied her face, finding it serene, beautiful, exotic, yet unnaturally still—the toll of her ordeal and magical exertion having clearly drawn her into unconsciousness.

Meanwhile, Thorne, still grappling with the abruptness of the attack, had regained his footing. He stood, dripping wet, a cut on his temple bleeding slightly and mixing with the water. He tried to shake off the seawater from his attire, a futile attempt at best.

"Are you all right?" Alaric asked.

"I am…" Thorne looked up and eyed Rikka warily. "That was something."

Nodding, Alaric hoisted Rikka with a gentle yet resolute grip, picking her up and into his arms. She weighed almost nothing.

Her head settled into and rested against his shoulder, her chest rising and falling with shallow breaths.

"I think we found the lumina," Thorne commented as he retrieved his sword from the water. Looking back, he shook his head as he warily regarded the woman in Alaric's arms. "I've never seen anything like that. Have you?"

"I'd say she's the real thing, no hoaxer."

Thorne could only nod.

The ship groaned deeply, the boards creaking and popping loudly. Alaric began sloshing forward, out and into the corridor and around the body of the man Rikka had just killed. The water was almost up to his knees and clearly rising steadily. "Now, let's get out of here before the ship sinks around us."

9

Alaric stifled a yawn. He was leaning heavily on *Magerie*'s railing, his gaze locked onto the spot where *Mysteeri* was making her final, begrudging descent into the abyss. As the tip of the bow, the last visible fragment of the once formidable vessel, succumbed to the icy waves, the water around where the ship had gone down churned and frothed with a violence that spoke of the ocean's unforgiving nature. But just as quickly as the turmoil had erupted, a serene calm soon spread across the surface, as if the ocean were smoothing things away.

"The Well of Tears," he said to himself. Alaric now knew why the cove had gotten its name, for it was filled with the tears of the lost. He pondered the fates of countless other galleys, each with their own stories of valor and tragedy, now lying upon the ocean floor. Storms, battles, unforeseen calamities—so many had met their demise, maybe not here, but somewhere else, swallowed whole by a realm that was as beautiful as it was merciless.

The ocean jealously guarded the graves of those ships, a guardian over the lost and the damned. Alaric stood there, a witness to the sea's latest claim, contemplating the fleeting nature of glory, mortality, and the eternal grip of the ocean's dark depths.

Gazing upward, he observed the sun asserting its dominance in the sky, perched almost directly overhead in a clear declaration of midday. Its radiance was unyielding, casting a blanket of warmth over the day that had begun with a promise of heat. The sea beneath mirrored this brilliance, its surface a mosaic of dazzling reflections, each wave capturing and throwing back the sunlight in brilliant, fleeting flashes.

Despite the beauty of the day, Alaric was acutely aware of the weight of exhaustion that hung over him, an unwelcome cloak that seemed to draw tighter with each passing moment. The previous night had offered little rest, with only an hour's sleep—hardly enough to fend off the tiredness that now gnawed at him.

Though weary to the bone and exhausted from the fight, Alaric and his men, along with Bramwell's, had worked tirelessly. They had descended upon *Mysteeri* like a swarm of hungry ants, determined to salvage any item of value from the wreckage. Weapons, supplies, lengths of cordage, longboats, live animals, chests, and the strongboxes from Fina's quarters, even trinkets and jewelry from the dead that might fetch a price—nothing was overlooked in their thorough scouring of the warship.

Locked fast by the imposing rams of Bramwell's vessels and buoyed by the structural support of the two larger galleys, *Mysteeri* stubbornly refused to succumb to the waiting deep and had remained afloat long enough to complete the job. Once both ships had pulled away, she'd begun to sink, and rapidly at that.

Bramwell's third galley missed the fight. By the time her captain and crew navigated into position for a ram, the outcome was all but decided, particularly sealed by the demise of the warship's captain. Bramwell had waved her off.

Faced with the grim reality of their defeat and the loss of their leader, the majority of the enemy had opted against surrender—a decision that might have offered them a sliver of hope for survival, as slaves, which wasn't really an option. They chose instead to abandon ship. One by one, the survivors cast themselves into the sea's uncertain mercy, swimming desperately toward the distant promise of shore and whatever fate awaited them there along this barren and remote stretch of coastline.

The echoes of the fight still lingered on, manifesting through the agonized screams that permeated the lower decks of Bramwell's ships. On *Magerie*, Bramwell's doctor and Father Ava worked tirelessly, tending to one injured man after another, treating the wounds they could. Alaric had learned that each scream, while the two men worked, marked not just pain, but a chance—an opportunity—for survival.

He had gone to see the wounded and found the experience quite depressing. Below decks where both men, Ava and the doctor, worked to save lives, the air was thick with the metallic scent of blood. It overpowered everything else. The number of injured was nearly overwhelming, requiring as many as twenty assistants to tend to them. Cuts, arrow wounds, burns, broken bones, blunt trauma, and deeper, unseen wounds—they were dealing with it all.

The unmistakable sound of footsteps against the wooden deck pulled Alaric from his grim contemplations, and his gaze shifted from the blue of the sea to the figure approaching him. It was Grayson, his features etched with fatigue, the toll of the day's events evident in the weary slump of his shoulders and the shadows under his eyes. In the unspoken language of battle-worn comrades, Alaric immediately read the purpose of Grayson's visit in the man's gaze, before a word was exchanged.

"Did you manage any sleep?" Alaric asked, seeking a brief reprieve for the conversation ahead. He was not ready for that yet.

"I stole maybe two hours. You?"

"Just a short nap deck-side," Alaric admitted.

"Then, might I suggest you get some?" Grayson jerked his head toward the aft of the ship where their cabin waited.

"I will," Alaric said, "as soon as we are done with our business here—what you have come to discuss."

"Good, the cabin is yours, then." Grayson looked up at the sky. "It is warm enough that I might lie down in the sun for a while myself." The older man sucked in a deep breath and slowly let it out. "Ever since I was a boy, I've always enjoyed napping in the sun, out in the open."

"Maybe that's why you ultimately became a soldier," Alaric suggested.

"That was my father's doing," Grayson said. "And your grandfather's too, now that I think about it. He encouraged and even saw me promoted to a lieutenant in one of his companies. Your father was the one who raised me up to captain before sending me off with you to the holy land."

Talk of Alaric's father made him straighten and step back from the railing. Alaric loved his father, but at the same time, had always had a difficult relationship with the man. He never seemed to measure up to the old man's ideals and expectations. It was one of the reasons why Alaric figured he had been sent away. He grew grave and decided it was time to confront the inevitable. "So, what's the butcher's bill?"

"We lost ten men. One was knocked overboard and could not swim," Grayson began. "The rest were the result of a mix of arrow and sword wounds. Another fifteen were injured, to varying degrees. Two more will not live through the night. One man will be disabled for life and will not walk again—that is, if he survives the amputation. Father Ava gives him a fifty-fifty chance."

Grayson's words hit Alaric with the force of a physical blow, a visceral reminder of the price paid in flesh and blood for the decisions he made. He let go an unhappy breath. Twelve more men who would never see Dekar again, their dreams and hopes lost. The injustice of it lay heavy on his heart, a cruel fate for those who had been mere weeks away from the safety and familiarity of home.

This loss, this grievous toll, stirred a deep turmoil within Alaric. It was a burden he knew all too well, one that leadership demanded he bear, yet it did little to ease the personal anguish and guilt that came with the cost of command and ordering his men into battle. The knowledge that these men, these individuals under his care, had paid the ultimate price or faced a future marred by the scars of war, was a weight that, over years, had settled deep in his soul. It was a haunting reality that would linger in his thoughts, robbing him of sleep and peace as he wrestled with the inevitable questions of what might have been done differently, of whether the victory was worth the price paid.

"I will have a detailed accounting for you later today, fully listing and detailing our casualties. Tomorrow, after I am rested, I will adjust the company books to properly reflect our losses." Grayson paused. "It never gets any easier."

"No, it doesn't," Alaric said, his voice almost a whisper. "Perhaps, when we get home, the company can be discharged, the men allowed to retire and live out their lives in peace."

"That would be nice," Grayson said. "I could stand some peace, to see my wife and daughters again. Long has it been since I received news of them. My oldest, Tara, had her first baby last year. I like babies... so innocent..."

Alaric gave a nod. He'd heard Grayson talk about this before, many times. Whenever he brought the subject up, Alaric made a point to listen. Ever since his oldest daughter had married the miller and had a baby, Grayson had been itching to return home. But duty compelled him to remain at Alaric's side. And Alaric's duty to the Cardinal King had kept him chained to Hawkani.

"You will see your family again," Alaric assured the older man.

"This voyage cannot come to its conclusion soon enough,"

Grayson said, gazing almost forlornly at the shoreline. A group of perhaps twenty men was huddled there on the beach. All were the enemy, sailors who abandoned the fight and made the long swim to shore. Bramwell did not seem terribly concerned by them. The truth was that everyone was too tired and spent to do much of anything.

"I will see the men get the land they were promised," Alaric said, deciding to move the conversation along, "and some funds to set up a farm, maybe even a regular pension for their long and dedicated service."

"Instruction would be helpful too," Grayson suggested. "These are soldiers we are talking about. Most likely don't know how to farm or, if they ever did, forgot how."

Alaric gave a nod. "That's something to consider."

They both fell into silence for several heartbeats, each lost to their own thoughts. Alaric's gaze returned to the enemy clustered ashore. There had been as many as a hundred an hour ago. He supposed a good number of those had wandered off. Where to, he had no idea.

"Bramwell did much worse than we did," Grayson said. "The butcher's bill for his people was far steeper."

"They did go into the attack first, and we both know that's not the best place to be if you wish to keep your casualties down." A yawn overcame Alaric. "How bad was it for them?"

"Between the two ships, he lost seventy-five men," Grayson said. "Another hundred injured. I am not sure how many of those will survive their wounds or be crippled for life."

It was worse than Alaric had thought.

"Caxatarus took a shallow wound to his leg and should survive," Grayson added. "Father Ava cleaned it with vinegar and sewed the wound up. He's resting in his cabin—drank himself silly before the good father went to work with the needle and thread."

Alaric gave a nod but did not speak. He'd known Caxatarus had been injured, seen the man fighting on, blood streaming down his leg. It was good the man would recover. He was a fighter and Alaric liked fighters.

"Bramwell asked if we could spare some men to help operate the ship. I already told him we would."

"Good," Alaric said, yawning powerfully. There were tears in his eyes from the exhaustion. "What of the woman, the lumina?"

"Is she really a holy magic user?" Grayson asked curiously. "Thorne said she was…"

"She dropped a man dead by just holding out her hand and speaking magic. Light flew from that hand. It was rather incredible."

Grayson shook his head as if in disbelief. "I thought there weren't any luminas left, that they were more legend than anything else."

"It seems there are."

"Bramwell gave her a cabin next to ours. She's recovered and been allowed to bathe and clean up. I understand she is resting. I will make a point of checking in on her later."

"All right. Is there anything else?"

"We rescued six nobles who were destined to be ransomed, along with thirty common folk who were headed for the blocks."

"At least we did some good," Alaric said in an attempt to find solace amid the aftermath of battle. As he surveyed the deck, his gaze captured the efforts to erase the physical reminders of their recent conflict. The sand, once strewn across the wooden planks to soak up the blood and prevent slipping during the fight, had already been swept away, cast into the ocean.

Yet the deck bore the tangible scars of battle. Dark stains, the remnants of bloodshed, marked the places where men had fought, bled, suffered, and died. There were also scorch marks from the enemy's fire arrows.

Not far off, a solitary figure knelt on the deck, diligently working at one of the darker stains with a scrub brush and bucket. The methodical scrubbing was not just an act of cleaning; it was a ritual of healing, an attempt to return the ship to her former state, to wash away the reminders of suffering and loss. The sight of the man cleaning, the sound of the brush scraping against the wood, was a reminder of how life soldiered on.

"For a change," Grayson said, "I suppose we ultimately saved more than we lost."

"What do you mean?" Alaric asked.

"*Mysteeri* and Captain Fina will no longer be plaguing these waters," Grayson said plainly, gesturing at the cove with a hand. "Bramwell said she's taken dozens of ships this year alone. There's no telling how many more she would have gotten given the chance."

Alaric thought on that for several moments, then gave a nod. "That does make me feel a tad better."

"Me as well," Grayson admitted as Alaric stifled another yawn. "Now, why don't you go get some sleep."

"All right. I will grab a few hours' rest," Alaric said, the weight of their losses and the day's toll weighing heavily upon his shoulders. He moved off, leaving Grayson and making his way aft. As he approached the bridge, the figure of Bramwell came into view. The captain offered him a weary nod, then turned away as another officer on the bridge called for his attention.

Then, Alaric was at the stairs. Descending into the ship's interior, he was enveloped by the pungent fug that clung to the close quarters below deck—a mélange of sweat, salt, and the powerful iron tang of blood. The muffled screams of the wounded crawled through the wood, as the ship's doctor and Ava worked farther forward. He quickly moved down two flights of stairs, the darkness intermittently pierced by the dim light of lanterns.

As silent and unobtrusive as usual, Ezran followed a few steps behind. At the bottom of the stairs, Jasper stood guard, posted outside Alaric's cabin. Without a word, Jasper opened the door.

"Thank you," Alaric said.

Once inside, the door closed with a soft, definitive *thunk* and *click* as the latch fell into place, sealing Alaric away from the world outside. This small sanctuary offered a brief respite. Here, in the solitude of his cabin, he could surrender, however briefly, to the exhaustion that clawed at his edges, allowing himself a few precious hours of rest.

Alaric and Grayson's cabin was defined by its simplicity. The space was compact, dominated by a single hard bunk that stood unadorned, without the comfort—or risk—of a mattress. Their deliberate choice to forego such a basic amenity was the result of prior experience and the hard lessons learned on other ships. A mattress would likely have become ridden with lice and filled with other vermin, the kind that bit and made one itch.

After the battle, Alaric had taken time to wash and clean up. Michael had provided him fresh clothes, taking the soiled ones for cleaning. Each day, he took pains to bathe and wash himself so as not to become infested, which, shipboard, was a real possibility and concern. He had picked up this habit of regularly bathing in the holy land, where staying clean often meant the difference between remaining healthy or growing sick and diseased.

The cabin, though Spartan, was afforded a luxury few others on the ship enjoyed—a good-sized window. Located just under Bramwell's cabin, this aperture to the world outside was left unlatched and open, a conduit for the fresh air that swept away the stifling closeness of the ship's interior and much of the stink that came with it.

The breeze that whispered through the opening was a balm to the senses, carrying the briny scent of the ocean and the promise of a world beyond the wooden confines of the ship. Alaric's cabin was one of the privileged few that boasted such a connection to the outside, allowing natural light to spill into the otherwise dim space.

In this moment of solitude, the absence of the oil lamp's glow was notable. Its darkened state left the room bathed solely in the soft, diffused light filtering in through the window, casting shadows that danced with the gentle sway of the ship.

Alaric unbuckled Oathbreaker and propped the weapon up in the corner. The warmth of the room, amplified by the enclosed space and the heat of the day, prompted Alaric to shed his tunic, seeking some relief from the oppressive stuffiness that even the open window could not fully dispel. His boots followed. Yet just as he stood, ready to climb into his bunk and surrender to sleep, a knock at the door arrested his motion. It opened a moment later and Jasper stuck his head in.

"Someone to see you, my lord."

Wondering what problem needed attending, Alaric let go a heavy breath, one filled with resignation. "Send him in."

As Jasper respectfully made way, the door swung open to reveal Rikka entering the cabin with an air that seemed to command the very space around her. She was attired in the practical garb of a sailor. Her wool tunic and pants spoke more to utility than fashion, yet on her, they almost took on a character of their own. Her hair, brushed straight, framed her face in a simple, unadorned style. She was also barefoot.

Rikka looked meaningfully at Jasper, a silent command. It was enough to convey her wish for privacy, prompting Jasper to retreat back into the corridor and close the door behind him, as if commanded. Once alone with Alaric, Rikka faced him, her dark eyes locking onto his with an intensity that momentarily robbed him of speech.

Bruises marred her cheek and neck, evidence of the recent attack, but they did nothing to diminish her striking appearance or undeniable presence about her, a blend of strength and vulner-ability.

For a moment, Alaric found himself caught in the whirlwind of her beauty, a beauty that defied her captivity and the hardship she'd endured. It was a reminder of the complex layers of human resilience, of the ability to emerge from adversity with a dignity that transcended physical and often emotional scars.

"How can I help you, my lady?" Alaric managed, his voice regaining steadiness only after he cleared his throat, an attempt to mask the sudden surge of emotions Rikka's presence invoked. All sense of weariness and exhaustion had fled.

Rikka's response was not immediate. Instead, she chose to close the distance between them, her steps measured and deliber-ate, shrinking the realm of personal space to a mere whisper. Her gaze, intense and probing, seemed to traverse the contours of his face, seeking, perhaps, an understanding deeper than words could afford. It was in this proximity, with her almost within arm's reach, that Alaric felt an undeniable acceleration in his heartbeat.

She glanced down at his naked chest, her gaze lingering on an old scar along his right side. She then drew even closer, a bold encroachment that heightened Alaric's senses to a keen edge. His pulse raced as if preparing for battle, yet this was a confrontation of an entirely different nature. She reached out and, with a finger, traced the scar. Her touch felt like fire against his skin. Looking up into his eyes, Rikka exuded an aura that was at once mesmer-izing, disarming, and intoxicating. Her exotic appearance, coupled with the air of mystery that surrounded her, painted her as a figure not entirely of this world—a perception further reinforced by the whispers of holy magic that she wielded. This was a power Alaric found both intriguing and unfathomable, a force that tran-scended the martial prowess and strategy with which he was familiar. He also found it more than a little unsettling.

"As were you—I was drawn, led to this moment, to our meeting," Rikka breathed, her voice slightly husky. "At first, I did not know why Eldanar wished me to voyage to the holy land. Now, I do."

"What?" Alaric asked, not understanding.

"Are you a good man, Alaric of Dekar?"

Alaric was thoroughly confused by what was happening. "What?"

"I asked if you are a good man," Rikka pressed, her voice hardening slightly. "This is important. Do not make me repeat myself again. So, are you?"

"I try to be," Alaric admitted.

"And where are you going? Why are you on this ship?"

The question surprised him. "Right now, I am just trying to get my people home."

"Home?"

"Dekar. I chartered Bramwell's three ships to bring my people home."

She gave a slow nod. "And that's how Bramwell found *Mysteeri* and you rescued me—saved me from that animal, one of my captors?"

"Yes," Alaric answered.

"Then it is as *HE* wills… destiny's done." She eyed him a moment more, then abruptly reached up, grabbed his face with both hands, and pulled him down to her. He found himself powerless to resist. She kissed him, pressing her soft lips firmly against his, her tongue exploring. The kiss was passionate, intense. It was a connection that went beyond the physical, a melding of souls that had traversed their own journeys to find this point of convergence. The ring on Alaric's hand grew warm to the point of hotness, but he did not notice… not much.

After all that had happened in the last day, Alaric found himself responding with an unexpected hunger, wrapping his arms around this exotic and beautiful woman, and kissing her back. He felt her hard and erect nipples beneath her tunic press against his chest, and with it, a powerful stirring rose within him, his body responding.

She gently withdrew, pushing him back and away. With a tender yet determined grasp, she took his hand, directing his gaze toward the bunk with a look that conveyed volumes. Alaric, understanding the silent cue, swiftly gathered her into his arms as he had once before. The world around them seemed to blur into insignificance, their focus narrowing to the connection sparking between them.

As he carried Rikka, her eyes, deep and captivating, never strayed from his. Gently, he laid her down upon the bunk. She scooted over to make room. Climbing in beside her, he captured her lips in a kiss, profound and consuming. She responded with equal fervor, her arms winding around him in an impassioned embrace, pulling him closer, as if trying to merge their very souls.

In that moment, Alaric lost himself completely to the sensation, the emotion, and the overwhelming presence of her. The world outside their embrace ceased to exist, even the occasional muffled scream of a wounded man receiving treatment, leaving only the profound connection that thrummed through them with every heartbeat. It was a moment of unguarded vulnerability, of giving and receiving, a dance as old as time itself, yet as fresh and thrilling as if they were the first to discover its steps. Under the dim light, within the confines of that small bunk, they found an oasis of intimacy, a haven from the tumult of the world outside, where only the moment mattered, fierce and unyielding.

10

"I wish you good fortune, my friend," Bramwell said, his voice carrying the weight of the long sea journey they had endured together. He extended his hand, a gesture of friendship and respect.

Alaric paused to regard the offered hand, his gaze lingering on the captain's face. The lines there spoke of years spent battling the tempests of the sea and other adversities. Now, as the shores of home loomed large, so close at hand, mere yards away, the moment felt both triumphant and bittersweet.

Ezran, Thorne, and Kiera stood close by, patiently waiting and watchful for deceit. Caxatarus was next to his captain, looking on. Though he still limped slightly, he was as active as ever. Around them, the ship's crew, those who were freemen and not the slaves who rowed below decks, moved with the efficiency of long practice, the deck alive with the sounds of their labor.

A rope ladder dangled over the side, the bridge between their floating world and the longboat that would finally take him home. In the longboat, twelve sailors sat with disciplined patience, their oars held upright at the ready. Beside them, Grayson and ten of his men sat, also waiting. The rest of Alaric's people, their supplies, equipment, and the hard-won treasure of a decade had already made the transition from ship to shore, a painstaking process that consumed the better part of the day. With the last few boats, Rikka had gone too.

Obscured by an evening fog that had rolled in less than an hour ago, the three ships that had carried his people home now rode safely at anchor, each separated by a few hundred yards. The distant crash of waves against the shore played a constant, rhythmic backdrop to the scene.

"As usual, I enjoyed your stay aboard my ship," Bramwell said. There was a subtle warmth in his eyes belying the usual sternness. "In the morning, when the tide changes, we set sail. Before we do, I will send men ashore for fresh water." He gestured vaguely toward the unseen land, hidden by the fog, shrouding their surroundings in mystery and dampening the sounds of the coming night. "This place is called Smuggler's Cove. I am unashamed to admit I have used it a time or two." He glanced outward, the fog, thick and impenetrable, concealing the coast that lay just a few hundred yards away.

The natural harbor they found themselves in was a hidden gem among a rugged and difficult coastline of Dekar. Towering cliffs on either side formed a protective barrier against the relentless ocean waves, creating a secluded sanctuary for those who knew of its existence, which obviously Bramwell did.

"And now, it is time for you to go."

Alaric took the captain's hand, the shake firm and meaningful. "And where will you go from here?" Alaric asked, curiosity mingling with a tinge of concern for his friend's future endeavors.

"I will head for Gress to reprovision," Bramwell mused, his gaze drifting toward the horizon to the east, lost in thoughts of what lay ahead. "Sanenik's Landing is the closest port. Then I suppose… who knows. I am thinking we will head back south, though maybe not." A shrug accompanied his words, a gesture of acceptance toward the unpredictable nature of life at sea. "Maybe it is time to see new lands and what they have to offer. But—you need to put ashore before the tide shifts and I change my mind about selling you into a life of bondage," Bramwell added with a light chuckle, the threat more jest than earnest warning. "I am more than certain Sunara would pay dearly for your head." The humor in his voice did little to mask the underlying truth of his statement, a reminder of the dangers that lurked in their world, where loyalties, especially in the south, were often bought and sold, and lives were as much a currency as gold.

Ezran and Thorne tensed. Kiera remained unfazed, her expression unreadable as she gazed upon Bramwell. Alaric grinned, and without hesitation, he stepped forward, wrapping the captain in a hearty embrace, a gesture that transcended mere friendship and spoke to the brotherhood forged in the face of adversity. They thumped each other's back in a series of fond pats.

After a moment, both stepped back from one another.

"I told you I'd honor my word," Bramwell said. "I have too few genuine friends. I'd not lose one over money."

"You did honor it," Alaric acknowledged, his tone laden with gratitude. "And I am pleased. You will come back one day?"

"Build that port you spoke of, and I will come," Bramwell responded with a decisive nod, eyes sweeping over the obscured landscape, as if envisioning the future they had dared to dream. He gestured toward the fog, thick and enveloping, as if it were a curtain waiting to be drawn back. "I am thinking this may not be such a bad spot."

"Smuggler's Cove?" Alaric's voice was tinged with a mixture of surprise and contemplation, the name of the anchorage sparking a flurry of thoughts about its potential and its past. "I might have to come up with a better name for the place."

"Yes, you might," Bramwell agreed with a hint of fond reminiscence. "There are worse spots, and whenever I had business with your father, I came here. This cove is where we met."

"My father?" Alaric was both surprised and intrigued at the mention of his father. It was a connection he hadn't expected, a hidden thread tying his family to Bramwell in ways he had yet to fully understand.

"Build me that port and you will see me again."

"As long as my father approves," Alaric said.

The captain's eyes narrowed. "I wager, from those twelve heavy chests winched down to the longboats, you have enough treasure to see that happen. Besides, if he says no, one day, you will be the Earl of Dekar and then the decision will be solely yours. Now, you have wasted enough time and so have I."

Alaric grasped Oathbreaker's scabbard firmly to keep the weapon from becoming entangled as he climbed over the railing and moved with a deliberate intention. The rope ladder swayed gently beneath him, each rung a step away from the life he had known aboard the ship and a step toward the uncertain future that awaited him ashore.

As he began his descent, the sturdy ropes and wooden rungs of the ladder creaked softly under his weight. A few feet down, Alaric paused. He looked back up toward the deck where Bramwell stood, watching him.

"Take care of yourself, my friend," Alaric said.

"Always," Bramwell replied with a slight smirk.

Alaric continued his descent, each movement bringing him closer to the dark waters and the waiting longboat below. He was glad he wasn't wearing his armor. Had he fallen in, the heavy metal would drag him into the depths without mercy.

The longboat bobbed on the swells, its movements unpredictable and challenging as he neared the end of the ladder. The sight of a sailor extending a hand upward was a welcome one, offering a semblance of stability. Alaric accepted the assistance, jumping the final distance with a practiced ease that belied the risk involved. His boots met the boat's wooden bottom with a slight splash, for there was an inch of water inside.

"Over here, my lord," Grayson's voice cut through the sound of waves and creaking wood. Alaric moved toward the bow of the boat, each step a negotiation with the rocking vessel. He made it without stumbling and took the seat offered.

Thorne and Ezran followed next and found a seat just behind them. Alaric looked back and up. Kiera and Bramwell stood staring at one another. During the voyage, they had more than made up. Kiera had spent almost as much time with Bramwell as Alaric had. The exchange between them, though silent to Alaric, was clearly heavy with meaning, a final shared moment before parting ways. Then she turned away abruptly and clambered over the side and onto the rope ladder.

Kiera's descent was a spectacle of independence and strength. The same sailor who had offered a hand to Alaric extended one to her. Kiera's refusal was punctuated by a heated glare. She jumped down into the rocking boat and then made her way forward to a bench just behind Alaric, where an open space waited next to Ezran.

"I do believe he will miss you," Ezran said, leaning toward her. "Did I see a tear in his eye?"

"Shut up, you," Kiera said and shot him a hard look.

This mist, dense and enveloping, draped itself heavily over the water, casting the anchored galley in an almost otherworldly silence. The only sounds to puncture this veil of tranquility were the creaks and groans from the ship's timbers as she rocked with the swells and the distant, rhythmic crash of the waves against the shoreline.

The ship, with her oars shipped and away, was a towering presence against the backdrop of the fog-enveloped sea, looming over the longboat like a spectral guardian of the deep. The longboat, in comparison, appeared almost fragile and tiny.

Alaric spotted motion above. Bramwell was now making his way down the ladder with ease to join them. That surprised him.

"Oh, look, Kiera," Ezran said in a low tone. "I think he can't bear to live without you."

Kiera shot him another hard look that spoke of warning. "Don't force me to test the sharpness of my blades upon you."

Ezran grinned at her. "I believe you already know how well they cut, Lady Luminary."

"Then you may wish to watch your mouth."

Bramwell's boots splashed and *thunked* down into the boat, having leapt the last foot, timing the swells right as the longboat rose. He made the movement look almost easy. The captain worked his way carefully to the stern of the longboat. Once there, his gaze fixed upon the crew assembled before him. The sailors waited in anticipation, their hands gripping the oars, which were out of the water and pointed straight up at the sky. They were a raggedy bunch, their tunics bleached by the sun, almost threadbare and stained with tar and food.

"Listen up, lads." The captain's voice broke the silence, commanding and clear. "We're heading to shore, and I'll not have us be the day's spectacle. Row with strength but keep your pace even. We'll push off on my command and make for the beach with all the grace this miserable craft can muster."

He turned his attention to the mate, who stood ready by the ladder and the rope that secured them to the galley.

"Thomas, on my mark, release us and take the tiller."

"Aye, Captain," Thomas replied, his hands steady on the rope.

Bramwell's eyes swept over his crew once more, ensuring every man was prepared. "This is it, gentlemen. Ready your oars... and... shove off!"

At his command, Thomas untied the rope with a swift motion,

releasing the longboat from the galley's embrace. With a heavy grunt, he pushed off from the galley, then made his way back to the tiller and took it in hand, standing next to his captain.

"Starboard side, oars shove off."

The rowers there lowered their oars and placed the ends against the hull of the ship as the gap widened. They shoved mightily and, suddenly, the boat was moving away, the distance between ship and longboat growing with every passing moment.

Bramwell waited several heartbeats. "Ready oars… deploy oars."

A moment later, the rowers plunged their oars into the water.

"Row."

Their movements synchronized under Bramwell's orders and watchful eye. The longboat began to glide away from the galley, the gap between them rapidly widening with each and every stroke.

"Steady, lads. Keep her steady," Bramwell instructed, his voice a blend of encouragement and authority as the longboat accelerated, moving into the fog. The ship behind them began to rapidly disappear. "Let's show the old girl we can handle her with tender care. Strongly now. Keep rowing. That's it. Keep up the pace."

The rowers responded with a rhythmic cadence, their oars dipping and rising in perfect harmony. The longboat moved gracefully through the water, her crew working as one. Bramwell stood tall at the aft of the longboat, his orders now softening to words of guidance and encouragement as the boat cut its way toward the shore.

Alaric felt the experience almost otherworldly, as if he was moving to a new chapter in his life, which he supposed he was.

The longboat continued her journey away from the galley. The outline of the shore, at first a mere shadow within the fog, slowly clarified into a landscape both daunting and somehow welcoming.

Alaric's heart raced as the coast drew nearer, each beat a drum heralding his return. The sight that unfolded before him was one of hard beauty—jagged rocks and steep cliffs, monuments to the timeless battle between land and sea.

The beach, with its sand and rocks, offered a welcome after the long journey at sea. The sight of Dekar, his home, evoked a surge of powerful emotion—relief, anticipation, and an underlying current of apprehension for what awaited him on land.

Captain Bramwell's eyes narrowed as he assessed the rapidly approaching shoreline, clearly calculating the best approach. After a long moment, he pointed.

"There! Between those two rock outcroppings." The captain was indicating a narrow inlet where the rocks gave way to a small, pebbled beach. "Thomas, that's our landing. Steer toward it and mind the currents. They can be treacherous here."

"Aye, sar," Thomas said, hand on the tiller, making a minute adjustment as they drew closer.

"Row, boys, faster now," Bramwell said. "That's it. Faster."

The rowers picked up the pace of their strokes, their oars slicing through the water with renewed purpose. The longboat veered slightly, aligning with the captain's chosen path, as the crew braced themselves against the pull of the sea.

As they neared the shore, the sounds of the ocean grew louder. The crash of waves against rock and beach became a constant beat that filled the air. Seabirds circled overhead, their cries mingling with the wind and waves, as if heralding the arrival of the longboat and her crew.

Alaric found himself hungrily devouring the view. He recognized these cliffs and this beach, this very spot. His mother had taken him here, more than once, to play in the water as a child. This was Dekar, his home. If memory served, his family keep was only twenty miles distant from where they were being landed, a day's march.

Many of those who had already landed had made their way up a narrow trail to the cliffs above. Several were standing at the edge of the cliff, looking down upon them as they came in for a landing. Alaric could see smoke from fires that had been set to drive the cold away. Only one person waited upon the beach for their arrival, and somehow Alaric was not terribly surprised.

Rikka.

"Ready yourselves!" Bramwell's voice cut through the noise. "We'll need to pull hard to make it through the surf. On my command, give it everything you've got and then some. Pull! I said, bloody pull at those oars! That's it… pull!"

The longboat hit the first of the breaking waves, water splashing over the sides and drenching the men in a frigid spray. The oarsmen rowed with all their might, muscles straining, as Thomas steered them through the frothy turmoil of the surf zone.

"Pull!"

Another wave lifted the boat, propelling it forward with a surge of power.

"Now! Pull!" Bramwell shouted, and the rowers obeyed, their coordinated effort driving the longboat up and onto the pebbled beach with a final, triumphant effort.

The craft ground against the small stones and sand, its momentum carrying it farther up the shore until it came to rest, lodged firmly on the shoreline. The rowers, along with the passengers, panting and soaked, looked up to see the rugged and forbidding cliffs towering over them.

"Well done, lads," Bramwell praised and then turned to look at Alaric. "May I be the first to welcome you home, my lord."

"Thank you." Standing, Alaric leapt from the longboat. His boots met the soft yet unforgiving soil of the beach—a mixture of sand and millions of pebbles that told tales of the sea's relentless sculpting. The sensation of solid ground beneath his feet felt odd, almost unnatural. That he was no longer on the swaying deck of a ship anchored him to the moment, to the reality of his homecoming.

Kneeling, he scooped up a handful of the cold, damp sand, filled liberally with small, rounded stones and pebbles, along with shells. This simple act was his way of reconnecting with the land that had shaped him.

Beside him, Grayson's presence was announced by the crunch of heavy boots landing on the beach. "Home," Grayson breathed. "At long last, we are home, my lord."

In this sacred moment, Alaric bowed his head, his voice barely above a whisper, yet carrying the weight of his gratitude. "I give thanks to you, holy God, for our deliverance, for our return. For those who could not make the journey and fell in your name along the difficult path we traveled, look after them in the here-after. On this, I pray."

Dropping the handful of beach, Alaric stood as the others began to climb out of the longboat. Behind them, still in the boat with Thomas, Captain Bramwell issued the order to push back into the sea. The sailors, having jumped out and accustomed to working in unison under their captain's command, set about the task with practiced ease.

Alaric turned and watched, along with Grayson, as the crew, with concerted effort, lifted and pushed the heavy boat, her hull scraping against the pebbles and rocks with a grating sound that echoed off the nearest cliff walls. Slowly, the longboat began to move, inching her way back toward the water's edge under the collective strength of the men.

Once the boat reached the shallows, the rowers waded into the surf, pushing and pulling, manhandling, until the craft was afloat once more. They maneuvered it carefully through the breaking waves, their bodies bracing against the push and pull of the frigid ocean until they were past the initial surf line. There, they clambered aboard.

Several more orders were shouted by Bramwell in quick succession, and the oars were rapidly taken back up. They dipped in unison into the water, and within moments, the boat was pulling back out to sea toward the anchored galley hidden by the fog. Bramwell half turned back and waved at Alaric. Then he looked to Kiera, staring long and hard at her. A moment later, he turned his gaze to his men.

"Pull, you bloody dogs. I said, pull."

As the longboat disappeared into the distance, melding with the mist and the vastness of the sea beyond, Alaric felt a sense of finality, a chapter closing as firmly as the waves closed over the longboat's wake. Kiera stood, silent as if in vigil, staring out at where the longboat had been. Alaric's heart tugged with empathy for her. If anyone deserved to be happy, it was her. But, as a Luminary, her path in life had been set. There was no changing that or the vows she had made to her god and order.

Turning his attention from the sea, Alaric's eyes met the rugged beauty of the fog-shrouded cliffs. There were still barrels and crates stacked farther up along the beach. Two men were tying crates to a mule, while several others carried additional crates toward the trailhead. One of their horses was being led up the narrow trail.

Alaric's gaze moved to Rikka. She was still wearing the sailor's shirt and pants. She had been given boots. Her dark hair blew with the wind, making her look even more captivating than usual. She was staring at him, her gaze deep and unfathomable. Though they had spent their nights together for the past two and a half weeks, she was still an enigma to him, a mystery beyond solving. Steadfastly, Rikka had refused to talk about herself. She had spent her days alone, isolated, locked within her cabin or standing upon the deck of the ship, staring out to sea, as if searching for something. Oddly, when she was out and about on the ship, Alaric had often found Kiera in her presence, neither talking. He had a strong suspicion of what that potentially represented and that made him deeply uncomfortable.

A cold gust of wind whirled around them. It was biting and unforgiving and seemed to cut right through Alaric, a sharp reminder of the season's change.

"I forgot how cold winter could be," Alaric remarked, a shiver passing through him.

"This isn't winter, not yet," Grayson said. "But if I am any judge, soon the snows will fall. Then it will really get cold."

"It already is cold," Ezran groused, "and likely to get colder when night fully falls. We should find a fire to warm ourselves and dry our clothing."

"We will camp above tonight," Alaric declared, his voice firm with the resolve of leadership. "Then, in the morning, we'll push on to my parents' keep. There, we will find food, drink, and warmth aplenty."

"Do you wish a fortified camp built, for security, my lord?" Grayson asked.

Alaric thought for a moment, then shook his head. "No, we're home." He sucked in a breath and let out, "We're finally home."

11

With a firm yet gentle hand gripping the worn leather reins, Alaric coaxed his horse, Fire, into a patient halt. The horse, named for the fiery streak of his spirit, snorted softly, breath misting in the cool early morning air. After being confined for so long in the ship's hold, Fire wanted to ride, to run. The horse pawed at the ground. Beside him, Grayson brought his own mount—a robust dapple gray named Storm—to a stop alongside Alaric. Both men wore their armor and heavy cloaks, which draped over the horses' rumps.

They had been threading their way along a meandering dirt track for the last several hours, a path so rugged and untamed, it scoffed at the notion of being termed, even remotely, a road. It was a vein of dirt, nothing more, carved and hacked through the forest.

The forest had been a canvas of untamed beauty, with towering trees whose canopies wore a drapery of brightly colored fall leaves—yellow, deep purple, and red—that at times worked to take one's breath away. Already, there was a carpet of leaves that had fallen. Alaric had forgotten how pretty fall could be. In the south, he had missed the changing of the seasons.

Alaric's gaze drifted over his shoulder, looking back along the path. Just behind them, Thorne, Ezran, and Jasper had also reined in their mounts. Beyond them, three hundred yards back, the head of the column was rounding a bend in the forest. With his soldiers marching at the van, the column stretched for nearly a quarter-mile as it snaked its way after them through the forest.

Somewhere within the trailing procession walked Rikka and Kiera. Both women had elected to go by foot, rather than by horseback and the comfort a ride might afford. Kiera had her own horse. Alaric had extended the courtesy of a mount to Rikka so the two could ride, yet she had declined with a polite nod, her eyes reflecting a determination to remain grounded, connected to the land she traversed. Kiera had decided to join Rikka.

"After so long shipbound, I wish to stretch these wonderful things I call legs," Rikka had told him. After spending his nights with her, he had to admit she did have fine legs.

Turning his attention forward, Alaric faced the threshold of the forest's embrace. They stood on a hill, looking down upon the cusp of civilization's touch. Surrounded by partially harvested fields, the village was a patchwork of thatched roofs and cobblestone paths, with smoke curling lazily from a handful of chimneys into the crisp air, signifying the life that simmered quietly within. Here, the untamed wilderness, with its cryptic shadows and ancient secrets, gave way to the chaos of habitation.

The air carried the scent of woodsmoke.

"Thornwicke," Grayson said.

"What?" Alaric inquired, his curiosity piqued as he shifted in the saddle and looked at Grayson.

"That's the name of this place, the village, Thornwicke." Grayson shielded his eyes against the brilliance of the sun, which hung low yet ascendant in the blue expanse of the sky. He pointed. "Just beyond it, on the other side, is a good road that will take us straight to the keep and your father. It will be an improvement over this miserable track."

Alaric squinted in the direction indicated, beyond the village. There was the road, off in the distance, as a brown line that disappeared back into the forest after a few hundred yards. He sucked in a cold breath of air, as underneath him, Fire shifted, clearly eager to be off once again. Alaric took a firmer hold of the reins and stilled the animal.

They had broken camp at the earliest hint of dawn, starting out on the twenty-mile trek toward Alaric's ancestral keep. With only a couple of breaks to rest, they had been marching ever since. Alaric figured they were about halfway to their destination, which should see them arriving around dusk.

The wind gusted, the biting cold swirling and stinging exposed flesh. It rustled the tree branches overhead and sent a flurry of leaves to flight. Alaric glanced up as the leaves fell around them as the gust died off. The sun, in its steady ascent toward its zenith, offered scant warmth to the ground and those below.

Alaric found himself frowning as he gazed out at the village. Thornwicke itself seemed to recoil from the chill, its assortment of dilapidated buildings displaying their wear as if it were a badge of honor. At the village's threshold stood a modest, thatched cottage, its once robust structure succumbing to time's relentless march. The roof sagged despondently in the center, its thatch faded to a lifeless gray, with gaping patches revealing the brittle wooden skeleton beneath. The cottage's walls, crafted from wattle and daub, bore the scars of relentless weathering, fissures webbing through the material like the veins of a leaf. One of the windows was boarded up, suggesting long abandonment.

Beyond the cottage, the track, more mud than dirt now from a recent rain, meandered through the village, which consisted of more than two dozen buildings. Among them, near the edge of town, stood a building that bore the telltale signs of a blacksmith's forge.

What appeared to be a good-sized tavern languished nearby, its sign hanging desolately by a single hinge, creaking in the wind —a mournful dirge for better days now long past. Farther still, the heart of the village, a square that might once have pulsed with the vibrant chaos of market days, lay barren, empty. Encircled by shuttered stalls and forsaken stands. There was not a soul in sight.

"This place appears abandoned," Thorne observed, his voice tinged with a blend of disappointment and intrigue as he scanned the village from the hill upon which they were perched. "They've not even fully gathered in the harvest. A good portion of it has been left to rot."

Alaric was troubled by that.

"It's not completely deserted," Alaric corrected, and pointed. "Look there—smoke rises from the chimney of the blacksmith's forge. It's not much of a fire, but someone lit the forge this morning, and the tavern, along with a handful of other homes."

Alaric felt a mix of curiosity and melancholy as he surveyed the scene. The village, with its decaying buildings and sense of abandonment, seemed to stand as a memorial to a forgotten people and broken dreams. Yet beneath the ruin and disrepair, there was a story here, a tale. Something bad had happened. What that was, Alaric knew not.

The ring on his finger began to emanate a subtle warmth, its temperature gradually increasing as if reacting to the secrets Thornwicke held. At the same time, it was as though an invisible force was drawing him deeper into the heart of the village, compelling him to peel back the layers of obscurity and bring to light the truths that lay hidden within.

Or was the ring trying to tell him something? Was it warning him?

"Thornwicke was thriving and full of life when we left,"

Grayson remarked, his voice laced with plain concern. With a sweeping gesture that encompassed the depressing village, he added, "I don't ever recall this village looking rundown… We used to recruit here… there were children, families."

"That was ten years ago," Alaric said.

"It was," Grayson acknowledged sadly. "God knows what's happened since then."

"It's possible disease ravaged these lands," Ezran suggested, a hint of worry in his tone. "This village bears an eerie resemblance to Kol'tech."

At the mention of Kol'tech, Thorne visibly tensed, a shiver coursing through him, causing his horse to sidestep. Alaric stiffened slightly in the saddle and glanced back at the former ash man. "I hoped to forget that place."

"That was a town cursed by fortune herself," Thorne said.

"Disease…" The idea struck a chord with Alaric, stirring memories of the plague he witnessed ravage the holy lands—visions of suffering and death that haunted his nights still as the healthy by the thousands sickened and died. It had been bad, very bad in Kol'tech. He cast a glance back at the column, drawing nearer with every passing moment. They were almost on top of them.

"I suspect our arrival did not go unnoticed," Grayson observed, breaking into Alaric's contemplations. "Hence no one in view."

Alaric, pondering Grayson's insight, looked over. "You mean to say the villagers have fled?"

With a nod, Grayson confirmed Alaric's understanding. The behavior was not uncommon in times of strife and difficulty; communities would often flee to the safety of hidden retreats at the first sign of potential danger or strange soldiers appearing on the horizon.

"We may have been spotted by a hunter out in the forest," Grayson added, gesturing at the town with a wave of his hand.

"I'd run too if I didn't know who we were," Thorne said. "Then again, if it is disease…"

"Have the standard unfurled," Alaric ordered. "Though the inhabitants have likely run for the hills, let's let them, and anyone else who sees us in the coming hours, know we are friendly and not a threat to hide from."

"As you command, my lord," Grayson said. "I will see it done."

"I want no falling out of the column of march, no straggling," Alaric ordered. "I know we've not had fresh food in some time, but we will not take what little these people have through scavenging. Besides, they are our own, and from the looks of things, they have little enough as it is and likely nothing to spare."

"My lord," Grayson said, "there are undoubtedly men who have or had relatives in this village. They may have nothing left, especially if disease has ravaged Dekar."

Was the possibility of disease why he had not heard from his parents? Surely, someone would have written.

"That's a good point," Alaric conceded, "and all the more reason to keep the men on a tight leash. No one is to be released from service until I say so. Is that understood?"

"Understood, my lord," Grayson said.

"Perhaps we should not march through the village, but around it?" Thorne suggested. "Less temptation that way."

"Should we send scouts into the village?" Grayson asked. "Learn the news?"

Alaric turned his gaze upon Thornwicke, considering his captain's suggestion. After a moment, he shook his head. "No. I think we have already frightened the inhabitants enough. We're only ten—maybe twelve miles from the keep. Let us push on. We will learn all we need soon enough. We will find food and shelter there. Make it so, Grayson."

Grayson turned in his saddle, barked a series of orders, and pointed with his hand at the lead of his column. He shifted his horse around and began to personally direct and guide the column wide to the right of the village, marching around the partially harvested fields. Alaric remained where he was, holding the reins of his horse lightly. Behind him waited Ezran, Thorne, and Jasper.

"Not the homecoming you expected," Thorne said.

"Definitely not," Alaric said with a shake of his head. "I pray Thornwicke is not indicative of the rest of Dekar, for if it is…"

As the column continued its march, the sounds of the soldiers' lighthearted voices, a mixture of speculation and camaraderie, filled the air, punctuating the otherwise silent village. The chink of armor and equipment was strong as they passed by.

Soon the soldiers gave way to the families and camp followers. Amidst this procession, a solitary figure made a deliberate departure from the line of march. Father Ava disengaged himself and walked up next to Alaric's horse, his gaze fixed upon the village. Clad in coarse brown robes that spoke of the humility of his vocation, the fabric worn to a near whisper of its former self and faded, he carried nothing but a light traveling pack.

"Father Ava," Alaric greeted, gazing down at the priest. Ava, in his seventies, was in good health and fit, though Alaric thought a tad lean. The hair on his head was bushy and had long since gone gray. Alaric had known the man for nearly ten years, and in all that time, unlike the other priests, Ava had never demanded or even asked for money. He had always been very humble in Alaric's presence.

"My lord, do you believe there to be a church in village?" the elderly priest asked, looking up.

"There should be." Alaric shifted in his saddle to see if he could spot the steeple. After a moment, he pointed. "It is there, on the far side of village. Do you see it?"

The older man squinted, searching for a long moment, then gave a nod. "Do you mind if I depart the column? Do I have your permission, my lord?"

"You don't need it," Alaric said.

"But still, I feel compelled to ask."

"You intend on visiting the church?" Thorne asked plainly.

Father Ava gave a nod as he scratched at an itch upon his neck. "I would honor God and give thanks properly for our safe deliverance."

"My lord," Thorne said, giving the old priest a meaningful stare. "You have long been gone from these lands. We don't know if there are bandits, cutpurses, thugs, or whatnot about in that village down there. It looks rather mean, if you take my meaning."

"Jasper," Alaric said, heaving a heavy sigh. "I've changed my mind. I am going into the village and to the church. Ride to Grayson and inform him where I am headed. We will meet him on the far side of the village."

"Yes, my lord." Jasper pulled on his reins and guided his horse off the track before nudging her into a trot, moving along the column, heading for Grayson, who was now more than five hundred yards away.

"Father Ava," Alaric said. "We will escort you to the church to make certain it is safe."

"Thank you, my lord," the priest said. "I appreciate that. Though anyone harming a pauper priest like myself would face everlasting damnation. I think there is little risk and reason to trouble yourself."

"You are most likely correct. But better safe than sorry." Alaric started his horse forward into a slow walk. The priest began walking as Thorne and Ezran nudged their horses forward.

After a few yards moving through the fields, Alaric was able to maneuver his mount along the sodden path that wound through the harvested fields and merged onto the main thoroughfare leading into the heart of Thornwicke. He kept the pace slow so that Ava could keep up.

Not another word was spoken until they reached the edge of town. The desolate view he had initially perceived from afar began to manifest with unsettling clarity. The village, which was once a vibrant hub of activity and communal life, now presented itself as a clear scene of neglect and decay. Many of the buildings, their structures compromised by time, disuse, and clear lack of maintenance, seemed to lean upon one another for support, embodying a collective grief and sadness for the souls they no longer sheltered.

The farther they went into the village, passing building after building, the more pronounced the signs of abandonment became. It was evident from the state of the outer buildings that very few dared to call this place home.

What had happened here? Why had people left? Was it disease? Or worse, war?

He imagined those who remained eking out an existence on the very margins of survival. The atmosphere was heavy with a profound silence, the kind that felt almost tangible, as if the very air mourned the loss of laughter, of footsteps, of life. With every clopping step forward by his horse, Alaric began to feel a mounting sense of unease.

The oppressive quietude was occasionally broken by the mournful creak of timeworn wood protesting against the wind or the distant, solitary caw of a crow. Not even a dog emerged to bark at them.

As they passed what once were animal pens and enclosures, Alaric noted their emptiness with a heavy heart. The absence of pigs rooting in the mud, sheep grazing contentedly, or chickens pecking at the dirt underscored the complete abandonment of domesticity and sustenance. These empty spaces, once clearly teeming with life and the daily rhythms of rural existence, were a sign of the unraveling of a community, of a way of life that had withered and faded like the last echoes of an ancient song.

Weeds had sprung up everywhere. They passed the blacksmith's shop, where he imagined the ringing of hammer on anvil had once signified industry and progress. Now, only the lingering scent of burnt coal hinted at past labors, with the forge's embers offering only a feeble glow, marking the absence of its keeper, who had clearly gone into hiding.

A cold gust of wind swept through the empty streets, telling of the coming winter. A shutter, loosened from its fastenings by time and neglect, clattered against a window frame, punctuating the silence with its erratic beat. Alaric's keen eyes caught a hint of movement behind a window—a fleeting shadow that vanished as quickly as it appeared, suggesting that they were not entirely alone in this forgotten place.

Continuing their solemn and silent procession, they reached the village square, dominated by the church on the far side, a tavern on the other. For a moment, he thought he heard the discordant sound of someone snoring from that direction. Alaric considered going to the tavern first. He disregarded that idea. He imagined someone overcome with drink in an attempt to drown their sorrows. Instead, he kept Fire moving forward. He had agreed to bring Ava to the church, and that was what he would do.

Answers would come later.

The church, which might once have stood as a pillar of faith and a gathering place for the community, now, like the rest of the village, bore the marks of decay and abandonment. The steeple, which had ambitiously pierced the sky, now leaned precariously, a symbol that spoke of lost hope and direction.

The stained-glass windows, once vibrant with color and light, telling stories of faith, hope, and charity, were now dulled by dust and neglect, with many of the panes broken, leaving the interior exposed to the elements. These windows, designed to illuminate the church with divine light during the day, now offered only a fragmented glimpse into the interior, echoing the shattered spirit of Thornwicke itself.

Despite its dilapidation, the church door stood ajar, as if inviting Alaric and company into its sorrowful and lonely embrace. Before the entrance, he pulled his horse to a stop and dismounted, glancing over at Father Ava, who was gazing upon the building with plain, unfiltered sadness.

"Thorne," Alaric said as he handed his reins to Ezran, "since you are a believer, you're with me."

In a jingle of armor and tack, Thorne dismounted and then handed his reins up to Ezran before joining Alaric, who led the way, ascending the steps to the church's entrance. He looked through the open door. The interior was bathed in the soft, dim glow of a single candle, mixed with the natural light that flowed in through the windows.

A lone figure, draped in robes that spoke of a clerical life, knelt before the main altar, his posture one of deep, fervent prayer. This man, so absorbed in his communion with the divine, seemed very much like the last keeper of faith in a village lost to time and despair.

As Alaric stepped over the threshold, the change in atmosphere was palpable. The air inside was cool and tinged with the musty odor of disuse and mold, different from the vibrant community spaces of worship he had known in the south. The absence of pews and the lack of silver vessels for the sacramental wine marked a departure from the traditional adornments associated with such sacred places.

The walls, bereft of tapestries, and the altar, missing its customary golden compass, spoke of a simplicity that verged on destitution. The candle, its flickering flame almost a testament to some enduring hope, rested in a humble wooden holder, far removed from the grandeur typically associated with the church's rituals.

Yet the presence of the praying priest suggested that even in the deepest reaches of despair, faith—or at least the search for it —persisted. And where that happened, hope remained.

Alaric continued forward, his approach, marked by the sound of the hobnails of his boots against the stone floor, reverberated through the hushed interior of the church, announcing their presence to its solitary occupant.

As the elderly priest made a painstaking effort to rise, his frailty became painfully evident. The robes that once might have draped with dignity over a healthier frame now engulfed him, accentuating his emaciated condition. His face was gaunt, and the man was clearly hungry. Yet, despite his evident weakness, the priest's demeanor bore no trace of fear. His eyes, though dimmed by age and clouded with caution, fixed upon the newcomers with an intensity born of years spent guarding his faith against the encroaching darkness.

"Who are you?" The question, delivered in a raspy voice that carried the weight of countless solitary days and an age-born weariness, cut through the silence of the church.

Alaric stopped, with a gesture of introduction that bridged the gap between their worlds. "This is Thorne"—he indicated the companion to his right, then to his left—"and this is Father Ava." The priest's eyes flicked from Thorne to Ava. His shoulders relaxed slightly at the sight of another priest. Alaric touched his own armored chest with his palm. "I am Viscount Alaric, returned home from the Crusades, Holy Father."

It seemed to take a moment for his words to penetrate. Hands trembling and shaking violently, the priest took a step forward, eyes narrowing as if in disbelief as he peered at Alaric. "Truly?"

"Aye," Alaric said. "We landed last evening. I am on my way to the keep to see my parents." He gestured at Ava. "I thought I would personally escort Father Ava to this church before pressing on. He wished to pay his respects to God in a holy house."

"We have been traveling by sea for weeks, and this is the first proper house of prayer we have happened across," Ava said.

The priest eyed Alaric, then Ava. His hand went to his mouth as if in disbelief as his gaze returned to Alaric. The priest was missing several teeth, with others browned. "You are Alaric?"

"I am."

The priest dropped shakily to his knees on the dusty stone floor and bowed his head, which shook, as his hands had. "My lord earl. You have come at last."

Alaric's expression darkened into a scowl as he faced the frail figure of the priest kneeling before him on the hard stone. He glanced over. Thorne's nonchalant shrug in reply offered little in the way of comfort or solutions, prompting Alaric to take a more direct approach. He stepped forward and, with a gentleness, grasped the elderly priest's arm, drawing the man back to his feet. Beneath the threadbare robes, the priest's body felt alarmingly insubstantial, as if he were more a specter of the past, a wraith imitating life, than a living, breathing individual.

"Why did you name him earl?" Thorne's straightforward inquiry, posed with a mixture of curiosity and concern, echoed slightly off the walls of the church.

"He is old and clearly mistaken," Alaric offered by way of explanation, addressing Thorne but keeping his gaze on the priest. He felt a sick worry begin to worm its way into his gut. "What is your name?"

"Father Boatman, my lord." The elderly priest's introduction came amidst the tremors of palsy that gripped his hands, an affliction that lent his manner a certain vulnerability. Yet, in his acknowledgment of Alaric, there was a clarity and conviction that pierced through the haze of time and frailty. "I knew you as a lad, my lord."

Alaric's mind raced to place the name, the face, but found no foothold in his memory for Father Boatman.

"Your mother used to bring you about occasionally, as did your father," Boatman added, then hesitated, his hands shaking even more violently than before. "And you are the earl. There is none other."

The words were like a key turning in a lock, and with them, Alaric felt a cold dread seep into his marrow. The realization that his father, the indomitable pillar of strength and authority in his life, might be gone, left him reeling.

"My father is dead?" Alaric echoed, the question hollow, as if saying the words aloud might somehow refute their truth.

"Yes, my lord, over a year ago," came Father Boatman's somber confirmation, his voice imbued with a sorrow that mirrored the gravity of his news. "I am sorry that I am the one to break the news to you. Truly I am. We, the people, loved your father."

Gone?

The impact of this revelation left Alaric staggered, both physically and emotionally. The world seemed to tilt under his feet, unmoored by the loss of a man he had deemed invincible. His father had been a foundational force in his life and in the life of their lands, a man whose presence was as unyielding as the stone walls of their keep. To imagine he was no longer a part of this world, that he had been gone for more than a year, all while Alaric remained oblivious in a distant land, was a concept too vast and painful to fully encompass. "No, that cannot be."

This moment of stark revelation marked not just the loss of a father, but the beginning of a profound transformation in Alaric's life. He was now thrust into a role he had not anticipated assuming so soon.

"I understand your mother sent word for you to return soon after his passing," Boatman said, "to bring your companies home, to help defend us, to protect us."

"I never got the message," Alaric said, absolutely stunned. "You must be mistaken."

"I am not, Lord Earl," Boatman said.

"What do you mean *defend*?" Thorne asked, glancing back the way they came at the open door. "Defend from whom?"

"The raiders, bandits," Boatman said. "They've taken everything and roam the land freely without fear. There is no longer strength of will to stand up to them."

Alaric rubbed the back of his neck. This was not welcome news. When he'd left, Dekar had been strong and safe, rich. There had been no bandits, no raiding. Everyone respected and feared his father, even their fellow and neighboring lords. He'd had knights and men-at-arms at his beck and call for such trouble.

"What of my father's bannermen?" Alaric asked.

"They have their own problems," Boatman said with a shrug, "and have done little."

"Earl," Alaric breathed to himself, still scarcely able to believe what he was learning. He regarded the priest, and his heart hardened in anger before turning to Thorne. "Go inform Grayson. Tell him I want men posted here to protect the town, at least fifty of our best. They can set up in some of the abandoned homes, but I want a guard at all times, understand me?"

Thorne gave a hard nod.

"They are also to work on a defensive wall for the village. Have him break out some of our rations for the men and those who still call Thornwicke home. I also want scouts put out around the column. We are not in friendly lands, not any longer. Warn him. Go... now."

"Yes, my lord earl." Thorne turned, his hobnailed boots clicking against the stone floor as he hurried from the church.

The priest was staring at him in astonishment, his lower jaw trembling. "You will defend us?"

"I will do more than that, Father," Alaric said, his anger growing by the moment. "I will make Dekar safe and strong again."

"I prayed for your coming, my lord," Boatman said. "But many gave up and left. Those who remained are terrified."

Alaric slapped his palm against his thigh. He glanced at the altar and knew without a doubt he should have come home sooner. He was needed here.

"The bandits took everything from the church?" Alaric asked, glancing around.

"They did, my lord," Boatman said. "And… and… the thugs who run the town took what little was left."

Ezran stepped into the church, his gaze flicking about before settling upon Alaric. The sound of hooves could be heard as Thorne rode off. "Thugs? Where?"

"In the tavern," Boatman said, looking to the former ash man. "They live there and have chased most everyone off."

"They won't be running the town much longer." Alaric's tone was rock-hard. "You are sure my father is dead?"

The priest nodded.

"How?"

"They said sickness," the priest said. "But…"

"But what?"

"Others said it was poison, my lord earl," Boatman said. "I don't know for certain…"

This revelation struck Alaric with the force of a winter gale, chilling him to his core. His father had always had enemies, people who wanted to claim Dekar as their own. "And my mother? Is she dead also?"

"No one has seen your mother for weeks," Father Boatman said. "She has retreated into the keep. Some say she is being held prisoner by her guard, that they have become opportunists. Others say she is in mourning, lost to her grief." Father Boatman paused. "I went myself to the keep to see her, to beg for help, and was turned away at the gate. The guards told me she was seeing no one. The people in the town have not seen her either."

Alaric's mother had always been strong. His father had even feared her temper. She would have grieved for her husband but not let it consume her. He could not see her turning from her duty to the people. The very idea that his mother might be suffering at the hands of turncoat guards spurred a mix of dread and resolve within Alaric. Feeling terrible frustration, he let go an unhappy breath that sounded explosive in the confines of the church.

"Many have fled Dekar for hope of safety elsewhere."

"Why did you stay?" Ava asked.

"This is my home," Boatman said and held out his hands. "This church is *HIS* home. What would it say of my faith if I left this holy place unattended, even in the state it is now? I am an old man... no threat to them, to anyone."

"They took everything, chased most of your flock off, and yet you remained," Ava said.

Boatman nodded. "They took nearly everything but my faith."

The ring on Alaric's finger began to grow warm. He glanced down at it, moving it around his finger with his thumb. It had been incredibly active of late, speaking to him with greater frequency. He looked back up on the old priest, racked by palsy. That he'd elected to remain when so many others fled was no small thing. He clearly believed and was strong with the faith.

Driven by an instinct he perhaps didn't fully understand, almost an impulse, Alaric reached into a pocket and produced Father Kemm's golden compass. As he did, the air seemed suddenly charged with an unseen energy, a power that made the little hairs on the back of his neck stand on end. Father Boatman's eyes widened, and his mouth fell agape, a reaction that went beyond mere admiration for its beauty.

Even Ava was taken aback, for he blinked rapidly.

"It is so beautiful," Boatman breathed, taking a shaking step forward to get a better look. "In all my years—I have only seen one other like her."

"Take it," Alaric said, offering the compass to the man.

"My lord, I cannot accept such a gift," Boatman rasped, his gaze going from the compass to Alaric. "This is too rich for me."

"On impulse, I took it from one who was not worthy of bearing such a symbol, a man who professed to be a priest but had no faith. I claimed it with the intention of giving it to one who was a believer. I..." Alaric hesitated, feeling the object in his hand growing warm like the ring upon his finger. He looked upon it and knew what he was doing was right—more than right. His gaze shifted to Boatman. "This is now yours, Father. I... I think it is—was always—meant for you."

"Take it," Father Ava urged firmly. There was an intense light in the other's gaze, almost an eagerness.

As Alaric extended the compass toward the elderly priest, the significance of the act seemed to magnify within the confines of the church's crumbling and decrepit walls. The priest's hand trembled violently as he accepted the gift.

The compass flared with golden light when his hand closed about it, bathing the church in an otherworldly glow. This illumination lasted but a moment, a mere flash. Brief as it was, it transcended the physical decay of their surroundings, hinting at a deeper magic or divine favor at play. Boatman's expression of open wonder mirrored Alaric's own astonishment as they witnessed this manifestation of power.

The palsy that caused the priest to tremble ceased as the light died off, his hands and body growing suddenly rock-steady, his gaze firm. The gaunt and starved look faded and the priest's eyes became shaper, clearer, as did his stature as he stood straight. The man looked as if he'd grown slightly younger, losing at least five years.

For a long moment, there was absolute silence.

"Eldanar has judged him worthy," Father Ava breathed, his words spoken with a reverent awe. "In *HIS* holy light, we are blessed."

Alaric glanced over at Ava. The man had tears in his eyes.

"I felt the lord our god," Boatman breathed, still staring at the compass in his hand. "I felt his love. I have work yet that needs doing—*HE* told me so."

"Long has it been since I have seen a true miracle," Ava breathed as he wiped the tears away with the back of his forearm. "That compass is a relic from an age past, and it recognizes its own. You have been blessed this day, blessed by our god, and so have we all, who stood witness to our lord's judgment."

Alaric glanced back at Ezran. The man's eyes were wide. Godless, he too had clearly been stunned by what just transpired. Rikka and Kiera had joined them. Both were standing in the entrance. How long they had been there, he did not know, but the look in Rikka's gaze was intense, fierce.

The profound moment shared within the shadowed confines of the church left Alaric deeply moved, yet it also reignited the embers of resolve and anger within him, especially for his father, mother, and the land he called home. Confronted with the neglect and decay all around him, Alaric felt the weight of his newly inherited responsibilities upon his shoulders. He had one company at his command, but they were all hardened veterans. More importantly, they were loyal. He turned his gaze back to the priest. It was time he claimed his mantle, his legacy.

"I will rebuild this church and bring your parishioners back, Father. I will do the same for all of Dekar." Alaric's tone was as hard as granite. "No one will live in fear again, not on my land. On this I swear before our god."

"And I will help," Rikka said from the doorway, drawing his attention. Ezran jumped as he realized they were not alone. "So has Eldanar called me."

Alaric returned his attention to the priest, who was still staring at the compass. "You said they are in the tavern? These thugs?"

The priest, with effort, tore his gaze from the compass he clutched. "There are six of them, my lord."

"Well, then," Alaric said, turning to Ezran, "let us start there."

12

Alaric's stride faltered as he crossed the threshold of the church and stepped outside, where he came to an abrupt halt. Before him, arrayed with threatening intent, stood six men. Each was armed, their swords unsheathed and glinting ominously under the sunlight. They were strategically positioned before the horses in a semicircle facing the church and Alaric, with one imposing figure notably advanced slightly ahead of the others.

"And who do we have here?" It came from the man who stepped forward from the group, distinguishing himself not just by his stature, but by the air of authority he exuded. His voice was coarse, rough, and hard, as if he were accustomed to raising it. He was markedly larger than his companions, his chest broad and barrel-like, arms bulging with the kind of muscle born from relentless physical toil, perhaps the countless hefts of a sword and shield.

Rikka and Kiera, still just inside the church, caught off guard, spun around, their reactions a mirror to the sudden tension that filled the air. Alaric, however, fueled by an undiminished storm of rage, took measured and confident steps forward, stopping at the top of the stairs that led down to the muddy dirt. With deliberate slowness, he placed his hands upon his hips, adopting a posture of defiance as he looked down upon the six men before him.

Despite their attire, which consisted of simple tunics and trousers, all worn and weathered from heavy use, paired with boots that had seen better days, there was an unmistakable military bearing to their stances, a confidence that long service brought. Their demeanor spoke of order and being accustomed to listening to authority. He got the feeling they were former soldiers, which potentially made them more dangerous, as they would be skilled with a sword.

Alaric's gaze lingered on the man who had spoken, noting the web of scars that adorned his forearms from extensive weapons training, years of taking little nicks and cuts during practice and drill. These were not mere brigands or thieves; their presence spoke of a purpose, a mission driven by motives yet to be unveiled. Alaric was sure of it.

With deliberate caution, Ezran emerged from the shadowed confines of the church, his hand resting assuredly on the hilt of his scimitar. His dark eyes, deep and calculating, swept over the six men with a gaze as piercing as it was evaluating, dissecting their intentions and sizing them up. Silently, he positioned himself to Alaric's right.

Kiera moved to his left. Her plate armor gleamed dully in the light, each piece a finely crafted shell that encased her form. Her eyes were hard as they swept across the group confronting them.

"I said, who the bloody fuck are you?" The leader's voice cut through the air once more, tinged with an edge of growing impatience. His tone, laced with authority and expectation, sought to command an answer. He reminded Alaric very much of a company sergeant.

From the backdrop of tension, a voice, unmistakably that of Boatman, emerged from behind the door. "That is them. The ones I spoke of that live in the tavern."

"Well, well, well, I was just about to come find you," Alaric responded calmly. He placed his hand upon the hilt of his sword. With a fluid motion, he drew Oathbreaker and glanced at the cold steel before turning his gaze back upon the men and their leader. "That makes it quite convenient, then. We no longer have to go get them."

Two of the men shared an uneasy glance.

Ezran's movements were a blend of fluid grace as he drew his scimitar, the blade singing a soft, ominous note as it left its sheath. Beside him, Kiera's expression was set into a mask of grim determination. With a resolute grip, she wrapped her hand around her longsword and pulled it out.

The leader scowled. His posture, though still imposing, betrayed a flicker of uncertainty at the bold proposition laid before him. "You were searching for us?"

"Not until we met Father Boatman, but yes, I was coming to find you." Alaric paused for a heartbeat and raised his voice. "You six will lower your swords and surrender."

The notion of surrendering astonished the leader. Disbelief etched his features as he turned to gauge the reaction of his men —a collective of toughs momentarily taken aback by the unexpected challenge, someone actually standing up to them. Regaining his composure, he scoffed at Alaric's demand, the laugh he emitted harsh and devoid of humor. "Surrender?" He pointed his sword at Alaric. "It's you who should bloody surrender. You're outnumbered six to one."

"That doesn't much concern him," Ezran stated, nodding toward Alaric. "He's having quite the bad day, and you, my friends, are about to make it much better."

"There are three of you, including a woman, and an ugly one at that in that ancient armor, with all those scars and tattoos ruining what likely once was a fair face." The leader's taunt sliced through the tense air, targeting Kiera with disdain sharpened by his clear ignorance of who and what she had survived. "You three think you can stand against us? A woman, a foreigner, and a petty noble."

The men with him laughed.

Kiera stiffened, an instinctual reaction to the insult, but then, almost imperceptibly, her demeanor shifted. Her face, already set in hard lines, became even more impenetrable, colder. Alaric had seen that look before and knew it would end in blood.

"They're not very smart," Rikka observed as she came to stand next to Kiera, her voice tinged with both contempt and a touch of amusement.

"Smart?" scoffed another of the men, his voice dripping with derision. "What do you know, you uppity bitch? She's likely of noble birth too, boss."

"Quite the insult," Rikka said. "Crude and unimaginative—a nightsoil man could have done better, been wittier."

"You are correct, my lady," Kiera replied, her voice cool and steady. "These men are clearly dumber than most farm animals."

"When we deal with him"—the leader made a threatening gesture with his sword toward Alaric—"and the other one in black"—he waved his sword at Ezran—"we are going to have fun with you two bitches, teach you some humility. Then, we will see how funny you are."

Father Ava, having emerged from the church alongside Father Boatman, addressed the armed men with an air of serene authority that was out of place amid the brewing storm, "I encourage you to lower your weapons," his tone imbued a grave sincerity, "before it is too late. You men know not who you are dealing with here."

"And you don't bloody know who *you* are dealing with," the leader retorted, his tone becoming nasty. "We run this village now. Our word is law in these parts."

"Though I shouldn't, I am going to give you one last chance," Alaric declared, the undercurrent of danger in his tone impossible to ignore. "Drop your weapons and surrender. You have my word you will live." It was a pledge spoken with the solemnity of one who understood the weight of his words, a vow made by a man accustomed to being both judged and bound by his honor.

"Your word?" The leader's reaction was one of pure contempt, his disdain evident as he spat upon the ground. "I don't even know who you are. But I really don't care either. You are noble born—that much I can tell—and I hate nobles. Your kind think you are better than us. But I bet the purse you carry is fat with gold and silver. Mine is on the light side."

"I would be careful with your words. You are addressing Viscount Alaric of Dekar, just returned from the Crusade," Ezran stated helpfully. The former ash man grinned wickedly at them.

This sent a shock through the opposing men. The leader stiffened visibly, the earlier confidence in his posture evaporating into a wary tension. Then his eyes narrowed into slits of calculation, as if reassessing the situation.

The men beside him, who had until that moment worn smirks of an easy and coming victory, found their expressions dissolving into seriousness. The grins that had adorned their faces vanishing with the breeze.

"We will be rewarded for this one, boys," the leader said, "especially if we bring him in alive."

"Let this be your final warning, then—with a day like he's having, people like you tend to die." Ezran's follow-up was chilling in its simplicity. "But then again, I don't think the world will mourn the loss of you bunch very much. Shall we cease this wasteful talking and begin this dance?"

"Fuck you," the leader, uncowed, hissed with venom. His tone hardened into something more dangerous and committed. He pointed his sword again at Alaric. "A silver piece to the one who brings me his head. Take them!"

There was a moment of hesitation, then the men began to

advance with grim determination. Alaric almost allowed himself a grin, a silent acknowledgment of the challenge before him.

With the agility of a predator, Alaric launched himself off the steps. He leapt at the nearest of the advancing adversaries. As he flew through the air, Oathbreaker rose in a graceful arc before descending in a swift, decisive motion as he landed. His opponent, caught completely off guard by the suddenness of the attack, barely managed a hasty block.

Their two swords met with a ringing clang. Alaric rapidly shifted his sword and, pushing the other's aside, maneuvered past the block with an elegance that belied the ferocity of his assault. Oathbreaker found its mark, the edge slicing into the man's leg.

The cut was deep, and the leg immediately gave out. The man dropped to the ground with an agonized cry, falling to his knees. Before he could react, Alaric reversed his blade and stabbed downward, his sword point driving deep into the other's collar. The man gave a pained grunt, stiffened, and then his eyes rolled back into his head as he went limp, Alaric's sword holding him upright on his knees. Alaric ripped the blade free and stepped past, focusing on his next target—the leader, just steps away.

Their swords clashed in a crash of metal, the sound a clear, resonant clang that reverberated on the air and sent a jolt of pain through Alaric's hand. Ignoring the discomfort and refusing to give his opponent a chance to recover, Alaric continued his attack, launching a strike at the man's left thigh. The leader, biceps bulging, blocked and backed up a step to gain room. Now on the defensive, he parried desperately as Alaric attacked again and again, launching a flurry of strikes to keep the man off-balance and on his heels.

To his right, the metallic clang of Ezran's engagement was a familiar comfort. On his left, a deep grunt of agony signaled Kiera's lethal prowess, her own victory claimed in the striking down of one of the enemy. And somewhere ahead, in the midst of combat, a meaty thwack was followed by a heavy grunt that announced help from another quarter, though Alaric dared not look.

His focus remained on the leader. It had to. Each movement, each attack and block, was a step toward victory or defeat, a balance he navigated with the skill of a warrior born and trained for this moment, for the fight.

The clash with the leader was a crescendo of metal and might, their swords meeting with repeated clangs and flat clunks that resonated on the air with sparks that flew forth from each impact. The other man was skilled and well-trained, yet it was Alaric's relentless assault and sustained attack that drove the leader back, step by desperate step.

Then, unexpectedly, a flash of light, followed by a low hissing, and a resulting crack rang out, almost deafening in its loudness. The air seemed to vibrate with the concussion of impact that blew a blast of hot air past and around them. Surprised, Alaric hesitated in his next strike. He almost turned to see what happened, but his opponent clearly saw what had occurred.

The leader's eyes were wide, and his mouth fell open. He rapidly retreated two steps, his sword point lowering, almost touching the ground.

"Sorcery..." The man's gaze was plainly filled with worry, doubt, and blatant fear. He turned on his heel and ran, sprinting madly away. He only made it five feet before an arrow hammered powerfully into his chest, the point emerging from his back, right where the heart was located. He went down in a tumble, thrashed about for a moment or two, and then fell still.

Ten yards away, Alaric spotted Jasper, mounted on his horse, lowering his bow. He gave the man a nod, which was returned, as he pulled forth another missile and nocked it.

Alaric looked around, just as an agonized scream rang out, signaling the end of the last opponent by Kiera's hand. Her decisive blow was one of both brute power and precision as she cut her opponent down, literally chopping the man with a blow to the shoulder. Her heavy sword, cleaving through muscle and bone, sank deep and drove her opponent to the ground. She ripped the blade free with a grunt, then stabbed into his exposed neck to finish him, silencing a second scream before it even came.

Alaric glanced around. All six were down. In the aftermath of the whirlwind clash, Alaric found himself surprisingly unburdened by fatigue, his breath almost steady, as if the dance of death he'd just engaged in was no more taxing than a stroll through the gardens of Hawkani. He doubted the struggle had lasted more than a fifty count.

The six assailants who just moments ago bristled with hostile intent now lay motionless, each deader than a doornail, their life blood spilling onto the muddy ground. Among the fallen, one man bore a serene countenance, as if in a deep slumber, rather than the throes of death. His body lay supine, a peaceful expression etched on his features, incongruously at odds with the large, ugly hole that had burned into his chest, all the way to the spine. Alaric required no further evidence to attribute his demise to Rikka, whose mastery of arcane forces had clearly claimed yet another life.

Turning his gaze toward the church, Alaric observed the two priests. Their expressions were etched with shock and disbelief at the bloodshed and unrestrained violence that unfolded on the church's very steps and likely the rapidity and one-sidedness of the resolution.

"Feel better?" Ezran asked Alaric as he cleaned his own blade free of blood and gore on the tunic of one of the dead.

"No," Alaric admitted after a moment's thought. His rage still pounded within his chest, as did the adrenaline from the fight. His pulse was racing. "It will take a lot more than this to put me at peace, but it is a step in the right direction."

"I told you."

Alaric turned to see Thorne had ridden up. Like Jasper, he'd clearly returned after passing along Alaric's orders to Grayson. His gaze flickered over the aftermath of the fight with interest, raising an eyebrow. He was leaning forward on his saddle.

"I guess I missed out on the fun."

"Told me what?" Alaric asked, drawing the other's gaze.

"That you'd find people who needed killing. You always do."

Alaric ran his gaze over the fallen men, a complex tapestry of emotions running through him. There was no triumph in his heart, only a deepening resolve, a steeling of his spirit for the path that lay ahead. Each unmoving body, life extinguished, spoke not just to the immediate struggle—bringing order and safety to his lands—but to addressing the broader decay festering within Dekar, now his domain and responsibility. The presence of bandits, thugs, and raiders, once mere whispers and rumors, had manifested into a grim reality, painting a picture of a land in turmoil, her people preyed upon by lawlessness and those who willingly took from the weak.

His father, the once steadfast protector of their lands, was gone, swallowed by the shadows of an untimely death. The uncertainty surrounding his mother's fate—a potential captive in her own keep—added a personal anguish to the broader canvas of the chaos playing out within his lands. It was a situation that cried out for rectification, for someone to rise up and confront the darkness, someone who was not afraid to stand up for others.

Alaric's response to this turmoil was not merely reactive; it was a conscious, deliberate stand. The cold resolve that had driven him through the Crusade was now fueled by a deeper, more personal vendetta against the injustice that had taken root in his home. Thornwicke was merely the starting point, a symbol of the initial push against the tide of corruption that threatened to swallow Dekar. Alaric would lend his people some of his strength, enough to stand with him against the darkness, and then together, they would force it back.

As he eyed the dead leader, Alaric knew they should have tried to take a prisoner. He was sure the man was a soldier, likely a deserter, but it still would have been good to have one of these bastards questioned, for he recognized that a larger plot against his family might be afoot. One of their neighboring lords might be involved.

He turned his gaze back to Thorne. "This is only the beginning."

13

"Report," Alaric ordered as he dismounted from his horse and led Fire off to the side of the road and up to the waiting scout. "What did you learn?"

A few dozen feet away, Grayson had drawn his horse to a halt and also slid off, his boots landing amidst the layer of leaves carpeting the ground. "Keep marching, boys," he said to the head of the column. "We're almost there."

The scout, Krebbs, had drawn himself up to attention and, fist to chest, saluted Alaric.

"Well?" Alaric, impatient for news, asked.

"My lord," Krebbs said, "the town is garrisoned by the local militia. The militia is patrolling the streets and manning the walls. I saw no thugs about on the streets, and I looked good and hard. The mayor is still in charge. At least that's what me mum said."

"Dark Forge is under friendly control?" Grayson pressed the scout as he joined them, leading his horse by the reins. The captain's eyes searched Krebbs's face for any trace of uncertainty as he walked his horse off the road and out of the way of the marching column. "That's what you are telling us?"

After what had happened in Thornwicke, Alaric had sent

Krebbs on ahead to gather intelligence on what they would encounter when they got to the town outside his family's keep. They had expected him back more than an hour ago and feared something had happened to him.

Alaric held the reins of his horse loosely as the animal nosed at the leaves lying upon the ground in search of a snack. The surrounding trees of the forest, ancient and towering, seemed to lean in, crowding close, as if eager to overhear the tidings that Krebbs brought. The Stonebridge Road was an ancient artery, winding through the dense forest like a serpent, leading them inexorably toward Dark Forge and, beyond that, Alaric's familial seat at Dragon Bone's Rest.

The column of march stretched back through the forest, a weary procession plodding steadily one step after another, crunching the fallen leaves underfoot. As the men passed, they picked up their heads and stared at Alaric, wearily and with mild curiosity, and then they were by, their boots carrying them onward, farther up the road.

Alaric knew they would be speculating and gossiping about what Krebbs was reporting. In a short while, there would be dozens of stories, all wrong and not even close to the truth, running up and down the marching column. The wilder the tale, the more it was believed. There was no stopping it. That was just how things were in the army.

"Is the captain right?" Alaric asked. "Is Dark Forge friendly and loyal?"

"It seems that way, sir," Krebbs affirmed to Grayson and then Alaric with a nod, his voice carrying the weight of personal witness. "I seen me mum. She lives there and said things had got dangerous out in the countryside. There now be hundreds of people in town, all on the streets or in others' barns. I seen that with me own eyes too. It ain't gonna be a good winter for them when it comes and gets cold."

"Refugees?" The word fell from Alaric's lips. It was a term that carried the echo of desperation, of lives uprooted by unseen storms of conflict and hardship. During his campaigning in the holy land, he had seen plenty of refugees—people, families fleeing war, homeless and desperate for a safe haven along with the next meal.

"Yes, my lord," Krebbs confirmed, his gaze dropping momentarily before meeting Alaric's once more. "Mostly farmers and those from remote villages seeking protection of the town's walls —scared, frightened. There's talk about the Duke of Laval sending soldiers to help restore order. Me mum told me some think it might be better if he took over."

"You are talking Dekar?" Alaric asked.

Krebbs gave a slow nod. "Yes, my lord. I am."

That stirred a ripple of unease within Alaric. His knowledge of the duke was limited, framed largely by his father's disdain for the man—a disdain whose origins Alaric had never fully understood. What he did know was that Laval was no friend of his family. He might even be an enemy.

A gust of wind swept through the forest, stirring the canopy overhead into a whispering frenzy. Golden leaves danced around them in a flurry of autumnal splendor, casting the moment in a fleeting, ethereal beauty that belied the gravity of their discussion and the news being passed along.

"Laval…" Alaric echoed, mind racing to piece together the scant information he had about the duke, trying to gauge the implications of his potential involvement. "Are you certain that his was the name mentioned?"

"Yes, my lord, I am," Krebbs continued, his voice a somber note against the rustling backdrop. "Things are bad. Food is in short supply, as much of the harvest was not taken in, and there are many mouths needing feeding."

Along their march, they had passed several abandoned farms.

For the most part, their crops had been allowed to rot in the fields. Alaric had not liked what he saw. He had a flash of one farm that had been burned to the ground, the crops torched.

"Me mum says it wasn't safe for many of the villages and outer farms to take in the harvest," Krebbs continued. "There are bandits and raiders all over Dekar and they've been pretty brutal, killing and raping. Now there be hunger in the town. I am sorry to tell you, my lord, some of your people are starving."

Alaric and Grayson shared a glance, a silent exchange that conveyed volumes between them. Alaric was deeply worried by what he was hearing. In Grayson's gaze flickered the recognition of the complexity of the situation before them, a tangled web of political intrigue, social upheaval, and crisis—the bandits and raiders, refugees, the specter of hunger, the uncertain role of the Duke of Laval mixed into it all. Alaric wished he had a better grasp on what was happening.

"Did you tell your mother Alaric has returned with the Iron Guard?" Grayson's question cut through the ambient murmur of the forest and the backdrop of crunching boots passing them by, his gaze fixed on the scout with an intensity that conveyed the seriousness of their venture and the worry the man had said too much.

"No, sir," Krebbs replied, a trace of resolve in his voice. "You told me to say nothin'. I said nothin', not even to me mum. I swear by our lord and all that's holy and true, I said nothin'."

Alaric, his mind strategizing, shifted the topic to another crucial piece of information Krebbs had brought him. "You mentioned the town mayor. Did you get his name?"

"Nightwell," came Krebbs's prompt response. "Mum said he's been mayor for a good long time… well before your da died, my lord."

"That means he was appointed by my father." Alaric thought it a good sign, that some of the news was encouraging.

"Edmond Nightwell?" Grayson probed further, recognition of the name clearly sparking interest. "Is that the man or his son, Kana?"

"Edmond, sir," Krebbs confirmed. "That's be the man. Me mum told me so. She likes him. Said he be doing his best in a bad time, trying to feed as many as he can."

"I take it you know him?" Alaric's question was directed at Grayson. When Alaric had left Dekar, he had only been a wet-behind-the-ears teenager. In truth, he knew little of the inner workings of Dekar, especially after so long away, let alone the political machinations of his fellow nobility. However, having served the Cardinal King, Alaric had become a quick study. He'd learned the backstabbing game of politics and had become quite an astute player himself. Now, he only needed to know who he was playing against. Was it Laval or someone else? One of their neighbors?

"I do know him, my lord," Grayson affirmed as the wind chose that moment to gust once more, this time strongly, not only stirring the leaves on the forest floor, but sending a shower of them cascading from the branches overhead. "He's a good man— or was—and served your father as one of his company captains before my time. If my memory is good, he is seven years my senior, maybe a little older."

"So, he should be loyal to me, then," Alaric surmised, trying to piece together the puzzle of allegiances that would be critical to their cause—that would help him rebuild Dekar. "Especially if my father appointed him to his current position."

"He should be, but with what we are learning about the condition of Dekar and Laval's potential intent or involvement..." Grayson trailed off for a couple of heartbeats as another strong wind rustled the leaves overhead and swirled them around at their feet. He gave a slight shrug of his armored shoulders. "We've also been gone ten years. Who is to say where Nightwell's loyalties now lie?"

"That is a good point." Alaric's nod was one of contemplation. He turned his gaze back to Krebbs, his eyes lingering on the scout, thinking. "What of Dragon Bone's Rest? Did you learn anything of my mother?"

Krebbs's response was hesitant, a reflection of the uneasy news he bore. "No one has seen her for some time, my lord, months," he admitted with a shake of his head. "Rumors are she's alive and being held against her will by her guard. My mother said no one in the town likes them much, the keep guard, that is. The captain of the guard is a man named Masterson. He was brought on after your father died and is a shady sort of fellow. At least that's what me mum says. She doesn't much like the look of that man. It's said he fought in the Crusade, but no one knows for sure. He frightens people and is likely a bully. For his part, Masterson and the other guards claim your mum's in mourning and wants to see no one."

"And people don't believe that?" Alaric asked.

"No, my lord," Krebbs confirmed. "They think Masterson is living like a king in the keep with his men while your mum is locked up. Few are allowed into the keep."

Alaric felt a cold sensation slither down his spine. If true, this was not good news, not at all. He was more worried for his mother than ever before. Worse, if they closed the gate to him, he would have to force his way in and find a way to rescue her—if that was even possible. As if in response to that thought, the ring on his hand began growing warm. He glanced down at it and idly moved it around with his thumb.

"They don't even see the keep servants anymore," Krebbs added, "and them lot have kin in Dark Forge. They are not allowed to leave the keep."

The thought of his mother, isolated or possibly held against her will within the very walls meant to protect and shelter her, kindled a flame of righteous indignation within his chest. He was already angry, but that fire was beginning to grow hot to a true rage.

The hot glance he spared with Grayson was laden with a mix of frustration and determination, an unspoken vow passing between them in the brief exchange. The wind, ever present, seemed to echo the tumultuous emotions stirring within Alaric, whipping through the trees with a renewed and bitter vigor.

The stakes were clear, and the path forward, though fraught with uncertainty, was also one that could lead to the reclamation of Dragon Bone's Rest, along with the restoration of Dekar. In fact, Alaric meant to do just that. He would not rest until his family's rule and order was restored fully to his lands. Anyone standing in his way—and that included his fellow nobles—would soon learn to regret it.

"How far are we from Dark Forge?" Alaric asked, his voice imbued with a newfound sense of urgency.

"By foot, no more than an hour, my lord, much shorter by horseback," Krebbs responded promptly. He turned and pointed in the direction the column was marching. "The forest ends in about a quarter-mile and then gives over to fields. The town is just past that. Few are out beyond the walls."

"Because it is not safe," Grayson said.

"Yes, sir," the scout responded.

In the brief silence that followed, Alaric's thoughts weaved through the possibilities and outcomes the next hours might hold. It was a moment of decision-making, underlined by the gravity of his responsibility and the anticipation of what awaited them in Dark Forge, not to mention his family keep.

Turning, Alaric's gaze found Thorne, still astride his horse. With him, Ezran and Jasper also remained mounted. All three were waiting patiently as the column of soldiers continued to march steadily by. Kiera was somewhere back in the column, walking with Rikka.

"Thorne… loan Krebbs your horse." Alaric's command was swift, a clear directive that brooked no hesitation.

Thorne immediately dismounted. Moving forward, he handed the reins over to Krebbs.

"Krebbs, I want you to ride with all possible haste to Dark Forge. Find Mayor Nightwell. You are to tell him and anyone else you encounter in the town that I have returned home with the Iron Guard and will be at the town's gates in less than an hour." The mandate was more than a mere announcement; it was a declaration of Alaric's intent, a harbinger of the changes poised to unfold. "You tell the mayor that, as the earl, I expect to be welcomed properly. Can you do that?"

Krebbs's response, a grin accompanied by a confident nod, was more than an affirmation of his ability to carry out the task. It was a promise it would be done right.

"Good," Alaric stated, a decisive note in his tone as he turned yet again. "Jasper, go with him. Make sure there is no trouble, and if there is, deal with it."

"And what if the mayor refuses to see him?" Jasper asked. "What then, my lord?"

"Tell the mayor he is commanded by his earl," Alaric said. "If he still refuses to see you, then tell everyone in town I am coming, that the earl has come home. You tell them all that I have returned to save Dekar."

"And what of the mayor in that instance?" Jasper asked.

"He will answer to me afterwards for his actions if he refuses to see you both."

"And what of the keep, my lord?" Jasper asked. "What of your mother? Shall we tell them too?"

"No. I will deal with that after the town and mayor have knuckled under," Alaric said. "Now, we've wasted enough time.

Both of you, get going. Ride hard and fast. I want word to spread concerning my arrival before I get there. I need the people excited. If Nightwell is against us, it will make any move on his part more difficult."

Jasper's nod was swift, a silent vow of commitment to the task. As Krebbs spurred the horse into a trot, the animal's hooves kicking up small clumps of dirt along the road, Jasper followed. Both rode alongside the column, rapidly overtaking it.

Together, both men would became the vanguard of Alaric's intentions, speeding ahead to lay the groundwork for his arrival and what was to come. Alaric's eyes lingered on the departing figures, determination and concern swirling in his heart. In a town where there was little hope, Alaric intended to give some.

Grayson's voice cut through the silence. "I don't like it."

Alaric's gaze drifted back down the length of the column, looking in the direction from which they had just come, where the train of civilians was just now rounding a bend in the road and approaching. Behind them, and out of sight, was the supply train and rearguard. Out in the forest around the column worked a team of scouts searching for any potential threats.

"I don't like it either," Alaric admitted. "Dekar is not in good shape. This is not the homecoming I envisioned."

"We have our work cut out for us," Grayson added, his voice a blend of realism and resolve, "and I am thinking it will not be easy righting the cart."

"No, it will not." Alaric's thoughts turned to the Duke of Laval. Was he an instigator or merely an opportunist in the unfolding crisis? As one of the two dukes of the kingdom, the man was powerful and rich beyond compare. He could easily be behind the troubles afflicting Alaric's lands. Or—he could simply be taking advantage of the situation, the instability. Either way, it wasn't good that the man's name was being bandied about.

Unlike the other earldoms in Kevahn, Dekar owed her allegiance directly to the king and not to one of the dukes. Alaric needed to demonstrate strength, and quickly, to solidify his hold upon Dekar. Otherwise, he would be viewed as weak by the other lords of the realm, and that could not be allowed to happen, for they would seek to take advantage of his perceived vulnerability. The imperative was clear: to restore order, to reassert control over the chaos that had taken root, and to rule with a firm hand, one that could not be mistaken by anyone. That would require examples to be made.

Alaric sucked in a breath and let it out slowly through his nose.

"First, we secure the town, then we tackle the keep, this Masterson, and find my mother. After that, we worry about the rest and Laval's involvement. Understand?"

"Yes, my lord," Grayson said.

Reins in hand, Alaric moved back to the side of his horse. Mounting in a single graceful motion, he settled into the saddle. He took a moment, shifting his seat, to get himself comfortable. Casting a final glance down at Grayson, he commanded, "Let's get moving."

14

Alaric pulled Fire to a halt, pausing on the crest of a small, sloping hill. He was less than a half-mile from the town. His heart began beating faster at what lay before him. It had been more than ten years since he'd set eyes upon Dark Forge, and Alaric felt strangely moved. He had not expected this feeling… the emotion of the moment.

The late fall air was crisp, biting at his cheeks with an invisible cold. As the day had progressed, it grew colder, almost frigid. The sun hung low in the sky, preparing to set, offering light but little warmth. The wind, playful yet chilling, ruffled his hair and danced around him, carrying with it the faint scents of woodsmoke, the sour stench of civilization, and the smell of harvested fields alongside the decaying vegetation left behind.

Below him, encircled by sturdy stone walls, lay the town. Its layout was familiar to him, but as a boy, had always held a hint of mystery in the shadows of the narrow streets. He'd once loved exploring Dark Forge. That seemed like another lifetime.

The town walls, aged and weathered, bore the marks of time and the scars of past conflicts, standing as guardians over the inhabitants sheltering within. The only break in this formidable barrier was the town gate, which appeared welcoming, for it was open and not barred. Alaric thought that a very good sign.

On the far side of the town was the keep, his home. Its silhouette, marked by towers and battlements, cut a stark figure against the softening sky in the distance. A moat, its waters dark and still, encircled the fortress, the parts he could see reflecting the last rays of the sun like a mirror to the heavens. This castle watched over the town with an air of silent authority, a symbol of power and protection perched upon its own hill.

Surrounding the town and stretching into the wide lands were farm and pasture fields. They sprawled like a patchwork quilt laid upon the ground, some sections with the remnants of autumn's harvest, others bare and exposed, revealing the dark, fertile soil beneath. Alaric's gaze traveled from the fields to the town and then back to the castle.

"That is no keep," Ezran said plainly.

Alaric glanced over at the former ash man, who was staring outward, beyond the town.

"That is a full castle, a fortress that would make those we knew in the holy land blush in embarrassment," Ezran continued.

"It is my family home." Alaric's voice held a quiet reverence as he spoke of the towering structure, the fortress he had inherited, that had been his father's and grandfather's before him. His ancestors had called it their home for centuries.

Though it was a distance away, the castle loomed before them, its age evident in the weathered stones that had witnessed generations come and go. Its grandeur spoke of a time long past, when craftsmanship was revered. For a moment, he could see it through Ezran's eyes, someone who had never laid eyes upon Dragon Bone's Rest. In that instant, Alaric couldn't help but marvel at its size, a sudden connection to the legacy his ancestors had left behind washing over him.

Memories stirred as he recalled tales of the castle's construction, passed down through the generations like cherished heirlooms. Dragon Bone's Rest had been built during the last days of the Ordinate, a stronghold meant to secure the empire's northern frontier from the barbarians. At the end, it had been one of the last holdouts of the empire.

Built upon a slight rise in the landscape, the castle commanded views in all directions, ensuring that any approach could be seen well in advance. Its walls, constructed from massive blocks of granite, were thick and high, designed to repel sieges and resist the ambitions of would-be invaders. It had never been conquered and had withstood all tests when enemies marched against it.

The stones, darkened by time and the elements, bore the weight of history, their surfaces occasionally broken by arrow slits through which defenders could observe and attack without exposing themselves. At strategic points along the walls, sturdy towers rose, their tops crenellated for protection of archers and guardsmen. These towers served not only as lookout points, but also as symbols of strength, their presence a reminder of the lord's power over the surrounding lands or, at the moment, the lack of it.

The largest of these towers, the keep, what he actually called his home, stood at the heart of the castle, its walls even thicker and its defenses more elaborate. Within the keep were the lord's quarters, along with rooms for his family, guests, and the administrative heart of the domain. The keep was the last line of defense in Dragon Bone's Rest, a place of refuge should the outer walls be breached.

Encircling the castle was the moat. The moat served as both a physical barrier to attackers and a psychological one, its presence making the castle seem even more unassailable. A drawbridge, heavy and reinforced, spanned the moat, capable of being raised to cut off access and turn the castle into an island unto itself.

The castle grounds included a courtyard, where daily activities took place, from training exercises for soldiers to gatherings for the castle's inhabitants. From his current vantage point, Alaric could not see the courtyard, but he had spent countless hours there working the sword and shield under the direct oversight of his arms master and his tutors. Within these walls, too, were the essential services that sustained castle life: blacksmiths, stables, kitchens, and storerooms, each playing its role to keep things functioning.

Though worn by years of weathering, detail was evident in the aesthetic touches of the castle's construction as well—the intricate stonework around windows and battlements and the occasional stained-glass window that told an ancient and mostly forgotten story or heralded an alliance of some sort that was lost to the mists of time.

Alaric felt himself scowl. There were normally banners and flags that flew from the battlements and the top of the keep, each bearing the colors and crest of the lord's family, his family. There were none in view. That was clear confirmation something wasn't quite right.

Yet, for all its strength and majesty, the castle was not just a military fortress. It was a home, a place of courtly life where feasts were held, where troubadours sang, and where the court engaged in the intricate dance of politics and diplomacy, not to mention family life. It stood as a center of power, a protector of the realm, and a symbol of the lord's authority and responsibility to his people.

And Alaric meant to get it all back.

Lifting himself slightly in the stirrups, he cast a glance over his shoulder. The column behind him was a formidable sight, a procession of armored figures. They climbed the hill with purpose. The rhythmic crunch and thud of boots and the creak of leather filled the air as they steadily advanced toward the crest. At the forefront rode Grayson beside the standard-bearer, his presence commanding respect as the column stretched back along the road to the forest's edge, where the civilians were just beginning to emerge.

"Your family home is quite impressive." Ezran's voice broke through Alaric's thoughts, drawing his attention back to the castle.

Alaric nodded, a wistful smile playing at the corners of his lips. "Honestly, I had forgotten how large Dragon Bone's Rest was."

"Isn't it supposed to be that when you return to your childhood home you are surprised by how small it is, yes? This makes Hawkani's keep seem tiny."

Alaric gave an amused grunt. "I believe you are correct."

Movement on the town's wall caught his attention. Squinting against the fading light, he strained to make out the figures gathered there. His heart quickened with excitement as he realized the significance of what he saw. Hundreds of civilians were lining the battlements, their presence signaling the success of Krebbs and Jasper's mission. They had come to watch their lord return.

His gaze was drawn as a pennant was raised and hoisted over the town's gate. It was a striking display of artistry and history, over-large and unfurling gracefully. Alaric knew it only too well. The pennant's field, a rich tapestry of blue and gold, was split vertically, symbolizing the union of two powerful ancient lineages that had centuries ago forged an unbreakable and powerful alliance through marriage and shared conquests that had lasted centuries.

On the blue side, a majestic golden lion signified courage, strength, and the noble spirit of the family's warrior ancestors. The lion's mane was detailed with such intricacy that even from afar, Alaric could almost sense its wild majesty and untamed fury.

On the golden half, a castle was embossed in sable. The castle was not that of Dragon Bone's Rest but signified the unbreaking spirit of the alliance that had been forged, the walls upon which all struggles and conflicts would crash and be turned away.

Bordering the pennant was a delicate trim of silver, reflecting the light of the sun with a brilliance that seemed almost magical. Alaric's heart began beating faster. This was his family's pennant, their crest. The shimmering boundary symbolized a commitment to purity, honor, and the pursuit of enlightenment, to God—ideals that they had upheld for generations.

At the very top of the pennant, a crown rested, not just as an ornament, but as a declaration of the family's regal status and their divine right to govern. It was a right they traced all the way back to the Ordinate. As the overly large pennant danced in the wind, it seemed to Alaric not just a piece of fabric, but a living chronicle of history, each thread woven with the stories of those who had come before him, those who had blazed the path Alaric now rode.

"It seems they are welcoming you home," Ezran remarked with a side glance.

"That it does." Alaric's gaze remained fixed ahead, his expression solemn yet resolute. "That it most certainly does…"

Ezran's gaze shifted back to the pennant fluttering over the town's gate. He gestured at it. "Not many know the history of that banner."

"No, they don't," Alaric admitted quietly, his thoughts drifting to the countless souls who had rallied to its call, their stories now lost to the annals of time and history. "I think that a good thing…"

Ezran's gaze met Alaric's, an understanding passing between them. "Your people don't know either, and that includes Grayson."

A somber silence settled over them before Alaric spoke again, his voice firm with conviction. "It means something to me."

Ezran's expression softened, a flicker of solidarity in his eyes. "As it does to me."

"I've told you—I am not the one mentioned in prophecy," Alaric said, feeling a stab of unhappiness.

"That is to be seen."

Alaric scowled again. The rhythmic sound of boots and the steady clop of hooves pulled their attention away from the town as Grayson, accompanied by Thorne marching just behind the captain, arrived at the head of the column. The company's standard waved proudly in the cold breeze.

"Column, halt!" Grayson's command echoed across the hill as he and the head of the column reached the crest, the words carrying the weight of authority. Behind him, the column came to a grinding halt.

Drawing alongside Alaric, Grayson brought his horse to a stop, his expression one of solemn respect. "My lord. At long last, we have arrived home."

Alaric acknowledged Grayson with a simple nod, his gaze still fixed upon the town below and his thoughts on the conversation with Ezran. Through the open gate, a procession of men emerged, their purposeful strides halting just before the threshold as they turned their attention toward the hill where Alaric sat astride his horse.

"A welcoming committee," Grayson remarked, tone laced with cautious optimism.

"Yes, it is," Alaric affirmed. He turned his attention back to the column, gaze sweeping over his soldiers as he thought ahead to their pending arrival. "Many of the men will have family within the town."

"Undoubtedly, my lord," Grayson concurred, his own gaze following Alaric's. "Is that a problem?"

"It might be," Alaric said. "We will not dismiss them when we arrive before the town. We may need them when it comes to the castle."

"I understand, my lord," Grayson said "Once you have

concluded matters with the mayor and town officials, I will form the company up and explain why they won't be released. They won't like it, though."

"I know. But that can't be helped. We will make camp outside the town tonight. The men's families can come to them. Once the castle is secured, we will consider releasing them on a limited-pass basis."

"Very good, my lord. That will make things much easier." The captain paused. "There are undoubtedly relatives in town who will be looking for their own amongst our ranks. They will not know their loved ones have fallen in battle."

Alaric gave a nod, his thoughts already turning to the challenges that awaited them within the walls of the castle. What was he dealing with here?

A sudden eruption of cheers from the town walls cut through the crisp afternoon air, their hearty resonance carrying even across the distance to Alaric and his companions. The sound echoed once more, a chorus of joyous celebration that reverberated through the surrounding landscape.

"Shall we go, my lord?" Grayson's voice broke through the jubilant din, his tone expectant as he awaited Alaric's command. "It seems a shame to keep them waiting."

Alaric nodded, his steely resolve undeterred by the cacophony of cheers. There were serious matters that needed attending, and he was now wasting time. With a gentle nudge of his heels, he urged his horse into a slow, deliberate walk, Ezran matching his pace at his side.

"Column!" Grayson's voice rang out, commanding attention as he raised his hand high into the air, a signal to the men behind him. For a moment, he held the gesture before pointing forward toward the town. "March!"

With that directive, the column began moving once more, the rhythmic cadence of their footsteps echoing the steady beat of

Alaric's heart. Each heavy clop of his horse brought them closer to their destination, the town looming larger with every passing moment.

Alaric stole a glance over his shoulder, taking in the sight of the company marching behind him down the hill and road, moving steadily toward the town. Grayson had tightened the march up, ensuring that every man moved as one, their feet in step. They were not just soldiers; they were a symbol of strength and solidarity, a power that his enemies would have to reckon with.

Under the golden hues of the late afternoon sunlight, the gleaming armor of the men caught the light, casting dazzling reflections that danced across the landscape. It was a sight to behold. He felt a surge of pride in them, for they were his men, and he was their lord, their ultimate leader.

As they advanced down the road, flanked by farm fields and pastureland, Alaric's gaze remained fixed ahead, anticipation coiling in his chest as they neared the main gate and the waiting reception committee. The figures came into clearer view as they drew closer, each one bearing the weight of their respective roles in the town's hierarchy.

At the forefront clearly stood the mayor, his distinguished presence marked by the regal robes of his office and the wisdom etched into the lines of his aged face. Beside him stood the solemn figure of a priest, clad in pristine white robes that spoke of his sacred calling as the spiritual leader of the community. The priest's hands were clasped before his chest and a golden compass hung from his rope belt. Alaric's eyes shifted to the man in light armor who stood with them, recognizing him as the likely commander of the local militia, those who were guarding the town.

Behind these key figures stood a group of men adorned in civilian attire, their expressions displaying both curiosity and anticipation. Among them, Alaric supposed, was the bailiff, responsible for administrative matters within the town, and the reeve, tasked with overseeing and catering to the needs of the local peasantry. The remaining individuals were likely prominent members of the community—business owners, leaders of influential guilds, and esteemed and wealthy citizens whose voices carried weight in matters of governance and commerce.

Alaric reined in Fire a dozen yards before the assembled group, both scrutiny and respect in his sweeping gaze. To rule, he would need these people. If they worked against him, it would complicate the job that needed doing. He then acknowledged the onlookers lining the battlements above. There were hundreds, perhaps even thousands—the populace of the town mixed in with the militia. All stared downward. A heavy silence hung on the air, thick with anticipation and expectation, as Alaric assessed the gathering before him.

"Column, halt!" Grayson's voice rang out, cutting through the tension like a clarion call.

Alaric's gaze lingered on the assemblage, noting the undercurrent of nervous tension. Unease was etched into the lines of their faces, their postures betraying the weight of responsibility they bore and the uncertainty of what lay ahead.

With a fluid motion, Alaric swung his leg over the back of his horse, dismounting with a sense of purpose that seemed to infuse the air around him. Ezran mirrored his actions, dropping to the ground. At Grayson's direction, a man from the ranks dashed forward and took the reins of both of their horses.

Alaric approached the man he presumed to be the mayor, his gaze meeting the older man's with curiosity and respect. The mayor's appearance spoke volumes, his weary countenance bearing the unmistakable marks of adversity. It was clear that he carried the burdens of leadership with a heavy heart, a weight that Alaric could empathize with all too well.

"Earl Alaric, I presume," the man spoke, his voice raspy with age and laden with deference and apprehension.

"You presume correct, Nightwell," Grayson confirmed, joining Alaric and stopping at his side with a steady presence that lent reassurance to the tense atmosphere. Grayson offered a nod to the mayor, which was returned before Nightwell shifted his gaze back upon Alaric.

"It is my pleasure to welcome you home, Lord Earl." With visible effort, and shaking slightly, Nightwell lowered himself to a knee before Alaric. The gesture of respect was tinged with the weariness of someone who had borne the weight of their duties for far too long. Beside him, the others followed suit, their actions an acknowledgment of Alaric's authority and the gravity of the moment.

Alaric regarded them for several long heartbeats, his gaze piercing yet measured as he assessed each individual before him. He had the sense these were all frightened men, looking for not only help, but leadership.

"Rise," Alaric commanded, his voice carrying the weight of authority tempered by understanding.

As the others rose to their feet, Nightwell remained kneeling. He made an attempt to stand, but his old and shaky legs failed him. His cheeks flushed. Alaric approached him, extending a hand. The mayor took it gratefully. Gently, Alaric pulled Nightwell to his feet.

"Thank you, my lord," Nightwell murmured gratefully as Alaric stepped back, allowing the mayor to regain his footing. "We are pleased you have returned. We are here to serve. Will you accept our humble offer of service?"

The last were formal words. If Alaric rejected the offer, these men would lose nearly everything, most of their wealth and power. But he could not do that. He needed them as much as they needed him.

Alaric took note of the lingering unease that still clung to the assembled men. To them, Alaric represented the unknown, but also the hope that the world could be put right again and Dekar made safe. He understood their apprehension—they stood before a leader they did not know, one who had spent a decade at war, yet the weight of their allegiance remained unquestioned. For they understood, as he did, the immutable bond that tied them to their rightful lord, the Earl of Dekar, and he to the people and land.

With a sense of conviction burning within him, Alaric raised his voice, projecting it so that all could hear, especially those lining the town walls. "I have returned home! Together, we shall make Dekar right again! We will push back the darkness that threatens our home."

The proclamation was met with an enthusiastic cheer from the gathered crowd upon the town's wall, their voices rising in fervent agreement and thundering down upon them. Alaric turned his attention back to Nightwell, and a glimmer of hope showed through his steely resolve as he met the mayor's gaze.

"The town is yours, my lord," Nightwell declared, a solemn acceptance of Alaric's rightful authority. There was a note of relief within his voice.

"And what of the keep?" Alaric inquired.

"That is a different matter, my lord," Nightwell conceded with a look of sadness. "You may need to reclaim your ancestral home by force of arms."

Alaric glanced over at Grayson unhappily. It was a moment of shared understanding. They would have to free his mother the hard way. That much was clear. It was something he had feared might become necessary.

"So be it," Alaric affirmed, his voice steady with resolve. "So be it."

15

"What do you lot bloody want?" The harsh shout had come from the top of the gate. "You wanted to speak with me, so speak."

Alaric had halted his stride mere yards before the castle's drawbridge, which lay lowered before him. They had been waiting for almost a quarter of an hour. Alongside him stood Grayson and Nightwell, accompanied by his Shadow Guard. Ezran and Thorne both carried shields and had positioned themselves just before him. With the shields, they were ready to provide cover for him should it be needed. Rikka had joined them and was standing next to Kiera off to Alaric's right. Twenty-five yards back were thirty of Grayson's men, still formed up into a marching column.

The day's sunlight was fading, and fast, bathing the scene in an increasingly dim twilight. The temperature was also dropping. Winter was clearly just around the corner.

"That is Masterson, the man I told you of," Nightwell whispered, his voice a deliberate murmur designed not to carry beyond their immediate vicinity. "He is quite a disagreeable man, my lord. I never much liked him and told your mother as much when she engaged his services."

In the failing light, Alaric strained his eyes, barely discerning the features of the man. Leaning casually with his elbows against the battlement above, he wore a red tunic and had a prominent bushy mustache, which he was idly playing with. From his elevated position, Masterson was surveying the scene, as if feigning disinterest and boredom. Beside him was another figure, equally intent on observing the gathering just before the drawbridge. The second man pointed at Grayson's men and then said something to Masterson, who replied curtly. Alaric could not hear what was said between them.

Immediately below the top of the walls to either side of the gate, the ominous presence of several arrow slits carved into the stone of the gatehouse caught Alaric's attention. Peering into the darkness that filled each opening, he couldn't shake the unsettling feeling that unseen archers lay in wait, their bows drawn and aimed at him and the others. This added a real sense of danger, but Alaric felt compelled to take the risk. If he could get a resolution without resorting to bloodshed, all the better, especially if his mother was released unharmed.

"Well?" Masterson demanded, his tone coarse and hard. His manner reminded Alaric very much of a bully. "What do you lot want? You're already boring me to death. Speak, so I can go back to my dinner and eat in peace."

"Open the gate," Alaric commanded. He was not accustomed to being spoken to this way, but that wasn't what irritated him. It was what had happened—and was happening still—to Dekar. Masterson was a direct symbol of that decay. The rot needed rooting out, and Alaric aimed to do just that. It would begin here.

"No," came the brusque reply from above. Masterson, with a glance at his companion, lowered his voice for a private remark, yet his words still managed to carry, and that told Alaric the tone and level was intentional. "They must be foolish to think we would open the gates for them."

"I could hit him from here with my bow," Jasper stated quietly with an edge of readiness. In one hand, he grasped his strung bow, in the other three arrows. "Just for the insolence, I can take him down. Give the word, my lord, and it shall be my pleasure. It is an easy shot for me."

"I know it." Alaric surveyed the land to either side of the road that led up to the drawbridge and gate, noting the encroaching wilderness with a sense of dismay. The forest, once a cherished family reserve behind the castle, was now steadily advancing around it. When he'd left, there had been extensive manicured gardens alongside the road, along with a handful of farms that provided fresh produce to Dragon Bone's Rest.

Nature was asserting her dominion, weaving the wild back into what had once been neat and ordered. The outskirts of the town, merely a quarter-mile behind them and down the hill, seemed almost a distant memory amidst nature's steady encroachment, with the nearest homes and barns outside the walls lying abandoned in ruin.

Turning back to the castle, his gaze lifted to the once majestic edifice that had sheltered generations of his family. The castle, now a dark silhouette against the dimming sky, bore the weight of neglect on its shoulders. The outer wall's stones, etched with the passage of time, seemed to whisper past tales of glory and despair in the same breath. The turrets, which had once pierced the sky with their might, now appeared jagged and weary, their wooden roofs rotting away and the proud pennants missing. Even some of the stone facing had come loose and dropped away, along with chunks of mortar.

The heavy and reinforced wooden gates stood open, the left side hanging askew on its hinges, creaking mournfully with every gust of wind. However, the portcullis was closed. The drawbridge over the moat was down, one of its heavy chains broken, long ago having snapped. The other was badly rusted and appeared to not have been used in some time. A thick and frayed rope had been fitted in the missing chain's place. The entrance—once bustling with the comings and goings of noble guests, bannermen, and civilians from the town—was now overtaken by creeping ivy and weeds.

The moat, which had stood as a formidable barrier, was now choked with lilies, reeds, and other detritus, reflecting the failing light in its stagnant waters. Eyeing the moat, Alaric thought one might simply be able to wade across, but there was no telling how muddy the bottom was. Neglect was quite apparent in everything before him.

As daylight retreated with every passing heartbeat, casting long shadows across the derelict courtyard beyond the portcullis, Alaric could see the remnants of one of his mother's many gardens, once meticulously groomed, now overgrown. The sight saddened him, for his mother always loved her gardens. Around it, wildflowers and grass peeked through cracked paving stones, and vines clambered over statues and the inner walls. It seemed nothing was being maintained by the castle servants and had not been for some time.

The scene was a reminder of impermanence, a tangible sign of his family's rise and apparent fall. It was clear to him that Dekar herself, years before his father's death, had fallen into hard times.

Over the years, he had received a few letters from his mother and father. Why had they not said anything about the declining state of Dekar? He found it maddening. Yet, in the encroaching gloom, Alaric felt a stir of something indefinable—a connection to the land about him and its history, a powerful resolve to reclaim and restore what had been lost.

The castle wall ran for more than a quarter of a mile in either direction. Running his eyes over the walls, he counted only six men manning the defensive platform. Those six did not take into account Masterson or the man standing by his side.

"Well?" Masterson demanded. "You are really beginning to bore me already."

"Open the gate and call for the Lady Elara," Grayson shouted. "Her son has returned from the Crusade."

The two men above stiffened and then turned to one another and began speaking urgently in hushed tones. After several moments, Masterson made a chopping motion with his hand and turned back to regard them, even leaning forward for a better view of Alaric.

"I don't care who you claim to be," Masterson called back down, sounding surly and coarse. He pointed a finger down at them. "She's not seeing no one, not today, not tomorrow, not anytime soon. Go away and leave us in peace."

"Given time, we could build scaling ladders and storm the walls," Grayson suggested, his tone low as he spoke to Alaric. "I doubt there are very many holding the castle. They certainly don't look like fighters."

Alaric's gaze briefly swept behind them, where the small contingent of Grayson's men waited. Back before the town and out of view, the rest of the company was building a fortified camp. There was no way they could be ready for a ladder assault by dawn or even, in his estimation, by tomorrow evening, for they would have to manufacture ladders tall enough to overcome the walls. Turning his attention back to the castle, Alaric noticed the area behind the portcullis remained eerily devoid of any presence or activity. The courtyard should have servants and craftsmen in view. The entire time they had been standing here waiting, he'd seen no one pass.

"You dare deny the rightful ruler of these lands?" Grayson demanded.

"The Lady Elara told me personally her son died in the holy land. So your man down there is an imposter."

"This is the real Alaric and Earl of Dekar," Nightwell called back up, his voice raspy. "There is no denying that. I knew him as a boy."

The two men atop the gate turned to one another and spoke between themselves again. Once more, Alaric could not hear what was being said.

"The game is up," Nightwell said. "He has brought his soldiers home. Defy him at your own risk."

Masterson and the other man looked down at them before speaking again. This time, they were more animated. Masterson gestured off to the north, away from the town, pointing emphatically. Alaric wondered what was passing between them.

"Open the gate, surrender my mother," Alaric called, "and I will allow you and your men to walk away—to go free." Just the thought of doing that turned Alaric's stomach. Still, if he could end this standoff without putting his mother or any of his men at risk, then it would be worth it.

"And you expect us to take your word on that?" the other man said, doubt heavily lacing his tone. "I think not."

"Shut up, you," Masterson hissed loud enough for Alaric to hear. "I will handle this."

"I give you my word as Lord of Dekar," Alaric replied. "Open the gate and you will go free."

There was silence at that.

"You would be wise to listen, Masterson," Nightwell called.

"Old fool," Masterson sneered. "I heed my own bloody counsel and don't need your advice."

"If they had a larger force, we'd surely see more of them on the walls," Alaric said to Grayson, careful to keep his voice low enough that those above would not be able to overhear.

"I agree, my lord." Grayson gave a nod. "I think it quite evident they've taken your mother captive and are holding her against her will. I can't imagine the Lady Elara refusing to see anyone, especially her son, let alone claiming you had died."

"I concur," Nightwell added, his tone grave.

"Do you know how many men he might have in there?" Alaric asked the mayor.

"Masterson commands a force of no more than thirty men. They are trained but, from what I have seen, are mostly ruffians, thugs, rogues, and scoundrels."

"Why did you not try to help the Lady Elara?" Grayson asked.

"We've been talking about it, my lord… but those few men we have are all that protect us, the town, that is… My militia are not regular soldiers," Nightwell added. "They are the old and young—poorly trained at that. By the time we realized what was really happening here at the castle, they had locked themselves in, and well…"

Alaric nodded his understanding. There was the real chance that if they attacked the castle, the militia would be slaughtered by Masterson's men or, if successful, badly mauled to the point where there would be few left to defend the town.

"But to what purpose are they holding her?" Alaric pondered, struggling to understand the strategic advantage here. "This does not make sense to me. Should the other nobles within the kingdom catch wind of this, they would undoubtedly unite to make an example out of such defiance, for if it can happen to my mother, it can happen to them. That is something that cannot be tolerated."

"Normally, I would agree with such sentiment, my lord." Grayson shook his head sadly. "However, I'm not entirely sure about that, especially if one of the dukes is involved."

Alaric's thoughts immediately went to Laval. Grayson's words laid bare the precariousness of their situation, highlighting the politics that might be at play within the kingdom itself. Once more, Alaric was reminded that he did not know the rules of the game being played. Worse, he had to learn fast, before it was too late.

"You will let me in." Alaric had grown tired of being toyed with.

"Or what?"

"Resist me on this and we do it the hard way. None of you will walk out of the castle alive. On that, you also have my solemn word."

"Her son died. She ain't seeing no one," Masterson called down. "Go away and stop wasting my time."

"You are holding my mother against her will," Alaric declared. "We know that, and you know that. Stop playing games."

"And if I am?" The man barked a harsh laugh. "What are you going to do about it? You're out there, and I am in here, fool, with more than a hundred guardsmen standing between you and her."

"He lies," Nightwell breathed. "As I told you, he came with no more than thirty men."

"This is your last chance. Release my mother and you will live, Masterson," Alaric said. "You have my word as lord of these lands."

"From up here, you are master of very little. Now, go fuck off, you noble prick."

Alaric sucked in a heated breath, his anger firing. He was about to reply when Masterson spoke again.

"Come in here and I will see the old bag dead before you can free her."

"He is bold," Rikka whispered with a hint of acerbity, her voice barely carrying. "Bold and scared."

Alaric's gaze shifted toward her. Still dressed in the rugged garb of a sailor, she seemed out of place amongst them. He made a mental note to find her attire more befitting her status. He found himself once more wondering why she had come with them. Why had she even gotten off the boat? Why had she spent her nights with him? He had so many questions. She was a mystery, one he was keen to solve.

During their passage from the town to the castle, Nightwell's curious glances toward Rikka had not gone unnoticed. Though the man held his tongue, it was clear he was curious as to who she was and why she had been allowed to tag along.

"Is there anything you can do about that portcullis?" Kiera inquired of Rikka.

Rikka's dark eyes moved from the heavy iron bars to the stone archway above, her expression contemplative. "I might be able to do something, but I am thinking not without causing considerable damage to the castle."

Alaric's gaze oscillated between the gate and Rikka, pondering the implications of her words. "Were you to use your powers, how extensive would the damage be?"

Nightwell, overhearing the conversation, voiced his confusion. "Powers, my lord?"

"She is a lumina," Kiera explained plainly.

The revelation caused the color to drain from the mayor's aged face. He instinctively stepped back from Rikka, his mouth falling open in apparent horror. "Surely you jest with this old man."

"Do not worry, Mayor," Rikka said, her tone reassuring as she gestured toward Alaric. "I am only dangerous to his enemies and those who wish me harm."

Nightwell's gaze went from Rikka to Kiera. His eyes narrowed as he stared at her face. It was as if, for the first time, he really noticed the tattoos and scars. He gave a slight gasp. "And you are her Luminary?"

"How much damage?" Alaric asked again, pressing for an answer, while shooting Nightwell a slight scowl.

"Were I to employ the spell I am of a mind to, the gate might come down, perhaps even some of the adjoining wall," Rikka said plainly. "I have only ever used it once. The results were… quite impressive. I am not sure you would want that."

"Which could ultimately see the way still blocked," Grayson said. "Our people would have to climb the rubble to get into the castle. That would take time, perhaps long enough for Masterson to hurt the Lady Elara."

"That is not an option, then," Alaric declared, slightly disappointed. The prospect of damaging the castle, his seat of power, was unthinkable to him. Any harm inflicted upon the structure would necessitate repairs, demanding resources and wealth that were perhaps better allocated elsewhere, like rebuilding his lands and holdings.

"This castle is ancient. It speaks of the Ordinate," Rikka observed, her voice laced with a reverence that hinted at her connection to things unseen. She closed her eyes and held her hand out toward the gate, as if consulting with unseen forces or tapping into a hidden well of knowledge. When her eyes fluttered open, she added almost breathlessly, "The walls might be warded. I—I am not sure, but I think the binding likely to be old."

Grayson, puzzled, sought clarification. "What do you mean warded, a binding, and old?"

Ezran intervened, "She means magically protected."

"Yes, and there's no telling what those defenses might actually do in response to my intrusion," Rikka confirmed, her acknowledgment sending a shiver down Alaric's spine, a sensation almost detached from the encroaching chill of the coming night. "There are magics that have long since been lost. I—I think that is what we are dealing with here."

Grayson sought to gauge the certainty of their predicament. "How sure are you about that?"

Nightwell, still grappling with the revelation of Rikka's true nature, expressed his astonishment. "She is a lumina? I thought they were no more."

"I am a lumina," Rikka responded to the mayor, her affirmation serene yet firm. She turned her attention to Grayson. "Though I don't fully recognize what I am sensing, I'm also sure. It may be dangerous for me to even try to crack open that gate using my spells."

Alaric, digesting the implications, concluded, "Definitely not an option then."

The realization that the castle might be protected by ancient magics added a layer of complexity to the already daunting task of reclaiming what was his own. It was something he'd never even suspected possible. Had his father and grandfather known about the warding? Alaric had his doubts about that.

"I could still shoot him dead," Jasper murmured with a dangerous edge, barely concealing his eagerness for action.

"And I could end him as well," Rikka added, her voice calm yet carrying a chilling undertone. "But if we did, you'd lose the opportunity to interrogate him and find out if he is working for someone or simply operating on his own."

"Good point." Alaric's gaze shifted between Jasper and Rikka, the rising tide of anger within him almost a physical thing.

From above, Masterson's taunting voice broke the tense silence that had grown between them. "See," he called down with a smug assurance, "I am in here, and you are out there with no easy way to get in. Go away and stop wasting my time. Now, I am done talking. Come back tomorrow if you wish to bore me some more."

Masterson said something inaudible to the man beside him and gestured down at Alaric almost dismissively. The other replied, then Masterson stepped out of view.

"I thought I saw movement in one of the arrow slits. We should move back out of missile range," Jasper suggested, his eyes upon the stone walls. Thorne and Ezran raised their shields to protect Alaric.

Acknowledging the wisdom in Jasper's advice, Alaric gave a curt nod. Together, they retreated, moving back, stopping just before Grayson's contingent. From this new vantage point and position of relative safety, Alaric cast one more glance at the castle that was his birthright, a new surge of frustration rising. The fortress was more than just stone and mortar; it was a legacy that had been usurped, a home that felt increasingly distant no matter how close he got.

"What are you thinking, my lord?" Grayson inquired.

"That we're going in there and freeing my mother," Alaric responded with determined resolve. He inhaled deeply, the cool evening air infused with the rich scent of soil and vegetation. This breath was more than a mere intake of air; it was a silent pledge, a tacit commitment to revitalize the very essence of his familial stronghold. Yet before he could breathe new life into these ancient stones, he faced the immediate challenge of penetrating the castle's defenses and rescuing his mother.

"How?" Grayson's question pierced the thickening shadows of the evening.

"Do we have rope with us?" Alaric asked, having already formulated a plan.

"We do," Grayson confirmed, "in the train, and I'm sure there is more to be found in town if needed."

"Sufficient for it to be knotted and lowered down the wall?" Alaric asked. "To be used for the men to climb up and into the castle?"

"I believe so," Grayson said with a nod. "Though that would mean our needing someone inside to do the lowering."

"Grayson is correct, there is also rope in the town, my lord," Nightwell confirmed. "We will provide all you require."

"Good." Alaric turned back to Grayson. "Let us move some of the men up, create a decoy camp about a hundred yards from here, and make a show of it. Light several fires, pitch the tents, and post a watch. We'll keep those inside the castle distracted and their attention fixed on the camp."

"To what purpose? Even aged as they are, those walls don't seem climbable." Grayson gestured back at the castle. "The stone facing is too smooth, the blocks too large for handholds."

"There's another way in, one that's known only to me," Alaric confessed.

"A bolt hole?" Grayson quickly deduced.

With a nod, Alaric confirmed Grayson's guess. His eyes then shifted upward, observing the clouds. As the sun had started to set, it had begun clouding over. The possibility of rain lingered in his mind, adding another layer of complexity to their plans.

"The moon won't be full tonight, and what light there is will be obscured by clouds. Just before dawn, when the darkness is most dense, I'll take my Shadow Guard and we'll infiltrate the castle. Our aim will be to reach the back wall, opposite from here, and lower ropes. Select twenty men, no armor—swords and daggers only. Make sure they can swim in case the moat is deeper than it appears. Once inside, their objective will be to reach the gatehouse, open the portcullis and let the rest of the company into the castle. Meanwhile, the Shadow Guard and I will rescue my mother."

"I think you should take more men with you, my lord," Grayson suggested and glanced at Nightwell. "Especially if there are thirty of them in there. You might be overwhelmed by numbers if you are prematurely discovered."

"I can't risk bringing anyone else," Alaric firmly stated. "After we take the castle back, the location of the bolt hole must remain a closely guarded secret."

"And your Shadow Guard are bound by oath; we will not speak of it, to anyone," Ezran added, reinforcing the point with a loyalty that left no room for doubt.

"No, we won't," Thorne chimed in, his voice echoing the

solemn commitment and pact the Shadow Guard had made with Alaric.

Grayson, though visibly uneasy with the plan, acknowledged the inevitable by shifting the stance of his feet and glancing down at the ground before looking back up. "I don't like it, but you are the earl now, and no longer my ward. The decision is yours to make."

"I am going with you too," Rikka announced, catching Alaric off guard. "You may need my services before this is done. Besides, where you go, I go. That is now the way of things."

Kiera looked over sharply at Rikka.

Recovering, Alaric shook his head. "No, Lady Lumina, you are not going. It is too risky and dangerous."

"She is going," Kiera interjected with an unwavering firmness that took Alaric thoroughly by surprise as she turned her intense gaze upon him. Never before had Kiera openly contradicted him, especially not in matters of strategy, let alone personal risk. "She goes if that is her wish."

Before Alaric could formulate a response, Rikka asserted herself with finality, "I am not some helpless girl. You should know that by now. My place is at your side, and that is where I will remain, as has been foretold. I am going, and that is the end of it. You will not try to stop me, Lord Alaric. You may dictate orders to your people, but you do not command me, not in the slightest. I answer to a higher power."

Alaric still felt like saying no. However, faced with the determined stances of both Rikka and Kiera, he found himself somewhat outmaneuvered. Kiera's look was particularly intense as she stared back at him. It was clear her mind was set. Though he could refuse them, to do so would be a mistake, something he would pay for later. More importantly, Rikka was correct; she was far from helpless. In fact, she was quite dangerous. With a resigned nod and still feeling uneasy, he conceded to their will.

Grayson grinned and barked out a laugh. He turned his gaze back toward the keep, a spark seeming to light up his eyes.

"What?" Alaric asked.

"Masterson made a terrible mistake," Grayson remarked.

"He did," Alaric agreed, determination growing. "All of them in there made a mistake, and we are going to show them the error of their ways."

16

The sound of cascading and running water filled the air with a pleasant sound. It seemed more pronounced in the near-enveloping darkness of the night. Alaric led the others through the forest, his senses heightened. Each step was taken with deliberate care and caution, ensuring that not a leaf crackled, nor a branch snapped underfoot to betray their presence to the sentries on the wall two hundred yards away. He also did not want to trip over undergrowth.

They were walking beside a fast-moving stream, one Alaric knew well. As a child, he'd played in it on hot days. The stream wound down an incline, tumbling over a series of rocks and into pools, creating mini waterfalls, before ultimately emptying into the moat that ringed the castle.

Following behind him in a line as he weaved his way around the trees, his Shadow Guard moved almost as extensions of the night itself. Thorne and Jasper each carried knotted coils of rope over their shoulders. Close on their heels, Ezran and Kiera glided through the underbrush, their movements as silent as the whispers of the wind through the trees. Rikka was bringing up the rear. When he occasionally turned to look to make sure they were all still with him, she was nearly invisible in the darkness. She seemed to move through the forest with ease the others, including Jasper, could not match.

They were working their way through the dense forest that lay off the castle's back side and bordered the moat. The forest was ancient beyond conception. The trees were nearly all hardwoods, their trunks massive and straight as if reaching for the stars.

Alaric's grandfather had once told him that elves, the chosen and first worshippers of Eldanar, had once lived here amongst the trees. Unlike humans, they had called the forest their home. Alaric had trouble imagining how one would live exposed to the elements without a roof over their head. In winter, that would have been exceptionally hard. Still, the stories said the elves were magical beings, so who knew.

It was they who had supposedly first introduced humans to their god. Extinct and now gone from the world, elves were more legend and myth than anything else, in Alaric's mind. But now, as he stepped around the thick trunk of a tree that was at least ten feet around and ancient beyond belief, he found himself wondering if the stories had a bit of truth to them. Had these trees borne witness to the first race?

The elves had reputedly been masters of the forests. The old tales told of them being veritable wraiths amongst the trees. If they did not want you to find them, you would not. And now, they had vanished into the mists of time. That was, if they ever existed in the first place.

Here, amidst the trees, it was Alaric and his companions who had become the phantoms, the forest wraiths, seeming to flit between reality and shadow. With every carefully measured step, they maintained a harmonious balance with their surroundings, mindful of the dry twigs and rustling foliage that threatened to unmask their silent procession.

In the embrace of near-total darkness, the world around Alaric was reduced to shades and hints of shapes. The moon and stars were hidden behind a cloak of dense cloud cover. Yet his steps were sure, guided by the murmuring stream a few feet to his left —a constant companion in this near-opaque world. When he maneuvered around another ancient tree, its rough bark seemingly filled with the wisdom of centuries, an abrupt change in the landscape unfolded before him.

The forest opened to a wide clearing. Alaric remembered this spot and almost sighed with relief at finally having found it. Bald rock covered the ground, over which lay a carpet of fallen leaves. A large outcropping of rock, the size of a small house, rose from the ground in the center of the clearing. The top was almost flat, as if a statue had once stood there and the rock was the pedestal.

"This is it," Alaric announced, his voice barely more than a breath on the breeze. He moved into the clearing and up to the outcropping. He reached out to touch the rock face, hesitating a moment, then placed his palm against it. The granite was cold against his skin, colder than the frigid air itself.

Looking over the rock before him, Alaric scanned it, squinting, searching. His eyes, although accustomed to the dark, could not discern the details he so desperately sought. Without the option of illuminating their surroundings with the unlit torch Kiera was carrying, for fear of drawing unwanted attention from the sentries, Alaric resorted to his sense of touch, fingers just above the ground, gliding over the stone's smooth surface in search of a small notch—a legacy from the generations before him.

Yet the more he searched, the more the notch eluded him. He moved completely around the rock, feeling for it, and found nothing. He did a second circuit, bending low and running his hand along the smoothed face, knowing it had to be there... somewhere.

The others, silent, waited and watched.

Feeling frustration tinged with unease, Alaric took a step back, gaze piercing into the darkness, willing the rock to yield its secrets before him. It didn't.

Memories echoed in his mind, of a time long past when his father and grandfather had stood here with him, pointing out this very rock as an important guidepost, the secret way into their ancestral home. The lesson had been clear, the location unmistakable, and yet, so many years later, the notch eluded him.

So, where was it? It should be right before him, about a foot from the ground. He reached down and once more felt for it, moving completely around the monolith.

Nothing.

The absence of the notch was an enigma, stirring a whirlpool of emotions and questions. Had the landscape changed so much since he'd been here last? Had the years cloaked his memory? Or had exposure and the elements simply worn the notch away? The rock face stood mute in reply, indifferent to his scrutiny, to his questions.

Under the cloak of night, with only the faint whispers of the forest and the occasional distant call of a nocturnal creature, Alaric delved deep into his reservoir of memories, trying to stitch together the fragments from that pivotal day when his father and grandfather had brought him here, to show him the way.

It was his thirteenth birthday, a day marked by both personal transformation and the solemn rituals of ascension, becoming a man in the eyes of the community. After the ceremonies, under the watchful eyes of Eldanar's priests, he had been bestowed the family ring, what he wore now—a symbol of his newfound status and responsibilities as a viscount of the realm and Dekar's heir in waiting.

The ring suddenly pulsed with an inner heat that almost made him jump.

"What are we looking for?" Thorne's whispered inquiry cut through the night.

Alaric raised a hand as a silent command for patience, his mind racing. The ring's warmth surged, its heat intensifying as if in response to the secrets that lay hidden before them and his thoughts on the past.

The memories of his Ascension Day came back to him. It had been a day that began and ended with solemn supplications, prayer, and devotion to Eldanar. Alaric had a sudden flash of his grandfather. He remembered the man kneeling in reverence before this very rock, as if the ground it stood on was sacred, holy… as if the elves themselves had once worshipped here.

Alaric let go a breath and moved to the spot where he thought his grandfather had knelt. He took a knee, mirroring the posture of humble supplication he once observed and been taught. Around him, the forest seemed to hold its breath in anticipation. As he bowed his head and closed his eyes, the ring's heat increased to an almost unbearable intensity. Alaric's heart began beating faster.

"Eldanar, god of my father and forefathers, light in the darkness, steer me this day, show me the true way forward," he whispered into the darkness, his voice a mere thread of sound. "Guide us in ridding my ancestral home of taint and bathe us in your radiance this night."

His words, fervent and sincere, seemed to resonate with the world around him, a plea for guidance in the shadowed thicket of uncertainty. The heat of the ring reached a fevered pitch, burning almost unbearably, to the point where he felt like removing it. Alaric dared not do that.

He heard the others shift, disturbing the leaves that covered the stone, as if suddenly uncomfortable. Alaric opened his eyes and blinked. The ring had begun glowing softly with an otherworldly luminescence that bathed his hand in a ghostly white light.

Rikka stepped forward. "You have been blessed this night, for Eldanar has answered," she whispered, awe coloring her tone. She placed her hand on his shoulder and pointed ahead at the rock, slightly to his right and a foot above the ground. "You have been shown the way."

A previously unseen indent on the rock outcropping had revealed itself. That too was glowing in the same pale light as his hand. His heart pounded in his chest with a mixture of adrenaline, reverence, and awe. Drawn as if by a force beyond his own will, he extended his hand and ring toward the glowing indent. The moment the ring touched the spot, there was a soft click. A heartbeat later, the night was punctured by the muffled sound of mechanisms within the rock outcropping, long dormant, springing to life. It was followed by a heavy, resonant clunk that vibrated through the ground beneath their feet.

The seam of a small doorway revealed itself, then all at once, the glow from the ring and Alaric's hand dissipated, taking with it the mild glowing light from the indent on the rock, leaving them back in darkness.

"That," Jasper said, "was impressive." His voice was barely above a whisper, yet it carried through the sudden silence with the weight of shared astonishment.

"A miracle, my lord," Thorne breathed.

"Holy magic," Kiera said.

"Old magic," Rikka said.

Ezran did not speak.

Alaric stood and stooped down to place his hands against the cold, unyielding surface of the stone, then pushed where the outline of the door was located. At first, the stone resisted him, refusing to give. Alaric's determination did not waver; his push became a concerted effort, muscles straining powerfully as he increased the force against the door.

Yet it did not budge. Alaric pushed harder, with more force, and then, almost imperceptibly at first, there was movement—a slight yielding that escalated into a low, grating sound of protest from hinges hidden from view for generations. The sound, discordant—metal grinding against metal and stone—seemed almost sacrilegious amidst the night's silence. Alaric, gritting his teeth, pushed against the weight of history and disuse, a resistance that tested both his physical strength and resolve.

The sudden rush of cold, stale air that burst forth from the newly opened passage was like the exhalation of the depths itself—a breath held in for far too long, laden with secrets and the dust and musk of ages. The darkness that spilled out from the opening was a dense entity, an invitation and a challenge all at once.

Thorne joined Alaric, throwing his shoulder into it. Together, grunting, they pushed against the stone door, their combined strength gradually overcoming the resistance until the pathway was opened wide enough to grant passage. They stepped back, their chests heaving from the effort. The doorway now stood ajar, an invitation into the depths of the world, a gateway to mysteries long hidden from view.

"Do you think they heard anything?" Alaric asked, glancing in the direction of the wall, which wasn't that far off. He could see nothing through the trees and darkness, not even the light of a torch or lantern. He could not hear the sound of an alarm bell either.

"I doubt it," Ezran said quietly. "The forest about us will have muffled the sound. At least, it should, and it wasn't all that loud to begin with. It only seemed so."

"Things always seem louder at night when you are trying to be stealthy," Kiera said.

Alaric gave a nod then signaled Kiera, the bearer of their

torch, gesturing toward the opening. She moved forward and, ducking her head, stepped into the darkness of the tunnel, her silhouette merging with the shadows as she approached the threshold of the unknown, and knelt. There was a rough scraping sound, a spark of light, hidden by her body, momentarily illuminating her frame within the bolt-hole's entrance.

Another scrape, then a strong hissing as light flared and the torch lit, revealing a tunnel that led downward at a steep angle into the ground. The tunnel beckoned them with its ancient, unspoken secrets. It was a path not taken by many, a passage through time as much as space.

Alaric stepped over the threshold and past her as she stood holding the torch up to see the way ahead. The tunnel was reminiscent of the mines he'd seen in the holy land, with its rough-hewn walls and the claustrophobic closeness of its ceiling. The air was thick with the scent of dampness and decay, a musty reminder of the tunnel's age and disuse.

Off in the distance, the dripping of water played a haunting melody that echoed off the stone walls. This sound, intertwined with the faint rustling of their movements, created an echo. Alaric motioned the others inside. They brushed past him.

Behind the door, he spotted a thick, rusted iron handle. With the last of their party safely within the secret passageway, the urgency of sealing their entrance from the outside world became Alaric's immediate focus. He gripped the handle firmly. With the hinges loosened, the door's closure was much easier. It was marked by a grating squeal, echoing more loudly through the tunnel's confines before settling with a definitive *thunk* and a reassuring, heavy click of the lock. They were now isolated from the world above, enveloped in the tunnel's ancient and cold embrace, with the hissing and spitting torch their only light.

The air within was thick with the dust of ages and the scent of neglect and abandonment. Taking the torch from Kiera, Alaric assumed his role as leader, guiding his companions deeper into the tunnel. Their footsteps, amplified by the narrow confines of the walls, created a rhythmic and echoing cadence.

The angled tunnel, though steep, was not an impossible grade, the hissing torch illuminating the way ahead. Pickaxe and chisel marks from those who had dug the tunnel were plain. In places along the ceiling, there were also dark soot and scorch marks, from when the rock had been intentionally heated before being quenched with cold water. Such a practice caused the rock to break and crack, making tunneling easier. Alaric also spotted a couple ventilation shafts and niches for tools. He had seen such things before in mines.

After five hundred yards, the path forked, offering them a choice between veils of darkness, one to the left and the other to the right. Alaric knew the two passages led to different parts of the castle. The one he wanted led to the bottom levels, where they were unlikely to find anyone. The other traveled to the kitchens. Alaric did not want to go there, for the possibility of encountering someone was high. He took the right fork. His father and grandfather had made a point of showing him both.

The tunnel's downward grade soon gave way to a level path and, after a short distance, ended at a narrow stone staircase leading upward. He turned to the others and held a finger up. They nodded and froze.

At the bottom of the staircase, Alaric listened, straining his ears. He heard nothing coming from above. Satisfied, he motioned for the others to follow and began climbing the steps. There were more than two dozen. The staircase terminated at a heavy wooden trapdoor, an unassuming barrier between them and the world above.

From the other side, it was designed to look like a simple drainage grate. Above the wood, there were iron grates. Alaric knew the trapdoor opened into a storeroom, one that had been disused and seemingly forgotten the last time he'd been home. That was intentional.

The iron ring nailed into the door's underside was cold and heavy in Alaric's grasp. He handed the torch to Kiera. The flickering light cast ominous shadows on the walls, the soft hiss of the flame punctuating the silence.

With a firm grip on the ring, Alaric pushed upward, the trapdoor's hinges protesting with a painful creak that seemed loud in the stillness. The sound could easily betray their presence. Despite its initial resistance, the door yielded surprisingly easily, rapidly swinging open.

Alaric climbed up, cautious and careful, his senses heightened as he scanned the storage room—a dimly remembered location from his childhood explorations. The room was small and the door to it, as expected, closed.

As Kiera climbed out next, the torch lighting the room, Alaric listened intently for any sign of movement or hint of alarm beyond the door. The absence of sound was a tentative assurance, yet the tension of potential discovery lingered like a specter.

Drawing his sword with a soft rasp of steel, he approached the door leading out of the storage room as the others emerged from the trapdoor, one after another. Rikka was the last to join them, her presence completing their number.

Alaric pressed his ear against the cold wood of the door, seeking any whisper—any breath of danger that might lurk beyond. The silence that greeted him was a cautious ally and, he thought, encouraging.

"We must move quickly," he said, turning to the others. "It will be light soon."

Ezran had one of his throwing daggers in hand, while Thorne had drawn his sword, a long, narrow, and lethal blade. Kiera and Jasper, too, had armed themselves with daggers, their expressions set in determination. Their swords remained sheathed. Only

Rikka was unarmed, though Alaric could not say she was defenseless.

With a cautious push and slight squeaking, Alaric opened the door, the darkness of the hallway swallowing them as they stepped out from the relative safety of the storage room. The under levels of the castle lay in oppressive silence, dark and foreboding. This was a different realm, one of secrets and shadows, where every sound became magnified and the silence was heavy with anticipation. Kiera joined him with the torch, providing some illumination that pushed back against the inky darkness.

Turning right, Alaric led his group down the hallway, their footsteps echoing softly, their presence a ghostly intrusion in the night. The long corridor was flanked on either side by doors, each of which was closed, holding its own secrets. At the end of the corridor, a spiraling staircase wound its way up into the heart of the keep and the upper levels. Only one door stood open, and that was just before the stairs. It led to the castle's dungeon, a dismal place of suffering, and one he avoided as a child. It was where the criminals were kept.

He moved down the hallway, pausing before the open door and looking in, searching for a threat. He was greeted with a sight of despair and suffering. The dim light from a solitary lantern hanging from the ceiling threw elongated shadows across the floor, barely illuminating the three large iron cages that lined the wall. Each was filled with people. Inside the room on the left and right were two more doors, both of which were closed. Alaric did not recall where those led but supposed it was to additional cages and holding pens for prisoners.

As Alaric, with Kiera at his side, stepped closer and into the room, the figures within the cells began to stir as if coming to life, their movements slow and laden with the weight of their captivity as they sat up or pulled themselves with some effort to their feet. Eyes, sockets hollow and sunken from suffering and hunger, looked out through the bars, their gazes meeting Alaric's with a mixture of hope and fear.

The stench that wafted from the cells was overwhelming, a noxious blend of despair, neglect, and human misery. The prisoners, their bodies emaciated and dirt-encrusted, clothed in rags, were barely recognizable as human. Their condition spoke of prolonged suffering and neglect.

In short, Alaric was certain, Masterson's work.

Alaric moved closer, his heart heavy with the sight before him. These were not just prisoners; they were his subjects, his people. He was horrified.

How had it become this bad?

"Hamlin?" Alaric asked, recognizing one of the men, who rose and stepped up to the cage door. At least he thought he recognized him. The figure before him looked like half the man Alaric had known. "Arms Master Hamlin? Is that you?"

"Alaric?" Hamlin's recognition of Alaric in the dim light of the dungeon was a moment fraught with emotion, the man's disbelief and desperation clear. The arms master, once a robust figure of towering strength, experience, and discipline—a force to be reckoned with—was now a shadow of his former self. He had been one of Alaric's first tutors and a man he greatly respected, one who had achieved his position through hard service and work.

The transformation of the man before him spoke of the ordeal he and the others had endured, and also the passage of ten years. His once dark beard had turned white, and the dirt and grime that now marred his visage could not hide the deep age lines.

While the rest of the prisoners shrank away from the sudden intrusion of light and Alaric's party, Hamlin's approach to the cage door, his hands gripping the bars, told of his enduring spirit. "Is that you, my boy? By Eldanar, my eyes must be deceiving me. This cannot be! I must be dreaming."

"It is I, and you are not dreaming," Alaric affirmed, his voice steady, though his heart ached at the sight of his once great mentor reduced to such dire straits. The dungeon held not just Hamlin, but others known to him, faces from the past, each bearing marks of their captivity, though he could not recall many of their names—members of the castle staff, servants, guards—all now united in their suffering.

"Masterson," Hamlin said, confirming Alaric's suspicion, his voice a raspy whisper of its former command. "The bastard took over."

"I'm here to fix that and make the bastard pay," Alaric stated, a declaration that carried weight and purpose.

"Your mother, she hired him to run the guard, after your father passed." Hamlin glanced down at the ground. "He brought in men I did not like. I—I was helpless to… stop it…" The old man's shoulders shook. A sob escaped him. "I should have stood up to him, challenged him to a duel. I regret that I did not."

Alaric patted the man's arm through the bars. "Do you know where they are holding my mother? Do you know where we can find her?"

"We've been down here an awful long time, but I'd guess her suite, upstairs in the keep," Hamlin said. "She's not in the dungeon. We'd have known. Our jailor, Thensus, would have said something. He would have bragged about it."

"That's true," another man said as he moved up next to Hamlin. Alaric did not know him.

"We need to get moving," Thorne said, "before the sun comes up, my lord. Our men should be across the moat and at the base of the wall by now. They're waiting for us, relying upon us to be there."

Alaric gave a nod. He took a step back and turned away.

"Don't leave us here," someone fairly yelled from behind Hamlin. "Please! Don't leave us."

"Quiet," Rikka hissed angrily. "Don't give us away or we all die."

"I won't leave you." Alaric turned back toward the cages and ran his gaze over those confined. Recognizing he was a friend and not one of their captors, several had overcome their initial trepidation and had stepped up eagerly to the bars. "I've brought the Iron Vanguard home with me. They're outside the castle and waiting for us. We're going to let them in and retake what is ours."

"Free us," Hamlin said, a fierce light igniting in his gaze. "We can fight, my lord, with bare hands if needed. Give us that chance!"

"I—" Alaric's words were cut short by the sudden, jarring sound of a door to the left of the entrance being thrown open. He whirled. A burly figure emerged from the door, his stance unsteady, movements sluggish, betraying what was clearly an inebriated state. His bleary and red eyes struggled to focus as he looked around, squinting as he tried to make sense of the scene before him, of those standing by the nearest cages, people he did not know, people who were armed.

The confusion etched on his face morphed into suspicion as he confronted the intruders who had barged into his domain, his words slurred and disjointed. "Who is you? Whash's going on here?"

The dungeon's stagnant and foul air was suddenly split by a swift, deadly motion—a dagger flying with lethal precision from Ezran's extended hand. It found its mark in the guard's chest with a meaty thump, the impact halting his words. His shock was a frozen mask as he staggered backward and into the room from which he had just stumbled. It was sparsely furnished, a cot and table with a large decanter barely visible in the dim light of the lantern. His collapse onto the cot inside was a cacophony of chaos, a crash as it gave way under his bulk, sending splinters and echoes flying outward.

Ezran was there before Alaric could even move. He jerked the throwing dagger out of the guard's chest as the man made to cry out. Ezran grabbed the man's hair in a firm hold and sawed the serrated edge across his throat. The cry ended in a sickening gurgle. Ezran let go the hair and stood up as the man choked on his own blood and expired.

"That," Hamlin said, "was Thensus, our guard. He was a real bastard of a man. I am glad he's dead. Thank you for that kindness."

There was a murmur of agreement from the others in the cages.

"Kiera," Alaric said, hoping the element of surprise had not been lost. He pointed at the door to the cage holding Hamlin. "Find the keys, free them. The armory should be on the next floor up. Hamlin can show you. Give them weapons and a chance to reclaim their honor, to help retake the castle."

"We won't fail you, my lord," Hamlin said fervently as the others in the cages grumbled their deep agreement.

"As you command." Kiera moved into the room with Thensus's body as Ezran stepped out, clearly intent on searching.

Alaric turned away and retraced his steps into the outer hallway, moving for the stairs that led upward. The spiral staircase loomed before him. He started up, taking the steps rapidly, two at a time. Bloody dagger in hand, Ezran hustled up behind. Thorne and Jasper followed. Rikka was a few steps after. Alaric had one thing on his mind: getting to the wall, and quickly. Once his men were over, he'd find Masterson and kill him.

17

The stairs, shrouded in an eerie silence, wound higher into the heart of the ancient keep, Alaric's childhood home. The stillness enveloped them, an ominous prelude to the unknown. Not a single flicker of light dared to pierce the all-encompassing darkness, save for the lantern that Ezran had taken from a wall mount. It was a lone light pushing against the shadows as they climbed, step by cautious step, bypassing one deserted floor after another.

Upon reaching the main landing on the ground floor, Alaric paused, casting a wary glance along the corridor that stretched out before them, shrouded in mystery and potential hidden threats. Only two oil lanterns along the entire length of the corridor were lit. These provided a meager light.

To the left, a few yards away, lay the entrance to the great hall, its once grandiose splendor now hidden behind the cloak of night. To the right was a closed door that led to the courtyard and, beyond it, the castle walls—their objective.

"That's the exit," Alaric breathed to Ezran. "The lantern will have to be left here."

Ezran nodded and set the lantern on the ground against the wall, leaving it to burn with a ghostly glow set against the cold stone floor. Sword at the ready, Alaric led the way down the hallway toward the exit.

Upon reaching the door at the corridor's end, he lifted the iron latch and, with a gentle push, opened the door, slipping outside and into the cold night. Along the outer defensive walls were several torches that fought back the darkness, their light shifting across the stones. A handful of sentries stood vigil near the torches, their figures casting long, sinister shadows, yet none were close enough to notice them.

Concealed within the deeper shadows, Alaric and his party, with the stealth of the shadows themselves, veered right and navigated around the keep's imposing perimeter to the castle's rear. The sky, a tapestry of the coming dawn, had just begun to shed its night-time hues, heralding the approach of day with subtle strokes of light. Alaric knew they had to hurry.

Finding the staircase they sought at the back wall, the group ascended the dark stairs, climbing rapidly. The staircase led them to the fighting platform above at the top of the wall. Remarkably, they encountered no one; the path was deserted, as if the castle itself held its breath in anticipation of what was coming.

Upon their arrival at the top of the stairs, their footsteps echoed hollowly against the wooden expanse of the platform. This elevated and protected walkway, cloaked under the protective awning of a sturdy roof, served as a sanctuary from the elements and enemy missile fire if it ever came to a siege.

The wall itself stretched out like a sleeping dragon, its spine running for five hundred yards in either direction, a formidable barrier against the threats that lurked beyond the castle's heart. The ancient stones whispered tales of past sieges and silent watchers, bearing the scars of time, the elements, and conflict with stoic resilience.

Thorne, with a subtle urgency, tapped Alaric on the shoulder, his gesture drawing attention to the leftmost reaches of the wall.

There, at the far corner, a lone torch flickered—a flare in the oppressive gloom of the early morning. Beneath its halo of light, two sentries stood in casual conversation, their guard lowered. The torch unwittingly served to blind them to the shadows beyond its reach, a critical oversight in the cloak of night, a serious lapse in discipline.

Alaric's eyes, sharp and calculating, lifted to assess the interplay of light and shadow around them. The roof overhead cast a deep, enveloping shadow, making the platform beneath a realm of near-absolute darkness. In this hidden world, they were mere phantoms, their presence as insubstantial as the whispers of the wind. The realization of their advantage, the perfect cloak provided by the night and the structure itself, almost coaxed a grin from Alaric's lips. Here they were unseen, moving with the freedom of the dark itself.

Alaric, with a predator's grace and the silence of the night cloaked around him, led the way toward their objective, a mere hundred yards to their left and away from the sentries. Each step was measured, his body hunched to better meld with the shadows cast by the roof.

The sentries, bathed in their false sense of security under the torchlight, remained blissfully unaware of the shadowy figures moving with intent along the wall. Alaric, mindful of their gaze, hoped their attention remained tethered to their idle chatter, their eyes dulled by the comforting and warm glow of their torch.

Pausing in his tracks, Alaric straightened up between two battlements. Leaning, he peered over the edge of the wall, looking straight down the other side. Below, hidden within the embrace of night's deepest shadows, were twenty men—his men—who had braved the moat to reach the castle's base. Among them was Grayson, who gave a wave. Alaric waved back as Grayson began moving, leading the others so that he and they were directly under Alaric.

"Here," Alaric said to Jasper and Thorne, his voice barely above a whisper. "This is the spot. Tie the ropes to the battlements and lower them down, quickly now."

His words set them into motion, their movements a blend of urgency and stealth. Under the protective veil of darkness, they fastened the ropes securely to the ancient stone, their hands deft and experienced in the task. The knotted lengths of rope, lifelines to their compatriots, were soon dropping to the ground below. Within moments, they became taut as the first of those waiting with Grayson began to scale the wall.

Throughout this endeavor, Alaric's gaze remained fixed on the distant sentries, his senses honed to any shift in their languid posture or the slightest break in their conversation, which he could not overhear due to the distance. They continued their talk, oblivious to the drama unfolding mere yards away. Alaric held his breath, acutely aware of the razor's edge upon which their fate balanced.

The sudden scuff of movement against the ancient stone momentarily pierced the veil of night's stillness, redirecting Alaric's gaze. As if conjured from the darkness, a figure emerged from the shadows of the other side of the wall. First a head, then an arm, materialized with the quiet determination of a ghost transitioning through the veil between the world of the dead and living.

Thorne and Ezran moved to aid the newcomer, their hands grasping and pulling, helping him over the lip of the wall. The man who emerged onto the platform was Grayson, his tunic soaked and clinging to his skin from crossing the moat, with a sword strapped to his back. His face, masked in charcoal, melded with the darkness.

"I never thought we'd be storming our own keep," Grayson remarked, his voice a low blend of irony and resolve as he crouched beside Alaric in the shadows. Almost in tandem with his words, another man came over the wall, Thorne and Ezran helping him.

"Neither did I," Alaric responded, the weight of his words reflecting the gravity of their situation. He turned to Grayson, a silent question in his eyes. "Think you can handle things from here?"

"I do," came Grayson's reply.

"Good. We're going to free my mother. As soon as you have enough men over the wall, go for the gate and, as planned, open it," Alaric instructed.

"I will." The resolve in Grayson's voice was matched by the firmness of his grip on Alaric's shoulder, a gesture of solidarity and concern. "Be careful, and good fortune."

"Always," Alaric replied with the terse assurance of a man who had long made peace with the peril that shadowed his every step. With a determined gesture, he beckoned Ezran, Thorne, Jasper, and Rikka to his side. "Let's go."

Together, they retraced their steps with a swiftness born of necessity, each a shadow flitting through the darkness. Alaric spared a fleeting glance toward the sentries, noting with a mix of relief and satisfaction that they remained engrossed in their conversation, blissfully unaware of the storm quietly brewing under their watch.

With not a moment wasted on further observation, Alaric led his companions back down the staircase, their descent swift. Circling back around to the side entrance of the keep, he found the door as they had left it, ajar and inviting. The lantern Ezran had set down was still there, a few yards inside the entrance and sitting against the wall, its light dim and low. As they stepped into the keep's shadowy embrace, the stillness that greeted them was profound.

The corridor stretched before them, a veiled path leading toward the great hall. Alaric started moving down it. As they approached the hall, the soft, rhythmic sounds of snoring drifted to their ears, a discordant lullaby. Slowing their advance, Alaric paused at the corridor's end, caution tempering his momentum. Peering around the corner, he looked into and surveyed the hall.

Before the dying embers of the hearth, two men lay in a state of unguarded repose, sprawled across benches and overtaken with sleep. The low, flickering light of the fire from the main hearth cast long shadows across the hall, painting a scene of peace.

Alaric leaned back and gestured, pointing two fingers to his eyes. That was all it took to be understood by his companions. As Alaric's gaze swept across the hall once more, the weight of memories, both bitter and sweet, pressed upon him. The hall, a custodian of his family's legacy, stood much as he remembered it —dozens of tables arranged in orderly rows for feasts and councils of days long past. The walls, adorned with old standards and trophies, spoke of valor and the victories of his ancestors, his family's history. Large iron candelabras and the imposing silhouettes of chandeliers loomed in the darkness, their candles unlit, as if in mourning for the splendor and life that had once filled the space.

The pang of sadness that gripped Alaric as he spied his father's chair at the head table was unexpected, a sharp reminder of unhealed wounds and lost opportunities, ones he'd never have back. Part of him had harbored the hope of reconciliation, of bridging the chasm that had grown between them with time and misunderstandings. Now, with that possibility forever out of reach, the weight of what could have been pressing down upon his heart.

Directly across from him were a set of stairs. Those were the ones he wanted, for they led higher up and into the keep, to the personal quarters. With a resolve forged from necessity and the urgency of their mission, Alaric steeled himself against the tide of emotions threatening to undermine his focus. He stepped out into the great hall and moved across it, a spectral figure against the backdrop of history and heritage within these stone walls. His companions, shadows in his wake, followed with equal care.

The sleeping enemy, Masterson's men, lost to the world in their slumber, remained snoring and oblivious to their presence.

Ascending the staircase, Alaric and his companions embarked on a climb that was as much a journey through the corridors of his memory as it was a physical ascent within the stone heart of the keep. The staircase appeared to stretch endlessly into the shadows above, each flight a step closer to the past that Alaric had left behind and the future he hoped to claim.

Three flights they conquered in near silence, the only sound the muffled echo of their footsteps until they reached the fourth and highest level—a sanctum of private lives and personal histories, where the echoes of his family's existence still lingered on the air like ghosts of the past.

The corridor into which they emerged was hauntingly familiar to Alaric, a pathway lined with doors that held within them the remnants of his childhood, his upbringing, and the many lives that had intertwined with his own, the servants'. Near the middle of this corridor, guarding the threshold to his parents' quarters, sat a lone figure. He was slumped in a chair—also lost to the grip of sleep.

With the urgency of their mission renewed by the proximity to his goal, Alaric advanced. The distance between them closed rapidly, the element of surprise firmly on his side. However, fate, with its capricious twist, intervened—a muffled cry shattered the silence, followed by the piercing clamor of an alarm bell being rung desperately somewhere in the distance. An agonized scream sounded. Alaric thought it might have come from somewhere in the keep.

Startled from his slumber, the guard snorted and jolted awake, his disorientation lasting only a moment before the grim reality of his situation became clear as he turned his head toward death, eyes going wide. Alaric was upon him and drove his sword, Oathbreaker, into the man's chest, blade diving between ribs. He forced it in, deep, even as the man made to stand. Then the blade pierced the heart, rupturing it, and the guard let go a breath and collapsed in a heap, the chair toppling in his wake with a crash.

Placing a foot upon the man's chest, Alaric withdrew his blade. The air behind him was split by a heavy thud. Turning, he witnessed Thorne delivering a formidable kick to the heavy oak door of his parents' quarters. A scream from within pierced the tumult, a harrowing sound that spoke of fear and confusion. Another determined kick from Thorne and the door yielded, its lock cracking and breaking under the assault. The two doors violently swung inward with a resounding crash.

Light from the corridor flooded into the darkened room beyond. In the bed, a woman was sitting up, clearly startled from her slumber into a world turned abruptly chaotic, fear and confusion plain upon her face. The disarray of her silvered hair and the protective clutch of the blanket around her spoke of her vulnerability in that moment of alarm. Yet it was the wildness in her eyes, a primal response to the unexpected, that captured the essence of the scene—raw human emotion laid bare.

Alaric, standing on the threshold of the room, the harbinger of the upheaval that had shattered the night's peace, found himself overwhelmed by a surge of emotions. The sight of his mother, alive and before him after all the trials and tribulations that had led to this moment, ignited a flame of relief so intense, it manifested as a grin, an incongruous expression amidst the tension of their circumstances.

"Mother, I'm home," he announced.

Under the dim illumination that invaded the room, his mother's recognition was hesitant, her voice tinged with disbelief as her eyes narrowed. "Alaric?" she queried, as if saying his name could conjure the reality of his presence from the shadows of doubt.

"None other," he affirmed, his response lightened with an extravagant bow.

Behind him, shouts filled the air, a cacophony of urgency and alarm. Feet were pounding on the stairs, climbing, coming for them. Thorne, Ezran, and Jasper were already moving in that direction.

"Who the bloody fuck are you?" The abrupt challenge, a crude bellow, tore through the tense air. Alaric spun around to confront the new threat, his posture instinctively shifting to one of readiness. Three men had reached the top of the stairs. Their advance, however, faltered at the sight that greeted them—their comrade fallen, a growing pool of blood around the body, and Alaric's party, of which Jasper, Ezran, and Thorne were facing them, swords drawn with grim looks.

Rikka, with a gesture of her hand, whispered an incantation, her voice a soft thread on the air. The words passed from hearing and memory instantly, like water through one's open fingers. From her outstretched hand, a dart of light surged forth with unerring precision, striking the man who'd spoken in the center of his chest. He collapsed, a puppet severed from its strings, the shock of his abrupt downfall sowing a momentary hesitation among his comrades, who, in sudden uncertainty, took a step back in unison.

This hesitation was all the opening that Thorne and Jasper needed. They launched themselves into the attack with a ferocity born of necessity and the understanding that hesitation was a luxury that could ill be afforded.

The man on the left, his reactions a beat too slow against the seasoned warrior he faced, managed a block. Thorne easily circumvented this defense with a speed that bordered on the unnatural. His blade edge, a flash of silver in the dim lamplight, twisted around and found its mark on the sword arm of his adversary. The impact was swift, merciless, a surgical strike that severed the man's ability to fight as effectively as it cut through flesh and tendons of the arm. His opponent's sword was dropped by nerveless fingers. The sound of it hitting the floor, a metallic lament, was quickly overshadowed by the man's scream, a raw expression of pain and shock as he looked down upon his ruined arm.

Jasper, with a powerful strike, easily batted his opponent's sword away. Fear plain in his eyes, the man took a step back toward the stairs. Jasper followed up with a powerful kick that landed squarely to the chest—sending the man reeling backward with such force that he disappeared down the stairs, his retreat marked by the tumultuous echo of his fall and a scream.

Thorne stabbed the disarmed man in the chest. He fell to the floor and gasped in pure agony. Thorne yanked his blade out and stabbed downward, opening the man's throat and ending him.

There were more shouts within the keep. Jasper and Thorne stepped to the edge of the stairs and looked down. At the same time, Alaric's attention was snatched by a peripheral flicker of motion. Ezran was turning as well, his scimitar held at the ready. A new threat emerged from the other side of the hallway.

Alaric found himself confronted with the sight of five more men advancing toward them. Behind him, in the direction of the stairs, there was more shouting, and he had a glimpse of both Jasper and Thorne starting down the stairs, charging toward the threat from that direction.

"Who are you?" one of the men in the center demanded as he stopped several feet from Alaric and Ezran.

"Didn't we just get asked that?" Ezran asked Alaric.

"You know who I am." Sword held ready, Alaric moved up to Ezran's side. He recognized the bushy mustache. He pointed his sword at the man. "And you are in my home."

Masterson's eyes narrowed under the low light as he understood who he now faced.

"Am I?" the other man asked with a mocking laugh. "What are you going to do about it?"

"You are trespassing, Masterson," Alaric said. His enemy was dressed only in a tunic. His feet were bare as he stood on the cold stone. Alaric looked at the other four men. They were similarly attired and had clearly been awoken from a cold sleep. "My company is even now breaking into the castle. It's over. Drop your weapons and surrender."

"So that you might hang me?" Masterson asked, his tone mocking. "Or torture me and my men? I think not."

The men flanking Masterson stiffened as realization of what they faced hammered home, the consequences of their actions. They glanced uncertainly amongst themselves.

"Kill him," Alaric's mother ordered as she emerged from her room clothed in a nightdress. "Kill him for all he's done to me and Dekar… to our family and people."

Alaric glanced over at his mother. She stood somewhat smaller than he by a head. She was older and frailer than when he'd last seen her. She even seemed gaunt with hunger. His heart hardened with that.

"Shut up, Elara," Masterson said. "When I am done with your son, I will tend to you as I should have from the start."

Alaric's resolve crystallized in the heat of the moment, his patience worn thin by the weight of the stakes before him and what this man had done. Deciding to take the head from the snake, he launched himself at Masterson. Almost instinctively, Masterson took several steps back, retreating and placing his own men between himself and danger.

Alaric, with a warrior's focus, shifted his attack, singling out an opponent. The man, surprised by the sudden attack, was clumsy, and his sword was easily forced aside. Before that man could recover, Alaric was stabbing down into his extended left leg, delivering a crippling blow. He fell as the leg gave out, dropping his weapon.

Alaric saw a blade jabbing out for him. It flashed under the dim light. He jumped to the left, and the sword point only met air. Alaric took a step back as Masterson advanced, following up the strike, stepping over his injured man, who was rocking on the floor in agony and gripping his leg, even as he bled fatally out.

"Kill them!" Masterson roared to the other men with him.

Behind Alaric, the sound of battle rang out on the stairs, the clash of swords a grim backdrop to the fight he and Ezran now faced. Jasper and Thorne were each engaged in their own struggles.

With the ancient stones of the keep echoing the clash of steel, Alaric found himself on the receiving end of Masterson's aggressive onslaught. Two of the men with Masterson started forward, both attacking Ezran, while the other two hesitated, even taking a step backward. Ezran, locked in his own dance of death, faced his two opponents with a measure of skill that made their fight a perilous ballet of rapid strikes and parries.

Behind Alaric, the sounds of battle intensified. It was punctuated by screams and much shouting. Yet, for Alaric, there was no opportunity to glance backward, no moment to spare for concern beyond the immediate threat that Masterson posed. Each jab and strike from Masterson was met with a desperate parry, Alaric's focus narrowed to the singular task of survival.

Masterson, emboldened by his initial success, pressed his advantage with a ferocity that forced Alaric off-balance and into a defensive posture. But Alaric soon found his rhythm, his defense solidifying into a wall that Masterson could not penetrate. Alaric could easily read the frustration in the other's eyes. Then, he launched a counterattack. With a series of swift, precise blows, he turned the tide, his offensive a storm unleashed upon his enemy, the man who thought to usurp his home. The momentum shifted, with his enemy now the one retreating under the weight of the attack, one grudging step, then another.

There was a snap, a flash of light, and a crack. Alaric had a glimpse of one of the men engaging Ezran being flung violently to the ground, his sword clattering away and down the hallway. Surprised, Masterson glanced away from Alaric.

That was a mistake.

"Bastard," Masterson hissed venomously, recoiling as Alaric, with the precision of a seasoned fighter, managed a small yet deliberate nick on the other man's forearm.

Masterson danced back several paces and gazed down at the thin line of blood that began its journey from the shallow cut, tracing a red path along his skin.

"Bastard," Masterson repeated, the word laced with a blend of hatred and begrudging respect as he turned his gaze back to Alaric.

"I've been called worse," Alaric responded, tone steady and unnervingly calm. His eyes, sharp and focused, never left his enemy, betraying none of the fatigue that clung to his limbs from lack of sleep and the effort of the fight.

In the background, the repeated clang and clash of steel and the shouts of combatants filled the air. The man Ezran was locked in combat with gave a strangled cry, a sound of despair and finality, his belly cut wide open, entrails spilling out. His body hit the ground with a thud that echoed ominously, signaling the end of his fight, not to mention his life.

Behind them, the tumult of the battle on the stairs dwindled as yet another scream rang out. Then there was silence, except for the muffled sounds of fighting off in the distance. The last two men standing with Masterson, the two who had not come forward to fight, witnessing the tide of battle turn, made a split-second decision. Their courage failing, they both turned and ran, their footsteps echoing off the walls.

Masterson watched them go, his expression morphing into one of utter disgust mixed with bitterness. The abandonment by his allies seemed to carve deeper wounds than any blade could inflict. With a heavy sigh, masked by the sound of his labored breathing from the fight, he faced Alaric, the resolve in his stance unwavering even as the inevitability of his situation dawned upon him.

"Surrender," Alaric said, his voice clear and authoritative. It was not a request, but a command.

"Never," Masterson declared with a defiance that belied the vulnerability of his position, his words forced through clenched teeth as he inched another step backward. The blood continued to run down his arm, dripping to splash upon the stone floor. "I'd rather die by the sword blade than by the hangman's noose."

"That can be arranged," Alaric replied, a chilling promise hanging in the air between them. He advanced a step. Masterson retreated once more, his movements hesitant, the sword he held a faltering extension of his dwindling resolve. The steel of his gaze, once sharp and unyielding, wavered, a crack in the armor of his defiance.

"What if I tell you who sent me... who gave me my orders?" Masterson ventured, desperation creeping into his voice. "Will that matter? On your honor as a noble, will you let me go, free me to go my own way?" His eyes searched Alaric's for a sign of concession, of mercy, a lifeline in the dire straits in which he found himself. "I will disappear, and you will never see me again."

Alaric's advance halted as he contemplated the proposition. His gaze, penetrating and calculating, studied Masterson with a new intensity. This moment of hesitation was not born of uncertainty, but of strategy, weighing the value of the information against the principle of justice. He thought of what the man had done to his mother, Hamlin, and Dekar. Masterson was but a pawn, a fact now crystal clear and unassailable, sent to enact the will of another, a puppet whose strings were pulled by hands shrouded in shadows.

But what was the endgame? To destabilize Dekar? To sow discord and weakness? To strike at the heart of his family's legacy? To take the land that was Alaric's ancestral right? He pondered this and more, mind racing through the possibilities. His father, the leader of their house, had always been a focus for envy and animosity amongst their peers. The identity of the mastermind, a rival noble or perhaps an unknown adversary or a foreign threat, was a puzzle yet to be solved, one Alaric desperately wanted. He needed to know the game being played and his ultimate opponent.

"No," Masterson abruptly declared before Alaric could articulate his thoughts, his voice suddenly resolute. "Were you to let me live, I would not survive long, even if I went into hiding. My employer would see to that. He would find me, hunt me down. Besides, he would make my family pay first, and I can't have that. No, on second thought, I will not tell you anything. Death is my only escape, my only true choice."

In this declaration, there was a grim acceptance, a surrender, not to Alaric, but to the inevitable fate that awaited him beyond the confines of this confrontation. Masterson's resolve hardened as his eyes narrowed, crystallizing in the fatalistic understanding of his doomed fate, regardless of the outcome of their duel.

With a deliberate step backward, a step that carried the weight of a final decision, Masterson dropped his sword. The blade hit the stone floor in an echoing clatter. In one swift, fluid motion, he drew his dagger from his belt and, without hesitation, plunged it into his own belly. The action was shockingly swift.

Alaric was taken aback by the suddenness of Masterson's self-inflicted wound. He had never seen anything like it, never seen anyone do that. He shared a look of disbelief with Ezran, their eyes locking in an exchange of astonishment.

Blood, dark and relentless, flowed from the terrible wound Masterson had inflicted upon himself, spilling out and painting the ancient stones beneath him in unforgiving crimson. Masterson doubled over, grunting in agony as he fell to his knees, a grimace of pain etched upon his face as his lifeblood continued to spill out.

After a moment, with an effort that seemed superhuman, Masterson looked up at Alaric. Sweat beaded his brow. It ran down his face, mingling with the blood that frothed at his mouth, a grotesque smile revealing rotten teeth stained red. The dagger, still embedded in his body, became an instrument of further torment as he twisted the hilt, inflicting horrendous damage upon himself, a final act of defiance and control over his own fate.

"At last," Masterson breathed softly to himself. "I am free."

He twitched from the agony he had visited upon himself, a visceral reaction to the unbearable pain, before pulling the dagger out with a final act of will. He tossed it away. The weapon clattered across the floor, stopping at Alaric's feet.

A scream pierced the heavy air behind them, an interruption to the grim scene unfolding between Alaric and the dying Masterson. The tension momentarily shifted, eyes darting toward the source of the disturbance, but it was quickly resolved as Thorne's voice cut through the uncertainty. "It's clear," he shouted from somewhere out of view on the stairs below, a declaration that the immediate threat had been neutralized, that their position was, for the moment, secure.

Masterson, his strength visibly waning as his lifeblood continued its relentless escape, pooling on the floor around him, attempted to speak again, his voice a hoarse whisper, strained with pain and the effort to impart something of significance. "I—

go to my—death—with the know—knowledge you need…" The words trailed off, an incomplete confession, a tantalizing hint at secrets unshared. The effort to continue proved too much, the pain overwhelming, silencing him with its brutal finality. Trembling, he rocked, caught in the throes of agony, his breathing heavy and labored, a man on the precipice of death yet burdened with untold truths, ones Alaric desperately wanted and needed.

"My lord," came another voice, this time from Grayson, calling from somewhere on the stairs below. "We have the gate and it's open. The company is inside the walls!" This news carried with it the weight of victory, of a battle turning decisively in their favor. The castle would soon be theirs, and more importantly, his mother was safe.

Alaric, absorbing the significance of these developments, turned back to Masterson. Despite the gravity of the moment, a sense of inevitability settled over him, the knowledge that their victory was near, that their efforts had not been in vain.

"You've lost," Alaric stated, a simple declaration of fact.

"I have, but not my master," Masterson managed to articulate in a low, strangled voice. "You will not—cannot—beat—him."

Masterson's body wavered, barely maintaining its kneel; yet even in these final moments, his spirit fought on, a gruesome grin etched on his face as bloody spittle drooled from his mouth. It was a sight that stirred a complex whirl of emotions in Alaric, an acknowledgment of the end drawing near. He lowered the point of his sword to the floor, an unspoken declaration that the justice to be meted out would not be by his hand, not this time. For all the crimes this man had committed, he was to be left to suffer his final moments in agony and defeat. Alaric would not speed him on his way. He did not deserve such a kindness.

A hand, swift and determined, snatched the dagger from Alaric's belt. As it was yanked out, his mother rushed past him. Before he could react, she had already plunged the dagger deep into the side of Masterson's neck. The man stiffened, a look of shock fleeting across his face as he looked up at his new tormentor. Elara mercilessly grabbed his hair tightly in a fist, pulling his head back to expose his throat. With deliberate care and a grimace, she slowly opened his neck from one side to the other, a final act of retribution. Blood flowed and sprayed outward, painting her white nightgown in crimson.

"That is for what you did to me and our people," Elara declared, her voice a cold echo of finality as Masterson's eyes rolled back, his life extinguished by her hands. With a rough toss, she discarded him like a piece of refuse, his body hitting the stone floor with a decisiveness that underscored her contempt. A spit upon his corpse was her last insult.

Then, turning to face Alaric, she regarded her son with an intensity that bridged the gap between them, a silent conversation passing in the space of a look. The look spoke of justice done. Her nod was more than an acknowledgment; it was a conclusion to an internal debate, a decision made and acted upon. Dropping the bloodied dagger, she turned away, her movements resonating a resolve as steadfast as the blade she had wielded.

"I am going to change," she stated. With that, she entered her chamber and closed both doors, which had been broken open by Thorne. The lock would need repairing, for they refused to completely close.

"I like her," Rikka's voice cut through the heavy atmosphere. The lumina gave a nod. "Oh yes, I like your mother very much."

Ezran placed the point of his saber upon the stone floor with a heavy click. "Now I understand."

"Understand what?" Alaric asked, looking over.

Ezran glanced at the two closed doors. "What I just witnessed explains a lot about you. I thought you had gotten your drive and passion from your father, but now I know it came from your mother, especially that killer instinct of yours. That is something I have always admired."

Alaric felt a scowl forming as he looked up the hallway in the direction Masterson had come and the two men had fled, his thoughts briefly diverted to the awaiting concerns. With the gate secured and their forces sweeping through the castle, victory was imminent, yet the necessity of vigilance remained paramount. Some of the enemy were bound to hide, especially since there was nowhere to run. The faint sounds of distant fighting and shouts served as a reminder of the ongoing struggle, even as confidence in their eventual triumph remained unshaken.

The hallway, with its familiar doors and haunting memories, especially that of his sister's room, served as a poignant reminder of what had been lost, of the family and his childhood that had once filled these spaces with life and laughter.

Jasper and Thorne had come back up the stairs. Swords, arms, chests, and faces splattered with the enemy's blood, they looked grimly upon him and waited. Alaric understood that a new chapter was about to be written, not only for Dragon Bone's Rest, but also Dekar. Though he'd thought to have put his sword away, the killing was far from done, his job far from finished.

"Check the other rooms on this floor," Alaric ordered. "Make sure no one is lying in wait."

Without question, they moved past him to carry out his orders. Alaric was left with Rikka and the bodies of the fallen, along with the overturned chair. He glanced over at her. She looked exhausted, weary, and spent. Was that the result of using her magic? Rikka's eyes were deep, captivating, and Alaric found a strong stirring of desire within him. Though they spent their nights together, he still knew so very little about her, but like a moth to a flame, he was drawn to her, captivated in a way he could not easily explain. Oddly, the ring on his finger began to warm with his thoughts.

Alaric forced his gaze away and to the blood-drenched and body-strewn corridor. The triumph of reclaiming his home was bittersweet, tinged with the loss of his father and the heavy mantle of responsibility that now rested squarely upon his shoulders. Today's victory was not just a reclaiming of stone and mortar, but the start of reclaiming his legacy, his ancestral right—by a sword's edge.

There was work to be done. He understood he could not rest after this, not for long. For Dekar, overrun with bandits and raiders, was far from safe. More importantly, someone meant his family ill. Of that, there was no longer any doubt. He had to find out who, and fast.

"You are now truly the Earl of Dekar," Rikka breathed, drawing his attention once more. She took a step closer to him, her gaze seeming to grow more intense. "Destiny brought us together, destiny has its stamp upon you, destiny is the path you walk—Child of the Ordinate and last true heir of the empire."

Alaric looked over at her sharply. He considered her for several long moments. The Ordinate and his ties to it were not something he wished to discuss, not now, not ever. "The empire no longer exists. It collapsed and is done."

"You are heir nonetheless, heir to the Obsidian Throne," Rikka said fiercely. "You know that to be true. It is why you and I were brought together."

Alaric almost felt sick to his stomach. "You are my lumina? The heir's lumina? Is that it? That is what you are telling me?"

She gave a slow nod. "I was led to you, Alaric of Dekar. As Eldanar wills, so has it been done."

"And what of the other gods?" Alaric asked. "The Ordinate honored many. There was once tolerance, acceptance, or so the histories say, before the Great Rift and Crusade."

She gave a shrug. "I worship only one god. It is he to whom I answer and respond."

Alaric rubbed his jaw as he continued to regard her. He shook his head sadly. "The killing will never end, will it?"

"Not until the coming of the Second Ordinate, not until you ascend the throne that is rightfully yours."

"No," Alaric said with a firm shake of his head. "That is not my destiny, not my torch to bear. I will not raise that banner, not now, not ever."

With a fierce look, her hand went to her belly. "Then, Lord Alaric, it will be your child's destiny."

18

"Mother," Alaric greeted, his voice echoing slightly as he crossed the threshold of the great hall. He stepped past two guardsmen standing just inside the doorway, both his men, and worked his way around the tables to the hearth at the back of the hall. Alaric himself bore the marks of battle, bruises, scrapes, and slight cuts on his arms, legs, neck, and face, yet now presented a cleansed visage, having washed away the vestiges of the fight earlier in the day. He'd even managed to grab some sleep and felt moderately rested.

Despite the warmth radiated by the roaring hearth, a pervasive chill lingered within the cavernous space, seeping into the very stones of the hall. Enveloped in a heavy gray woolen blanket that seemed to swallow her diminutive form, his mother occupied a chair of ancient make, positioned close to the fire.

The fire's flickering light cast dancing shadows across Elara's features, momentarily dispelling the weight of years and worry that lined her face. The hall, vast and echoing with the memories of countless gatherings, felt desolately empty. The only other soul present was Ezran, who halted at the entrance with the guards, his presence unobtrusive yet vigilant.

Alaric grabbed a stool, its legs scraping softly against the stone floor, and positioned himself beside his mother. Since she had not spoken in reply, he joined her in companionable contemplation of the fire, which crackled and occasionally popped loudly, the only source of sound in the otherwise oppressive silence. The moment stretched on, until the amplified quiet felt almost tangible.

That silence between them was a reflective pool, deep and still, allowing unspoken thoughts and emotions to swirl beneath its surface. In this sanctuary of stone and shadow, mother and son sat together, united not just by blood, but by the unyielding bonds of survival and the understanding that only those who have faced the precipice together can truly know.

Elara's voice finally broke the stillness, her words weaving through the air like a delicate yet somber melody. "I wrote you multiple letters." A faint tremor of her chin betrayed the steadfast calm of her demeanor. "You did not come. I would know why."

"I never got them," he confessed, his voice a low rumble, akin to distant thunder. "Had I received your summons, you know I would have returned sooner and on the fastest ship I could have found."

She did not reply to that and the air between them thickened with unvoiced thoughts, the silence once again descending like a shroud, heavy and impenetrable.

Alaric exhaled deeply, the weight of his next words pressing down upon him. "The Crusade is lost, the Cardinal King done," he admitted, the defeat resonating in his voice. It was a fact he had come to terms with, and yet he still had unresolved feelings rooted in guilt. "I brought less than half of my people home, and then some, warriors we picked up and adopted as our own, commoners too, families made, some sundered, refugees, skilled craftsmen who did not want to see the enemy rule over them."

Alaric paused. "I left too many behind… those who fell in service of a lost cause."

Elara's response was a sorrowful shake of her head.

"How did he die?" Alaric broached the subject that lay like a shadow between them. His voice, though steady, was laced with a pain that had not yet found its full expression.

"Your father?" Elara's voice was a whisper, barely audible above the crackle of the fire.

"Yes, I'd like to know how he died."

A profound sadness enveloped her; the plain sorrow in her eyes was as tangible as the cold that gripped the hall. She diverted her gaze back to the fire, its light painting her face with hues of orange and gold.

"It came on sudden," she began, voice steady but laced with grief. "He grew sick and died two days later. The doctor said it was an inflammation of the bowels—a bad spirit had wormed its way into him." She paused, her eyes distant. "Priests were called, but by then, there was nothing to be done." Her voice broke on the last words, a fragile whisper lost to the crackling of the flames. "One moment, he was strong and healthy; the next, he was gone." She shook her head slowly as she sucked in a breath that shuddered. "My great love was gone… leaving me behind and alone."

Alaric's gaze dropped, settling on the hands clasped tightly in his lap—sadness and regret churning within. The revelation of his father's mortality, the man who had been an immovable force in his early life, stirred a whirlwind of emotions. His father had been a bastion of strength and resilience, an indomitable presence that shaped the very foundations of his world. Tough, demanding, and seemingly invincible—that his father was dead still in a way did not seem quite real.

"For a long time, I resented him for sending me away," Alaric confided, his voice a soft murmur against the backdrop of the fire's lively crackle. "I hated him for that."

"I know. We had no choice."

"But at the same time, I owe him a great deal," Alaric continued, the words pulled from a place of deep reflection. "I would not be the man I am today without him. It took me years away from home to realize that."

Elara's gaze met his, her eyes shimmering with unshed tears reflected by the dancing firelight. "He loved you. It was painful for him to send you away, painful for us both, but the king ordered it done. He specifically asked for Dekar's best for the Crusade, and your father sent you."

"I was the firstborn and of age," Alaric said, acknowledging the burden and expectation that came with his birthright. "With no brothers and sisters to speak of."

"I bore your father six children. You were the only one that survived," Elara revealed, her voice a delicate thread of sorrow. The magnitude of her loss, the depth of her resilience, was laid bare in those few words. "I thought your sister would live past infanthood, but… but… that was not to be."

"And now I am home."

"And as your father's son, you are the earl." Though spoken softly, her words resonated with the gravity of the role Alaric was to assume. "You will need to go to Royal Bridge and swear loyalty to the king."

"I will," Alaric affirmed, his tone resolute, a hardness creeping in. "But first, I will begin putting our house in order, straightening out things here. Then, when I am ready, I shall approach the king from a position of strength, not weakness."

"Our house is broke. Banditry is rampant. Most of our people have fled or sought shelter somewhere. There is little strength left in Dekar."

"What of our bannermen?" Alaric inquired, seeking to gauge the extent of their support or, from what he had seen, lack thereof.

"What of them?" Elara's response was tinged with disgust, a clear reflection of the desolation that had befallen their allies as well.

"Are there any left?" Alaric pressed, seeking a glimmer of hope in the dire situation. He'd take any help he could get. "Anyone who'd lift a sword and stand by our side?"

"Jourgan, Duncan, Keever," Elara enumerated. "They are all that remain, and they are just as impoverished as we are. They have little, if any, strength left. They hide behind the walls of their keeps and strongholds, barely daring to come out in the light of day. They do nothing to help deal with the lawlessness and banditry that has overtaken our and their lands."

Alaric felt a flaring of disappointment at this news. "I have soldiers, all veterans." A spark of defiance lit his eyes. "We will find the bandits, the rabble, and deal with them. I will bring order back to our lands, make them prosperous once more. The people will return, and more will come. We will rebuild and Dekar will flourish." His words were not just a plan of action, but a vow, a pledge to restore the glory and prosperity of their ancestral lands.

"Strong words," Elara observed, filled with both skepticism and hope.

"True words," Alaric affirmed, his commitment unwavering.

"That will take money." Elara's gaze, sharp and assessing, sought to divine Alaric's plans amidst the uncertainty that shrouded their future. Her practicality was born of years navigating the treacherous waters of nobility and the stewardship of their holdings. "How will you pay your soldiers? Where will the money come from to rebuild? Will you take a loan out from one of the dukes? Will you beggar yourself in debt? Neither of the kingdom's dukes has ever been overly friendly to our house. The other earls, mostly yes, but not the dukes, the higher nobility."

"We will need no loans. I returned home with a king's ransom, literally."

"What?" Elara's reaction was immediate, her interest clearly piqued as she sat up straighter. "How? How did you manage that?"

"It does not matter how," Alaric said, dismissing the particulars of his fortune as irrelevant to the current conversation. His focus aimed solely on the future. "All that is important is I have the funds we will need to restore our house and lands to their rightful place, perhaps, in the process, making our family stronger than it was."

Elara reached out, her hand coming to rest on his arm, a gesture that bridged the gap of years and hardships they'd both endured. In that touch, there was strength, support, and the unspoken understanding that had always defined their relationship. She eyed him for a long moment, her gaze delving deep, seeking the son she had sent away, now returned a man changed by time and the hard trials of life. Alaric found her gaze almost painfully intense, noting the gauntness of her face, the lines that time had etched into her skin, marking the passage of years and the burdens they brought, making a once beautiful woman look frail and old. Then her gaze hardened once more, and she removed her hand.

"We have enemies," Elara said bitterly, "amongst the nobility."

It was Alaric's turn to straighten at her words.

"I cannot help but think there are those who covet our lands, who seek to enrich themselves off our misfortune." Her statement reflected the harsh realities of their world, where power vacuums were exploited by the ambitious and the ruthless. "They did this to us after your father passed, created the lawlessness, sent the bandits, undermined our authority, and in the process, bled us nearly dry to the point where we have been unable to pay the king's taxes."

Alaric's response was a measured nod, his expression grave. The weight of his newfound responsibilities pressed upon him, not just to rebuild, but to protect what remained of their legacy. "Do you know who is responsible?"

"I have no proof, but I believe it to be Duke Laval. Masterson mentioned him a time or two in passing, as if he'd known the man. But still, we have no proof with which to go to the king. But even if we had such proof—that would be a wasted effort. You are an earl, he is a duke, and the king is weak, easily swayed."

"Then he will bear watching, and we will take steps to limit what he can do to us," Alaric declared, his decision immediate. The absence of proof did not equate to inaction; rather, it necessitated vigilance and action when required.

In the complex web of politics, Alaric knew that observation, patience, and information often proved as valuable as the sword. And acting when one needed to was just as important. Alaric had learned how to play such games, to be utterly ruthless when needed. Life amidst the Cardinal King's court had taught him only too well. To be strong, you had to project strength. Showing weakness invited others to try to take advantage of you, and Alaric would not have that. If Laval wanted to play with Dekar, he would be playing with fire. And when one played with fire, it was easy to get burned.

"How many prisoners were taken?" Elara's question shifted the focus. "They were an ignorant and brutish lot, but I'd know. How many of Masterson's men survived?"

"Six surrendered to our forces. Three of those have sustained wounds which are mortal. They will not make it through the night."

"What will you do with those that do?" The query, though

simple, was laden with the complexities of leadership and the moral quandaries it entailed.

"They will be publicly executed," Alaric stated simply, a harsh decree but one he deemed necessary. "We will make an example of them. But right now, they are being questioned. If there is anything useful to be learned, Grayson will find out. He has people skilled in interrogation."

Elara nodded, her approval unequivocal. In the calculus of survival, such decisions, though grim, were often indispensable.

"There is hunger across our lands." Alaric's declaration was not just an observation, but a prelude to action. "I will send people to Kanar to buy what food and seed we can for spring. Do you believe the Earl of Kanar still friendly? I remember him as a kindly man, but that was more than a decade ago."

"As far as I know, he is still a friend, though I have not corresponded with him for some time. He was always a friend of your father, a near-brother. They campaigned together in their youth. I believe he will welcome not only your gold, but also your friendship. He may even be convinced to offer support through strength of arms."

Alaric's nod was an affirmation of their shared understanding, an unspoken vow to leverage all avenues of support in the daunting task of restoration that lay before him.

The moment of strategic contemplation was interrupted by movement at the periphery of their awareness. Michael and Missa emerged from a side door that led to the kitchens. Together, they approached the fire's light. Their subsequent bows were marks of respect and fealty.

"Do you require anything, my lord, my lady?" asked Michael. "The food stores from the supply train have been moved into the castle. I am told the cook died in the cells. If you wish, Missa can make you something or at least heat up some rations to make them more palatable."

"No, thank you, I do not require anything." Alaric dismissed the offer with a gentle wave of his hand, his attention swiftly shifting to his mother as he arched an eyebrow in inquiry regarding her own needs.

"Grayson saw me fed a short while ago," Elara assured. "Camp rations are far from the worst fare I have ever had. I need nothing more for now."

"Missa." Alaric turned toward the girl with a decisive tone. "My mother needs a personal servant. You will act in that capacity, until otherwise told."

"Yes, my lord," Missa said, bowing her head in acceptance.

Alaric's mother cast a curious glance at the foreign girl, then to him, her eyebrows knitting together in a mix of surprise and mild protest that he should make such decisions for her. "I did not say I needed someone," she pointed out, her independence surfacing in her gentle objection.

"You did not have to," Alaric countered firmly. "The staff that survived the dungeons are mere skeletons. Many are sick. They will need to recover before they are able to resume their positions and work."

Elara, understanding the necessity behind Alaric's decision, nodded in acquiescence. "Very well," she agreed almost reluctantly, her gaze once more drifting to Missa, her eyes narrowing in appraisal.

Alaric decided he would follow up with both Michael and Missa to find out how his mother received her new servant. Elara was not an easy woman, and she could be quite difficult.

"Leave us," Alaric said, signaling an end to the conversation. "Michael, I will send for you if I require anything further."

With a final bow, Michael and Missa withdrew from the great hall, their movements respectful and measured. Their departure left Alaric and Elara alone once more, enveloped in the warm glow of the fire and the heavy silence.

"You must send to the king in the morning," Elara reiterated. "He must confirm you as earl. Securing your title as earl is not just a formality; it is a critical step in securing our house's future and legitimacy."

"I heard there is a new king," Alaric said. A change in the throne might complicate their plans. "Two years ago, right?"

"There is. His name is Silas. He is barely more than a boy, and weak at that, but still, he must confirm you. If he doesn't, we have a problem."

"He will confirm me," Alaric asserted confidently. "I will be bringing a gift of gold."

"When we asked for aid, he never sent any help," Elara said bitterly. "In our time of need, our darkest hour, he did not come. No one was willing to step forward."

Alaric found the young king's inaction troubling. A ruler who did not support his subjects, especially his own sworn nobility, was failing in one of the fundamental duties of kingship. Such behavior did not bode well for the strength and unity of the realm.

"And if he doesn't confirm you as earl?" Elara pressed. "What then?"

"Then he and I will have a problem," Alaric stated plainly. The determination in his tone left no room for doubt; he was prepared to defend his claim and position, regardless of the opposition. He hardened his tone. "He will confirm me. I will give him no other choice but to do so."

Elara eyed him for a long moment. "You have changed much since I last saw you."

"I have," Alaric acknowledged, a simple affirmation that carried the depth of countless battles, decisions, and sacrifices that had honed his resolve, sharpened his vision for the future, and shaped his views on life and how to make one's way through it.

"And who is this woman you have brought home?" Elara asked. "Who is this Rikka?"

Alaric let go a breath. He glanced toward where Ezran stood at the other end of the hall with the two guards. He lowered his voice so that they would not be overheard. "You saw what she did outside your room against Masterson's men, yes?"

Elara nodded and, in the same low tone, responded, "Magic."

"She is a lumina," Alaric said quietly so that only the two of them could hear.

Elara's gaze sharpened. "She sought you out, didn't she?"

"Not quite, but close enough. She said she was led to me."

"And you have a Luminary within your retinue? I've seen her tattoos and ritual scars."

"I do," Alaric admitted.

Elara turned her gaze to the fire and stared into its depths. For a time, she did not speak, clearly thinking. Eventually, she looked back at him. "You know what this means?"

"Trouble," Alaric said. "Something Grandfather and Father were looking to avoid and advised the same of me."

Elara gave a slow nod as the heavy tread of boots against stone interrupted their conversation, heralding the arrival of Grayson. His entrance was marked by the urgency in his stride as he moved briskly across the hall and up to them.

"My Lady Elara, my lord," Grayson addressed Alaric and his mother with a mixture of deference, respect, and concern. "We have a problem that will not wait."

"Of course we do," Alaric sighed, a brief closure of his eyes serving as a momentary respite before facing the latest headache. He reopened his eyes, ready to tackle whatever lay ahead. "This has to do with the prisoners and your questioning them?"

"It does, my lord," Grayson said.

"Then speak. Let us get this out and into the open."

"Until yesterday, it seems Masterson kept his plans to himself.

His men did not really understand why they were here, other than for personal gain, or for that matter, who was really directing efforts to take control of Dragon Bone's Rest and Dekar, who would profit from the disorder that's been created."

"What changed?" Elara's query, sharp and direct, sought to uncover the root of this sudden shift.

"We did," Alaric surmised. "My arrival changed the equation."

"That is correct," Grayson affirmed with a nod. "When we showed up, his men wanted to leave and were thinking of doing just that, abandoning him. They are mostly thugs and hired muscle. They wanted out before our company arrived to lay siege to the castle and trap them inside. A spy in town informed them a half hour before we came to the keep that you had come home with lots of men, veterans back from campaign. Masterson talked his men into remaining. He told them in three days' time they were due to be relieved by an even larger force and there was nothing to worry about."

"Relieved by whom?" Alaric asked.

"By Duke Laval. Masterson told them the duke was coming to return order to Dekar and take control. He said he had just received a message to that effect, that the duke would soon be on his way."

Elara's hiss was a visceral response to the mention of Laval. "I never liked that bastard. As a child, I could not stand Laval, not in the slightest. He is the worst of pigs."

"The feeling apparently wasn't mutual. Laval very much wanted you alive, my lady, or so Masterson claimed. That was the reason he never had you killed or harmed in any way."

"Why?" Alaric asked, puzzled by the motives of their adversary, someone he could not recall ever having met. "Why would he do that, especially after turning Dekar upside down? Surely it would be easier to take control if my mother was dead."

Elara was silent for a long moment, her gaze shifting to the fire. "Partly, I think it goes back to my youth. He courted me, sought my hand in marriage. I fell for your father, not him. He resented that and always has been holding a grudge."

"I thought your marriage was arranged?" Alaric, surprised, sought clarification. "At least Father always said so."

"It was," Elara confirmed, her sigh conveying the weight of memories and decisions long past. "Our marriage was arranged by my father. He believed in a happy marriage for me, one based upon love, and knew my heart, who I wanted. So he made it happen, joined our two houses in union."

"Grandfather did that?" Alaric asked. He had always recalled his grandfather as a hard man, much more difficult and overbearing than his father.

Elara gave a nod. "Laval never forgave him for that, or me."

Alaric, attempting to grasp the full implications, wondered aloud, "So, this is over scorn and settling a score on account of you, Mother?"

"No," Elara clarified. "Laval is only interested in power and wealth. Even back then, it was clear that was all he cared about. Mark my words, he means to take Dekar and increase his own holdings. That is his ultimate endgame. I'm just a prize he was denied, and he does not like being denied anything."

"I agree with Lady Elara," Grayson said, drawing Alaric's attention. "By intentionally fostering disorder, he has a pretext to move in and scoop up Dekar. He could claim the instability and lawlessness had spread to his own lands, that his hand was forced, that he had to take action."

"Without a man to lead this house, he would take me under his protection," Elara said sourly, "effectively making him ruler of Dekar by proxy."

Her words propelled Alaric to his feet. Just thinking about it disgusted him, but the more he thought about it, the more it seemed plausible. He began pacing before the fire.

"With you alive, my lady," Grayson added, his gaze on Alaric before shifting to Elara, "the king would be hesitant to displace you by raising up and appointing a new earl. More importantly, he would hesitate in upsetting one of his most powerful vassals, Laval."

"The bastard," Elara said. "I would be nothing more than a prisoner in my own home, while he lorded over everything. It would be a miserable existence, one much worse than Masterson provided."

"So, Laval is marching on us now? He is coming here with soldiers?" Alaric sought confirmation, thinking ahead to what must be done.

"Not quite," Grayson said. "I don't think he has arrived yet to lead his men. They are apparently in disguise, at least four hundred men camping just over the border, on our side of the river, at a village called Tyfel. It is they who have been supposedly raiding our lands, creating havoc. It apparently began as a small force and over the months grew larger. They've been raping and pillaging, sending the goods they've taken back to Laval. At least, Masterson told the others that. But... he's dead and can't answer for himself."

The revelation that four hundred men lay in wait, disguised and encamped within the boundaries of Dekar, painted a concerning picture, one that Alaric found very disturbing. These were not distant threats, but immediate dangers, orchestrators of the raids that had plagued their lands, sowing chaos, and weakening Dekar's defenses, forcing his people to flee their homes and fear for their lives. Alaric rubbed his jaw and stopped pacing. "Are you sure about this, certain?"

"Certain?" Grayson asked with a shake of his head. "No, I am not certain. Most of what we got from interrogation was second-hand, and likely some of it is nothing more than rumor, exaggeration, men jawing amongst themselves after Masterson told them what he did and why, blowing things out of proportion. However, what I told you is what I was able to piece together. I feel it is fairly accurate, enough for us to reasonably act upon." Grayson paused. "Then again, to be honest, there may be others who are involved, some of our neighbors, who seek gain in the destruction of your house, my lord. They may be working with Laval or even against him. We don't yet know the full story."

"As you said, Grayson, we now know enough to act," Elara said, "and they grew bolder with their success, bold enough that Laval himself is coming to take my home. We cannot allow that to happen."

Grayson nodded his agreement. "All Masterson's men needed was to hang on for three days, maybe four at most, and then they would all be rewarded, well paid for their work when Laval arrived. With the walls of the castle, Masterson did not think holding out would be a problem."

"Obviously, he was wrong," Elara said.

"Tyfel, you said?" Alaric asked, to which Grayson gave a nod. "I recall that being a forest village on Laval's border. My father took me there once on a hunting and fishing trip. The village sits along a wide river."

"That is correct," Grayson said. "The river is the boundary between Dekar and Laval."

"Tyfel has been abandoned for some time," Elara said. "Since the troubles began. From Laval's point of view, it is a good place to establish a base, remote and hidden away from prying eyes. There used to be a wooden bridge there, built in your grandfather's time, but it washed away during a bad storm when I was a child. A ferry was set up in its place."

Alaric looked to Grayson. "How long of a ride is it to Tyfel? Do you recall?"

"Maybe half a day's hard ride. Two and a half marching depending upon the condition of the road. We can probably do it in two, maybe less if we push the men some. What are you thinking, my lord?"

"If we move fast enough," Alaric said, "before word of what happened here reaches them, we might be able to surprise this force, wipe it out, and send a message to Laval and anyone else that we are not to be messed with."

"You would be attacking Laval's men, his soldiers," Elara cautioned. "The king and our peers might frown upon that."

"I don't care if they do." Alaric pointed at the stone floor. "They are on our lands, and it's time to show strength, real power, set an example that cannot be mistaken. If I don't demonstrate it now, no one will respect me or our family again. Laval will only be the start of our troubles. Besides, they are acting as bandits, raiders, and that is all the provocation and justification I need. If we can get to them before Laval does, all the better."

"You could be starting a war," Elara warned. "Especially if Laval or one of his children is amongst them."

"Maybe," Alaric said, thinking about all that needed doing. "If he was among them, they'd already be marching."

"And what happens if he's already on his way?" Elara said. "What will you do if you encounter him and his soldiers on the road to the keep?"

"Then I will convince him to return from whence he came," Alaric said in a hard tone, "by sword if needed."

Elara's look was a hard one. "That is something your father would have said."

"What are your orders, my lord?" Grayson asked.

Alaric thought for a moment. "Send our best scouts. Give them the fastest horses we have, mine included. I want eyes on this force at Tyfel. I need to know exactly what we are facing."

"Yes, my lord,"

"Get the men ready to go, along with sufficient supplies, food, and water. We will give them a few hours of rest, then we march before dawn, and we march hard. I know it has been difficult for our boys, but this cannot be helped."

"I understand, my lord," Grayson said. "They will handle it."

"Notify Mayor Nightwell that the militia will be going with us, but don't tell anyone where we're headed or what we will be up to. We are going to need every available sword for this, along with the element of surprise."

"I will also post men outside the town to watch for messengers that might run to this force with the intent of bringing word, my lord," Grayson said.

"Good idea," Alaric said with a pleased nod.

"Anything else, my lord?" Grayson asked.

"The bannermen—"

"What of them?" Elara said, interrupting before Alaric could continue. "They are useless. When help was needed, they came not."

Alaric sucked in a breath. He turned back to Grayson. "Send a messenger to each. Like the militia, do not tell them where we are going or why. Designate a point and a specific time for them to meet up with us en route, somewhere not too obvious, in the event they have been working with Laval and cutting side deals. My orders to them: They are to immediately march. I expect no hesitation and will not tolerate delay."

"What if they don't come, my lord?" Grayson glanced at Alaric's mother. "What if they sit tight?"

"Instruct the messengers to inform them in no uncertain terms that when I am done restoring order to Dekar and putting down our enemies, I will march on their keeps and remove them by force. Their families will be turned out and all they own will be confiscated. I will have bannermen who are loyal to me and Dekar, not to mention responsive. I will tolerate nothing less."

"Yes, my lord."

"Now," Alaric said, "carry out my orders."

"As you command, my lord, so shall it be done." Grayson bowed and retreated, leaving him with his mother.

Alaric moved to the fire once more and held out his hands, warming them against the chill on the air.

"You risk a lot, my son. If this goes badly, we could lose everything."

Alaric gave an understanding nod as he glanced over at his mother. "I well know it. But if I do nothing, we are certain to lose everything. In my book, action is always preferable to inaction."

"This may lead to war."

Alaric turned his gaze back to the fire, staring into its depths. "Mother, war and killing is something I have become quite good at. It does not frighten me."

19

As the late afternoon sun dipped toward the horizon, casting long shadows across the winding forest road, Alaric, with Grayson at his side, marched. The column stretched out of view, disappearing behind them around a bend and into the dense thicket of ancient trees that made up the forest. Each step they took was accompanied by the massed crunch of boots against the rough terrain of dirt and a carpet of freshly fallen leaves.

Throughout the day, they had taken several regular brief respites to allow the men to rest their weary legs and dip into haversacks. Despite the urgency pulsing through Alaric's veins, a driven need to reach Tyfel with the swiftest haste, he recognized the importance of ensuring his men remained in fighting form. He could not afford to meet the enemy with overly fatigued men. That, simply, would not be wise.

The air was sharply cold, each breath forming fleeting clouds of mist. Winter's imminent arrival was undeniable, a change in season that edged ever closer with each passing moment. Memories of snow, a blanket of serene white that he hadn't laid eyes upon in over a decade, flickered through Alaric's mind.

He wondered what that might be like, for a child's memory wasn't always accurate.

Their surroundings were alive with the muted colors of late autumn, the leaves transitioning from greens to oranges, reds, and browns. The forest itself seemed to watch over them, the ancient trees' branches swaying gently in the breeze when it gusted.

He glanced over at Grayson.

"When the snows come, how deep will it get?" Alaric recalled snow blanketing the ground and playing in it as a kid. During the heart of winter, he remembered being bored as they huddled indoors for much of it, usually around a fire, for the keep was frightfully cold. Still, he was unsure exactly what kind of impact it would have on his efforts going forward when the snows arrived. From what he knew, it would not be good. "What are your thoughts on snow?"

"It's not that cold, if that is what you are asking." Grayson's gaze briefly met Alaric's.

"It's not," Alaric said.

"I don't think it will snow for some weeks yet, but I've been wrong before. At least we should not see significant snowfall."

"I am thinking from a military standpoint, tactically and strategically," Alaric clarified. "I am wondering how heavily it will affect military operations, marching, supply, and whatnot, especially if I have to create outposts, forts, and garrisons." He scanned the path ahead, as if envisioning the army's march through the thick cloak of winter that was to ultimately envelop the land in its firm grip.

"Ah." Understanding dawned on Grayson. He navigated around a large pothole in the road, its true depths obscured by a layer of yellow and brown leaves. "Some winters are worse than others, the snow deeper. As you well know, Dekar usually gets several feet over the course of the entire winter. Campaigning typically stops after the first snows here in the north, in all of

Kevahn, and the neighboring kingdoms. Late spring, summer, and fall are the fighting months."

Grayson paused as he stepped over another pothole. "It is kind of like in the south when the intense heat comes in summer, in all its oppressive force, and the sands kick up. Only, the cold is worse. Any outposts and forts that are established will need to be supplied and fully stocked before the full force of winter arrives." He looked over at Alaric again. "The snow piles up, and moving troops anywhere becomes very difficult, if not outright impossible."

"I see." It was as he'd figured. Winter would be a great hindrance. Alaric's mind raced through scenarios, adjustments, and strategies as to how he would have to manage things in the winter, especially if he was to restore order to his lands.

"The snow needs to be shoveled out of the way." Grayson gestured toward the road beneath their feet, his movements painting a picture of the logistical nightmares that winter brought. "Clearing roads like this one becomes a near impossibility. The snow can be heavy and, when it gets very cold, freezes solid. I've seen main roads cleared, but it takes time and a lot of manpower to get it done. Keeping them clear all winter is even more challenging."

Alaric absorbed the gravity of Grayson's words. "So," he mused aloud, the strategist within piecing together the puzzle, "if it comes to a fight, and war, once the snows come, there won't be much action. There will be no real fights for a while, at least until the warmth returns in spring and it all melts."

After a long moment, Grayson nodded, affirming the assessment with the seriousness it warranted. "That and the ground firms up. Dekar was not at war when you were younger and there was no internal strife worth mentioning. There was no need to establish forts or outposts or, for that matter, move large bodies of troops and supply in winter. The bannermen took care of basic security. When I entered service, before you were born, it wasn't like that. There were some troubles, problems only soldiers could solve. After the snows melt, the ground becomes the enemy as mud season arrives. As you can imagine, that brings its own complications. During both seasons, small groups of men will be able to move and operate, but nothing major happens. Armies don't march but sit things out until it becomes practical to move." His tone shifted, hinting at the underlying dangers beyond the tactical inconveniences. "Not only is it difficult to campaign in winter, but the cold becomes dangerous. Men can easily get frost-bite, lose digits and limbs, not to mention freeze to death."

Alaric's thoughtful nod marked his acceptance of the new challenge that lay before him. Though he was well-versed in the arid and dry climate and trials of the far south, the north presented a somewhat unfamiliar battleground, its icy climes and treach-erous landscapes demanding a different kind of understanding, one he needed to master.

This realization fully dawned on him as he navigated the uneven terrain of the road, his boots stepping over a particularly large pothole that the wagon ruts seemed to embrace and run right through. The road, a secondary artery through the heart of Dekar, was in a poor state, mirroring the broader neglect that the region had suffered.

"This is a sorry excuse for a road," Alaric remarked unhappily as he kicked at a small stone. It went skittering ahead. The road, after all, was more than just a path; it was a lifeline, crucial for not only the flow of commerce and trade, but also the movement of his soldiers in the event of an emergency or crisis. They'd already passed places where streams had completely washed the road out. It had taken them time to cross with their supply train, more than he'd expected.

The road's condition was a symptom of larger issues that

afflicted Dekar, a land left to languish. Like everything else, it would require attending to.

"It needs some work, is all," Grayson concurred.

"All of Dekar needs work." Alaric's comment hung in the air between them, heavy with implications. Grayson's silence in response was telling, a tacit acknowledgment of the daunting task that awaited those who dared to dream of a better future for this seemingly forsaken and broken land.

As they continued their march, the road ahead veiled by a bend, a sudden gust of wind swept through the towering trees and their branches overhead, stirring them to motion. It was a wild, whispering force, one that seemed to call out to him. Alaric's gaze lifted to the sky, noting the dark overcast clouds that had moved in throughout the day. He found himself pondering the whims of nature, wondering at what precise point the cold would tip the scales, transforming a normal rain into a blanket of snow.

In that moment, as the wind gusted and the chill bit into his exposed skin, Alaric was reminded of the fragile balance between human ambition and the indomitable will of nature. The road beneath his feet, the deteriorating state of Dekar, and the threat of a conflict with Laval—all were intertwined in a dance with the elements, one in which the coming winter would play a role, if it came to war.

"How far do you want to go this evening?" Grayson asked. "When would you like to stop to camp?"

Alaric weighed his answer with the consideration it deserved. "We can call a halt an hour before the sun sets."

"That early? You're thinking of a proper marching camp, complete with defensive walls, then?"

"I want to take no chances, especially with an enemy force within a day's march. Besides, it's been a while since we spent the time to construct a fortified encampment. Not only do I want dirt walls with a wooden barricade, but also an outer trench, complete with sharpened stakes."

Grayson nodded. "That will require clearing a portion of the forest. Fortified camps take time, maybe two hours of work for the size force we have."

"I know. We need to get into the habit of doing this, even small detachments that are sent out. I won't lose men to laxness. We cannot afford to. We will make up for the loss of time by breaking camp earlier in the morning."

Grayson's glance drifted behind them, running down the length of the long serpent that followed in their wake, the men marching in a column of two. "The militia are having a difficult time of it, the pace we set. Last I checked, there were several dozen stragglers who had fallen out."

"I know it," Alaric responded, his tone a mix of resignation and empathy. "It's only to be expected. They're not accustomed to this sort of thing, hard marching."

"No, they are accustomed to a far easier and sedate lifestyle."

The militia's struggles were a reminder of the gap between the ideal of regular trained soldiers and the reality of ordinary men called during unexpected times to serve. They were not professional soldiers, trained for the rigors of the march and battle, but rather individuals drawn from their everyday lives. It was these men, along with his own, who would be thrown into the maelstrom of what was potentially waiting down the road, likely a sharp fight with an enemy who was trained.

The sudden appearance of movement ahead caught Alaric's attention. A figure had rounded the bend in the road and come into view. It was the first person they had seen since they'd set out that morning. As soon as he spotted the head of the column, the man broke into a jog, picking up his pace. Alaric's hand instinctively moved in a gesture toward Grayson, drawing the other's attention ahead and to the approaching figure.

Grayson's eyes narrowed. "One of our close-in scouts."

Alaric acknowledged this with a nod, expression remaining composed, yet his mind was alive with speculation. Their deployment of a light screen—scouts positioned ahead, behind, and to the sides of the marching column in the forest itself—was a tactical measure essential for safeguarding the column from the threats of ambush and surprise attacks. A marching column was vulnerable to a hostile force lurking amongst the trees. His scouts were not only the vanguard, but also his extended eyes and ears as they moved.

As Grayson and Alaric continued their measured advance with the column, Alaric wondered about the news the man brought. The scout, breathing heavily, came up and saluted.

"Fall in and report," Alaric ordered, not stopping, continuing down the road.

The scout seamlessly fell into pace beside them, his breath still heavy from the exertion. "The bannermen, they are ahead, just around the bend at the crossroads, waiting, my lord."

A surge of adrenaline quickened Alaric's heartbeat. The exchange of glances with Grayson was brief but loaded with significance.

They had come.

"How many bannermen are there?" Alaric pressed, seeking specifics, needing to gauge the strength they could rely upon. "How many men did they bring?"

"All three bannermen and fifty, maybe sixty soldiers between them," came the scout's estimation, a figure that resonated with a mix of relief and disappointment in Alaric's heart. The numbers were fewer than hoped for, a reminder of the limitations they faced, yet each bannerman represented a measure of support, a vital addition to their ranks.

"Very good," Alaric responded, maintaining the composure of

command despite the flicker of disappointment. "Carry on with your duty. Continue scouting ahead of the line of march."

"Yes, my lord." The scout gave a salute and started back the way he'd come. Watching the scout jog away, Alaric allowed himself a moment to breathe in the cold air, feeling it fill his lungs, before releasing it slowly through his nose, a physical attempt to steady the storm of thoughts and emotions the report stirred.

As they neared the bend in the road, the anticipation within him grew with each step.

"In truth, it is fifty or sixty men we did not have before," Grayson remarked.

Alaric acknowledged this wisdom with a simple "Agreed."

As they rounded the bend, the crossroads came into view. A hundred fifty yards ahead, campfires had been set, just off to the side of the road, with a gathering of men around them. Several figures rose to their feet as the column appeared, like a serpent, slowly revealing itself to the world.

Without speaking further, Alaric and Grayson continued their steady approach, leading the column, the distance between them and the bannermen steadily diminishing. Four figures, distinguished from the rest by their finer attire and the expensive armor they wore, stepped forward and gathered at the side of the road.

To Alaric, these men represented both the past and the future; they were the tangible connection to his father's reign and the potential pillars of his own. They had pledged their loyalty to his house, to his father, and now, as they stood waiting, the question of their allegiance loomed large. Would they extend the same fealty to him, the same wholehearted support? Could he place his trust in them, just as his father had? Those were questions that only time would answer.

This moment of first contact was laden with the weight of

history and the uncertainties of new beginnings. Alaric's eyes studied each bannerman, searching for signs of loyalty or dissent, knowing that the true test of their allegiance would unfold in the days to come, through their actions. The trust and support he sought could not be instantly won; it would need to be earned.

As they moved closer, the air tinged with the smoky scent of the campfires, Alaric faced not just the bannermen, but the broader challenge of leadership. The coming exchange would set the tone for his relationship with these key figures, a delicate dance of diplomacy and power where every gesture, every word, would be imbued with significance and read deeply into. In this meeting, the foundations for future loyalty, for unity or division, would be laid, marking the beginning of a new chapter in the saga of his house.

As Alaric closed the last of the distance between himself and the bannermen, their gazes met his with an intensity that spoke of their scrutiny and anticipation. His steps were more than physical movements; they were the closing of a gap between past allegiances and present loyalties. Grayson mirrored Alaric's movements, joining him. As always, his Shadow Guard was close at hand, as Ezran, Jasper, and Thorne positioned themselves off to the sides but within easy reach. Kiera and Rikka were somewhere behind in the column, riding together.

Alaric's silence as he assessed the bannermen was a deliberate choice, his gaze lingering on each in turn, taking the measure of the men before him. The three bannermen were older, into their late forties and fifties. They exuded a seasoned hardness, their appearances marked by lives of service and the toil of combat, the responsibilities that came with running their own houses—a visual affirmation of their capability and resilience. One youth stood amongst their number, barely beyond his teens.

The man who stepped forward, clad in a heavy gray wool

cloak and with a sheathed broadsword hanging at his side, assumed the role of spokesperson for the group. His gaze passed over Alaric, Grayson, and the Shadow Guard, taking them in. This was a moment of assessment, of judgment, and perhaps of recognition. The younger man's positioning by his side, coupled with their shared features, suggested a familial bond.

This opening exchange, filled with the unvoiced questions and answers that passed between them, set the stage for what was to come. Alaric, standing before these men, represented not just his own claim, but the legacy of his house. The dynamics at play, from the visible support of his companions to the subtle positioning of the bannermen, spoke to the complexities of power, loyalty, and leadership.

"Grayson," the man said, his voice gravelly and hard. "It has been a long time since we set eyes upon one another, old friend."

"Duncan." Grayson returned the acknowledgment with a measured nod, his posture relaxed yet unmistakably alert, as if prepared for any outcome this meeting might bring.

Duncan's gaze shifted. "And you must be Lord Alaric," he said, respect and scrutiny in his tone.

Another voice cut through the air. "Returned from the Crusade to save us, no doubt." The man's stance and sarcastic tone set him apart from the others. He stood tall, a presence to reckon with, his arms muscular, chest barrel-like. His armor, though bearing the marks of time and use, hugged his form with the ease of a second skin, its scars, nicks, and dents telling tales of survival and extensive use. The cord grip of his sword, frayed from years of faithful service, hinted at a warrior who valued the essence of the blade over its aesthetics. His face, etched with the hard lines of a life carved out on battlefields, remained unyielding under Alaric's scrutinizing gaze.

"I am Alaric," came the reply, simple, yet imbued with the unshakeable foundation of his claim.

"Come here to lord over us?" the same man challenged, his demeanor unflinching, as if daring Alaric to prove his worth beyond the title and birthright.

"I am your rightful lord," Alaric stated, his voice a calm assertion, "earl of these lands. I will tolerate none other."

"We don't know you," Duncan said. "You have been gone for many years, too many possibly."

"That was not my choice." Alaric was keenly aware that the respect and trust of these men would not be easily won. In this world of strife, nothing of value could be expected without effort and proof of worth.

"And yet you summon us like dogs," the other man retorted. "Threaten us to attend you."

Undeterred, Alaric closed the distance between them, each step measured and deliberate. Grayson moved with him, as did his Shadow Guard.

"What is your name?" Alaric asked.

"Keever," came the answer from Grayson, as if the name itself was a piece of the intricate puzzle unfolding between them.

Alaric's gaze then shifted to the third man, seeking to untangle the web of identities and allegiances. "You must be Jourgan," he surmised, receiving a simple affirmation in response. Turning to the younger man, he pieced another name to the mosaic of faces. "And you are Duncan's son."

"I am Jaxen, my lord," the younger man said, "and you are correct."

Acknowledging Jaxen with a nod, Alaric addressed the underlying currents of dissent. "I summoned you the way I did because you did not come when my mother called."

"We had our own problems," Keever stated.

"And now, I am yours, if you choose to make it so," Alaric informed them. This admission stirred a visible discomfort among the four men, a physical manifestation of the internal conflict each faced—a choice between skepticism born of past disappointments and the potential for a renewed allegiance. They shared glances amongst themselves and shifted their feet in clear discomfort. "I will not have bannermen who refuse to support me when I call for aid," Alaric continued, his words setting the terms of loyalty and mutual support, the cornerstone of his rule.

"And what about when *we* call for help?" Keever's question sliced through the tension, bringing to the surface the raw wounds of neglect. "None came when I called, when I begged for assistance. My man was turned away from your keep. Your mother would not even see him."

"I cannot change what has happened in the past," Alaric admitted, refusing to offer empty apologies for actions beyond his control. "Yet I can promise I will come when you call and will do so in strength."

"Will you?" Keever pressed, his skepticism plain.

Alaric stiffened. He was beginning to not like this man.

"He will," Grayson affirmed. "You have my word upon that, and if you decide to doubt me, then by my honor, I shall be forced to challenge you to a duel."

"I don't need Grayson to uphold my honor," Alaric said firmly. He looked directly at Keever, then shifted his gaze to the other two, looking at each in turn. "If you feel the need to challenge anyone, I will take up that gauntlet. You will be crossing swords with me, and we will settle matters as our ancestors of old did—with blood."

Jourgan cleared his throat and glanced over at Duncan.

"I don't believe that will be necessary," Duncan said, drawing Alaric's gaze as he sank to a knee. His son dropped to a knee a heartbeat later. "I will support you, my lord, if you will accept me as your bannerman. I have brought myself and my son. Sadly, that is all we could spare. I left two men, both disabled veterans, looking after my family and"—he paused and looked up—

"Grayson's family. They took shelter with us after the troubles began. We are kin, after all, and family looks after its own." Duncan glanced back at his son with this last bit.

Alaric, observing the subtle shift in the air, could almost feel the weight lifting from Grayson's shoulders as the man let out a slight breath of relief. The captain's shoulders slumped slightly. Alaric well knew what was running through Grayson's mind. His family was safe.

Alaric regarded Duncan. They were but two men. Yet, in the echo of Grayson's earlier sentiment, these two represented an increase to their ranks—a sign of growing support that, while modest, marked the beginning of Alaric's gathering strength. Two more was better than none, especially when every sword mattered.

"Rise, Sir Duncan. I will accept you into my service as a vassal and bannerman." Alaric's words, firm and decisive, were more than a mere acceptance; they were an affirmation of the bond between lord and vassal, a renewal of ancient ties that wove the fabric of their society.

As Duncan and his son stood, his response was immediate and unwavering. "Our swords are yours to command, my lord."

This solemn oath, simple yet profound, encapsulated the essence of fealty. It was a commitment that went beyond mere words, embodying a readiness to stand in battle, to support their lord at all costs. Their swords, and by extension, their lives, were now intertwined with Alaric's cause.

"My sword is yours as well, my lord," Jourgan said, taking a knee. "That is, if you will accept me. I brought twenty-one men, my lord, and I will hold you to your word as you will hold me to mine."

"That is only to be expected." Alaric nodded, pleased so far. "Rise, Sir Jourgan."

Jourgan stood, and then looked over at Keever. "It is time to take a side. You are the wealthiest of us knights and the strongest, with the number of men-at-arms at your disposal. Sitting on the fence is no longer an option."

Keever's eyes bored into Jourgan's with an intensity that pierced through the chilly air. It was a look fraught with unspoken words and history, including a bitter anger, one Alaric understood was directed at his own house. That was partly Masterson and Laval's work. After a long moment, Keever broke the gaze, slowly turning toward Alaric. His expression softened ever so slightly, but his eyes remained pools of hardened resolve and heat.

"I was raised up to a knight by your grandfather," Keever declared. "I will support you, just as I supported him, if only in his honor."

"Then bend the knee," Grayson commanded. "Show the proper respect for your lord."

These words seemed to strike Keever like a physical blow, his pride visibly bristling at the demand. Yet, almost as if propelled by a sheer force of will and bound by the invisible chains of duty and tradition, he begrudgingly complied. With a grimace, Keever slowly went down on one knee, bowing his head in a gesture of submission that appeared foreign to his nature. It was clear to Alaric that not only was Keever a proud man, but also a difficult one.

"My lord," Keever intoned, the words bitter on his tongue, "I have brought thirty-five men. My sword and theirs are yours to command."

Alaric, for his part, regarded the kneeling bannerman with a mixture of caution and newly kindled respect. In this man was a complex weave of loyalty, pride, and an unwavering sense of duty. He could either become a staunch pillar of support or a formidable obstacle, perhaps even an immovable object should he choose to be, one that might stand in Alaric's way. He hesitated, letting the silence stretch between them, a reminder of the delicate balance of power and fealty that defined their world.

"Rise, Sir Keever," Alaric finally said, his voice steady and commanding, yet not without a hint of respect for the man before him. "I accept your service to me and my house." Alaric knew that Keever's allegiance, while now sworn, would require more than mere words to fully secure. This man, with his fierce loyalty and proud spirit, would indeed bear watching.

As the tension of the moment began to dissipate, Alaric once more became aware of their surroundings. The steady rhythm of the column marching past served as a backdrop to the scene—the sound of armor and weapons chinking and clanking, feet grinding and crunching the dirt and leaves.

Those men standing by the roadside and campfires, loyal followers of Alaric's newly sworn bannermen, had been spectators to the solemn exchange of oaths. When Keever finally stood, a renewed sense of allegiance rent the air. Their pent-up breaths were released in a robust cheer, a collective expression of approval and solidarity. Alaric glanced around, assessing those men.

It was a beginning.

The sound of hooves clopping against the hard ground pulled Alaric's attention away from the men. He turned to see Kiera and Rikka making their way toward them. The latter had her long black hair tied back into a single braid and had donned a simple gray dress that Missa had found for her. The dress, though plain, could not dim the radiant beauty Rikka possessed. In the subdued light of the gray day, she stood out against the drabness. To Alaric, she appeared incredibly beautiful, so much so it almost took his breath away. Kiera was clad in her plate armor. Her bearing, as formidable as the steel she wore, was a declaration of her readiness to fight.

"We bring women to war now?" Keever groused. "This is something new to me."

Alaric held back a laugh. He looked forward to the day Keever got to witness Kiera and Rikka in battle. "Now, gentlemen, form your men up. We are pressed for time and have a long way to march. Once your men are in column and marching, I will explain where we are going, what we are going to do, and why."

20

As Alaric ate the last of his salted pork ration, he took a moment to allow the cool water from his canteen to wash it down. It was the beginning of the second day of their march and his leg muscles were stiff and sore from the prior day's exertions. The air, crisp from the night's embrace, carried the scent of dirt and the sour tang of rotting leaves, mingling with the smoky remnants of campfires. Alaric could also smell the foul stench from the latrines, which were on the other side of the camp.

It was still dark out and the forest was just starting to wake up, the birds calling to one another, but the encampment had been rousted more than a half hour before. Having eaten, all around, men were breaking down tents, packing up gear and equipment, and rolling blankets.

Though the sky was still dark, it was beginning to lighten a tad. The sun was likely about an hour, maybe a little longer, from peeking above the horizon and painting the sky in hues of orange and pink, setting the fallen dew-speckled leaves lying on the ground aglow and beginning to push back the night's chill.

Before eating, Alaric had restarted his campfire. Almost sullenly, as if it did not wish to wake, the fire was now low-burning, shedding barely a modicum of warmth. It was generating more smoke than anything else. That did not bother Alaric much, for once the march resumed, he knew he would warm up soon enough.

Around him, the temporary camp of canvas and rope had come to life amidst the rustle of fabric and the soft clinks and chinks of metal, the jawing of the men filling the air. There were coughs, barks of laughter, curses, and the shouts of sergeants trying to bring order to the chaos. Despite the early hour, there was a sense of efficiency amongst them as the men prepared to continue their march.

Within the brief span of half an hour, Alaric estimated that the entire column would once again be formed up on the road that ran alongside the camp and prepared to begin threading their way through the forest, a moving serpent of leather, steel, determination, and most importantly, Alaric's will.

Today's march would be harder as they pushed on the last leg toward Tyfel and hitting the enemy. There would be fewer stops and breaks. Speed would be the watchword of the day—speed and haste.

He took the opportunity to stretch, attempting to chase away the stiffness that the unforgiving, hard ground had bestowed upon him—that, and the exertions from the previous day's march. Rolling his neck, he felt a little better. Marching long distances while wearing armor was not the easiest of things. It took a toll upon the body, particularly the back and legs, not to mention the neck.

Behind him, Rikka emerged from their two-person tent. She looked up at the sky and then around at the forest outside the camp. She breathed in deeply and let it out slowly, as if being near the forest or just the act of camping recharged her being. Spotting him, she flashed a tired, slight smile and sat upon a log that had been placed before the fire as a seat. As if greeting her, the flame picked up a little, but not much. The fire was still putting out more smoke than anything else. As the breeze gusted, the smoke moved in her direction. She leaned away from it until the gust of wind subsided and the smoke moved away.

The night had offered little in the way of warmth as they slept on the ground, their only respite being the thick blankets they had shared and the natural heat emanating from Rikka's body. She was like a furnace in the chill of the night. He had never felt anything like it. When he'd mentioned it to her, she had seemed surprised, as if it were perfectly normal. Last night, as the temperature dropped, Alaric had not complained, not in the slightest.

"What?" Rikka's voice was tinged with fatigue. She'd caught him staring. Her appearance, though slightly disheveled, was captivating nonetheless. Strands of her dark hair twirled in the gentle morning breeze, framing her face in a wild, untamed manner.

"I was just enjoying the view."

"Is that all?"

"I've never campaigned with a woman before," Alaric admitted, his voice touched with bemusement. "I am finding it has its advantages, especially at night."

"I am rather enjoying it myself," Rikka confessed, tone infused with a warmth that pushed back the morning chill. "As long as you don't get distracted from your duty and what really matters."

He closed the distance between them, drawn by an invisible thread of companionship and something else that was growing within him, which he was hesitant to admit, even to himself. The world around them seemed to momentarily halt as he focused his entire attention upon her. Nearby, Ezran stood guard, his gaze watchful. Throughout the night, one of his Shadow Guard had stood sentry at all times.

"Why me?" Alaric asked plainly. "Why did you choose me?"

"We have already covered this, and you know well enough why." She let go a breath and patted the log beside her. "Come, sit with me, at least for a moment—until duty calls you away."

Figuring he had some time before Grayson came for him, Alaric obliged, settling onto the log next to her. Leaning into him, she placed her head against his shoulder, her body nestled closely against his. They sat there for a long moment, neither saying a thing. Though he was quite content, he suddenly felt a nagging sense of frustration about their relationship. The feeling had been growing by the day.

"Where are you from?" Alaric's inquiry, while gentle, carried a need to understand the origins of this enigmatic woman. She had unexpectedly become an integral part of his life, and in such a short span too. She'd ensnared him, almost as thoroughly as a spider does a fly caught in its web. Alaric wasn't a babe in the woods either. He'd had plenty of other women in his time, but none had gotten to him like Rikka.

Her voice was a soft murmur against the backdrop of the camp. "I already told you, I was drawn to find you. You may not have realized it, but you too were driven to find me. We were brought together for a purpose. Such is the way of our god, destiny."

"Okay, but from where? Where are you from? Who is your family, your mother and father? Do you have any sisters or brothers? I would know these things about you," Alaric pressed.

Rikka took her head from his shoulder and sat up straight. The air between them, a heartbeat ago filled with the warmth of their closeness, now held a tension. Her eyes were deep and mysterious as she looked at him, and in them, Alaric saw hesitation and something that almost looked like fear.

"No," Rikka said firmly.

"What do you mean, no?"

"You do not want to know these things. You would think less of me." She averted her eyes to the fire. "I think less of me."

"I would not think less of you," Alaric countered firmly, turning to face her fully. His gaze sought hers, an unspoken plea for trust. In his eyes, she was a mosaic of mysteries, a complex puzzle to be assembled, each piece more compelling than the last. Her cultured mannerisms, her refinement, her resilience, her inner strength—all these facets made her not just intriguing, but someone to be valued and understood on a deeper level. At least, he thought so. He reached up a hand and turned her face to look at him.

"I'm not so certain," Rikka confessed. "Is it not enough that we were brought together for a reason, a purpose, something larger than ourselves? Why complicate things when everything is good between us? You like me well enough and I you, more than you can possibly imagine. I ask you, is that not enough?"

"Don't you see? That is why I wish—I need to know more," Alaric said. His words were not just a request, but a vow of sorts, a promise to venture beyond the surface of their acquaintance into the depths of understanding and acceptance and possibly more. In his earnestness, there lay an offer of a sanctuary, a space where secrets could be shared without fear of censure or repercussion, where the past did not dictate the worth of one's character. If only she would trust him. If only she could see that.

"And if I was from the streets?" Rikka asked, her eyes alight with a defiant intensity. "Were you to learn I was born a commoner, a whore, or a thief, a murderer perhaps, a sinner, what then? Would I be more unattractive to your eyes, unpalatable, unacceptable in your presence?"

Alaric was taken aback, grappling with the hypotheticals she presented. The very notion seemed incongruous with the woman he had come to know and was beginning to care for deeply.

Indeed, she was a lumina, a wielder of holy magic, marked by their god for a higher purpose, one of the few, a chosen soul. Could his god have blessed someone so low? Would Eldanar have entrusted such a sacred gift to someone from the streets, someone society deemed unworthy, an untouchable? Or worse, someone from a profession that was considered sinful and wretched?

"Well?" she asked. "What would you do then? Cast me from your bed, your life? And if I carry your child, as Eldanar intends, what then? How will you see me? How will you view your child?"

"I am not sure," Alaric confessed, his honesty speaking to the complexity of his feelings and beliefs. The admission was difficult, laying bare his own uncertainties and prejudices. He had always assumed that he'd end up with a wife from the nobility, someone from his own station, likely an arranged marriage between houses. That had always been the only choice available, someone his mother and father deemed worthy. But now, he was the earl and, though he had not met the man yet, accountable only to a king and his god.

"So, why test that? Why test our relationship with such unwelcome truths, a reality you are unprepared to deal with?" Rikka countered, her question enveloping the heart of the matter. It was a reminder of the precariousness of his understanding of her. "Leave things well enough alone, my Alaric." She touched his chest armor. "I know who I am, my own worth. Our god knows too and has judged me acceptable for you. Leave it at that —please."

"If we are to be together," Alaric reasoned, "especially since you are growing in my heart, I would know you better."

For a long moment, her eyes searched his face, then became watery as a trace of a smirk flickered, her demeanor shifting as she absorbed his words. She blinked the unshed tears away. Lowering her chin, she looked up at him with a mix of amusement and challenge. "I think you know me well enough as it is."

"Do I?" Alaric pressed, his query more than a question—it was an entreaty, a yearning for deeper connection beyond the facades and the roles they played.

She opened her mouth to speak but was interrupted.

"Excuse me, my lord." The voice was respectful yet insistent.

Alaric's gaze shifted, locking onto Jaxen, who stood at a respectful distance from their campfire, next to Ezran, who was an immovable barrier barring the other's path.

"I hope I am not interrupting?" Jaxen's tone was laced with an undercurrent of unease. It was clear he had sensed something between him and Rikka.

Letting go a breath of resignation, Alaric stood. His eyes briefly met Rikka's. "We will finish this one day soon."

Almost reluctantly, she gave him a slight, sad nod.

"I can come back later," Jaxen suggested, looking between the two of them.

"No, you're not interrupting, not at all," Rikka said to Jaxen. She stood. "I need to ready myself for the march." With that, she made her retreat, ducking back into their tent and allowing the flap to fall back into place.

Ezran's gaze flickered between Alaric and the newcomer as he sought confirmation from his lord. Alaric's nod, subtle yet clear, was all the permission needed. The former ash man stepped aside, allowing Jaxen to proceed.

Alaric's attention shifted to the pack that Jaxen carried. Duncan's son set the pack down lightly on the ground at his feet.

"How can I help you?" Alaric inquired.

"I thought I might march with you today," Jaxen suggested, his words carefully spoken to convey both a request and a deference to Alaric's authority and right to say no. "That is, if you don't mind, my lord."

Realization dawned upon Alaric; Duncan's hand might be at play here. The bannermen didn't know him, not yet, and it was likely that Jaxen's father wanted his son to ingratiate himself with their new lord, to learn more about him and gain some advantage for their family, along with insight.

"Don't you have a horse?" Alaric asked.

"I do."

"And still, you would walk?" Alaric pressed.

"I've always enjoyed hiking, marching. Honestly, I am much better at walking than I am at riding. Yesterday's long journey to meet up with you left me with plenty of saddle sores." His words carried a hint of self-awareness and a lightness that spoke to his character—a young man comfortable in his choices and in sharing a laugh at his own expense. His cheeks colored slightly with the admission, and he shifted almost uncomfortably.

Alaric couldn't help but respond with a bark of a laugh. Jaxen's explanation was simple yet, Alaric thought, somewhat convincing. "I like your humor. And yes, you may march with me this day. I welcome your company."

"Thank you, my lord," Jaxen responded with some relief, his gratitude seeming genuine.

Alaric glanced around at his campsite. It had been set off to the side and away from most of the other tents, allowing him and Rikka a semblance of privacy, where in reality, there was none. Someone would be by shortly to break down their tent and see it packed and stowed with the supply train that was hauled by mules. He decided it was time to get moving and organized for the day. He'd wasted enough time. He picked up Oathbreaker by its scabbard. With a satisfying click, he secured the weapon to his harness, then tied the leather strap tight around his waist.

Next came his cloak, which he slung over his shoulders with an ease born of habit. It settled comfortingly around him. He observed the orchestrated chaos of the camp once more, of dismantling the tents and the preparations for departure of those nearest. The mules had been hitched with their tackle and harnesses. They were already being loaded with gear and equipment. One began braying loudly in protest.

Between his own men, the town's militia, and his bannermen, Alaric commanded a force of more than three hundred—a formidable number by any measure. Yet within that strength lay uncertainty, a segment of his force untested in the crucible of battle. The day ahead would be a trial by fire for many of the men not of Grayson's company, a test of their courage, steadfastness, and resolve. He'd know more about their quality after the sun set.

"You have led men into battle before?" Jaxen's question pierced through Alaric's contemplations. He turned, gaze lingering on Jaxen, taking in the mix of eagerness and apprehension that marked the younger man's demeanor.

It was a look he recognized from his own reflection of years past, before the realities of war and Crusade had tempered his youthful zeal, smothered it, really. Jaxen stood on the cusp of understanding, of experiences that would indelibly mark him, as they had Alaric. Under Alaric's gaze, the boy shifted uncomfortably.

"Have you been in a fight before? Not a rough-and-tumble scrum, boys' stuff, but a real fight—one with swords, where the other side is trying to kill you and yours stone dead?"

Jaxen hesitated a heartbeat. "I have." His gaze dropped to the ground beneath their feet, as if in search of the words to convey his experience properly. "This fall, my father and I came across bandits. They ambushed us and tried to kill us, to take what was ours. We got them, but not before they killed two of our number, loyal servants I had grown up with. That fight was not what I expected, what I thought killing would be like. I… I did not enjoy taking a life. I've thought of it often, for it was a close thing. Fate could have easily seen me and my father fodder for the worms."

Alaric nodded, understanding the weight of Jaxen's confession, the dissonance between expectation and reality, between the notion of valor and the visceral truth of violence and the consequences that followed, the shattering of youthful beliefs.

"Well," Alaric said with an unhappy breath as he thought back, "my first true fight where I took another's life was in a battle. That was certainly not what I thought it was going to be."

Jaxen gave a nod, his gaze locked on Alaric.

"The same goes for leading men into battle," Alaric shared, his voice carrying the burden of command, of decisions made in the heat of conflict. "Mistakes cost lives, and even when you do everything correct, people still manage to get killed. Afterwards, you have to live with that, with your choices or lack of them, and it is not a good feeling." Alaric paused for a moment as he sucked in a breath and then immediately released it. "I think it should not be a good feeling, but a bad one—one that keeps you up at night."

"So, you have led men in battle?" Jaxen pressed, seeking confirmation.

Was he perhaps looking for a mentor? A guide through the uncertain terrain of warfare and leadership? Alaric wasn't certain he was ready for a student, someone to teach. On the other hand, he might need to take the kid on, especially if he hoped to grow the number of men he had under arms, to increase Dekar's strength and military power. One company of infantry simply wasn't going to cut it. He'd need to raise more men in defense of his holdings.

Also, as Dekar prospered, so too would Duncan's holdings and the men who would serve his bannermen. Besides, eventually, Jaxen would succeed his father. He'd need to learn to lead, and Alaric would need effective leaders beyond Grayson. There was no doubt in his mind about that.

"Many times, I've led others into the fight," Alaric affirmed, thinking back to the question on leadership, the simplicity of his response belied by the gravity of his gaze. "It is not something I enjoy doing, but I've gotten good at it, better than some others

I've known." His admission was not one of pride, but of acceptance, a recognition of the role he played and the skills honed in service of necessity and one's duty.

Jaxen gave a grave nod. It was clear to Alaric he had impressed him, though that had not been his intention.

"Do you hope to lead men in battle one day?" Alaric turned the inquiry back on Jaxen, a question that was both a reflection and a challenge, inviting Jaxen to confront the realities behind his aspirations, whether he realized that or not. Regardless, Alaric already knew the answer he would receive. At Jaxen's age, he would have said the same.

"I do," Jaxen said.

"Then you have a lot to learn, more than you believe." Alaric spoke not only of the skills and strategies that command required, but also of the burdens it imposed—the decisions that would rest on Jaxen's shoulders, the lives that would depend on his wisdom and the courage needed to truly lead.

"My father says so too," Jaxen conceded.

"Then your father is wise. You should listen to him."

The moment was interrupted as Ezran called out, "My lord. Something has happened."

Alaric's gaze shifted to the former ash man, noticing the seriousness that marked his posture and the direction of his pointing hand. He followed Ezran's gesture and saw Grayson approaching, the captain's brisk pace and grim expression signaling the gravity of the situation. Something had indeed happened, and Alaric was sure whatever it was, was not good. Then Grayson was striding up to him.

"What is it?" Alaric asked, his voice steady despite the tension that the captain's demeanor evoked within him. Alaric had long since learned to keep his head, no matter how bad things got. That was one of the things others struggled with, but not him.

"The enemy at Tyfel," Grayson said. "They broke camp and are marching upon us."

"What?" Alaric demanded. That suggested the enemy knew he was on the way.

"One of our advance scouts just rode in to warn us. The enemy broke camp and began marching just after midnight. A rider had come in shortly before they formed up. It seems they got word of our coming for them, that we were on the way, and decided to come bring the fight to us."

Alaric glanced in the direction of the road. The evening before, he had received news from one of their scouts that the enemy was still at Tyfel, sitting tight and doing nothing much of anything. If they had marched just after midnight, that meant the enemy were now close at hand—that was, if they made good time of it. Alaric's mind was awhirl. Had one of the bannermen betrayed him and sent word, warning Laval's men? Was one or more in league with the duke? It was a troubling thought.

Alaric resisted glancing at Jaxen, who he knew was listening intently. Out of the corner of his eye, he could read the worry plastered across his youthful face. There was no proof that Alaric had been betrayed, but the thought of it nagged at him. For the moment, Alaric had to accept the oaths made were genuine. A messenger might have arrived from the town, another spy, one that had slipped around the line of march or, more likely, left before Alaric had even taken back the keep from Masterson. That he thought the more likely explanation.

"How close are they?" Alaric asked.

"The vanguard is a little more than a mile out, my lord." Grayson's response confirmed Alaric's worst fears. The enemy was not just approaching; they were almost upon him, the distance a mere whisper of space that separated the calm before the storm from the chaos of battle. "Our scout was pursued by one of theirs, up and to the camp itself."

That told him the enemy most definitely knew he was here and encamped. The immediacy of the threat left no room for doubt, hesitation, or second-guessing. Alaric found himself at the precipice of a decisive moment, one that would test the mettle of his leadership, the loyalty of his followers, and the strength of their collective resolve, not to mention the future of Dekar. With the enemy so near, each decision, each order, would be crucial in the orchestration of their defense and the outcome of the fight to come.

Alaric's tactical mind engaged, parsing the details to find some advantage in what appeared to be a bad situation. His men were rested, a significant benefit given the unexpected advance of the enemy, who would be badly fatigued after marching all night.

The presence of the defensive walls they had erected, not to mention the trench and the surrounding forest, provided not just a physical barrier, but tactical options. The forest could prove to be especially advantageous.

"Why did the scouts not report sooner, tell us the enemy was on the march?" Alaric asked. "What kept them? Surely our scouts should have made better time, especially since they were mounted."

"The enemy were marching along the road," Grayson reported. "Our men were forced to take to the forest and got turned around in the darkness. They had to work their way through the trees and about the enemy before they could make their way to us. That took time."

Rikka emerged from the tent, her expression mirroring the seriousness of their conversation. It was clear she had heard everything. She looked far from happy, worried even.

"How large is the enemy force?" Alaric asked, glancing from her back to Grayson. "Do we know?"

"At least five hundred foot, maybe slightly more," the captain reported, a number that dwarfed Alaric's force considerably.

"That many?" Alaric's reaction was not just one of surprise, but of recalibration, assessing their own capabilities against the daunting size of the approaching enemy infantry.

Grayson's nod, a silent affirmation of the challenge they faced, cemented the reality of their predicament. "The scouts seemed fairly confident in their count."

"What will we do?" Jaxen asked. "Fall back and retreat?"

Alaric glanced over at Jaxen and felt himself frown slightly, his thoughts awhirl as he looked away, thinking furiously. This information required a reassessment of their position, a strategic pivot that would leverage their advantages—the men, the defensive fortifications, and the surrounding forest—to counter the numerical superiority of their foes.

"Well," Alaric said, after a moment's more thought, "it will take some time for them to come up and get on line for an attack. I see no need to budge from the camp and fall back, to give up what we have, good defensive walls with plenty of men to man them and an outer trench to boot. More importantly, the enemy are coming to us, and we will have some time to prepare."

"Maybe a little more than a half hour before they arrive, then some more as they deploy, and yes, my lord," Grayson agreed, "we do have some advantages."

"We do." Alaric thought some more, scanning the forest that surrounded their camp. He was certain they were under direct observation. "Immediately push skirmishers out and into the trees about the camp. Any scouts the enemy have out there, I want them running for their lives and doing everything but their job of watching us. It must be done quickly, understand?"

"Yes, my lord," Grayson said. "And after that?"

"Take half of the company out and into the forest, the best of our veterans. Move to the east, work your way out around and behind the enemy. When the fighting begins, wait and then when you judge best"—Alaric brought his fist to his palm—"hit them from the rear, and hard. With any luck, you will catch them with their focus on us and unaware of your presence. I want you to come from the direction they marched, from the road. That should rob them of any feeling of safety and security from that quarter, letting them know that they've been cut off from possible retreat. I am hoping to generate a general panic."

"Yes, my lord," Grayson said eagerly.

"You mean to fight against a numerically superior force?" Jaxen asked. "One that is nearly twice our number?"

"I do, and it won't be the first time," Alaric said firmly and looked back at Grayson. "When they arrive, they will likely want to talk. I'll make sure I pick a fight and fix the enemy's attention firmly here, killing as many as I can as they throw themselves against our defenses. That should give you the time you need to loop around and behind."

"Yes, my lord. It should."

Alaric looked over at Jaxen. The younger man appeared worried, almost frightened. A thought struck Alaric. "Do you really want to learn how to lead?"

"I do," Jaxen affirmed with a nod.

"Then go with Grayson. He helped teach me. Watch and learn. More importantly, listen to him." Alaric shifted his attention to Grayson. "Keep him alive and from doing something stupid, like you did with me."

"As you command, my lord."

Alaric looked back at Jaxen, who suddenly seemed terribly excited by the prospect of what was to come. He had lost some of his apprehension. Alaric hardened his tone. "Do as he says, and not more, understand?"

"I do, my lord." Jaxen bowed his head in acceptance.

"Grayson." Alaric turned back to the captain. "We don't have a lot of time and need to get moving. Let's call the men to arms and put this plan into motion."

21

"Duncan." Alaric's voice carried the weight of command as he turned to the man standing beside him. His eyes swept across their encampment, a makeshift fortress of hastily constructed defenses nestled amidst the untamed wilderness. The sun was just up and moving higher, the sky brightening rapidly with its climb.

The enemy had arrived and were in the process of deploying around the camp, sealing them off. In short, they were encircled. There was no longer any getting out, no avenue of escape. But that was not Alaric's plan and certainly not his goal. He wanted the enemy to come to them, to throw themselves against his defenses. He badly wanted to destroy this enemy force and, given the chance, would do just that.

"My lord?" Duncan asked.

"You will lead our defense on the right flank, the east wall," Alaric declared, pointing in that direction.

"Aye, my lord. You can count upon me."

"Jourgan, you are to secure the rear, the west wall. Keever, the south is yours. As for myself, I shall stand firm in the north."

Gathered around him, his bannermen looked on with somber

and exceptionally grim expressions. Before any fight, no one was ever themselves or ready for what was to come, the violence, the maiming and killing. Emotion was always strong—unease, fear, worry—as were thoughts of one's mortality, faith, and the hereafter. There was no avoiding it, no helping it, and no alleviating such feelings, at least not easily. Keeping control of it all was what separated a man of action from one who was not, one who gibbered in fear.

His bannermen were looking not just grim, but unhappy and, Alaric conceded, they had a right to be. The enemy had gotten the jump on them and, more importantly, surprised him. Alaric knew in the future that could not happen, not again, for it could easily prove fatal. He would have to be more vigilant.

"I wish you had kept Grayson and his troops within the safety of our camp, my lord," Keever lamented, a note of frustration in his tone. He gestured toward the north, the direction from whence the enemy had come. "We have good defensive walls that will take serious effort to overcome, and we have the advantage of interior lines to shift reserves about as needed. By sending Grayson off with a hundred of your finest, you've thinned our numbers considerably, made the job of holding this camp much more difficult."

Alaric's gaze shifted to Keever, his eyes narrowing ever so slightly as he regarded the other man. It was rare for anyone to question his decisions, yet the critique was not without merit. By dispatching a portion of their number, Grayson and his contingent, beyond the confines of their encampment, Alaric had reduced their defensive capability and capacity. As Keever had said, he made it more difficult to hold the camp.

Instead of commanding a force of over three hundred strong, his defenders now numbered slightly over two hundred. Each man was tasked with defending a small stretch of wall. Their numbers had been so thinned that barely forty warriors could be spared for each wall, not accounting for the reserves he allocated for breaches in the line.

"Grayson knows what he's doing," Alaric countered firmly, betraying none of the uncertainty that the shadow of impending conflict often brought. It was critically important he remain in control of the situation, for he was their leader. They would look to him for strength in the coming hours. He could not afford to have that undermined.

He gestured broadly toward one of the walls. "We are at a disadvantage here, yes. The enemy is out there, surrounding us, boxing us in. If I had kept Grayson here, we would be without options, avenues of maneuver. I saw an opportunity and took it. With a force in the field and the way the enemy are currently deploying—that indicates they don't know about Grayson. It gives us a real chance to pull off a surprise, a serious upset on the gaming table, shocking our enemy to their core."

"And if this gamble doesn't pay off?" Jourgan asked.

"We worry about holding the walls of the camp," Alaric said, understanding he had to stamp out this kind of talk, for if given leeway, it would continue. "That, gentlemen, is our only concern. When Grayson hits—and trust that he will; we just need to give him time—we will go over the wall and take the fight to the enemy, hammering them straight in the teeth. They will not be expecting that."

"And when will he strike?" Keever interjected, his tone laced with skepticism, a mirror to the tension that gripped them all. "What if he gets lost out there and turned around, like our scouts did in the night?"

Grayson was on his own and effectively out of communication and contact. "He will attack when he's ready and not before. Our job will be to hold at all costs until then, and I seriously doubt he will get lost. Let me worry about Grayson. You worry about the walls you've been charged with holding."

"I don't like it," Keever confessed, his unease clear, a sentiment likely shared by the other two, though they didn't show it overly much.

Alaric was starting to become irritated. He did not need this headache right now, this division or questioning of his tactics. He hardened his tone so his bannermen could not mistake his meaning. "The die is cast, and we are bound to the path I've chosen. I've committed us to this course of action, and that is the end of the discussion. Our focus must be singular: defense, until Grayson strikes. Then, we go over to the attack."

"We will hold, my lord," Duncan declared firmly, carrying a blend of assurance and resolve. He cast a significant glance toward Keever, cutting off any potential rebuttal with a stern look.

"We will do it," Jourgan echoed. "There is simply no other option but to hold and force them back."

Alaric's gaze swept over the encampment, where his men stood vigilant, shields in hand and swords sheathed, ready to hastily move up to the defensive walls and behind the crude wooden barricade that had been constructed the night before. Only the sentries stood above and in view of the enemy. The air was thick with anticipation. He could feel it as the sergeants and corporals moved amongst the men working to soothe and cool nerves.

Alaric considered what he had on hand, reviewing his options. Beyond the reserve of fifty men at his command, he counted twenty bowmen amongst his forces. They'd already been given their orders, and once the fighting began, they would move to the walls. The value of skilled archers was clear to him, and Alaric felt they had too few.

"In the future, we need more bowmen," he mused to himself. Skilled men with bows could turn the tide of a battle, their arrows sowing discord and confusion, wrecking organization, not to mention thinning enemy ranks from a distance before the main lines even engaged one another.

Alaric made a mental note, when there was time, to prioritize the recruitment and training of such men. The effectiveness of archers in altering a battlefield's dynamics was undeniable. He had no idea how many bowmen the enemy had on hand and hoped it was not a goodly number, for they could make him pay dearly for holding this camp. For now, though, Alaric would make do with what they had on hand.

"Hello in there!" The call, unexpected and commanding attention, cut through the tension that hung like a thick fog over the encampment. It beckoned their attention toward the north wall, momentarily diverting their focus from the grim contemplations of the impending attack. "I would speak with your leader."

With a measured glance exchanged among his bannermen, Alaric took the initiative, his steps deliberate as he navigated through the painfully thin ranks of his men. These warriors, poised for battle with shields ready and swords resting in their sheaths, parted to allow him and his bannermen passage.

Ascending the reverse slope of the berm, Alaric climbed to the top and stopped at the barricade of tree trunks. An enemy line was arrayed before the north wall, much thicker than his own. Alaric scanned until his gaze fell upon the figures of two men standing a mere ten yards beyond the protective trench and ahead of the assault force. Alaric moved over so he was facing them more directly.

One of the two was a young man in his early twenties, accompanied by an older counterpart, who stood at his side. Both were armored, their attire a blend of practicality and status, with brown leather pants and helmets complementing their chest armor. The younger man, in particular, caught Alaric's eye. Fair of face and handsome, his armor so polished it gleamed under the newly risen sun, a display of wealth and care that spoke of noble birth, a pampered upbringing. He held his horse-plumed helmet casually under one arm, and his long, brown hair was neatly tied back into a single braid. Yet it was the smile, near perfect with overly white teeth, self-assured and bordering on arrogant, that solidified Alaric's immediate distaste for him.

Alaric glanced back at Jasper, who stood a few feet back and off to the side, bow in hand, staring outward at the enemy. Ezran and Thorne were with him. Alaric considered asking Jasper to cut down this arrogant bastard, then changed his mind. He needed to buy time for Grayson. He also needed the enemy to strike first and keep attacking. Killing their leader might see the opposite reaction. They might actually go home.

"Malvanis," Duncan murmured with a hint of disdain, clearly recognizing the young nobleman. The name alone was enough to elicit a collective unease amongst Alaric's bannermen.

"Who?" Alaric inquired, his gaze shifting to Duncan for clarification as he surveyed the scene before him.

"Laval's eldest son," Duncan returned. "He's a spoiled little shit, no better than his father, but much less bright and capable."

"He is at that," Jourgan chimed in, echoing the sentiment. "He is also a bully, a thug accustomed to getting his way."

Keever remained quiet, his expression souring further into a deep scowl. His discomfort was tangible, manifesting not in words, but in the restless shifting of his stance and the almost hateful glare he directed not just toward Malvanis, but also toward the enemy infantry arrayed into a battle line behind Laval's son.

Alaric's attention briefly returned to the enemy ranks to his front, noting the neat line they had formed up into and estimating it to be at least seventy-five strong. Their attire and armament were of a simpler make than that of his own men's: plain leather chest protection, mostly for warmth, paired with crude, inexpensive helmets and shields. A quick glance toward the other sections of the camp confirmed a similar deployment of enemy forces and dress—light infantry poised and ready for the attack, to be thrown against his defenses.

Despite the clear difference in equipment, Alaric could not help but weigh the strategic implications of what he was up against. His own men, clad in the more durable and expensive chainmail, offered a distinct advantage in terms of protection and combat effectiveness. His bannermen's men-at-arms and the local militia, though equipped in a manner more akin to the enemy, still benefitted from the defensive positioning provided by Alaric, placing them behind a trench and the walls, along with the barricade.

"Say there, is that you, Duncan?" Malvanis called out. "What are you doing in there?"

"Supporting my lord," Duncan's voice carried back firmly, a declaration of his allegiance that needed no further elaboration.

Malvanis's gaze swept over the group assembled atop the wall. However, his attention fixed upon Alaric, a mix of curiosity and calculation evident in his eyes, even from a distance. "I know all of you, Jourgan, and Keever, but I do not know you, sir," he said, pointing directly at Alaric.

"I am lord and earl of these lands, and you are trespassing," Alaric stated resolutely, leaving no room for ambiguity about the stakes at hand.

"Am I?" Malvanis responded, feigning surprise and innocence. "I had not realized that." He paused. "And that would make you Alaric, then. I had heard you'd returned from Crusade. Bad timing for you, if I might say so."

"You will turn your men around and leave my lands," Alaric commanded, his gaze flickering down into the trench before the wall. The previous night's labor, under his direct supervision, had seen the placement of sharpened stakes within the trench. Alaric had insisted upon it, a direct result of hard experience, campaigning in the holy land, and the paranoia he had acquired over the years when it came to moving through hostile lands. Though the number of stakes was modest, they were there none-theless, and the enemy would have to deal with them when they assaulted his camp.

A fleeting impulse to smile at the thought of the enemy assaulting his position crossed his mind, but he suppressed it. Instead, he focused on the immediate challenge, provoking Malvanis into initiating an immediate attack. When he did, Alaric would begin thinning the enemy's numbers.

"Is that all?" Malvanis asked. "Do you have any more demands of me?"

"No, not really. You will turn tail and leave my lands posthaste," Alaric reiterated. This time, he smiled broadly. "Tuck your tail between your legs and go home to your daddy. Tell him a man of strength rules these lands, one he should fear."

A grumble of approval ran through the men behind Alaric. He surveyed his men, running his gaze across the ranks, ready to move up and onto the wall.

"Turn tail?" Malvanis echoed, his voice laced with disbelief. "Surely you can't be serious?"

Alaric's response was unwavering, his tone cold as steel. "Leave, or I'll kill every single one of you I can get my hands on. I will murder you all stone dead." His rage swelled as he gazed out at Laval's son. Before him was one of the men directly responsible for the sorry state of his lands, the suffering his people had endured. It was even likely that Malvanis and the officer with him had personally directed those efforts, the raping, pillaging, and killing, not to mention directly participating. He made a point of looking directly at Laval's son and pointed with a finger. "If I get my hands on you, Malvanis, you'll personally wish I hadn't. That is a promise."

Malvanis, momentarily taken aback by the bold threat, turned to consult with the older man beside him. They spoke in low tones. This officer—clearly the commander of Malvanis's infantry—shared a brief, significant look with the young noble, gave a nod, gestured at the camp, and spoke some more. Alaric could not hear what was said. He got the feeling the officer was assuring Malvanis that they could take the camp from Alaric.

"We can expect no mercy from them," Duncan said. "They are here to seize Dekar."

"I agree," Alaric said.

"You are outnumbered and outmatched, sir," Malvanis retorted after he had finished speaking with the officer. "But— perhaps you mistake our intentions. We do not invade your lands but are here to restore order to Dekar."

"You expect me to believe that bullshit?" Alaric spat back. "Try selling it to someone else and see if they buy it."

"We can work together. My father wishes to return peace to this land."

"That is why I am here," Alaric countered, asserting his authority over his domain. "I had heard there were bandits oper- ating out of Tyfel. You wouldn't know anything about that, would you? Wait,"—Alaric gestured at Malvanis's men—"these are the bandits, aren't they? These are the pieces of shit that have been terrorizing Dekar."

"Tyfel, you say?" Malvanis asked, looking over at the officer with him. After a moment, the man simply shrugged. "I am afraid we don't know anything about that."

"This road only goes to one place, Tyfel, and that's where you're marching from," Duncan said.

"As I said, we know nothing about such things," Malvanis said. "Perhaps we can assist you in pacifying your lands."

"That will be the day," Jourgan grumbled.

Alaric raised his voice and gestured at Malvanis's line of soldiers. "Your men are going to find terrorizing regular people, civilians, is very different than tangling with my trained and experienced soldiers, my veterans of the Crusade. On that, you have my word." Alaric paused, then turned and shouted for all he was worth, "Man the walls!"

All around the camp, with armor chinking heavily, his men rushed up the reverse side of the berm to their positions on the wall, their shields held at the ready. Alaric imagined it looked impressive from the enemy's perspective. In fact, he hoped it had, for he wanted them to doubt what they were about to undertake.

The officer at Malvanis's side whispered something to him, prompting another series of words between the two. When they finished, Malvanis turned back to Alaric. He pointed at the ground. "We are here to stay. Dekar will be ours before the sun sets."

"Tell me, why are we even talking, then? Why are you wasting my time? Your daddy clearly sent you to do a man's job. As you will soon find out, he should have come himself, but I am sure he doesn't have the balls."

This blunt taunt elicited a ripple of laughter from the nearest of Alaric's men, a sound that carried defiance and camaraderie in the face of conflict.

Malvanis's reaction was instantaneous, a volcanic eruption, as his composure shattered with offense. His eyes, alight with indignation and rage, swept across the defenders manning the walls. "You bastard! No one talks to me or my family that way. We will see how smug you are after I am done with you and this little fort you've built. Today, we take no prisoners. We are going to kill every last one of you. On that, you have *my* personal word."

There was a deep unhappy grumbling at that last bit from Alaric's men. Malvanis could not have provided better motivation had he tried, for the man had just made plain what he'd do, and Alaric knew his men would fight harder for it, sell themselves dearly.

"Like your father, I don't think you have the balls," Alaric shot back, the dismissiveness in his voice stark as he turned his back on Malvanis, a final gesture of contempt. He rapidly descended the berm and stepped out of view, his bannermen following closely. He stopped a few paces down from the wall when he was completely out of sight of the enemy.

"You are mine, Alaric," Malvanis shouted in rage. "Do you hear me? You are mine, you bastard!"

"I think you pissed him off," Jourgan said.

"That was the plan," Alaric said calmly, though his rage still burned within his breast, fiery and hot. He intended to punish Malvanis and the men with him for all they had done.

"We are going to have a fight here soon enough," Duncan remarked with a note of certainty. "He will lose face if he backs down, and he can't have that. His father will surely punish him."

"The moment they crossed the border, a fight was inevitable, whether at Tyfel or here," Alaric responded. The die had been cast, and the time for words had passed. "Now, gentlemen, to your posts. Call for aid if you need it, but only if they make it up over the wall and are threatening to break into the camp proper."

As the bannermen dispersed, moving off to take up their positions, Alaric's attention was momentarily diverted. His eyes found Rikka, standing a short distance away, a figure of quiet strength. Bathed in sunlight, she looked otherworldly, intoxicating. Beside her was Kiera, both women talking amongst themselves.

Alaric's presence drew their attention as he moved toward them, his approach prompting Rikka to meet his gaze. The air between them was charged with unspoken words, a recognition of the stakes they faced—not just the impending battle, but the secrets that lay beneath the surface and hidden away.

"Do not ask me to use my magic in this fight," Rikka said before he could speak.

"Why?" Alaric asked, wondering what was wrong.

"The more energy I use, the more I cast, the longer it takes me to restore, to replace that which I have spent. In the last few days, I have used it to kill, and that takes time to replenish. I have a reserve, and spells I would prefer to save, but I do not wish to tap into that, not yet, not now. I use too much, and it may be months before I can cast another spell, be useful when the need is great."

"Then do not use your magic. I will solve this fight the old-fashioned way, with sword and shield."

"If the situation is dire and there is no other option," Rikka said, "I shall join the battle, but be warned, if it comes to that, what I have left is mainly nasty and powerful. It is not lightly used. Think of it as—a last resort, one I will use to protect you and you alone."

A massed shout came outside the walls of the camp, an ominous precursor to the storm of battle about to break. This thunderous shout pulled Alaric's focus sharply back to the immediacy of the looming conflict, to the north wall and his men manning it.

"My lord," Kiera began, drawing his attention. Her glance briefly met Rikka's, a silent exchange laden with shared understanding, before finding Alaric once more. "There is something we must discuss. It is important."

"Speak," Alaric said.

"I cannot fight at your side today. I—I now have a more important obligation, one I must honor above all else."

Alaric eyed her, understanding dawning as he looked between the two women. He had been expecting this conversation for some weeks. That it came now, on the eve of a fight, was a little concerning, but still not unexpected. Had it been Rikka's declaration of not using her magic? Had that been the catalyst for Kiera to finally make her move with him, to make her decision to move on? It did not matter, not now. "You are released from my service, then."

"What?" The surprise in Kiera's voice mirrored the shock in her gaze, along with some hurt. She had clearly expected him to argue, to protest. She opened her mouth to speak. Alaric held up a hand, forestalling her.

"I am not upset, let alone disappointed. You have served me with honor, done more than I could ever ask as part of my Shadow Guard." His gaze went to Rikka and lingered there. He looked back upon Kiera. "But a lumina needs her Luminary. You are her protector, her guardian, one of the last Luminaries around, the shield upon which the enemy's sword will break. That is the way of things, or at least the way they were during the last days of the Ordinate."

The enemy's fervor mounted outside the camp again as yet another shout rent the air, this one louder than the last. They were clearly working themselves up to a fevered pitch, a mounting storm about to break.

"Thank you, my lord," Kiera responded, her voice a mere whisper. There were tears in her eyes. Alaric took them to be tears of relief.

"Besides, you're not going anywhere, and Rikka has become —" Alaric stopped himself. What had Rikka become to him? He thought of the nights spent together, the touch of her skin against his when they lay next to one another, the warmth she generated, the smell of her hair, her very presence—the void that had been filled in his life, a companion who asked so little in return but who had given herself unreservedly. He did not fully know her, not yet, but it all somehow just felt correct... right, as if they had always been meant for one another. "Rikka has become dear to my heart. I would feel better with you watching over her, shadowing her, as you dogged my steps for all those years."

Rikka's gaze had locked with his, eyes watering and becoming glossy at his words. She gave him a slight nod of approval and thanks.

"You knew from the beginning?" Kiera accused, more as a statement than a question. "You knew this would happen!"

"When I saw you both repeatedly deck-side on *Magerie*, I suppose I did," Alaric confirmed, acknowledging the depth of his understanding of the growing bond between Kiera and Rikka—a lumina and her Luminary, a connection profound and essential. The old tales and histories spoke of such things. And looking at them, it felt right, correct. His ring had even begun to warm. "Or at least I suspected it would end up being so, that you two would become bonded in purpose and mission before our god. It is as it was meant to be. That's how I see things."

"Yes," Rikka agreed fervently. "It is."

Alaric turned away as another shout from the enemy roared over them. He felt himself scowl and decided it was time to return the favor.

"What are we going to do, boys?" Alaric called out, shouting loudly, rallying his men with a leader's resolve. "I want to hear it! What are we going to do?"

"Kill!" came the massed and expected response. The sound of the shout thundered on the air. It warmed his heart.

"I can't hear you!" Alaric shouted back. "What are we going to do?"

"Kill, kill, kill!" came the roar. "Kill… kill… KILL!"

Satisfied, Alaric bowed his head. It was time to commend his soul into his god's keeping. "Lord above and beyond, on this day of battle, we seek your favor, your blessing. Grant us the strength to vanquish the foes who stand before us. Watch over your brave warriors and spare them from the clutches of death and serious injury. May our victory be a testament to your glory. In your sacred name, I place my soul, trust, and hope, and those of my men."

"Amen," Rikka said quietly.

Alaric opened his eyes and looked at her. Her eyes were pools of deep emotion. Her gaze captivated his, locking him in place, freezing him in that moment. The world around them seemed to come to a complete stop. It was as if she were enchanting his soul. After a moment, he physically shook himself free, breaking the spell. He set his jaw as he regarded her. "Our conversation from earlier is far from done."

"I know it," Rikka said with a hint of sadness. "I know it only too well. It is inevitable."

"Then you will tell me everything?"

"I will," Rikka said, the sadness in her eyes growing. "Though in doing so, it may see the breaking of my heart."

A horn shattered the air. This was followed by another tremendous shout from the enemy.

"Here they come!"

22

A solitary arrow landed a few feet away, hammering down into the ground. Alaric barely paid it any mind. The noise of the fight was an entity in itself, a tempest of human turmoil, strife, and martial discord that rent the air, clawing painfully at the ears. Men's voices were raised in a tumultuous cacophony of agony and aggression—screams, intermingling with raw yells, oaths, and curses flung from one warrior to another.

Metal clashed against metal; swords met in a shrill chorus of steel, while shields produced deep, resonating *thunks* as blows were parried. Occasionally, arrows sliced through the tension-laden atmosphere, their presence announced by hissing and buzzing—ominous harbingers of death, the pitch and timbre of their flight altering eerily with their proximity.

Amidst this maelstrom of sound and fury, Alaric moved against the backdrop of chaos. His grip was firm on the shield he bore. With measured steps, he traversed the path behind the line holding the wall, gaze sweeping the fighting before him with keen scrutiny.

This assault marked the enemy's third attempt to overcome his defenses. The initial two attacks had been met and ultimately repelled, pushed back after a brutal and hard fight, the enemy having only tested two of the camp's walls during those assaults.

However, this time, the enemy had launched a powerful effort against all four walls at the same time. It was a clear attempt to put as much pressure as possible everywhere all at once and limit how Alaric could deploy his reserves. Despite having marched all night and launched two prior assaults, the enemy had come on with unchecked aggression. That spoke to their quality and motivation. Though poorly equipped, they were clearly well-trained and led.

Yet Alaric remained undaunted about their prospects. Though in the prior attacks he had drawn additional strength from the two walls not under attack, the reserves under his command were still uncommitted and waited to be called to action.

The fighting along his wall was brutal, hard, unrelenting savagery as man worked to kill his fellow man. The enemy were doggedly working their way up and out of the trench, scaling the wall to strike at those holding it.

Over a dozen of Alaric's men had already been wounded, some dragging themselves with the last vestiges of their strength to the aid station nestled within the camp's heart, where Father Ava worked. Others, who were too badly injured or had not the strength, were helped and carried back by comrades.

As he walked along the wall behind his men, he kept his shield up in the direction of the enemy, in the event someone took aim at him with a bow. The line he commanded, the one holding the north wall, was a fragile barrier of flesh and steel against the enemy's oncoming tide of rage. His men, using the crude barricade as cover, fought with a primal intensity behind it and their shields. With their swords, they thrust and jabbed at the enemy, for the closeness of the melee left little room for the wide arcs of slashing strikes.

Alaric saw an enemy combatant manage to claw his way out

of the trench's grasp, pulling himself up and over the barricade between two defenders who were engaged and could not deal with the man. He carried only a sword and was in the process of standing, when one of the corporals, moving behind the line, like Alaric, stepped forth and bashed the man directly in the face with his shield, knocking him violently into the trench. An agonized scream followed, likely the result of being impaled by one of the stakes below.

The sudden twang of a bowstring cut through the noise of battle, pulling Alaric's attention away from the melee at the wall. Just a yard off, Jasper, who had been following, had aimed and loosed, the missile flying through the narrow space between two men to his front to strike the enemy.

Alaric's gaze lingered on Jasper for a heartbeat, witnessing the focused calm as he rapidly nocked yet another arrow, aimed, and released. He had never met anyone better with a bow than Jasper. The man was freakishly good and rarely missed what he aimed at.

Alaric saw the arrow striking home—hitting a figure standing on the other side of the trench, likely a sergeant. The man had been encouraging his men forward, into the trench and attack. The arrow took him just above the hip and partially spun the sergeant around, sending him lurching forward. At the trench's edge, he lost his footing and tumbled headfirst, disappearing from sight, like a shadow at dusk.

Alaric whirled as one of his men, barely a breath away, crumpled to the ground, an arrow shaft protruding grotesquely from his left eye socket. Beside him, another dropped, struck down in rapid succession, then another. An arrow *thunked* heavily into the top portion of Alaric's shield, the point emerging out the back.

The breach in his line created by these losses did not go unexploited. Emboldened, three enemy combatants seized the moment, scrambling up and out of the trench, pulling themselves over the barricade and onto the wall.

"Close up the line!" Alaric shouted. He drew his sword and surged forward to directly confront this threat, this breach in his defenses. One of the men, having gotten to his feet, lunged at him with a sword. Alaric used his shield to block the attack and bat it away. He stabbed out, his blade biting into the shoulder of his enemy, the sword point punching through the leather of his tunic. It was a shallow wound, but sufficient to send his opponent reeling backward, where he tumbled over the barricade, falling back into the trench.

Alaric then turned his shield into a weapon, slamming the next man with a forceful blow that unbalanced him and sent him also tumbling into the trench. The third, a large and burly man much bigger than Alaric, gained his footing, his eyes burning with a crazed ferocity. With a guttural scream that sliced through the din, he hurled himself forward, just as Alaric began to turn and bring his shield up. It was too late, for this human projectile, driven by desperation and maddened by battle rage, tackled Alaric, taking him down to the ground.

Having lost his shield and sword, Alaric found himself in a desperate struggle, grappling as he and his adversary crashed to the ground. The fight became a maelstrom of close-quarters violence, a primal duel of flesh and fury as each man fought and battered at the other. Alaric unleashed a flurry of punches, striking the face, neck, and stomach, each blow an attempt to break free from the other's mad clawing.

A stray fist found its mark on Alaric's chin, a blow that sent a shockwave of disorientation coursing through him. His vision blazed with a burst of white, a momentary eclipse of his senses before determination surged within him, dragging back clarity of thought and purpose, the will to best his opponent and survive.

In that fraught instant of clarity, Alaric spotted Oathbreaker to his side. His fingers grasped the weapon's hilt, wrapping tightly around the cord grip. He attempted to wield it, to bring it to bear and turn the tide of the struggle with a decisive stroke, but his opponent was relentless and immediately recognized the threat.

The enemy soldier, leveraging his size, position, and weight, managed to get atop and straddle Alaric, a knee coming to press down heavily on his sword arm. At the same time, he fixed one meaty hand on Alaric's neck, leaning into it and squeezing powerfully, trying to choke the life out of him. The other hand fumbled for a dagger sheathed at his belt—a grim promise of a brutal end.

Alaric, his vision beginning to dim, struggled to breathe. Becoming desperate, he thrashed violently and managed to force the hand from his neck with a Herculean effort, batting it away, causing the other to drop, almost falling forward. Gasping for breath, Alaric propelled his helmeted head upward with all the force he could muster. The impact was powerful—a hollow *thunk*, followed by the sickening crunch of shattering bone as the enemy's jaw fractured. His opponent instantly went limp, falling forward and landing heavily on Alaric as pure dead weight.

Gasping for air and with effort, Alaric heaved the incapacitated enemy off his body and struggled to his knees. The wall around him was a maelstrom of chaos, a blur of friend and foe locked in deadly scrum. He raised his head, eyes darting about, endeavoring to discern the flow of battle amidst the tumult, to distinguish between ally and adversary in the swirling chaos of the fight.

It was in this moment of disoriented vigilance that an enemy brushed past. Instinctively, Alaric reacted, his sword slicing through the air and biting into the back of the man's calf. The blade sent his target crashing to the ground in screaming agony. He rolled down the reverse side of the wall and into camp. Almost instantly, Alaric lost sight of him.

With grim determination and groaning from discomfort, Alaric dragged himself upright, his body protesting every movement with a chorus of pain and fatigue. Then he was once more on his feet. However, his respite was short-lived; a forceful shove from a shield sent him reeling down the side of the berm, back toward the camp proper. The world tilted dangerously, yet somehow, he managed to recover his balance and remain on his feet.

There was fighting all around him. No sooner had he steadied himself than another enemy emerged from the chaos. This new opponent lunged, jabbing out, blade aimed with lethal intent, but Alaric, driven by a survivor's resolve and years of training, parried the thrust, knocking his opponent's blade aside. The two swords rang from the impact. Pain from the clashing of the blades radiated from his hand that held the grip of his sword.

Gritting his teeth and doing his best to ignore the discomfort, Alaric met his foe's gaze with a feral snarl. His opponent attacked and the swords clashed again, steel on steel, a song of survival where every note represented a potential final breath and at the same time the promise of life.

Alaric threw himself into the fight, launching a series of attacks. His opponent managed to block each. Then, Alaric feinted and his opponent went for it, overextending himself. Alaric's sword was a flash of lightning as he changed its trajectory, carving an arc that culminated in a thrust aimed at the man's hip. His enemy, realizing the error, hastily tried to correct his block, but it was too late. The strike was precise, slashing deeply. The side of the blade dug into the hip bone, then his adversary stumbled backward, and he was swallowed by the press of bodies that churned around them in a confused melee.

A sword hammered into him from behind, slamming against the sturdy metal of his armor and sending shockwaves of pain through his back. The force of the blow propelled him a grudging step forward. As he regained his balance and started to turn to face this new threat, a raw, agonized scream pierced the tumult of battle.

There, amidst the swirling chaos of friend and foe, were

Thorne and Ezran. Ezran had just taken down the man who had struck at Alaric from behind. The former ash man had already turned and engaged another enemy, batting away a sword and then stabbing deep into the other's stomach. Thorne stood to Ezran's left, locked in a struggle of his own with another opponent.

Alaric spotted an enemy moving past. He stabbed out, his sword sinking into the other's side, just below the ribcage. This man dropped, then suddenly, there was not an enemy within easy reach. Alaric glanced rapidly around, trying to get a sense for the fight, to see if there was anything he could do. The breach in the wall had widened, a gaping maw that threatened to swallow them whole as the enemy surged up from the trench and over the wall, literally throwing themselves into the fight with relentless fury.

His eyes locked onto another enemy who stumbled his way, momentarily exposed with his back partially turned. With a predator's precision, Alaric attacked, sword raised in a deadly arc. The blade descended, crashing onto the man's shoulder and collar with a bone-jarring impact. The force of the blow drove the enemy to his knees. Alaric felt the hot spray of blood across his face and tasted copper.

Without a moment's hesitation, he yanked his sword away and turned his attention to another enemy who had come near. Alaric's blade found its mark once more, slicing into the man's side just above the hip, finding the soft flesh there and cutting deep.

Then the fight was back on him as more of the enemy arrived and those on the wall around the gap were pushed back and down the reverse side of the wall, the melee of fighting once more crashing over him.

Alaric glanced back at the wall and the breach. "Commit the reserves! Commit the reserves!" His shout was swallowed up by the sound of the fight, then Alaric had no more time for thought.

He jabbed at an enemy, stabbing the man in the back, and dropped him.

More, Oathbreaker whispered, an entreaty to send their souls soaring on to Eldanar. This silent invocation stirred something primal within Alaric, igniting a ferocity, a matching hunger that transcended the mere physicality of the fight. His voice joined the cacophony of the battlefield, a raw, unbridled scream that was both a war cry and a release of all the pent-up fury and frustration that coursed through him. Each enemy became not just an opponent to be vanquished, but an obstacle in his path to be overcome.

In this frenzied state, Alaric was a whirlwind of death, unwilling to yield even an inch of the ground as he stabbed, jabbed, slashed, cut. His sword, stained with the blood of his enemies, rose and fell, struck out, and jabbed, again and again. He had flashes of Thorne and Ezran at the edges of his vision, their faces set in grim determination, anchoring him to the reality of their shared struggle. Yet, predominantly, his world was filled with the faces of the enemy, each one a challenge to be met, a threat to be nullified, someone to be cut down. The faces blended together into one great blur, a tide of violence and rage that spilled out from him and onto the enemy.

There was a massed shout and a mad rush, followed by a crash he could nearly feel. The tide of battle abruptly shifted with a thunderous surge of reinforcements—the arrival of the reserve. This sudden onslaught crashed into and against the enemy with overwhelming force.

As the fresh soldiers bounded past him, Alaric found a moment's respite, his breaths coming in heavy, ragged gasps as he surveyed the shifting battlefield. His eyes caught the figure of Keever cutting down an enemy from behind with the decisive swing of his longsword before he screamed in triumph over his kill. In that instant, surrounded by allies and buoyed by the resurgence of hope, Alaric felt the madness of the battle rage ebb and a heavy exhaustion overcome him.

"To the wall!" Keever was shouting as he fought his way forward, leading the reserves up the berm. At his side was Kiera, hacking and slashing as she fought with him. Rikka was nowhere in view. Alaric prayed she was all right. "Seal the breach!" Keever continued shouting. "Retake the wall! Shove them back and over the side!"

The reserve, under Keever's determined lead, surged like a tide of retribution into this gap, their swords singing of vengeance as they reclaimed the contested ground, once more sealing the breach.

In the brief respite that followed the frenetic clash, Alaric allowed himself a moment, taking in the full scope of the embattled fortifications that raged around him. He noted with a grim satisfaction that, save for a critical ten-yard breach, the majority of the wall, his defenders, still stood strong and defiant against the enemy's attempts to overcome them.

Alaric returned to the wall, climbing back up and joining Keever. Breathing heavily and catching his breath, the man was standing there with Kiera, both their swords bloodied. He gave her a nod, one that clearly conveyed his respect, and then turned to Alaric.

"That was a close thing, my lord," Keever remarked gruffly, acknowledging the razor's edge upon which victory and defeat had just danced. "Next time, send for help sooner."

"There was no time for that," Alaric explained wearily. "It happened too quickly, and I was caught up in the middle of it all."

The call of an enemy horn punctured the soundscape of battle. Like the subsiding of a violent storm, the clamor of combat began to rapidly dissipate as the enemy started to withdraw, pulling away from the walls.

Alaric stepped up to the barricade and looked over the wall's side, surveying the trench. It was nearly full of bodies, stacked one upon another. Behind him, there was a trail of dead and wounded where the breach had occurred, leading down and into the camp.

The horn sounded again.

"They're pulling back," came a shout. It was Duncan from the east wall. "They're pulling back, boys! Good job! Good bloody job!"

"We made them pay a steep price," Keever observed, his tone laden with satisfaction, "a very steep price."

Alaric, following Keever's line of sight, observed the enemy's wounded—men maimed and some most likely crippled for life—staggering away from the wall, dragging themselves out of the trench and moving toward the safety of the trees. Alaric did not see an aid station. It was almost as if the enemy did not care for their own, for no one was moving to assist the injured.

"It's always harder on the attacking force," Alaric mused aloud, a statement underpinned by the cold calculus of defensive warfare. "Especially if you are assaulting a fortified position."

"Aye," Keever concurred, his agreement carrying the weight of experience and the tacit acknowledgment of the harsh realities of warfare. "It is. They will regroup and come at us again until either they break us, or we break them." His words, while grim, were not defeatist, but rather a recognition of the inevitable cycle of conflict—a pause before the storm's resurgence. "They are not going to give up this effort easily."

Alaric could not deny that. His mind was already turning toward what was to come, to the inevitabilities that lay ahead. The enemy's near-success in breaching their defenses was a warning. Even having inflicted heavy losses upon Laval's men, the realization that they remained outnumbered, and the understanding that the enemy's resolve had not been shattered but merely checked, weighed heavily on him.

With the breach that had almost undone their defense, Malvanis would undoubtedly have taken stock of how close he had come to victory. Such knowledge would only serve to fuel his determination for a renewed assault and redoubling of effort.

In this moment, as the dust of battle settled and the din of combat receded into an uneasy near silence, save for the injured who cried out and moaned and screamed their agony to the world, Alaric was acutely aware of the fleeting nature of their reprieve. He was also terribly thirsty but had nothing at hand to drink.

"Reform," the enemy officer who had been with Malvanis before the fighting was shouting as he moved amongst his men. "Reform." The man was thirty yards away. Alaric could not see Malvanis. He must be elsewhere, along one of the other walls. Wooden whistles began to blow, and sergeants started to pick up the call, working to reinforce it.

"Form up, boys," the officer shouted again. "Come on, back into line."

"Assaulting is never an easy endeavor," Alaric remarked, the memory of battles past and the toll of the day's fight lending gravity to his words. With Oathbreaker in hand, he gestured toward the enemy coming back into a recognizable line of battle before the north wall. "It is hard and exhausting. They're tiring, and with each effort, we blood them greatly. Let them come again, let them throw themselves into the trench and against the wall. We just need to hold this next one."

"We do." Keever's response, though terse, was imbued with the gritty realism that characterized a veteran warrior's understanding of the situation. His sour tone belied the gravity of their situation, an acknowledgment of the daunting task that lay ahead. "My lord, with your permission, I will get back to my wall."

Alaric gave a nod of approval. Keever moved down the wall, leaving Alaric alone. His gaze drifted toward the forest as his thoughts wandered to Grayson. He and the men the captain had taken with him had been out there for over an hour and a half, maybe two at this point. It was hard to tell how much time had passed since the assaults had begun. He glanced skyward and was surprised to see the sun had risen significantly since he'd last looked. He turned his gaze back to the forest, into the trees, searching, scanning. How long before he came? Could they hold for another assault?

They had no choice but to hold.

The frenzied shouts of the enemy officer, slicing through the tense air, captured Alaric's attention again as he sought to organize his forces for the next assault. The man was moving along the line, shouting at stragglers, and physically forcing men back into the ranks. Alaric's gaze, sharp and calculating, focused on the source of the commands before glancing around.

"Jasper?" Alaric called out and waved for the other's attention. "Come over here."

Jasper made his way to join Alaric before the defensive barricade. "My lord? How can I help?"

"How many arrows do you have left?"

Jasper's answer was conveyed by holding up two arrows.

"See that officer?" Using a subtle gesture of his chin to avoid drawing unwanted attention, Alaric directed Jasper's gaze toward the enemy officer, the man who had stood with Malvanis.

Jasper, understanding the significance of the target, acknowledged the challenge. "It's a long shot, my lord, but I could hit him from here, stop him from organizing his men into an assault."

"No," Alaric said, dismissing the immediate elimination of the officer. "I don't want that, not yet."

"You want them to attack again?" Jasper asked, surprised. "That last effort nearly broke us."

"I know it, and I do want them to attack," Alaric confirmed. "Once it begins, take that officer out, drop him. He is the senior-most officer next to Malvanis, probably the guy who knows these soldiers the best. He should come closer once the assault begins, making your task of taking him down easier. I don't want him around to rally his men once Grayson attacks, understand?"

"I will make my shot count, then, my lord."

"Good man." Alaric clapped Jasper on the shoulder and moved off, walking along the line again. The weariness amongst his soldiers was a near-physical thing. After three assaults against the north wall, his men were tiring. Several had minor wounds. Alaric had to assume that his men on the other walls were tiring as well.

"Keep your heads up, boys!" Alaric shouted. "You've done good. Quite good! We'll give them more of the same and send them packing this time! These bastards aren't anywhere near as tough as Sunara's boys! You faced them, you can face anyone and put them in their place!"

The cheer that followed his words was more than a response; it was a reaffirmation of their collective resolve, a chorus of warriors ready to stand once again, united in purpose and will, to hold and throw back the enemy.

"What are we going to do?" Alaric shouted.

"Kill," the unified response came.

The enemy's horn sounded, blaring loudly, shockingly so. With a great cry, the opposing forces launched themselves forward, a wave of desperation and determination pouring forth and into the trench. Over the bodies of the fallen—the dead, the dying, and the injured who could not extricate themselves from the trench—the enemy advanced with murderous intent.

As they scrambled up the steep slope of the berm, the defenders braced, a collective tensing of bodies and spirits in anticipation of the imminent clash.

Alaric's focus momentarily shifted to Jasper, the embodiment of calm precision and focused intent amidst coming chaos. He held his bow with an arrow nocked, tension on the string. He drew a bead, leading his target as he pulled on the string to draw more tension onto the bow. Then with a suddenness… Jasper released.

The missile found its mark—the enemy officer. So powerful was the strike that the steel tip drove through the armored breastplate with a loud crack and knocked him back and to the ground. There he writhed in agony. Two men hurried to the officer's side and knelt to offer aid. Alaric felt a rush of triumph, for the man was badly injured and now effectively out of the fight.

He looked back at Jasper and nodded his approval.

Having made it over the trench, all along the walls, the enemy's assault crashed against the defense at the barricade with the force of a tempestuous storm breaking against a rocky shore. Alaric's men holding the wall fought with all they had, keeping the enemy from making it over the barricade. Along the north wall, Alaric, carrying Oathbreaker, once more resumed his pacing behind his line to watch the fighting. He called out encouragements and issued orders as he saw fit where there was need for some adjusting.

Observing the combat, Alaric sensed a shift in the tide. It was a subtle thing, a lessening of the sound of battle that came with previous attempts to overcome the wall. There was a sense of decline in the enemy's vigor, their energy and effort to push the assault home. Their attacks lacked the fervency of the previous ones, a sign that the relentless defense had begun to erode their resolve, a fact not lost on Alaric as he scrutinized the battlefield. His men were holding, and he suspected the enemy was finally beginning to flag. The march through the night had likely not helped. He stopped and looked at the other walls, studying the action there. As near as he could tell, it was the same story there as it was along the north wall.

He spotted idle bowmen huddled together within the safety of the camp, his mind quickly assessing their potential. They were all the reserve he had left, and not much of one. Their quivers were empty, having loosed all of their missiles, but these men were still armed with swords. He made a decision. They could contribute to the defense, not with arrows, but with steel in hand.

"Thorne," he directed, catching the other's attention and pointing toward the bowmen. "Go gather that lot up and have them draw swords. Divide them up evenly and send them to the walls as reinforcement. Make sure they get there too."

"Yes, my lord," Thorne said and moved off, jogging down the berm.

Turning back to the tumult of the fighting that was raging just feet away, Alaric's gaze swept across the north wall with the keenness of a hawk, searching for any weakness along his line, for any advantage he might be able to exploit. He saw nothing and continued to pace.

The battle wore on. The enemy, though their efforts were increasingly flagging, continued their assault. It was a clear attempt to wear down Alaric's defense through sheer force and numbers. He understood it could still work, but the enemy were now beginning to take heavy casualties, more with every passing moment. The power of his defense was showing.

Alaric heard alarmed shouting from behind and spun to look. On one of the other walls, the east side of the camp, a breach had been opened as two men had been cut down. Alaric's heart chilled at the sight of the gap in his line.

Several of the enemy were pulling themselves over the barricade and up and onto the wall. One made it over the barricade, followed rapidly by another. Then, Duncan was there amongst them. He surged into the gap, a force of will and vengeance, his heavy blade rising and falling as it chopped at the enemy making their way over the wall, causing them to hesitate and even recoil. His actions preserved the integrity of the line just long enough for additional men, one of Alaric's sergeants and a corporal, to join him. Together they began plugging the breach, throwing the enemy back and into the trench.

Alaric let go a relieved breath.

"My lord," Jasper called, drawing Alaric's attention. The other was pointing out and into the forest facing the north wall. "Look!"

Alaric turned, seeing nothing. Jasper pointed vigorously. He peered closer. There was movement out there. A line of men, formed into two ranks, materialized from the woodland's depth, the shadows of the forest. Were they enemy reinforcement? By God, he hoped not! He doubted they could hold against greater numbers.

He squinted harder, struggling to better see, to make out who they were. The advancing line bore the semblance of spectral avengers, forest wraiths. Alaric felt his heart begin to beat faster, hammering in his chest as he recognized the chainmail armor and standard.

Grayson had finally arrived!

Though Alaric felt a moment of triumph, the fight could still be lost, could still turn against him, for such was the fickleness of battles. Nothing was ever certain. Everything depended upon what happened next.

He watched these new figures, who were deployed and advancing in a line of battle, for several long heartbeats. They were at least two hundred yards from the camp and closing steadily, but their presence marked a significant shift in the day's narrative, the potential to turn things upside down for the enemy.

Malvanis's wounded, having settled amongst the nearest trees, were the first of the enemy to notice this new development. Their attempts to sound the alarm, a desperate bid to alert their comrades to the emerging threat, were swallowed by the relentless din of combat along the camp's walls. Their voices, strained and fading, failed to pierce the veil of noise that enveloped the battlefield, a sound that roared like a monster over the fight.

Those injured who could move tried to stagger or drag themselves out of the way of the advancing line. Those who couldn't make the effort simply waited for the inevitable. The line advanced, grinding mercilessly over them, Grayson's soldiers methodically stabbing down at the injured men as they passed, ending their lives and the potential threat they represented.

Grayson, leading his men from the front, was now a hundred yards out from the trench and the fighting. Alaric understood it was time to act, time to truly change the dynamic and take the initiative away from the enemy.

"Prepare to advance!" Alaric's command thundered across the battlefield, a call that galvanized his weary but resolute defenders. "Prepare to advance!"

The effect was immediate, a shift in the atmosphere, as his men tensed, a collective inhalation of purpose and resolve. The order was picked up by Jourgan and repeated, reinforcing the directive, a wave of anticipation rolling through the ranks, invigorating the weary. Then Duncan took up the call, and finally, Keever. The fighting along the walls abruptly slacked, the noise dying down somewhat, the enemy clearly wary that the defenders were about to come out from behind their defenses. Then, from the enemy's rear, along the north wall, a new cry emerged, a rhythmic chant that pierced the cacophony of battle with chilling precision.

"Kill... kill... kill!"

This unexpected rally, emanating from Grayson's men behind the enemy's lines, sowed confusion, fear, and utter shock in the hearts of their adversaries all along the north wall. Many looked around, clearly shocked at the unexpected appearance of enemy infantry behind them. It was then that Grayson's men began to beat their swords against the insides of their shields as they steadily continued to close the distance.

They were now fifty yards out.

The thumping of sword against shield was a sound that Alaric found quite ominous, and it clearly added to the enemy's terror, shock, and confusion at finding themselves flanked by a fresh force. Belatedly, enemy officers and sergeants started to shout orders, calling on their men to fall back, get out of the trench, and reform to face this new threat.

Alaric knew it was too little, too late.

"Advance!" Alaric shouted for all he was worth as he raised his sword high into the air, waving it around. "Advance! Push them, boys! Push them hard!"

With a collective roar, his men inside the camp and at the walls surged forward as one. They climbed over the barricade, shields battering at those enemy that had not fallen back and away from the wall, swords jabbing out and slashing down with unforgiving lethality, their movement a tidal wave of retribution and pent-up rage. The enemy faltered, caught off guard first by the appearance of Grayson's force, and now the sudden advance, their ranks at the north wall breaking.

The enemy gave way, falling from the berm in terror, going into the trench, clearly thinking now only of escape and their own lives. In their haste to unburden themselves, many threw their shields and swords away. Alaric's men followed with a vengeance, and he went with them.

As he climbed over the barricade, Alaric bent and scooped up a discarded shield. Then he was in the trench himself, he and his men stepping on and over the bodies of the wounded and dead as those before them fled.

There was a roaring shout from Grayson's line as his men were released. They charged forward madly, slamming into the fleeing enemy from the opposite direction, slashing and hacking at all those who came within reach. The real killing had begun, and the enemy, caught between two forces at the north wall, fell by the dozens as they were cut down in their frenzied flight.

Alaric stuck out his leg and tripped a man who was in the process of running by him. The man went down in a tumble. Alaric stepped over and stabbed downward into the back of the man's chest, aiming to pierce the heart. The man stiffened as the blade went in deep, easily penetrating the weak, inexpensive leather tunic and penetrating between the ribs. Then, he went limp, going still for all time. Alaric placed his boot upon the man's back and, with a hard pull, yanked the blade free.

Behind him, a massed shout caused him to turn. The west and east walls' assaults had given way under pressure from those who had come out from behind their defenses. The fear and confusion that had started in the north were now spreading like a plague amongst the rest of the enemy as they broke and ran for their lives to the trees, with Alaric's men giving a heated pursuit.

From his current point of view, he could not see the south wall but had to assume the same thing was happening there as well. A sense of triumph fully overcame him, though it was not yet over and the killing far from done. He had broken the enemy decisively.

They had won.

He had won.

Alaric knew it was only a start, a beginning of reclaiming his legacy at the edge of a sword.

"Grayson," Alaric shouted, having spotted the captain no more than twenty yards away as he cut down an enemy who had thought to stand and fight him. That had been a fatal mistake. Next to the captain was Jaxen, his sword bloodied. Alaric shouted again, "Grayson!"

"My lord?" Grayson called back, jogging over to him. Jaxen came along at his side. The young man's face was spattered with blood and bits of gore.

"We really caught them, my lord," Jaxen said, breathing heavily, his eyes a little crazed from the fight. "We really got them good."

"Yes, you did," Alaric said and turned to Grayson. "Good work!"

"Thank you, my lord. The flanking movement took longer than expected. Off the road, the forest is quite dense."

"I understand. Listen, I want an organized pursuit. Send runners to the bannermen. Catch as many of the bastards as we can, but don't let the men go too far into the forest, at least without the security of organized groups."

"Aye, my lord," Grayson said, looking around. "I will try to bring some order to this chaos."

"Very good. Again, excellent job. Your timing was perfect."

Grayson gave a firm nod. He looked over at Jaxen. "Come on. We have work to do."

With that, both men moved off to carry out his orders.

Ezran had appeared by his side. Jasper was there too. Alaric scanned for any sign of danger about them, any threat lurking nearby. He was also searching for Malvanis, scanning the trees for the man. He did not see the bastard anywhere amongst the fleeing enemy. Had he run off when his men had broken? If he had, where was he likely to go?

"If you were Malvanis, where would you run to?" Alaric asked Ezran, drawing the former ash man's attention. Before the other could reply, Alaric snapped his fingers and began heading toward the road, picking up his pace. "He'd go find a horse and then run for his father."

The enemy would have come with an organized supply train,

a lifeline for their forces carrying food rations and other essentials, like tents and tools for setting up camp. He understood all that would soon be his as the spoils of war. More importantly, there would also be horses for the officers, and they'd be kept with the train, which was likely parked along the road. If he was to find Malvanis amidst this chaos, he'd likely find him there, unless, of course, the bastard was already dead or, like his men, fleeing as fast as he could run into the heart of the forest.

As his men pursued the enemy into the trees, shouts of the hunters and cries from the hunted rang out, along with the occasional scream of agony. Entering the trees, Alaric glanced around as they moved, scanning for enemies hiding within the brush and undergrowth. He saw none. It had only been a short span of heartbeats, maybe a two hundred count, since he'd left Grayson, but no longer were any of Laval's soldiers in view. They'd all legged it.

Upon reaching the road, as expected, they found the supply train a short way off, with many of the supplies already unloaded and stacked neatly. Five heavy wagons, still partially loaded, were pulled by draft horses. The horses had been unhitched from the wagons and were picketed off to the side of the road in a large group, along with more than three dozen mules. Hay had been thrown at their feet.

Around the wagons, a handful of Alaric's soldiers were locked in combat with several enemy, their swords clashing in a deadly dance as they gave ground and his men pressed them. Even as he watched, one of the enemy dropped his sword and fled.

Amidst the fray, and close by, one figure stood out. A man had seized a horse from amongst several that had been picketed together, saddled it, and was in the process of climbing into the saddle. Under the light, the armor the man wore flashed, standing out from the other soldiers.

Malvanis.

The bastard was about to get away. Alaric could not, under any circumstances, allow the man to escape. "Jasper, do you have an arrow left?"

"I've been saving the last one, my lord," Jasper said as he nocked and aimed carefully, drawing a bead on Laval's son.

"I want him alive and off that horse," Alaric said as Malvanis settled himself into the saddle and wheeled his horse around, pointing the animal's nose down the road that led to Tyfel. "I made that man a promise and I would like to keep it."

Jasper did not bother replying. The bowstring's resonant twang was the only warning before the arrow sliced through the air, its flight a deadly hiss on the wind. Its mark was met with precision. The horse let out a harrowing scream of pain as the arrow burrowed into its rump. The animal reared up, its front legs pawing wildly at the air, and screamed again before bucking wildly several times.

Unprepared, Malvanis lost his hold on the reins and fell backward, off the horse. He hit the ground with a resounding thud that Alaric not only heard, but could almost feel himself. Freed from its rider and burden, the horse surrendered to its instincts and bolted, its hooves drumming a rapid retreat down the road, kicking up clods of dirt as it sped off and away.

"Good shot," Alaric said.

"Thank you, my lord," Jasper said.

Jogging, Alaric moved swiftly toward the fallen figure, who was rolling about on his back, even as the rest of the enemy, those who had been contesting Alaric's men around the wagons, broke and fled, running after the horse or heading for the safety of the trees that lined the road.

Alaric found Malvanis lying upon the ground, dazed by the fall, his senses scrambled. Blood ran from his nose down the side of his cheek. Alaric placed the cold, unyielding edge of his sword point against the man's armored chest. It was then that Malvanis's eyes finally focused, meeting Alaric's gaze. Shock, then fear, registered in the other man's eyes.

With a grim smile, Alaric shifted the point of his sword, moving it from Malvanis's chest to hover ominously at his neck, the point touching the skin and causing a bead of blood to appear.

"You, sir," Alaric said, "are my prisoner."

23

In the center of Tyfel's village square, Alaric eased himself onto a rough-hewn stool he had taken from the tavern. The stool's legs were slightly uneven from years of use. The square, once a hub of the community, now bore the marks of its occupation and subsequent abandonment by those who had once called the village home.

Tyfel had been transformed into a strategic point of operations. Its streets and alleys, which once echoed with the footsteps of its inhabitants, were now lined with makeshift barracks and warehouses. The latter had been constructed with an efficiency that spoke of military necessity rather than architectural beauty. These structures housed not only supplies for the men who had been quartered here, men Alaric had defeated in battle, but also the spoils plundered from Dekar, awaiting the meticulous process of inventory, allocation, and transport back to Laval's lands.

The sky overhead was a heavy blanket of gray, promising yet another cold, dreary day. Fleeting snowflakes drifted in the air, harbingers of the winter accumulating on the horizon, whispering of the harshness to come. It had been two days since the fight at the camp The thought of what Laval and Malvanis had attempted to do still enraged Alaric something fierce. His anger burned sullenly within. It took all his effort to just sit upon the stool and not pace while he waited. But in truth, he knew he did not have to wait that long. Scouts had spotted the approaching party.

To his right stood Rikka, with Kiera slightly behind her. On his left, Ezran's presence was more subdued, his gaze lost in thought, perhaps pondering the fate that had befallen Tyfel as his eyes casually swept the village square. Ezran's thoughts had always been an enigma to Alaric. The former ash man, though loyal to a fault, just thought differently.

They were facing the direction of the river, its waters hidden from view by the buildings of the village. Off to the left was a two-story tavern. It had once clearly been a way station for weary travelers, traders, and merchants moving along the road with their caravans and staying the night.

The enemy had used it as a mess hall and headquarters. The tavern's walls whispered tales of laughter and camaraderie that now seemed as distant and muted as the sky above. The absence of life in the village was a real thing, a sad thing, the heavy stillness a reminder of what Duke Laval had done to Dekar.

"Are you certain about this approach?" Rikka asked. "We could just kill him and be done with it."

"We could," Alaric conceded and wondered, once more, if the path he had chosen was the wrong one. "But there would be repercussions with the king. I do not know how that might play out, as I am answerable to him. Until I do, this is the safer trail to walk."

Jasper appeared at the far end of the street. He jogged up to them.

"He landed and has twenty men with him," Jasper reported. "They have the look of a personal guard. They are well-armed and seem competent enough."

Alaric gave a nod and gestured for Jasper to move behind

him. For once, the man did not have his bow in hand. He only carried a sword sheathed by his side and a dagger.

"Twenty is a lot, more than we expected," Rikka said. "It could come to a fight."

"It won't come to that." Alaric remained undeterred, his gaze locking with Rikka's. "At least, I don't think it will, and if it does, it will be a one-sided affair."

"This might be mildly interesting, then," Ezran quipped. "I personally think you should just kill him and be done with it. It is what I would do."

Alaric let go an unhappy breath. In truth, he did not think he could do that and get away with it, at least not yet.

"You have not seen enough blood?" Kiera asked.

"No," Ezran admitted. "I have not."

A heartbeat later, a group, all afoot, came into view. At their forefront was a figure who commanded attention, not only by his position as lead, but by the aura of authority he exuded. As the leader halted at the sight of Alaric and his companions in the middle of the square, his entourage followed suit.

The distinction of this man's attire was immediately noticeable: ornate chest armor that gleamed subtly under the muted light, meticulously tailored pants, and leather boots of fine craftsmanship. A heavy blue cloak was draped over his shoulders. Coupled with silvered hair and a groomed mustache, framing a mouth set in determination, his appearance painted the picture of a man who navigated the realms of power.

The escort had been marching in a tight column of two behind the man. A brief exchange, a muted query from one of the soldiers, likely the officer in command of the guard detail, was swiftly quelled by a gesture from their leader—his hand raised not in anger, but in command, demanding silence.

After a moment's more assessment, perhaps gauging the intent or the strength of Alaric's group, the leader motioned his men to spread out. His personal guard moved with calculated assurance. As they fanned out, their eyes swept over the shadowed facades of the surrounding buildings—each darkened window, each shadowed alley a potential threat.

Yet the leader's focus remained riveted, locked onto Alaric, who was still sitting upon the stool, waiting. After a moment's more hesitation, he started forward. His guard moved with him. They closed the distance rapidly before coming to a halt, a mere ten feet from Alaric and his party. The man's eyes, sharp and assessing, briefly scanned Rikka, Ezran, Jasper, and Kiera before settling back on Alaric.

"You would be Duke Laval," Alaric said.

"I am, and to whom do I have the pleasure of speaking?" Laval's voice was deep, refined, and as hard and unforgiving as granite.

Alaric's rise from his seated position was measured, a deliberate action that seemed to draw the very essence of command and authority around him like a cloak. "I am Alaric, Earl of Dekar."

The reaction to his introduction was immediate among the soldiers accompanying Laval. A current of unease swept through their ranks. It was a reaction born of instinct. Laval, however, remained an enigma, his response—or the lack thereof—a study in control.

The duke's expression did not waver, other than a slight and momentary flicker of his eyelids. His gaze retained its icy composure. He stood motionless, his stance suggesting a depth of calculation and resolve. In Laval's stillness lay a challenge, an assertion of his own power and authority.

Alaric already knew Laval was a dangerous man, but in this moment, he realized just how dangerous. He could easily see how Masterson would be frightened of such a man, for Laval was a cold-hearted killer and an opportunist, someone who would stoop to any lengths to see his objectives met. Alaric had known others just like him. Laval was someone who only respected strength.

Alaric would show him real strength.

"Your men are dead," Alaric stated plainly.

Laval stiffened ever so slightly. "What men?"

"Those led by your son, the ones who have been spreading disorder within my lands—raping, pillaging, looting Dekar."

"My son." Laval's cheeks began to color slightly with the heat of anger and a mounting rage. He took a deep breath and let it out. "You murdered my son?"

"He tried to kill me first," Alaric said.

"Captain," Laval hissed, glancing back at the officer who led the detachment, "I want him alive to answer for what he's done—kill the rest of them."

"Do you really believe I came alone or am as unprotected as I seem?" Alaric smirked at that, freezing the officer in place, who had opened his mouth to snap an order. "Grayson," Alaric called, "if you would."

Grayson emerged from behind one of the side buildings, stepping into the square. With him were more than a dozen bowmen, arrows nocked but pointing at the ground. More bowmen appeared in some of the windows of the nearest buildings. Laval eyed them sourly, then turned his gaze back to Alaric as it hardened even further. "Is that all you brought?"

"No, he brought me." Rikka, standing at Alaric's side, raised her hand, palm up, facing the heavens. A radiant sphere of golden light flared to life, a miniature sun cradled in her palm. Eyes going wide, Laval actually took a step backward.

"A witch," the officer with Laval hissed.

"My magic user." Alaric intentionally did not use the word "lumina." He was not prepared for that, though he was sure word would soon get out that one of the last users of holy magic, a conduit to Eldanar himself, had taken refuge within his keep. It was only a matter of time. There was simply no hiding it. "I think my point has been made. Rikka, that's enough. We don't want to really scare them."

"But I want to murder him dead for what he's done," Rikka said, a bloodthirsty hunger seeming to drip from her tongue. "Please, please, can I kill him? Can I kill them all?"

Laval took another uneasy step backward. So too did his men.

Alaric glanced over at Rikka in shock. Her eyes had begun to glow red. He had never seen her like this before. She was menace incarnate.

She looked at him with those glowing eyes. "Please. He deserves to die."

At those words, for a mere breath, his anger surged again at all the man had been responsible for. Alaric nearly gave in and said yes, then nearly forcefully shook his head. "No. Rikka, that's enough."

Rikka shook herself, and the glowing orb in her palm vanished. A moment later, the light within her eyes died off too, turning back to their normal black color. For a moment, she just stood there and breathed, her chest rising and falling as if shaking off whatever had overcome her.

Laval studied her for several heartbeats, eyes narrowing before returning his attention to Alaric. He seemed to recover a measure of himself. "You knew I was coming, that I would be here this day. You were waiting for me. How and why?"

With a simple, authoritative gesture, Alaric raised his hand, giving an expected signal. The sudden, jarring noise of the tavern door being flung open punctured the tense silence of Tyfel's square, drawing all eyes. Keever and Thorne emerged, their figures momentarily framed by the darkened interior of the tavern, before stepping into the muted light. Between them, they half-dragged, half-carried Malvanis. The man's appearance told all, for he was bound and clearly battered.

As they brought Malvanis to Alaric and released him, his collapse to the ground was not just a physical fall, but a symbol of utter defeat. With a groan, he rolled over onto his side and moaned weakly.

"You beat him," Laval accused.

Alaric noted that despite the duke's apparent anger, there was a hint of relief in his gaze, relief that his son lived. At the same time, the bruises and marks of violence on Malvanis's face told a story, an eloquent narrative of what had transpired. They also spoke to the lengths to which Alaric was prepared to go. In truth, he had almost killed Laval's son—had the bastard hanged like a common criminal. He had wanted to, and badly, but reluctantly decided otherwise, to take a different approach.

"I questioned him." Alaric made a show of looking at the back of his right hand. The knuckles were bruised and slightly swollen. The same could be said of his other hand. He looked back up and met Laval's gaze. "He told me everything. Do you wish him back? I have a mind to execute him for leading a war party upon my lands, for orchestrating what was done to my people—on your orders. He also attacked me and my men."

There was a long moment of silence.

"He is my son," Laval said. "Killing him would mean war between our two houses. You cannot be so foolish as to want such a thing to pass."

"That does not answer my question. And if I wanted you dead, you would be so." Alaric gestured to Rikka. "All I need do is give the word."

Laval did not reply, but his gaze flicked to Rikka.

"Let me simplify things between you and me," Alaric said, deciding to stop playing games with the man. "These are my terms. You can take your son and go. If you or anyone serving you ever sets foot upon my lands again, I will kill them. You leave me, my family, my holdings, and my people alone, and I will give you the same courtesy. Test me on this, and you will regret it. I shall not warn you a second time. Consider this your first and only warning."

"I am a duke and sit on the king's council. You are but a lowly earl. Killing me would have serious repercussions. The king would not stand for it."

"There," Alaric said, "we understand each other's rank. I believe we are making progress. Oh... and"—Alaric glanced over at his bannerman—"Keever is no longer yours. He is mine and I am claiming him as such. So, hands off."

Keever stiffened, his gaze going to Alaric, eyes widening in disbelief and clear alarm. The man's face had paled considerably. Alaric ignored him, for he would deal with Keever soon enough. He kept his gaze focused on Laval.

"It was Keever who sent your son word we were marching on Tyfel. Your son took it into his head to ambush us on the road. That," Alaric said, "was a mistake, one that might have cost him his life and may still if you refuse my terms."

Laval glanced down at his son, who was still lying upon the ground, moaning softly. A look of disgust overcame him. "That would not have happened were I leading."

"Maybe, maybe not," Alaric said with a shrug. "However, if you wish to test that theory, feel free to come back and try me. The choice is yours."

Laval clenched a fist. Murder was plain in the man's stare. After several heartbeats, his gaze shifted to his son.

"Very well," Laval said and glanced over at those with the bows before turning his attention to Rikka and then Alaric. "We understand one another. You and I will have peace."

Alaric clapped both hands together. "Then you may take your son and go."

"Take him to the ferry," Laval snapped. Almost instantly, two men stepped forward and grabbed Malvanis, each taking an arm. He moaned louder as they dragged him off.

"It was a pleasure meeting you, Duke Laval," Alaric said, inclining his head ever so slightly.

"I wish I could say the same," Laval said, then with a last parting glance at Rikka, he stalked off, his cloak swirling. His guards parted for him, then followed. In a few moments, they were gone from view.

"Jasper," Alaric said, "make sure they leave and cross the river. Then cut the ferry's rope once they are across. Going forward, we will have no trade with Laval or anyone associated with him. As such, I do not see the need to maintain a ferry."

"As you command, my lord." Jasper jogged hastily off.

Alaric turned to face Keever and took a step closer.

"Ultimately, he will never abide by your terms." Keever's face was hard as he met Alaric's gaze. Though the bannerman had paled, he stood tall and firm. Alaric found himself impressed. It was clear the man had inner strength. "He will come after you again and again," Keever added.

"Ultimately, I expect he won't abide by the terms I set this day, and he likely will test me again," Alaric said, "but for a time, there will be peace and a chance to rebuild. While I have it, I will take that opportunity."

Alaric did not mention he had greatly bluffed Laval. He only had his company of soldiers for real strength, his bannermen, and the militia to help back them up. He would need to raise more soldiers and soon—otherwise, he'd be in trouble when Laval realized just how weak he was. He glanced at Rikka. The show she had put on had been magnificent. That alone might buy him the time he needed.

"And what will you do with me?" Keever asked, his tone hard. "Now that you know I betrayed you, sent word to Malvanis."

Alaric took another step forward. He eyed the man for a long moment. "Nothing. I will do nothing with you." He moved around Keever and toward the tavern, with Rikka in tow.

"What do you mean, nothing?" Keever demanded. "I don't understand."

Alaric stopped and turned to look back. "From this point forward, you will serve me loyally. If Laval, his servants, agents, or anyone else dares to approach you to undermine me or in any way harm my family or Dekar, you will listen to what they have to say, then report it all to me. At that point, I will decide what will be done." Alaric took a couple steps back so he was facing Keever directly, almost in his personal space. "Betray me again and I will kill you and your family. I will bring your entire line to an end. Do we have an understanding?"

Keever swallowed and gave a nod. "I—I—we do, my lord."

"Good," Alaric said. "Then let us forget this bad business between us and move on. I am not one to hold grudges. You now have a clean slate with me."

"Yes, my lord," Keever said.

"Besides, before, you did not know me. Now, you do."

"That I do, my lord," Keever conceded and bowed his head. "Thank you."

Alaric glanced at Rikka. "I want some time alone with my lumina to talk. Thorne, Ezran, and Jasper, see that we are not disturbed."

"As you command, my lord," Thorne said.

Alaric looked at Kiera, who had moved to follow. "And I mean alone, Luminary, just the two of us, Rikka and I, no one else."

Kiera glanced at Rikka, hesitated, then gave a nod of acceptance. She took a step back. "As you wish, Lord Alaric."

With a determined stride, Alaric turned on his heel and made his way toward the tavern. The building was a quaint edifice of weathered stone and plastered-over timber, its door ajar as if in silent welcome. Pushing the door firmly open, he crossed the threshold with a measured step, the heavy wooden door creaking softly. Inside, the common room stretched out before him, bathed in the soft glow of the hearth's dying fire and a couple of lanterns hanging from the ceiling. The common room was deserted. A lone, unattended jar of wine sat upon a table near the fire, flanked by several clay mugs.

Moving with purpose, Alaric approached the table, his gaze lingering on the liquid bounty before him within the jar. He poured the rich, dark wine into a mug, the heady aroma rising to greet him. Just as he lifted the mug to his lips, the faint sound of footsteps heralded Rikka's entrance. The door thudded shut behind her, sealing them both away from the others. Alaric took a deliberate sip of the wine, the taste complex and slightly tart on his tongue.

Rikka paused just inside the door. She cast a quick glance around the empty room, her eyes eventually settling on Alaric, almost fixing upon him like a predator might prey. With a quiet sigh, one filled with resignation, Rikka moved to join him at the table.

"That," Rikka said, "might have been a mistake."

"Letting Keever live?"

She nodded.

"I need fighters," Alaric said, "and Keever is a fighter and a leader. He proved himself to me during the fight. He will bear watching, but I doubt he will betray me a second time, especially after this…"

"Perhaps," Rikka said.

"That was an impressive show you put on," Alaric said.

She scowled slightly as she gazed back at him. "What show?"

"With the eyes."

Her scowl deepened, and she seemed uncertain, almost afraid.

She glanced down at the ground. "That was no show. I—I... it..." She trailed off.

"It impressed Laval." Alaric took a sip of his wine. "That's all that matters."

"I suppose you are right," Rikka conceded. "What will you do now?"

"Now?" Alaric sucked in a deep breath and released it, allowing the tension to go with it. He considered his answer before speaking. "Now, I will turn my energies to rebuilding Dekar and making my domain strong and powerful once more, strong enough that Laval or anyone else dare not challenge me without fear for themselves." Alaric took another pull of the wine, draining the mug. He set it down upon the table with a hollow clunk. "And maybe building a port for a certain pirate I know. All that will be my focus, at least until the next crisis arrives."

"I will be here at your side for that."

"Will you?" Alaric asked.

She gave a nod.

"Then I want to know more about you. I would learn about the woman who wants me to take up a banner long since fallen, a woman who wants to have a child with me."

She did not immediately speak, but her gaze grew intense. Under the dim light of the common room, her eyes seemed blacker than night.

"Tell me, and one day, I might just raise that banner for all to rally to."

"I do not want that for me," Rikka said. "I think you know that."

"Then what do you want in return?"

She considered him, then her gaze went to the jar of wine. "Pour me a drink, will you?"

Alaric obliged, his movements fluid as he poured a generous measure of the wine into another mug and extended it toward her.

She accepted it with a nod, her hands wrapping around the mug, but rather than partake, she held it close, her attention captured by Alaric as he refilled his own with the dark, aromatic wine.

Breaking the momentary silence, Rikka's voice carried a hint of jest, tempered with an underlying seriousness. "I hope there's more wine where that came from," she mused, a slight smile playing on her lips. "For we have much to unravel tonight—should you truly demand it of me."

Casting a brief glance at the jar sitting on the table, now diminished in its contents, Alaric met her comment with a light-hearted grin. "Fear not, for our supplies are far from exhausted," he assured her, motioning toward two barrels that sat off to the side and against the left wall. One had been tapped, the other not.

Rikka took a cautious and almost nervous sip of her wine. Her gaze met Alaric's, a sudden storm of hesitation swirling in her eyes. "Are you certain you wish to delve into what I have to share? You may not like it. In fact, I expect you not to."

Alaric's response was immediate, a nod of earnest assurance, even though he was uneasy at what he might learn. Still, mutual trust was born of truth, and Alaric would have that if he was to have a life with her. "Speak, Lady Lumina. Lay bare the tales and truths that burden your heart. Show me the real you, the person I have begun to care deeply for."

"Show you? Is that what you really desire?"

Alaric gave a nod.

Rikka took a deep breath, the initial sip of wine seeming to fortify her resolve. She sat down upon a stool before the table with the jar of wine. She placed her mug upon the table's surface as Alaric pulled a stool over and sat opposite, gazing at her from across the table.

She drew in another breath, and as she exhaled, the air seemed to shimmer around her. Slowly, her features shifted, her face subtly contorting as if molded by invisible hands. Her eyes deepened and the pupils widened, her cheekbones slid upward, and her skin took on an ethereal glow.

Alaric blinked in disbelief, his body tensing as he straightened upon his stool.

"You are not human," Alaric breathed, his voice a whisper of fear and fascination as he stared back at her.

"No," Rikka responded calmly, her voice steady, despite the profound change she had just undergone. "I am not—what you call human."

The Claimed Realm continues in Book Two: A Call to Arms!

THANK YOU FOR READING LEGACY'S EDGE

We hope you enjoyed it as much as we enjoyed bringing it to you. We just wanted to take a moment to encourage you to review the book. Follow this link: Legacy's Edge to be directed to the book's Amazon product page to leave your review.

Every review helps further the author's reach and, ultimately, helps them continue writing fantastic books for us all to enjoy.

Also in series:

THE CLAIMED REALM
Legacy's Edge

Check out the entire series here! (Tap or Scan)

Want to discuss our books with other readers and even the authors? Join our Discord server today and be a part of the Aethon community.

Facebook | Instagram | Twitter | Website

You can also join our non-spam mailing list by visiting www.subscribepage.com/AethonReadersGroup and never miss out on future releases. You'll also receive three full books completely Free as our thanks to you.

Looking for more great sci-fi books?

Check out our new releases!

CONNECT WITH MARC

Marc works very hard on his writing. He aims to create high quality books to be not only enjoyed but devoured by you. Late into the night, he writes with a drink at his side, usually whiskey, gin and tonic, or beer.

It helps fuel the creativity... ***If you think he deserves one, you can help to encourage his creativity. Think of it as a tip for an entertaining experience!***

Cheers! www.maenovels.com

Patreon Legion: As a member, you get exclusive perks like early access to chapters, art crafted for your tech screens, beta reader opportunities, signed proofs, autographed final read through manuscripts, and live Zoom calls every quarter.

We are offering a 7-day free trial to Marc's official fan club. Dive in and experience our vibrant community firsthand AND be a part of our next contest!

www.patreon.com/marcalanedelheit

Facebook: Make sure you visit Marc's author page and smash the *like button*. He is very active on Facebook.
Marc Edelheit Author

Facebook Group: MAE Fantasy & SciFi Lounge is a group he created where members can come together to share a love for Fantasy and Sci-Fi.

Twitter: Marc Edelheit Author

Instagram: Marc Edelheit Author

Amazon Author Central: Marc Edelheit Author

Newsletter: Sign up to Marc's newsletter to get notifications on preorders, contests, and new releases. We do not spam subscribers. www.maenovels.com

<u>Reviews</u> keep Marc motivated and also help to drive sales. He makes a point to read each and every one, so please continue to post them.

www.ingramcontent.com/pod-product-compliance
Lightning Source LLC
Chambersburg PA
CBHW022302310726
48973CB00001B/179